To Thomasina

Alexandra Joel is a former editor of the Australian edition of *Harper's Bazaar* and of *Portfolio*, Australia's first magazine for working women. She has also contributed feature articles, interviews and reviews to many national and metropolitan publications.

Her first novel, the bestselling *The Paris Model*, was published around the world, including in the United States, Canada, Germany, Hungary and Romania, and was followed by *The Royal Correspondent* and now *The Artist's Secret*. Alexandra's biography *Rosetta: A Scandalous True Story* was optioned for the screen by a major US-owned production company. She is also the author of two books about the history of fashion in Australia.

With an honours degree from the University of Sydney and a graduate diploma from the Australian College of Applied Psychology, she has been a practising counsellor and psychotherapist.

Alexandra has two children and lives in Sydney with her husband. She has been fascinated by the history and meaning of art since she was a schoolgirl.

To connect with Alexandra, visit:

AlexandraJoel.com
f @AlexandraJoelAuthor
⬡ @AlexandraJoelAuthor

Also by Alexandra Joel

FICTION
The Paris Model
The Royal Correspondent

NON-FICTION
Best Dressed: 200 Years of Fashion in Australia
Parade: The Story of Fashion in Australia
Rosetta: A Scandalous True Story

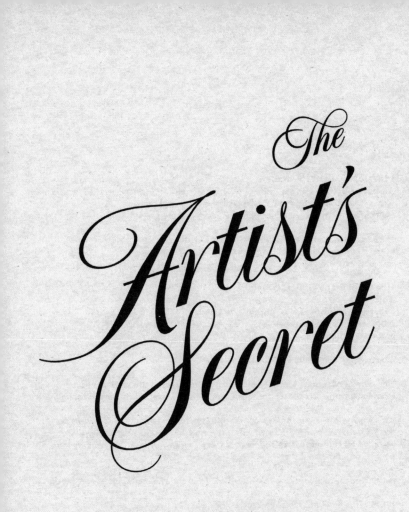

The
Artist's
Secret

ALEXANDRA JOEL

x

HarperCollins*Publishers*

HarperCollins*Publishers*

Australia • Brazil • Canada • France • Germany • Holland • India
Italy • Japan • Mexico • New Zealand • Poland • Spain • Sweden
Switzerland • United Kingdom • United States of America

HarperCollins acknowledges the Traditional Custodians
of the land upon which we live and work, and pays respect
to Elders past and present.

First published on Gadigal Country in Australia in 2023
This edition published in 2024
by HarperCollins*Publishers* Australia Pty Limited
ABN 36 009 913 517
harpercollins.com.au

A catalogue record for this book is available from the National Library of Australia

ISBN 978 1 4607 5819 9 (paperback)
ISBN 978 1 4607 1190 3 (ebook)
ISBN 978 1 4607 4660 8 (audiobook)

Cover design by Christine Armstrong, HarperCollins Design Studio
Cover images: Woman © plainpicture/beyond; Empire State Building
by Diarmid Weir/Alamy Stock Photo
Author photograph by Juli Balla
Typeset in Bembo Std by Kirby Jones

Printed and bound by CPI Group (UK) Ltd, Croydon, CR0 4YY

I have an idea that some are born out of their due place. Accident has cast them amid certain surroundings, but they have always a nostalgia for a home they know not.

W. Somerset Maugham

Art is the highest form of hope.

Gerhard Richter

PROLOGUE

New York, November 1988

Wren Summers breathed in deeply, savouring the atmosphere of the grand room from her place on the podium. Below her, the glamorous crowd buzzed with that particular brand of febrile excitement triggered only when a truly remarkable work was about to go on sale.

She told herself it wasn't important that her stomach fluttered – fear was inseparable from risk. All that mattered was whether she had the ability to make this room *hers*. Tonight she had to dominate her audience with the stealth of an eagle, feinting and gliding with such hypnotic grace that when finally she swooped, her prey would surrender not just willingly, but with delight.

Among those straining forward on their plush seats were some of the world's richest and most powerful individuals. She could feel the intensity of their gaze, sense them willing her to speak the familiar words that would signal the start of the drama.

Wren smoothed the jacket of her black satin Jean Paul Gaultier suit, confident that it provided a striking contrast to her pale skin and enhanced her cloud of dark hair. Just like her Charles Jourdan stilettos and luscious red Chanel lipstick, it had been chosen with one aim – to mesmerise.

Yet she hadn't reckoned on the power of the painting. A momentary glance at the masterpiece the porters had placed on a spot-lit easel was all it took to trigger her well of pain. Wren swept her eyes across the crowd, but to her horror saw only a featureless blur. Panic made her throat tighten. How was she to perform beyond all expectations if she could barely speak, let alone make out a single upturned face?

Blinking, she willed her unruly emotions away. Now was not the time to permit such distractions. She'd fought too hard for her chance to shine.

The room came back into focus. Wren held her head high. In a commanding voice subtly brushed by seduction, she began. 'Ladies and gentlemen …'

PART ONE

Sfumato

A painting technique that gradually blends tones and colours.
From the Italian sfumare, meaning 'to vanish'.

CHAPTER ONE

University of California, Berkeley, May 1965

The fair-haired girl with the face of an angel flinched as she struck the match. Although its tiny rasp sounded no different from the thousand other times she had scraped one red-tipped sliver of wood along the roughened side of a little box, nothing else was the same. This time hot bile rose in her throat as she tried to fathom a future without the boy by her side.

She was only nineteen, the blue-eyed boy twenty-three. He was holding the piece of thick paper he'd brought with him, the one bearing the words 'Registration Certificate' above the official crest of the United States of America. It looked such a dull, mundane document. How easy it would be to mistake it for an inoffensive government notice.

She leant so close to the boy she could smell the sweet scent of his skin. Then she put the match to the white rectangle, watching intently as the tiny lick of light crawled down one edge. Frowning, she wondered if the modest flame might expire, for the warm breeze coming in from the south on that hot spring night was making it flutter and wane. Instead, the yellow dart grew stronger, until it became a dancing orange flame.

The boy gave her a quick grin, then thrust the fiery draft card high. Within seconds his action was duplicated by the thirty-nine other young men ranged in front of the soaring white pillars of Berkeley's Sproul Hall. Each bore the same expression: intent, jubilant, united by a desire to resist. They would not enlist in the US army. They would not fight in a foreign land called Vietnam.

Entranced, the girl stood quite still, her hair streaming behind her in pale ribbons as the breeze intensified. The dramatic scene looked like an ancient rite, a trial by fire perhaps, or an unholy baptism.

The moment passed quickly. When flames threatened to scorch the young men's tender fingers, the burning draft cards fluttered to the ground. Her ears rang with their whooping and hollering as they stamped on the charred paper, their treasonous act now turned into ash.

She couldn't help sharing the euphoria; it throbbed in her chest like a chord wrenched from an electric guitar. Then came the fear, vanquishing her high spirits with a stab so sharp that she winced. A line had been crossed; a price was certain to be exacted.

Tensing, she turned her head in the direction of a high-pitched squeal – sirens. Any minute now, California's state troopers would swoop down upon the demonstrators.

Despite the balmy night, a shiver ran through her. The last thing she wanted was for her lover, with his quick mind and gentle hands, to be forced into military service, but surely an even worse outcome now awaited him.

Bile burned her throat once more as a parade of frightening images flashed into her mind. The boy she adored dragged away by a vicious officer. Standing handcuffed in court before a black-robed judge. Sentenced to be locked in a jail cell for who knew how many years of awful confinement. Unless he took off like some of the other draft dodgers they knew and hitchhiked across the border to Mexico – but surely he would never abandon her?

She swallowed hard, choking back the acid taste in her mouth. It must have been a couple of months now, but the sickness was yet to subside. With her hands cradling the newly rounded contours of her belly, she tried to imagine how the flame she had lit might change this new life.

CHAPTER TWO

Sydney, December 1987

Wren skipped up the sandstone steps of the Sydney Art Museum, trying not to grin like an idiot. 'Assistant Curator of Prints and Drawings,' she murmured to herself, enjoying the dignified sound of the title. She'd longed for a job like this for years and, finally, here she was, on the brink of seeing her dream realised.

Instinctively, she touched the gold locket she wore under her shirt. Her mother had given it to her when she'd still been a child, claiming it would bring Wren luck, though if that were the case it might have been better if Lily had kept it for herself. She made fewer and fewer paintings these days, although Wren still considered her a great artist. It pained her to know that she had never received the recognition she deserved.

Wren's smile melted away. It was on occasions like this, when she had her all-important interview with the museum's director, that she became aware of the aching void within her. If only she had some other special person besides her maddening mother in her life.

The last thing she needed was The Look. She was crossing the museum's vestibule when she noticed it: a guard swept his gaze over her, not bothering to hide his leering appreciation. Wren groaned inwardly but didn't break her stride. She had always considered herself riddled with defects – she was too tall, her chocolate-brown eyes were too wide, her lips too full, and that was without counting her hair's dark, unruly waves – which was just fine, because if there was one lesson Lily had taught her, it was the untrustworthy nature of men.

With that knowledge firmly in mind, Wren had left her all-girl boarding school and started university, determined to avoid even the slimmest chance of attracting what her more feminist-leaning lecturers termed 'the male gaze'. She'd tamed her hair by dragging it back into a ponytail, used no make-up and disguised her figure by wearing baggy men's clothes she found in op shops. It was, therefore, almost as shocking as it was alarming to discover the effect she still had upon the opposite sex. Fellow students, tutors and even the odd ageing professor gave her The Look, sometimes a sidelong glance, often an open stare.

Now it seemed that even here, in an art museum of all places, she still failed to fly under the radar. Well, she wasn't about to let that bother her, particularly as this just might be the day when her life would change forever. Walking purposefully into the ladies' room, she made her way to a wall-length mirror. First, she straightened her double-breasted suit. A recent charity store find, its soft grey fabric was of such superior quality she was sure the former owner must have been an overpaid city banker. Next, she took some hairspray from her shoulder bag and went to work taming a stray curl.

With just ten minutes left before her meeting, Wren squared her shoulders and strode out of the ladies' room. She had already submitted her résumé and survived an initial interview with two officials. Now she would face her final hurdle.

Alastair Stephenson was reputed to hail from Edinburgh, although his clipped British accent gave no hint of any Scottish origins. The slim, sandy-haired man wore a tweed suit and tortoiseshell glasses, through which he was now peering.

'Ah, Miss Summers,' he said, waving her towards a chair. 'May I call you Wren?'

'Yes, of course.' *Don't blow this*, she told herself as she sat down. *Stay focused.*

'And this is our Head of Collections, John Tremaine.' Stephenson gestured to the man sitting beside him. 'Though, of course, you have met already.'

'Indeed, we have,' Tremaine said loudly. He was on the heavy side and had entered early middle age, though looked to still fancy himself as a younger man, for he wore jeans with his slightly too tight striped shirt and navy blue sports jacket. Unlike the director, whose diffident manner endowed him with an old-fashioned charm, he seemed very sure of himself. It was Tremaine who'd conducted her previous interview, together with a stern-looking woman from the Public Service's personnel department.

'The formalities have already been well covered,' Stephenson said. 'I see your thesis on the Impressionists' brushwork was awarded first-class honours. Not only that, but you have already had a paper published in the *International Journal of Art Practice* on the same subject.'

He raised his eyebrows. 'That *is* impressive – it seems you are something of a prodigy. And I believe you had another article appear' – he glanced down – 'on the subject of Renaissance figure drawing.'

Stephenson looked at her quizzically. 'Naturally, that research would be very useful for this position, though I can't quite grasp the connection to your thesis topic. Can you explain?'

Wren smiled; the subject was dear to her heart. 'It's because drawings provide such an intimate understanding of the artist's process – they're so much more immediate than a considered painting.' Her eyes sparkled as she spoke.

'That same immediacy is what attracted me to the Impressionists,' she added. 'Nothing about their work is laboured or overthought. Of course, this technique can lead to flaws, but sometimes a so-called flaw is the element that illuminates the entire work.'

Stephenson nodded. 'Nicely put. Now, what else? Yes, you studied Italian – that's useful – and the State Library has provided an outstanding reference.' He tapped a piece of paper. 'I put great store by Eva Reiter's opinion.'

Dear Miss Reiter, Wren thought. She'd worked part-time throughout university and full-time during vacations assisting the elderly Viennese woman who oversaw the State Library's collection of prints and drawings. Despite the paltry wages, she would always be grateful that Miss Reiter had taken so much care training her how to catalogue and care for the works.

Stephenson adjusted a cufflink. 'You might as well know,' he said, 'we're down to just two candidates, so this little chat is more to assess whether you would be a good fit for our team than anything else.'

Wren nodded calmly. Seeing as she'd already faked her way through the exclusive Daneford school and then university, pretending to these men to be someone she wasn't was unlikely to present a problem. *Just act the part*, she told herself. *You've done it for long enough, and, thanks to Daneford's enforced elocution lessons, you have even picked up the right accent.* The urbane director and his offsider would never guess where she came from.

'Right, then,' Tremaine said, taking charge. 'Let's see how good you really are.' He gave her a look laden with condescension. 'Name ten paintings by Pablo Picasso – dates too if you don't mind.'

Wren struggled to conceal her irritation. Why would he ask her something that had absolutely no relevance to the job for which she was applying? Anyway, it was a ridiculous question to pose to someone with her academic credentials – she hadn't encountered such an elementary memory test since her first semester at university.

'*La Vie* and *The Old Guitarist*, both 1903,' she began.

'Are you quite sure about that?' Tremaine probed.

'Quite sure.' The annoying man was trying to put her off. '*Les Demoiselles d'Avignon*, 1907,' she continued, '*Girl Before a Mirror*, 1932—'

'That's quite enough,' Stephenson broke in. 'Frankly, I'm not terribly interested in a recitation of names and dates. I'm far more concerned with meaning.'

That was a relief. Expounding her views on the latest colour theory or the philosophical underpinnings of nineteenth-century art would at least give her a chance to display her grasp of artistic theory.

The director leant forward. 'For instance,' he said, 'tell me the painting you like best among all those this museum has in its collection.'

Wren swallowed. Here was another question she hadn't expected. For a split second, she wondered which work would be the safest choice. Perhaps an iconic Australian picture such as Frederick McCubbin's *On the Wallaby Track* – everyone liked that. Or would something European and dramatic have more appeal? *Three Bathers* by the German Expressionist Ernst Ludwig Kirchner had to be a possibility.

But she couldn't bring herself to nominate either of these works. There was something about the director's authentic curiosity that sparked an unusual recklessness in her. 'I've always loved *The Camp, Sirius Cove*,' she confessed.

'What, that tiny little Tom Roberts?' Tremaine blustered.

'An interesting choice,' Stephenson remarked. 'Could you tell me why?'

'Because it fills my soul with joy,' Wren said simply. 'I agree, the work is modest in size, but it captures the essence of Sydney Harbour. I think it's because of the way Roberts has filled his canvas with light, and his handling of the horizontal bands of colour. They're precise, yet completely alive.'

Stephenson coughed. 'Would you mind waiting outside?'

Well, she'd done it now, Wren thought as she sat up stiffly in an uncomfortable, modern chair, one of a neat row of three standing in the corridor outside. A single moment's loss of self-control and she'd ruined her best chance of breaking into the world of art museums. Permanent entry-level jobs such as assistant curator were rare in Australia and hardly ever became available.

Five minutes later she was called back into the director's office. Tremaine's expression was sullen, while Stephenson was preoccupied with flipping through the pages of his desk calendar. He looked up with a start when she came in, as if he'd forgotten he had asked her to return.

'The Head of Collections and I,' he said, composing himself, 'have decided that all things considered, you are the best qualified candidate for the position.'

Wren gripped her hands together, though she would have preferred to leap into the air with joy.

'If you are agreeable, please present yourself to our Curator of Prints and Drawings, Dr Robert Hawkins, on Monday morning.' Stephenson paused. 'Best make it ten-thirty.'

'Thank you, I'm very grateful,' Wren said, still endeavouring to maintain her restraint.

She was turning to go when she heard the director say, 'Oh, and Wren? About that little Roberts.'

She looked back. 'Yes?'

Stephenson smiled. 'It's always been one of my favourites.'

At last, Wren thought, as she took in the beauty of the paintings and sculptures she passed on her way out of the museum. She didn't care about the lurking guard's expression, or the fact that she was about to return to her lonely room in a rundown Bondi boarding house. She didn't even mind that all she could afford for dinner was toast and Vegemite. None of that mattered now.

She had finally won a role for herself in this temple of wonders. It was the only place in the world where, ever since the age of fourteen, she'd been quite certain she belonged.

CHAPTER THREE

November 1980

Wren peered forward as the lurching bus came to a stop outside a building of golden stone. With its classical columns and pediment, it looked to her like the photos of ancient sites of worship her Latin teacher had shown the class. She immediately checked that her navy blue plush hat was straight, her fawn socks pulled up and her gloves in her blazer pocket, ready to be donned. After nearly three years at Daneford, the process was automatic.

Once Wren and the other twenty-four identically dressed girls had filed out of the vehicle, they were directed by Miss Barnes – an art teacher who favoured asymmetrical black clothes of Japanese origin – to form a line in an orderly fashion.

Wren bubbled with curiosity. She'd never been to an art museum before.

'Did you listen when Mrs Chambers quoted the *Herald* in assembly?' she whispered to Mary-Jane Clarke, a tall, gawky girl with crinkly red hair who was commonly known as MJ. 'The paper reckons the Modern Masters show is the most important exhibition ever to come to Australia.'

Giggling, MJ tugged at one of her plaits. 'I'd stare at a blank wall if it meant missing geometry.'

Wren had been close to MJ ever since her first week at school when their bully of a boarding mistress, 'Captain' Hooke, had punished the pair for talking after lights out. Wren winced as she remembered the hours they'd spent kneeling on ice-cold tiles while they cleaned the communal bathroom. Hooke had forced them to use their toothbrushes.

Nobody at Woolahderra, the haphazard south coast commune where Wren had grown up, cared a fig about rules and regulations. They weren't cruel or mean, either. Maybe, she'd reflected, it was the Miss Hookes of this world that had driven them to seek a safe haven.

Wren had been so incensed she'd fired off a letter to Daneford's headmistress, setting out exactly what had happened. Then she'd made sure it was signed by as many other girls as she could muster. She'd fully expected to be thrown out. Instead, an announcement had been made in the following Friday's assembly that Miss Hooke had taken a sudden decision to embrace early retirement.

Wren had been MJ's personal hero ever since. The girl was chatty and full of fun, though as she struggled with schoolwork – especially Latin and maths – most afternoons Wren helped her out with her assignments. What Wren did not do was share the truth about her unruly home, or that her mum was a dope-smoking artist. The story she told everyone was that she'd grown up near the Queensland border on a remote cattle property efficiently run by her widowed mother – which was about as far from the truth as was possible.

Just thinking about her lie made Wren feel queasy, but she knew she couldn't trust the guileless MJ to stay silent. It was hard enough to fit in at Daneford without word getting out that Wren Summers was a dirt-poor hippie chick's kid – with no idea who her dad was.

'I know what you mean. Geometry sucks,' she said companionably, even though she quite enjoyed the precision imposed by set squares and compasses.

Miss Barnes escorted the girls inside the museum, then whisked them down a set of stairs with a flap of her arm.

'You are free to explore the show in your own time,' she said. 'But please refer to your worksheets. The questions have all been numbered, and you can see there is space for you to write the answers as you progress through the exhibition. We will meet by the poster display in the museum shop in exactly one hour.' She pursed her mouth. 'And remember, you are Daneford girls. Be on your best behaviour at all times.'

Wren entered the first hall fully expecting the paintings to resemble the reproductions pinned up in the art room at school. Then her eyes widened. These pictures were nothing like those muted images. They shone with colour and life.

She could hardly tear herself away from an exquisite rendition of lilac waterlilies by Monet, then felt a thrill when she spotted a sumptuous picture whose subject turned out to be Monet himself, captured by his friend Renoir while the artist worked at an easel in his riotous flower-filled garden.

Her heart beat faster when she arrived at a deep blue and green Matisse called *The Young Sailor*, the subject's shoulders and arms captured in one expressive curve. It beat faster still when she saw a jewel-toned composition by Bonnard in the next room. Her hand automatically moved to the narrow strip of skin between her collar and ponytail, for she was sure she'd felt a weird sort of prickle. Then she realised that when people said the hair on the back of their necks had stood up, this sensation was exactly what they meant.

Flushed and light-headed, she shook off her blazer, quickly undid her two top buttons and loosened her tie. She'd never felt more alive. The pictures captured so many vivid people and scenes: ballerinas and washerwomen and enchanting children; lush country landscapes, Paris theatres and bohemian cafés; all with such intense colour and verve it felt as if she could leap into any one of their burnished frames and become a part of their captivating world. If only she could live with art like this every day.

With a jolt, Wren stood still. She had spent her life surrounded by luminous canvases, filled with the bush and the river and the sky. Lily's paintings were just as stirring as these works. Why hadn't she realised it before?

It was not until Wren was in the last court, lost in a moving portrait by Modigliani, that she became aware she couldn't see anyone from her school. She'd been so engrossed in the paintings that time had stood still. With a final, lingering look over her shoulder, she reluctantly hurried out and found her classmates clustered in the museum shop.

'About time,' Miss Barnes said, tapping her foot. 'The bus will be leaving at any minute. Quick, hand me your worksheet.'

Wren did as she asked.

'But you haven't written a word!' Miss Barnes crumpled the piece of paper. 'That's not like you, Wren, you're usually such a diligent girl.' The teacher glared at her. 'And you look a mess. What on earth happened to you in there?'

Wren's face shone with a transcendent smile.

CHAPTER FOUR

December 1987

A polite knock on a door bearing the inscription *Prints and Drawings Department* brought no response. After a moment or two spent buttoning and then unbuttoning her jacket, Wren seized the knob and stepped inside.

'Who's there?' a faint voice called.

She scanned a room so dim she found it impossible to pick anyone out.

'Y-your new assistant.' Her confidence was starting to ebb.

She stood, momentarily uncertain, until her eyes adjusted to the gloom. Then her jaw dropped.

Wren found herself in a chaotic room, crowded with teetering piles of books, papers, journals and files. She had to inch her way between these unstable stacks until finally she located a tiny wisp of a man, presumably Hawkins, tucked in a corner. If it had not been for his carrot-coloured hair, she doubted she would have been able to pick him out from behind his laden desk, for the debris did not merely cover the floor. It was littered over every available surface.

Her new boss looked at her blankly before waving towards another paper-strewn desk in the opposite corner. 'You work over there' was all he said. Bewildered, she asked him what he wanted her to do.

'Suit yourself,' he replied with a shrug of his shoulders. Then as an afterthought, 'I suppose the place could do with a tidy-up.'

Wren raised her eyebrows. 'Where do you suggest I start, Dr Hawkins?'

'Search me.' This was accompanied by a timid smile. 'But why don't you call me Bobby?'

Wren immediately relaxed. Hawkins was no ogre. His offhand manner simply hid a shy man in need of a great deal of assistance. Taking charge was nothing new – she had been doing that, first in her mum's disordered shack and then in the library, for years.

It seemed that a proper filing system had not been applied to a single item for a very long time. Catalogues lay on top of receipts; bits of research had become mixed up with typed lists of potential acquisitions; and advertisements for upcoming shows were curled on top of obscure journals. Ageing messages from people who must have long since given up hope of having their telephone calls returned jostled with taxi receipts and photographs that nestled beneath government warnings regarding – she broke into a wry smile – occupational health and safety.

Only the department's precious prints and drawings were carefully stowed away, although Wren noticed there was not a single work on display. Most of the wall space was taken up with thumbtacked notices about long-past staff Christmas parties, out-of-date calendars and fading memos.

She frowned. Sorting anything out would be impossible as, other than the pool of light cast by the lamp on Bobby's desk, the room had no illumination. Trying the main switch did nothing to improve the situation.

'Had the overheads disconnected,' Bobby muttered when he saw her looking at him reproachfully. 'They ruin prints and drawings.'

'But how do you find anything?' she asked.

He gave her a sheepish grin. 'Well, if I'm really desperate I use this.' He produced a small silver flashlight.

'I think we'll have to make some changes,' she said with a slight shake of her head. This man might be her boss, but if she didn't find a speedy way of establishing some order it was going to be impossible to work here.

'Must we?' he asked nervously.

Wren offered a comforting smile. 'Don't worry, Bobby. I'll be gentle.'

She was in the kitchen, washing up half a dozen stained coffee mugs she'd unearthed from the debris, when a girl with cropped white-blonde hair and wearing a pair of black velvet jodhpurs and a hot pink shirt with a pussycat bow bounced in.

'Hi, I don't think we've met,' the girl said with a bright smile. She peered into the refrigerator and took out a plastic-wrapped sandwich. 'Late lunch,' she explained. 'My name's Jo Draper, by the way. I assist over in Contemporary Art.'

'How do you like it?' Wren asked. The girl's unguarded cheerfulness was disarming.

'I manage.' Jo laughed. 'Anyway, I'll be off in a few months. As soon as my US visa comes through I'm leaving for the States. Officially, I'll be advising the Russell Museum on contemporary Australian and Pacific works, though in reality I'm the assistant to the curatorial assistant.' She grinned. 'Which probably means general dogsbody. What's your name, by the way?'

'Sorry, it's Wren. Wren Summers.'

'You mean Wren, as in a bird? That's a new one.'

Wren was used to people's surprise. Normally she'd simply shrug, but Jo was so friendly she found herself explaining. 'It was my mother's idea. Knowing her, it's lucky I wasn't called Nightingale or something.'

'So, she's a nature lover?'

This conversation was getting a little too close to home. 'In a manner of speaking,' Wren said quickly.

'Look, I only have a minute now, but are you free for lunch tomorrow?' Jo asked. 'I'd love to catch up. I'm from Melbourne, you see, and I hardly know anyone up here. I could do with a friend.'

Wren felt her chest tighten. She'd been lonely for a long time.

Once school was done with, MJ had taken off back to her family's sprawling western New South Wales property with promises to write, but after a few scrawled letters her correspondence had petered out. At university, Wren had been so busy studying and working at the library there hadn't been time to befriend other girls. The inevitable stress that went with disguising who she really was and where she came from had been another good reason to keep to herself. But this exuberant new acquaintance was taking off soon, Wren thought. What would it matter if she made a slip?

'Sure.' She smiled. 'Sounds good.'

'I usually go to the park opposite at lunchtime,' Jo said as she headed out the door. 'Look for me on the bench under the big magnolia tree at, say, one o'clock.'

Wren stacked the clean coffee mugs on top of each other. It felt good to know that, even if for only a brief time, she wouldn't be quite so solitary.

That afternoon, Wren made a point of passing through the main exhibition court. A new show highlighting Chinese works from the collection was being assembled, and she wanted to observe the process.

She took up position in an unobtrusive corner, carrying a file so she didn't look like she was simply loitering. John Tremaine, barking orders in his jeans and tight shirt, was in charge.

'No, not there,' he shouted at the hapless curator of Asian art. 'Can't you see that scroll should be positioned behind the Ming vases – it gives a much clearer understanding of the period.'

He was officious and unpleasant, but Wren could see he knew what he was doing. Every decision Tremaine made helped illuminate the delicate works, so not only were they shown off to their best advantage, but they also told a more coherent story. It was a considerable skill.

'Wren!' With a start, she realised he had spotted her. 'Don't hide away. I'd like your opinion.'

Surprised, she stumbled into the centre of the court.

'Higher or lower?' he asked, pointing to a marvellous screen depicting cranes and long grasses, currently held by two attendants.

'Oh, as low as possible, I'd say,' she volunteered. 'I imagine it was designed to be seen that way.'

'Clever girl,' Tremaine said approvingly. 'You're quite right.'

'Thanks.'

That was nice, Wren thought, *even if a touch patronising*. Perhaps she'd been too quick to judge the man.

Jo was unlike anyone Wren knew. Two years older than herself, she was a cheeky ball of energy who'd grown up in a suburban home in Melbourne.

'There's not a single aspect of me or my family that's in the least bit exotic,' she announced from her spot on the park bench as a group of office workers played football in the background.

Wren raised an eyebrow. 'You mean, apart from the neon-yellow jumpsuit and those Space Age chrome earrings you're wearing?'

Jo laughed. 'Give me a break – it's no wonder I'm keen to make a statement. I'm the third child of four. We all went to the local state high, which meant that as poor Mum practically had us one after the other, the four of us Draper kids were all in senior school at the same time.'

Jo made a face. 'What else? Dad is an overworked GP and our dog, Scout, is a golden retriever with an uncontrollable appetite.' She turned to face Wren. 'On Mondays we eat spaghetti bolognaise and every Friday it's chicken and chips. See what I mean?' She threw her hands in the air. 'Totally unremarkable. We put the "average" into average Australia. What I wouldn't give for a fascinating past!'

'Be careful what you wish for,' Wren murmured darkly.

'Why do you say that?'

'It's just an expression.' Wren doubted she'd have much hope of getting on with someone who'd grown up in circumstances so far removed from weird Woolahderra.

'Well, what I'm wishing for right now is that my visa would arrive.' Jo plucked a glossy red apple from the paper bag on her knee, threw it in the air and caught it with a grin. 'I can't wait to get to New York and see the amazing museums and galleries. You'll think I'm mad,' she said in a confiding tone, 'but when I see really fabulous art, it makes the hairs stand up on the back of my neck.'

'Me too!'

It was only later, on the bus back to Bondi, that a shadow passed across Wren's face. She'd already had to reassess her impressions of two new colleagues – three, if she counted Jo. She told herself the cause must be sheer inexperience, which was at least a reversible condition. All the same, it was unsettling. She wondered how many more mistakes she would make.

Wren peered at the screen with a bemused expression. The closed-circuit television was broadcasting every move made by a nude man and woman who were occupying the stark white enclosed room sitting on the new-wave gallery floor like a huge opaque ice cube. She knew she was hopelessly old-fashioned, but painting and drawing would always be her first loves. Conceptual art like this installation just didn't speak to her soul.

'*So* interesting,' Jo said enthusiastically. She'd gelled her blonde hair so it stood up in punk-style spikes. 'Although from the look of those two's body language' – she giggled – 'I predict trouble.'

Wren decided she'd had enough. 'Feel like a pizza?' she asked. 'I don't think I can stomach any more of these openings' stale chips and cask wine. There's a place I spotted down the road we can try.'

They were sharing a margherita with extra cheese and a bottle of chianti, laughing as they bet each other how many days the naked couple would last before one of them either strangled the other or simply walked out, when it struck Wren that she was sick of pretending to be someone she was not. She'd become close to Jo during the past weeks – closer than she could ever have imagined. That story about the farm and her widowed mother belonged back in her student days. If she was ever to establish proper adult friendships, she'd have to risk a little more honesty.

By the time their chianti was finished, she had told Jo everything. She'd described Lily and her great talent, but also her usual, exasperating state of dreamy distraction. She'd spoken of what it was like to grow up in chaotic Woolahderra. She'd even touched on the aching emptiness she felt inside, blinking back tears when she said, 'It's been there ever since I can remember – as if I'm not whole.' Wren strayed from the truth only when it came to her father.

'A car accident?' Jo patted her hand. 'I'm so sorry. It must be awful for you, never knowing your dad.'

Wren felt sick to her stomach. Jo was right. It *was* awful, but so was her lie. If only she wasn't in this humiliating position. Sure, these days it didn't always mean much if someone's parents hadn't bothered with a legal marriage. But that someone still had a mum and dad, whereas she didn't have the faintest clue who her father was. There was something shameful about the not knowing.

'Jeez, with the commune and everything, now I can see what you meant about the challenges of a fascinating past,' Jo said. 'Do you miss Woolahderra?'

Wren nodded slowly. 'I guess so. At least bits of it,' she mused. 'I miss the smell of the bush and watching the birds and the river – and Mum, of course, even though she can be a nightmare.

'Mostly though, you know what terrifies me?' She paused, frowning. 'That one day something will drag me back and I'll find myself stuck there.'

CHAPTER FIVE

Woolahderra, September 1977

Kicking aside stones and sharp twigs with her sandalled feet, Wren picked her way down the steep incline that led to the Shoalhaven River. On an impulse, she touched the letter she'd thrust deep inside the pocket of her overalls, then pulled her fingers away as quickly as if they'd come into contact with a flame. It would keep.

On either side of her stretched dense green-grey bushland, a wilderness of jutting eucalypts and tangled vines. She screwed up her brown eyes, searching for evidence of the first red, spiky flowers of a bottlebrush. 'Nah,' she murmured. It was too early in spring; she could still make out brilliant smudges of golden wattle on the opposite hill.

Wren grasped a dead branch hanging diagonally across her path. Suddenly irritated, she broke the dry limb in two with a satisfying snap before casting the pieces into a clump of grevilleas. Her mother was driving her crazy.

She was used to Lily forgetting things, but lately she'd grown more absent-minded than ever. What made it particularly frustrating was that if Wren complained about there being no milk in their shack or pointed out that Lily had missed the latest parent–teacher meeting, her mother's lovely face would simply acquire a puzzled expression and she'd murmur, 'Chill out, baby girl,' in her soft American drawl. If she wasn't gliding around the commune doing God knew what, she might return to painting another of the big canvases that accumulated in the shack until, on a whim, she gave them away to whoever was interested.

Wren never knew when Lily would pick up a brush – like everything else she did in her life, there wasn't a schedule. But every now and then, when the urge struck her or the moon was in Venus or whatever, she would experience a spurt of near-manic energy, staying up all night to create colour-drenched canvases radiant with light.

Wren felt even more isolated when one of her mother's flowerchild friends was around, Starlight or Dewdrop or whatever bizarre names they'd invented. She could still hear the tiny silver bells they wore around their wrists and ankles tinkle as they'd point at her, saying, 'That's one freaky planet your girl is from.' They didn't mean freaky good, either, but freaky dull, freaky *conservative*, which was about the worst thing you could be called at Woolahderra.

Yeah, she was different from them, all right. While the floating group of thirty-odd commune dwellers she and her mum lived with wafted about in grubby jeans and crumpled kaftans, Wren washed her primary school uniform as soon as it was dirty. Then she'd drape the cotton dress over a bush to dry in the sun, before pressing it at night under her thin mattress. In the morning, while Lily slept, she made her own lunch. If she couldn't find anything to eat in their shack, she'd head over to bearded Elijah and his girlfriend Winnie's mud hut – at least they were always good for some cheese or maybe a leftover hardboiled egg. As for a bit of fruit, she'd been pinching fallen apples and pears from the neighbouring orchard for as long as she could remember.

No way was she was going to carry on drifting through life like Lily – sometimes she swapped that for 'Mum', even though she knew her mother preferred Wren to use her first name, claiming it was 'less hierarchical'. Hell, she'd been forced to look the word up in her school dictionary.

Pausing to extract a twig caught up in one of her sandals, Wren considered the bounty her friends took for granted – the gleaming refrigerators in spotless kitchens, matching lounge suites and television sets – all provided by their oh-so-normal mums and dads. She could get by without shiny appliances. She could even put up with the shack. But, God, what she wouldn't give for two regular, standard-issue parents.

Using both hands, Wren cautiously touched her bony ribcage. Somewhere tucked deep inside was the sore, unfilled space that nagged like a stitch whenever she thought of her father. But Lily wouldn't talk about him. For that matter, she wouldn't talk about growing up in America or just about anything else that had happened to her before she arrived at Woolahderra. It was all a giant blank, because whenever Wren asked any questions her mother would turn away or, worse, start smoking a roll-your-own cigarette stuffed with weed.

Only yesterday, Clara Johnson had made a crack after Wren once more came first in a test. 'The teachers feel sorry for you, Wren Summers – that's why they go easy,' Clara had sneered in a stage whisper just loud enough so that, although it didn't reach old Mr Madden's ears, the entire back row of 6M heard each word. 'My mum reckons your mum is such a big druggie slut that your dad killed himself.'

Wren had felt as if she'd been smacked in the face.

She sighed. No wonder there was spiteful gossip. Her mother wasn't just a hippie. Lily was so pretty – small and slim with blonde hair that hung down nearly to her waist – there was always some bloke hanging around her, only she made it clear she had no intention of staying with any of them for long.

'Don't ever fall in love.' She'd said it again and again. 'You and me, honey – that's all we have. It's all we need.'

Wren resumed trekking down the slope, her shoulders hunched.

'Shit!' she burst out as she pictured last night's confrontation. She'd charged home after school, still in a state, throwing her bag across the room so hard it nearly knocked over the painting her mother was working on.

'Why won't you tell me what happened between you and my dad?' she'd demanded.

Paling, Lily had looked up from the splotches of vermilion and chrome yellow she'd been mixing on a bit of broken board.

'I'll be thirteen next year – I'm not a kid anymore,' Wren had shouted. 'What did he do that made you take off and bring me here, of all places?' She'd narrowed her eyes. 'Or was it something *you* did?'

Wren still had a faint memory from when she was small of her mother always crying. She used to toddle over with her teddy and pat Lily's hand, wishing as hard as she could that she'd be able to make her smile again.

With a groan, her thoughts snapped back to last night's argument. The makeshift palette had slipped through Lily's hands, scattering splashes of colour onto their shack's wooden floor. There'd been shock in her mother's green eyes, but Wren had felt so overwhelmed by fury and grief and resentment, all mixed together, that she'd almost screamed her next question.

'*Is he even alive?*' She still felt the sting of Clara Johnson's words.

Lily had staggered towards her, capturing Wren's hands in her own.

'Darlin', I know you're damned smart when it comes to schoolwork,' she'd said, her voice at a higher pitch than usual. 'But you have no idea how the real world works – it's cruel out there. The answers you're looking for aren't worth the pain they'd bring.'

So many tears had slid onto Lily's cheeks that Wren had felt guilty. She loved her gentle mother, who still stroked her curls and sang her old gospel tunes when they sat together on the front step at night. They'd only ever had each other.

She had wrapped her arms around Lily, saying, 'It's okay,' as softly as a parent to a child.

Nearing the end of the path, Wren caught the sound of a currawong's wings skimming over the current and the faint splash of a beak being dipped. If only life was as simple as that bird's, she thought. If only she felt complete.

The river had dropped so low that hard-packed soil and twisted tree roots lay exposed along its parched banks. Humid air pressed against her cheeks as she walked along the water's edge.

Although Lily had insisted Wren join in a mad ceremony involving chants and the banging of drums, the storm clouds hovering overhead for the past week had stubbornly refused to produce anything other than an increasingly oppressive atmosphere. Now, her mum and the rest of Woolahderra's inhabitants were sure to be lazing around indulging in their usual panacea for any kind of setback – dope, and plenty of it. Wren looked up at the threatening sky. They'd be more unhinged than ever.

Turning, she clambered up through the dense undergrowth just far enough to reach a jutting rock. Hauling herself over one lichen-covered side, she found the smooth patch she liked to sit on, right at the top. From here she had a far better view of the water, though the stand of gums she peered through provided a useful shield from any curious eyes.

Once, when she was around six years old, a long black car had drawn up at the commune in a cloud of dust. She'd never been a shy child, but something had made her hide behind the clump of dense green murraya that grew at the side of their shack.

She had watched silently as Lily rushed out of the front door, wild-eyed. Wren had never seen her mild, dreamy mother look like that before. She'd been in a fury, had flung accusations at the man in the dark blue suit and shiny shoes who'd stepped out of the limousine. Wren thought he must be a kind of policeman – it wouldn't be the first time one of the 'lousy bastards', as the commune dwellers called them, had wanted to shut Woolahderra down.

At first he'd appeared to be reasonable, but then he'd grown angry, raising his voice and throwing his arms about. Wren had curled herself into a tight little ball, squeezing her eyes shut in an effort to shut out the explosive scene. She wasn't certain how long the noise went on; it could have been ten minutes though it might just as easily have lasted for an hour. But there was one thing she was sure of, and that was a strange, new word, thrown in among terms like 'court orders' and threats to 'remove the child so she could be looked after properly'.

'Varenna,' the man kept saying. But who or what was that? Finally, with her arms and legs stiff and sore, she'd heard the car door slam and its wheels grind the gravel as it roared away. Her mother had begun shrieking, 'Wren? Wren? Where are you?'

Only then had she emerged from her hiding place, hot and itchy from being pressed up against the shrubs. Lily was weeping. She'd wrapped her arms around Wren in the tightest embrace, but when Wren had asked who their furious visitor was she'd said only, 'He's a bad man, honey. If he ever comes round again, just you hide like you did this time.'

She'd never forgotten the sight of that long black car and the way the man's shoes shone. He'd made her terrified that, just when they least expected it, little girls like her with no proper house and no proper father could be taken away.

Wren hugged her knees to her chest. Elijah had told her Woolahderra meant 'safe harbour' in the language of the Shoalhaven's Indigenous people – perhaps that promise was what had attracted Lily to this strange little community. Yet, for a long time now, Wren had known she would have to escape one day.

A flame in her belly flared whenever she thought about her future. Although she didn't know exactly *where* she belonged, she was sure as hell it wasn't in Woolahderra. Staying too long in the commune with its healing crystals and weirdo rituals would mean she'd be likely to end up like the others, holed up in a shack or a dilapidated tent, living off the government's dole cheques. She might only be twelve years old, but she already knew she wanted more than that.

Wren tried to swallow the lump in her throat. Her father wasn't the only confusing figure in her life. Lily was also a mystery. Maybe she hadn't always been a drug-taking dreamer; perhaps something had changed her. Whatever had happened, it made Lily cling to Woolahderra as if she were drowning and the crazy commune was her life raft.

Wren heaved a sigh of resignation. She would never be able to persuade her mother to leave. She'd have to do it by herself.

Back in June she had volunteered to help Mr Madden set up for Open Day. They had been laying out projects on the Australian wheat industry when he'd told her she was clever. 'Far too clever for what we can offer around here' were his exact words.

Then he'd added, 'Anyway, Wren Summers, a bird has to learn to fly, and in your case sooner would be better than later.'

He had looked at her with a straightforward gaze. 'You know, it doesn't matter where you have come from. What counts is who you want to be.'

Something inside her had shifted. Mr Madden had revealed new possibilities.

As thunder rumbled ominously in the distance, she gingerly extracted the letter from her pocket and placed it on the palm of her hand. When her teacher had asked if she would like to sit for exams that might lead to a full boarding scholarship at Daneford she'd leapt at the chance. But its board of trustees only awarded a single academic scholarship for each new Year 7 intake and hundreds of the smartest kids in the state tried to win. What hope did she have?

A sudden spike of fear made her gasp. What if she did win the scholarship? How would she manage? She didn't have a clue about the way wealthy, respectable people lived.

Wren reminded herself of the inspiring stories Mr Madden told about adventurers such as Sir Edmund Hillary and his Sherpa guide Tenzing Norgay, conquering Mount Everest without either oxygen or modern gear. Then there were the brave astronauts on board *Apollo 13*, who'd made it back home even though they'd been forced to abandon their control module 200,000 miles from earth. If there was one thing these heroes had taught her, it was that achieving your dreams required taking risks.

With a surge of adrenaline, she ripped open the envelope, removed the single, folded page and smoothed it out against her knees. There wasn't a soul to hear the scream that tore from her lips as the first drops of rain fell onto her flushed cheeks.

CHAPTER SIX

Sydney, 31 January 1988

Wren's fingers tapped against the synthetic upholstery while the taxi driver edged forward in the snarl of traffic. If she wasn't in her seat before the official party's entrance, she'd be locked out. At this rate, she'd end up sitting on a step outside the Opera House, staring blankly at the city lights, instead of inside with Jo watching a once-in-a-lifetime parade.

She'd been amazed when Jo had danced into the Prints and Drawings Department a week earlier, brandishing two tickets to the Australian Wool Board's bicentennial fashion spectacular. As Bobby was viewing a new set of black and white Cartier-Bresson prints in Photography, Jo's elation was entirely unchecked.

'How on earth did you score those?' Wren had asked. 'I've just read a newspaper story saying that ticket holders are being offered up to five thousand dollars on the black market by desperate social climbers.' Then she'd grinned. 'Aren't you tempted?'

'No way!' Jo had performed a little skip of pure glee. 'The show will be incredible – there'll be six local designers and another nine of the world's best. As to how I got hold of them, I've a friend called Meg who's a fashion curator at the Powerhouse Museum. It seems there was some sort of muddle, and she was sent four tickets instead of two.'

Jo had beamed. 'Considering I set her up on a blind date with the guy she's now engaged to, she owes me big time. So – why don't you come with me?'

Finally, the taxi pulled up in front of the Opera House. Wren leapt out and sprinted for the main entrance, only to find herself trapped there by the raucous press pack. A man with a camera shoved her shoulder and someone else trod on her foot as the journalists jockeyed for position, their faces bearing the predatory expressions of big-game hunters.

Wren gulped. Just how late was she? The media was only after one person and, by the sound of it, her arrival was imminent. Wren felt them surge around her, thrusting their oversized telephoto lenses forward as they yelled, 'That's her car!' and 'Diana! Diana!'

Blinking in the glare of the television lights, Wren watched with alarm as the Prince and Princess of Wales swept up in their official limousine. She couldn't decide whether to hang back and attempt to sneak into the show after the royal couple or race up the stairs straight away.

The decision was made for her. Although Wren had managed to push her way out of the media scrum, the sheer force of a new swarm, made up of uniformed aides-de-camp, bustling ladies-in-waiting and the countless security guards who surrounded Charles and Diana, carried her along with it.

Suddenly, a flash of pink caught her eye. Spinning through the air was a rectangular evening bag, which bounced off a step before skittering towards her. Wren instinctively bent down and grabbed it, then looked up to see a mountainous security guard standing centimetres from her nose. 'Hand it over,' he growled.

Wren froze. Absurdly, she felt as guilty as a thief who'd been caught red-handed.

Then a distinctive voice, girlish, with an upper-class English accent, floated towards her. 'Thank you so much, I'm always fingers and thumbs on these big occasions.' Her Royal Highness, the Princess of Wales gave Wren a haunting smile, before adding,

'You look fabulous, by the way. Gosh, I wish they'd put me in what you're wearing.'

Stunned, Wren managed only an awkward bow before shuffling away.

Jo was looking around anxiously when Wren, hot and out of breath, slid into the seat beside her.

'What kept you?' she grumbled, adjusting one of the wildly exaggerated puff sleeves on her short black velvet and satin dress. 'I was beginning to think you wouldn't make it.'

'Traffic,' Wren panted. Her encounter with Diana didn't feel real.

As if on cue, the royal couple entered the cathedral-like auditorium. Thousands of eyes immediately turned in their direction.

Jo gave Wren a nudge. 'Do you know what I'm asking myself?'

'Is it where did Diana's sapphire and diamond necklace and earrings come from?'

'Oh, those – I believe they're a gift from the Sultan of Oman,' Jo said dismissively 'No, I was wondering what possessed Diana's advisers to force a twenty-something girl into that blue frock. The wide collar doesn't work and those mid-calf-length pleats on the skirt are plain dowdy. Poor Diana.'

Wren agreed. It made Diana's wistful admiration of her own vintage tuxedo – picked up for a song in the Paddington markets – even more poignant.

As the house lights dimmed, she heard the rustle of programs and faint noises of anticipation sweep through the audience. A glance back up to the dress circle revealed Diana on the edge of her seat. By contrast, Charles gave every appearance of anticipating a nap.

'Looks like the show's about to begin,' Jo whispered.

A trio of mannequins strode out wearing dresses with huge extended shoulders, nipped-in waists and short skirts in purple and orange. They were quickly followed by a dizzying number of outfits.

Jo gave Wren a nudge. 'See that statuesque girl in Donna Karan? She's one of ours – an Aussie model they call The Body.'

'Does she have a name?' Wren said testily. The iconic image of the headless torso on the cover of Germaine Greer's *The Female Eunuch* had immediately popped into her mind. It sounded as if the mannequin was not a real person but merely a conglomeration of breasts, hips and thighs.

'It's Elle Macpherson,' Jo replied in an undertone. 'And there's the famous American Pat Cleveland – she swore she wouldn't work in the US again until they put a black model on the cover of *Vogue*.'

Jo lowered her voice even more. 'According to Meg, there's been all sorts of carry-on backstage, mainly because Gianni Versace flew in yesterday and proceeded to steal all the best girls from Oscar de la Renta, who's had a total meltdown.

'And as for the French designers – they nearly caused a diplomatic incident when they boycotted Bob Hawke's prime ministerial cocktail party. Seems things are still iffy after the stand-off over the nuclear test ban treaty. Speaking of which' – she paused – 'here comes the Claude Montana section.'

For a moment, Wren thought how much she would adore wearing one of Montana's ingeniously cut black and white pieces, before reminding herself that figure-hugging clothes like those would only encourage the kind of interest she'd always sworn she would avoid.

She tried to imagine how the Princess of Wales felt about being permanently on show. She was rarely out of the spotlight, every detail of her life constantly picked apart and commented upon by the press and public alike. Maybe she'd been mistaken, but Wren could swear she had glimpsed a hint of desperation in Diana's limpid blue eyes.

CHAPTER SEVEN

April

Wren looked across the airy room, observing Bobby Hawkins. As usual, he was crouched behind his desk, his nose buried in an obscure journal.

He must have sensed her eyes on him, as he glanced up, his high forehead furrowed. 'What?' he muttered.

'Nothing, really,' she said with a grin. 'It's just that I was thinking how amazing it is to see the carpet. I mean, institutional grey probably isn't the colour I'd choose, but all the same, actually being able to view it – well, you have to admit, that's a novelty.'

Bobby threw a ball of screwed-up paper at her.

'Oh no you don't,' Wren said, wagging her finger. 'Now that I have finally sorted this place out, don't go cluttering it all up again.'

It had taken much hard work, plus endless tussles with Bobby about what was staying and what should be consigned to the rubbish, but at last, here they were, in an ordered, surprisingly spacious room. Best of all, there was now an entire long wall devoted to works on paper that changed on a six-weekly basis. Currently, a lovely group of eighteenth-century etchings depicting life at the French court was on display.

'I nearly forgot to tell you,' Bobby mumbled shyly. 'We have a meeting today with Roth.'

Wren nearly dropped the rare Japanese print she was holding. Dr Robert Hawkins was a brilliant man with an encyclopedic knowledge of his field, although these attributes came with pronounced eccentricities. Among them was a passionate aversion to admitting any of the supplicants who regularly begged for entry to what he undoubtedly regarded as his own, private collection.

'As in Herbert Roth, the art dealer?' she said, carefully laying the print on her desk. 'I thought you couldn't bear the man.'

Bobby's cheeks revealed an unusual flush of colour. 'Roth's tracked down something I've always wanted,' he said earnestly.

Wren leant forward. 'Tell me more.'

'You'll have to wait.' Bobby gave her a mischievous look. 'He'll be in this afternoon.'

'Will he really.' Knowing her boss, he'd change his mind and send the man away. 'Then I'd better wash up the china.'

As Wren went out the door, balancing several mugs, her ears caught a peculiar, high-pitched sound she'd not heard before. Bobby Hawkins was whistling.

'My God,' Roth said, coming to a halt in the middle of the room. 'Am I in the right place?' He pushed a pair of wire-framed spectacles up his nose. 'Where is everything?'

'That would be a question best directed to my new assistant,' Bobby muttered. 'Herbert Roth, meet Wren Summers.'

Roth was of medium height, with a prominent stomach and sharp black eyes. 'I can tell you're a force to be reckoned with, young lady,' he said smoothly, as he dropped into the visitor's chair opposite Bobby.

Ignoring Roth's attempt at a compliment – it made him sound more like a used-car salesman than her idea of an art dealer – she offered a quick greeting before excusing herself to make coffee. Once she'd set down a tray and two mugs on the curator's desk, Bobby asked her, 'Why don't you join us? You should hear this.'

Herbert Roth turned towards Wren. 'No doubt you're aware that Dr Hawkins has been after a particular work for some time.'

She nodded vaguely. There were many works that Bobby longed to add to the collection, although she had no idea which one Roth might be referring to.

'And now I've found it – or at least, my Italian associate has.' He looked back at Bobby. 'It's a fine sketch of a woman, probably created in the latter part of Raphael's life. The condition's not perfect, but that's reflected in the price.' He took a sip from his mug. 'It's not signed, either, although Signor Baretti and I are quite sure it was drawn by the master himself. I can show you several expert reports,' he added.

An actual *Raphael*? Wren felt a thrilling shiver. As for Bobby, she thought his rapturous expression made him look like a child anticipating Christmas.

Roth laid out various documents relating to the drawing's provenance, followed by a sheaf of glossy photographs. Some showed the work in full, others focused on the woman's hands and face.

As Wren gazed at the pictures her heart beat a little faster. 'The original must be exquisite,' she whispered.

'It can be had for a very fair sum – only four hundred thousand.' Roth said casually, mentioning the figure as if it were a trifle.

Wren tried not to show her disappointment. The department had recently become the beneficiary of a generous bequest from a patron who favoured the Renaissance, but it fell fifty thousand dollars short.

'Well?' Roth asked. 'I've come to you first,' he paused, 'in view of our long relationship.'

'That's very kind of you, Herbert,' Bobby said, 'especially considering our, uh, ups and downs.'

'What, you mean all those phone calls you never returned? Forget about it.' Roth waved one hand dismissively.

'Three hundred thousand.' Bobby was uncharacteristically firm.

'Three seventy-five,' Roth countered.

'Three fifty.'

'Done.' The two men shook hands.

Wren couldn't believe how coolly Bobby had conducted himself. The department was acquiring a Raphael! She was sure that if she'd just pulled off that deal she would have been punching the air with triumph.

'There is just one matter, though,' Bobby said. 'Naturally, we need to verify the drawing's authenticity. I assume sending it to us here at the museum will not be a problem?'

Roth shook his balding head. 'I'm afraid it's far too fragile. You'll have to go to Rome.'

Bobby merely nodded.

'Excellent.' Roth stood up. 'There's no need to show me out. I'll be in touch with your pretty assistant to sort out the details.' He glanced at Wren. 'I've known Dr Hawkins long enough to realise he's not overly fond of paperwork.'

As soon as Roth had departed, Wren went to give Bobby a pat on the back, only to see him shrink away. Cursing herself for failing to remember he had an irrational fear of being touched, she decided instead to raise one of the coffee mugs in a toast to his success. She stopped midway when she saw his face was as white as a sheet of acid-free paper.

'Is everything all right?' she asked. Bobby might be distinctly odd, but all the same, she'd expected him to be over the moon. 'Come on. We've been sharing this office for more than three months. What is it?'

Bobby buried his face in his hands, mumbling something she couldn't quite catch.

'Can you try that a little louder?' she asked.

A strangled voice said, 'I can't do it.'

'What do you mean, you can't do it? Bobby, please look at me.'

He dropped his hands. 'I can't get on a plane.'

Of course, Wren thought with dismay. Flying *would* be one of Bobby's phobias. But missing out on a superb drawing by a sixteenth-century master didn't bear thinking about. She felt almost as despondent as Bobby looked. But perhaps ... she was struck by a wonderful thought.

'There might be a solution,' she said.

Bobby appeared near to tears 'No, there isn't. We are going to lose that perfect Raphael, the very drawing I've been after for years. It's a disaster.' His voice filled with despair. 'When you get down to it, this museum is just a small, provincial institution that's dramatically understaffed. There's no one I'd trust to carry out the authentication.'

'Not even me?' Wren said. 'Renaissance drawing is one of my specialities.' She gave Bobby an encouraging look. 'I'd hate for you to miss out.'

He clapped his forehead. 'Good Lord! I don't know what's wrong with me. You certainly have the academic credentials.' Then he paused. 'But going all the way to Rome and authenticating an expensive work – you haven't done anything like that before.'

He blew his nose with a handkerchief. 'I don't know ... Do you really think you're up to it?'

Wren's mind worked quickly. Heading off to one of the world's great art capitals to verify a Raphael, appealing as that might be, was bound to carry risks for someone as inexperienced as she was. But it was also a fantastic chance to further her career. Hadn't she always told herself that she'd never be like Lily? Her lackadaisical, flower-child mother had a way of blowing opportunities.

'Yes, Bobby.' Wren produced her most reassuring smile. 'I'm positive.'

CHAPTER EIGHT

Daneford School, November 1980

Glancing at her cheap watch, Wren waited impatiently by the wall-mounted telephone in the front hall of the boarding house. Each boarder was allocated a set time and day when their parents were permitted to make a ten-minute phone call. As it was now 4.00 pm, Lily was due to ring any minute.

'Don't worry, babe,' she had assured Wren when the arrangement had first been set up. 'I'll make sure I always have plenty of change, so I never miss a single conversation.'

She didn't, either – at least at first. But as the months passed, Wren often ended up hanging about, anticipating a phone call that never came.

'Come on, come on,' Wren muttered under her breath as she paced up and down the hall, fervently hoping this was not one of those times when her mother had become lost in a world of her own.

Gazing at the dazzling pictures in the museum had ignited something inside Wren. It wasn't the urge to make paintings like Lily, but the desire to discover everything there was to know about art, to understand it, appreciate the way great works were devised and the intentions that lay behind their creation. To spend her days surrounded by the glorious output of exceptional artists seemed like the best possible way to live.

'I give up!' she muttered between clenched teeth. Then the phone rang.

Wren pounced on the receiver. 'Mum, I'm so glad you called,' she burst out. 'Something really special has happened.'

'What is it?' Her mother sounded just as excited as she was.

'It's about the art exhibition I saw.'

'An art exhibition?' Lily seemed delighted. 'Well, that can be a powerful thing. You'll have to tell me all about it.'

Wren heard a clatter as Lily fed more coins into the payphone.

'It's kind of a coincidence, too. A little gallery has opened in town,' Lily said. 'You know me, I never hang on to my pictures, but the owner, Maisie Jones, persuaded me to sell a couple I had hanging around, and now she's offered me my own show.'

'Wow, that's amazing!' Wren danced on the spot with the phone in her hand. Her own news could wait – this was just the opportunity Lily needed.

'I'll have to work really hard if I'm going to have everything finished in time,' she murmured.

Wren could hear the doubt in her mother's voice. 'You can do it,' she said, willing her mother to believe in herself. 'I know you can. When's it on? My holidays start on December the fourth – that's a Thursday.'

'Honey, the timing's perfect,' Lily said, immediately brightening. 'You can help me hang my pictures the next day, because the opening party is that Saturday night.'

She gave a nervous laugh. 'According to Maisie, the whole damned town's turning up.'

It was nearly dark when Wren hopped off the bus. Swinging her small suitcase in one hand, she ran all the way from the highway down the gravel road that led to Woolahderra. The first thing she'd do was to give Lily a giant hug and then see her new work. After that she'd tell her mum about the lightning bolt of insight that had struck her when she'd visited the museum.

As she approached their rundown shack, she noticed that every window was lit up. That was exciting. It meant Lily must be putting the finishing touches to some of the paintings. Wren was proud of her mother, thrilled that at last she had focused long enough to create enough work for an exhibition. Lily would have a chance to show everyone how gifted she really was – a talent like hers should be celebrated. And she was sure to make some money, maybe even enough to fix the shack up a bit.

Shouldering aside the front door, Wren ran through the cramped front room – and came to an abrupt halt.

Lily was lying passed out on her bed, her arms around a gangly guy with blue tattooed dragons curling across his bare chest. Wren took in the bong that lay next to them and the remains of blackish-brown wads of hash, the empty bottles of cheap bourbon and the cigarette packets scattered on the floor like crumpled flowers.

She lurched backwards, stumbling over discarded shoes and bits of clothing. God only knew how long Lily had been on this bender. There had to be well over a dozen canvases propped up against the shack's walls, but no more than two or three were anywhere near finished. The rest sported only random daubs of colour.

A swirl of nausea made her swallow. She should have known there would never be an exhibition. It was always going to end like this.

Wren rushed out of the hut. Looking up at the night sky through hot, tear-filled eyes, she swore that she was not about to waste her life. She was going to be a success – and nothing would hold her back.

CHAPTER NINE

Sydney, May 1988

Wren was wriggling her fingers into a pair of the white cotton gloves all the curatorial staff wore while handling works of art when the sound of a familiar voice made her turn around.

'Hi there,' Jo said brightly. 'Bobby told me you were coming across to collect a couple of the Warhols.'

Wren looked up from the screen prints she had laid out on a table. 'Hi yourself. You're looking swish.'

Jo was dressed completely in black – high heels, opaque tights, a little skirt and a boxy jacket – save for a pair of chunky faux-pearl earrings and a white silk camellia she'd pinned to her lapel. 'You have such an appreciation for design,' she said, smiling. 'I can't believe you keep wearing those shapeless men's clothes. Plus, they have zero sex appeal.'

Wren eased off her gloves. 'You know me.'

Jo gave her a cheeky look. 'Don't you ever want to get up close and personal with a guy? I've had lots of boyfriends. Nothing serious though – there's no way I'm ready to settle down.'

'I experimented a little bit at uni, but it was never great.' Wren shrugged. 'Anyway, if I did get involved with someone, I'd just end up getting hurt.'

Something deep inside her fragile mother was broken – she was sure it was the reason Lily lost herself so often in drug-induced highs. If that was the result of giving your heart to a man, she didn't want any part of it.

Jo put her arm around Wren. 'Look, I don't want to come over all Dr Freud on you, but I'm guessing this has something to do with losing your father. Relationships don't always end up in disaster. They can be fun, you know.'

'Maybe.' Wren looked unconvinced.

'You're way too cautious.' Jo's face lit up. 'Which is exactly why I should take you shopping for some new clothes.'

'I'm saving money,' Wren said. 'I can't stay in that dismal boarding house forever. One day I want to buy my own apartment.'

'You'll be waiting a bloody long time if you stick with a museum career.' Jo laughed. 'The pay's hopeless, even at senior levels. You'd be better off robbing a bank.'

Smiling, Wren swept her arm around the room. 'But at least I get to work alongside all this art. Speaking of which, seeing as you're so dressed up, why don't you come out with me tonight? There are some interesting pictures being auctioned at the InterContinental.'

Wren felt a swell of anticipation as she contemplated the sale. She'd started attending auctions at university, at first purely because she'd been curious to see the pictures, but soon she'd become addicted to the rush of adrenaline brought about by watching competing bidders do battle as the price of a lot spiralled. Assessing who might bid on which work and how high they might be prepared to go was a magical game she never tired of playing.

'Once the auction is over we could have a drink in the bar or maybe drop in at a club.' Wren winked. 'You said I should live a little.'

Jo pointed at the man's waistcoat, shirt and pants she was wearing. 'Dressed like that? You might be on a budget, but it's time you made the most of yourself. I'd kill for your long legs and your figure, not to mention your Botticelli face.' She wrinkled her nose. 'You can't go to Rome dressed like some sort of superannuated business executive.'

'Jo!' Wren said with mock indignation.

'Don't "Jo" me.' She put her hands on her hips. 'Pop up to my place after work and I'll find something that will make you look a bit more like a girl.'

'Nothing doing.'

'Just a few tweaks to your look?' she wheedled.

'We'll see.' Wren replaced her gloves and slid a pair of lurid turquoise and pink prints of Marilyn Monroe into a tissue-lined folder.

A distinct ripple of interest greeted the girls as they strode down the central aisle of the hotel ballroom and found a couple of seats. Heads swivelled at the dramatic pairing – Jo, small and shapely, with her short blonde hair catching the light, and Wren, whose sole concessions to Jo's pleas had been to wear her waistcoat without the shirt underneath and to brush out her cloud of dark curls.

For once, Wren didn't care about the whispers and stares. Her eyes were fixed upon the man who stood in the spotlight facing the room.

'Lot twenty-three, *The River* by Brett Whiteley,' he said in a resonant voice. 'The work comes from the Jones-Nagle collection.' A landscape replete with voluptuous lines and swirls of cobalt blue was hoisted up on an easel by a couple of attendants.

Wren's heart began to thud.

'Do I hear eighty thousand?' The man nodded towards someone sitting at the side of the room. 'Thank you, sir. I have eighty thousand on my left, eighty thousand on my left. Do I hear ninety?'

Wren gave Jo a nudge. 'Watch the guy with the moustache who just bid. He's after that painting at any price. The glazed expression in his eyes is a dead giveaway.'

'What do you mean?' whispered Jo as a man wearing a bow tie raised his paddle.

'Ooh, this is interesting,' Wren whispered back. 'Bow Tie Man has the same look. He's got his heart set on the Whiteley as well.'

'Let's say you're right,' Jo murmured. 'I still can't understand why the auctioneer's ignoring everyone else.'

'You'll see.' Wren gave her a quick smile 'He'll give Moustache Guy, otherwise known as the underbidder, first chance to up the ante. There he goes now,' she said, 'but something tells me he's going to fold in the end.'

'That bloke in the blue suit who's waving his hand in the air looks a winner,' Jo said.

'No way,' Wren murmured. 'I'll guarantee he's a one-bid only punter, hoping like hell he'll pick up a bargain.'

'But what about—'

'Shhh, Jo. I'm concentrating.'

The man on the dais was masterly, Wren thought, one of the best auctioneers she'd seen. His cultivated voice and well-cut suit gave him an air of authority, though the way he was working the room reminded her of a snake charmer.

'Well?' she asked Jo over a glass of red wine in the bar downstairs after the last lot had been sold. 'What did you think?'

'You're uncanny – practically every bidder did exactly what you predicted.' Jo grinned. 'It's like you've got second sight or something. Bow Tie Man paid a bomb for that Whiteley, just like you said he would.' She gave Wren a meaningful look.

'Weird, isn't it?' Wren laughed. 'Even though, God knows, I often get people wrong when I first meet them, I never seem to have the same problem at a sale.'

'Well, if you're ever going to buy that dream apartment, maybe you should think about a career in an auction house. The business seems like the ultimate marriage between art and commerce, with a dollop of scholarship thrown in for good measure.' Jo paused. 'You might find that's a place where you'd fit in.'

Wren gulped some wine. She knew Jo had merely made a throwaway comment, but that remark had resonated with her in a way her friend couldn't possibly imagine. The truth was, she'd been looking for a place to belong for a very long time.

Maybe, just maybe, it was at an auction house. She could still recall the excitement she had experienced at her very first sale and, now that she thought about it, the sensation had been remarkably similar to that stirring, long-ago moment when she'd first visited the art museum. Now she was actually employed there, surely that should satisfy her – it had been the culmination of all her hopes and dreams. So why did she still have the feeling that there was something more?

Wiping her mouth with a paper napkin, Wren told herself to let that notion go. Right now she had more than enough to contend with.

'Perhaps you're onto something,' she said, 'but I'm not after a new job. The museum's pay might be dismal, but just think' – her lips curved into a wide smile – 'I'll be in Rome next week.'

CHAPTER TEN

University of California, Berkeley, May 1965

Fifteen minutes went by, but the air remained charged. News of the protest had spread like a forest fire, bringing hundreds of passionate demonstrators to join those already grouped defiantly in front of Sproul Hall.

The fair-haired girl told herself she had nothing to worry about. They'd been in plenty of tight spots before and hadn't once been arrested. She began to feel better, inspired by the values she and the blue-eyed boy both believed in: peace and love, justice and the freedom to do your own thing. She hadn't smoked pot for weeks, not since she'd realised she had the baby coming, but the mood evoked by this night of rebellion made her feel as high as a kite.

Right now, thousands of miles away, those silver bombers President Johnson had sent to North Vietnam were releasing their lethal cargoes on a place that had never threatened the United States. LBJ had declared the targets were 'strategic' – fuel depots and the like – but it was all too easy to imagine his fire-filled weapons raining down from the stratosphere onto innocent men, women and children who lived in simple villages.

At least Berkeley's students had shown President Johnson and the rest of his cronies that they would have no part in the deadly mission dubbed Operation Rolling Thunder, she thought with a glow of pride.

Suddenly, a high-pitched yell sliced through the night. 'The pigs are here!'

The boy and girl linked arms as a surge of Californian troopers advanced on the students in a dark, roiling wave. Within minutes their batons were flying.

The boy pulled her closer. 'Let's run!' he yelled above the crowd's screams.

She wrenched her arm from his grasp. 'Go on without me,' she said urgently. 'You'll get away faster, and anyway, it's draft-card burners like you that they're after.'

'Are you sure?' he said.

She nodded. 'I'll find you later, at Arnie's.'

With a pair of thuggish-looking troopers bearing down on him, the boy took to his heels. He might have passed his master's degree with flying colours, the girl thought as she pushed her way through the melee, but thank God he'd always kept up his training for track and field.

She'd first spotted him inside that same building, back in December when a band of student demonstrators who stood for free speech dared to occupy the site. Even though he'd been wearing a pair of jeans and a faded T-shirt just like everyone else, she'd noticed an unusual elegance about him, a self-possession that, together with his dark thatch of hair and refined face, made him stand out.

'Hey, Joanie!' he'd called in an East Coast accent redolent of old money. She had recognised the folksinger Joan Baez, with her trademark bare feet and shining black hair, straightaway. Joan had waved at the blue-eyed boy before climbing onto a desk, where she'd started strumming her guitar. Then, in her stirring soprano, she'd launched into the best loved of protest songs, 'We Shall Overcome'.

The demonstrators had surged forward, knocking the fair-haired girl to the ground. She'd been gasping for air when the boy scooped her up in his arms. Taking her hand, he'd ushered her away from the crowd.

That was how it had begun. The beautiful boy had taken her back to the old, white-painted house she shared with four other students, made her hot tea and found ice for her bruises. They'd talked so long into the night that he'd stayed over, falling asleep in the worn velvet armchair next to her narrow bed.

They had been together ever since, their love forged as they walked shoulder to shoulder at free speech rallies and civil rights marches. She smiled, remembering how they had discovered the sweetness of each other's bodies during more intimate moments.

Free love was indulged in by most of the girls she knew. The Pill eliminated consequences, yet despite this advantage, she still didn't like the idea of spreading her favours. Anyway, who wanted to swallow an unnatural substance, synthesised in laboratories by greedy drug manufacturers?

This aversion should have been the perfect excuse for avoiding sex with the many young men who pursued her, though when she tried to push away their sweaty embraces, they accused her of everything from being repressed to neurotic. One swaggering boy, equipped with the requisite Californian tan and shaggy blond hair, had preserved his reputation for being a stud by putting out the rumour that she was an uptight, reactionary bitch.

The reality was, she'd still had too much of the good Southern girl in her to sleep around. The blue-eyed boy had been her first lover, revealing a new realm of sensual pleasure that had only deepened her feelings for him.

They shared the same passions, believed in a different kind of society, one that wasn't ruled by greedy capitalists and warmongers who circulated their odious views via a compliant network of news outlets.

Together, they could create their own world. Without him she would drift, alone. Her parents were dead. She had no brothers or sisters; she belonged only to the beautiful boy. If she wasn't with him, then where would she be? She pictured herself, unmoored and unprotected, like a fragile craft at the mercy of a monstrous sea.

It was with a sigh of relief that, hours afterwards, she recognised the boy's lean frame in the doorway of Arnie's, a smoky dive that catered mainly to the middle-aged beatniks who still hung around the San Francisco Bay area. He limped towards her, stopping only to speak to the bearded owner who stood behind the bar drying cups and saucers.

'If anyone asks, you never saw me,' she heard him say.

The man pulled up the neck of his black skivvy. 'I know how to keep my mouth shut.'

The boy caught her eye, indicating with a tilt of his head that she should move to another, less conspicuous table. Once they were seated next to each other in a dark alcove, he leant towards her. 'Well, I made it.' He gave her a lopsided smile.

She winced as she took in the bruises already blooming across one of his cheekbones. 'Thank the Lord,' she said in her soft drawl, pushing a glass of water towards him. 'Only, you don't look so good, honey.'

The boy's face was grim. 'There's plenty of guys who are worse off than me,' he muttered, rubbing one shoulder. 'At least I'm out on bail.'

'You were arrested?' she asked in a whisper.

'Yeah.'

Her hand flew to her mouth. 'No! They're trying to make you out to be a criminal, when the real criminals are in the US government – and that monster who fills his papers with right-wing propaganda.'

'I appreciate you not mentioning his name.' The boy laughed. He had regained some of his poise. 'Anyway, I gave the cops a fake identity, not that that's going to hold them off for long. I've heard the FBI has been brought in to help track us down.' He took her hand. 'Sweetheart, I went into this with my eyes open. We both did.'

Her pulse quickened. 'What does that mean?'

'It means that we're leaving.' His expression gave nothing away. She couldn't tell what lay behind those shadowed blue eyes.

'Leaving? To go where?' She sat back. 'I'm not returning to Louisiana, if that's what you're thinking. I want to live around people who feel the same way about the world as we do.' She put her head to one side. 'How about Greenwich Village? That's a cool place.'

'No way.' The boy recoiled. 'Too easy to be found.'

'Honey, you're sounding paranoid,' she said gently. 'Millions of people live in New York. How would anyone even know we were there?'

'You haven't met my father,' he said. 'Dad never stops until he gets what he's after. He's even worse since Mom died – I don't want anything to do with him.'

She sipped from her cup, even though she'd already had so many of Arnie's bitter coffees that her heart had started to skitter. All she knew about the boy's parents was that he'd been close to his mother, but he and his dad – some kind of businessman – had a volatile relationship. He didn't much like talking about either one of them.

The boy gave her a serious look. 'You did get your passport, didn't you?'

'Sure.' She twisted a strand of her blonde hair around one finger. 'But I thought that was for our holiday in Jamaica. We were going to dive in the ocean and check out the music. Don't tell me you're actually planning for us to live there?'

He looked intently into her sea-green eyes. 'The place we're heading for isn't a tropical island, but it's just as magical,' he said in a low voice. 'We'll fly out tomorrow.'

The girl stared back. 'Tomorrow!' She shook her head. 'We can't just run off to some foreign country.'

The boy responded with a smile. 'I've come into a bit of money. It's a legacy Mom left me. Which means …'

'What, exactly?'

'It means we can do whatever we like.'

CHAPTER ELEVEN

Rome, May 1988

Wren quivered with excitement as the Qantas jet circled above the lapis blue Mediterranean, then banked towards Leonardo da Vinci airport.

Today, she'd only have time for a special pilgrimage to see Raphael's tomb in the Pantheon, because the appointment with Alessandro Baretti had been set for 3.00 pm. Her stomach clenched. Whenever she thought of facing the Italian dealer and his precious drawing she felt slightly ill. She had a picture of him in her mind, a sort of Mediterranean version of Herbert Roth, although older, even stouter and certainly more impatient.

Once the verification process was completed, she'd have just two days left to explore the Vatican, including Michelangelo's Sistine Chapel. Then there was the Borghese Gallery and the Capitoline Hill, as well as Trajan's Column and the Forum. But she couldn't miss the Arch of Constantine or Piazza Navona, let alone the Trevi Fountain. Her shoulders slumped. She hadn't landed yet and she was already overwhelmed.

Swallowing hard as the plane descended, she wondered if the Italian she'd learnt from books would be sufficient for her to navigate her way around. She'd forgotten to ask whether Roth's partner spoke English.

Her brow wrinkled. She had never left Australia before, never encountered a foreign dealer, nor – and most significant of all –

had she ever viewed a genuine Raphael. Just like the language, her knowledge was entirely theoretical. On the other hand, she reflected, she'd pored over countless reproductions and read everything about Raphael she could get her hands on. 'Nothing ventured, nothing gained' was a motto that had worked pretty well for her so far. Why should the task ahead prove any different?

After collecting her bag from the carousel, she made her way through the busy terminal, dodging tired families trailing small children, tourists with cameras slung around their necks and well-heeled businessmen clutching briefcases. '*Scusi, scusi,*' she muttered self-consciously as she headed for the exit.

The queue for the taxi was long and the disgruntled woman immediately in front of her kept up a loud stream of complaints in rapid Italian. Yawning as she shuffled along, Wren cursed the hours-long delay she'd endured at the Bahrain transit stop. She felt as if she'd been travelling forever and, now that she'd finally arrived in Italy, she had a major case of jet lag. *Whatever you do, don't fall asleep*, she told herself once she was sitting on the back seat of a taxi. She couldn't afford to miss a minute.

'Whoa!' Wren reeled back. As soon as the car reached central Rome, she was blasted by a roar of noise and a wave of heat. The city pulsed with chaotic energy. Horns blared and brakes screeched. Revving motorbikes whipped in front of pedestrians, who dashed heedlessly across choked streets. Rome had a staccato music all of its own.

Wren's head swivelled from left to right as the taxi passed a bridge lined with statues striking heroic poses, followed by an ornate wedding cake of a building decorated with marble figures. And wasn't that vast arena, more awesome than she had imagined, the fabled Colosseum? She had the sense that history had escaped from the dusty pages of textbooks and come dramatically alive, just for her.

By contrast, her hotel was a quiet, modest little place. Pinkish with green shutters, it was tucked away in a side street behind the majestic sweep of the Spanish Steps. As soon as she'd checked in, Wren headed for her tiny room, dumped her suitcase on the floor and threw open the window. Below her was a small square with a bubbling stone fountain at its centre. The brilliant colours of the surrounding buildings – golden yellow, a deep rose and blood red, the last draped with looping vines of crimson bougainvillea – brought a delighted smile to her face. Lily would have adored these brilliant shades.

Wren's smile fell away. Her mother never went anywhere. There were so many amazing experiences she might have had if she could only bring herself to leave Woolahderra. Strangely, when Wren had told Lily she was visiting Rome, her only response was a quick intake of breath before changing the subject. It had been enough, though, for Wren to gain the impression that Lily had been disturbed by her news. Shrugging, she reminded herself that it had always been impossible to fathom her mother's unpredictable moods.

As Wren glanced back at her room, her drooping eyes settled on the ornate bed's ruby coverlet, turned back to display an inviting triangle of cool white sheet. Surely she could afford to put her head down for ten minutes. She pulled off her jacket, kicked off her shoes and sank into the welcome softness.

Wren woke with a jolt. She was in Rome – *Rome*! She jumped out of bed and rushed back to the window. Curiously, the courtyard looked different. She didn't remember that golden-yellow wall being in shadow.

Glancing at her watch, she muttered, 'I don't believe it.'

Unless she'd made a mistake when she'd adjusted the time after landing – which wasn't likely as she'd checked it against one of the clocks in the terminal – she'd been asleep for hours. She hadn't set foot outside her hotel, let alone visited any sights. Worse, if she didn't hurry, she'd be keeping Signor Baretti waiting. The last thing she wanted was to be confronted by an irate Italian art dealer.

By now, she felt so flustered that her flailing fingers failed to fathom the bathroom's complicated plumbing. An unsatisfactory wash standing up with a cloth doused in tepid water was all she had time for.

At least dressing was easy. Having ignored Jo's entreaties to exchange her severe style for something more appealing, she threw her hair up in a tortoiseshell clasp and pulled on a pair of navy blue trousers. Then she added sturdy shoes and a light blue cotton shirt. Better wear the suit's matching jacket as well, she decided. It would look more professional, though she could already feel a trickle of perspiration working its way down her back.

Her stomach growled, but there was nothing to eat in the room and there'd be no time to stop on the way to her appointment. After a hurried swig from a bottle of mineral water, she grabbed her black leather shoulder bag and ran downstairs.

Screwing up her eyes in the fierce sunlight, she set off down the street. The afternoon heat radiated from the buildings, forcing her to remove her coat and fold it over one arm. How she wished she were dressed in shorts and a T-shirt like the tourists she passed, strung out in a meandering line behind their guide's bobbing red parasol.

Wren cursed when the unfamiliar cobblestones made her trip. Righting herself, she flew down an ancient street lined with dark green pines and intriguing shops selling leather goods, old books and Panama hats. If only she had the time to linger, to soak up every bit of this beautiful city. Most of all, though, she longed to enter one of the cafés that were dotted along her route. She was so hungry she could barely think.

Wren stopped at a corner, feeling disorientated. Peering down at the map she'd found in her hotel room, she reminded herself that the way to Baretti's had been straightforward. She had merely needed to take a turn to the right, then a left at the next corner, go down a lane, across a square and there, over the next street, should be the gallery.

She looked up with dismay at the church rearing in front of her. There was no sign of anything resembling an art gallery.

'Hey!' Wren spun around. A young man in a black T-shirt turned his head back and winked, then continued strolling nonchalantly across the street. Wren glowered. A girl at the museum had told her that bottom pinching was still a common experience for women visiting Italy, but she'd thought that sticking to her shapeless men's clothes would eliminate this indignity. If she wasn't so late and in entirely the wrong place, she would have caught up with the creep and told him to go to hell.

A split-second later her frown dissolved into a smile. Unknowingly, the man had done her a good turn for there, on the opposite side of the street, the word *Baretti* was written in elegant black letters across a white awning. As she drew closer, she saw that its window contained a single etching of a fantastical structure by the renowned eighteenth-century printmaker Piranesi, thereby announcing to the world this was an establishment that dealt with only the choicest work.

Inside, a chic middle-aged woman wearing a sleeveless black dress with a chunky gold necklace sat behind a counter. '*Si?*' she said pleasantly. '*Desidera?*'

Wren responded in halting Italian, explaining that she was Miss Summers from the Sydney Art Museum, here to see Signor Baretti about a Raphael drawing.

'But of course.' The woman responded in flawless English. 'I will show you into his office.'

Wren found herself staring. The man sitting in front of her could not be the dealer. Surely he was another visitor, almost certainly one who'd come straight from an Italian film set. In his early thirties, with thick dark hair brushed back from a bronzed face, he had a fine, straight nose and bright azure eyes.

A tide of attraction swept through her. She'd never felt so drawn to a man.

'*Benvenuta a Roma, Signorina Summers.*' Baretti rose to his feet, strode forward and shook her hand. 'If you prefer,' he added in a voice inflected with a lilting accent, 'we can speak in English.'

'Thank you, that's very kind.' Wren's head was swimming. The heat, the rush to arrive, jet lag and an empty stomach were all part of it, but she felt fairly sure it was the dealer himself who was the main cause of her alarming condition.

'Are you quite well, Miss Summers?' he asked, looking worried.

Wren felt herself begin to totter. She could still hear Baretti's voice, though it sounded as if it was coming from somewhere far away. Suddenly, her knees buckled.

She looked up, bewildered to find the handsome dealer holding her in his arms.

'*Grazie a Dio*, you are all right, Miss Summers. I'm afraid you fainted.' He helped her into a chair.

'This is so embarrassing,' Wren said weakly. 'I'm terribly sorry.'

'Not at all. It is I who should ask forgiveness for our Roman weather, which is absurdly hot for this time of year.' He held out his hands in an apologetic gesture. 'Plus, I believe you only arrived from Australia this morning, and that is a very long journey. I should have waited until tomorrow to see you, but I was due to fly to Milan later today.'

'If I could just have some water,' Wren murmured.

'*Sì, naturalmente, signorina*.' Baretti poured a glass of San Pellegrino from the bottle standing on a side table.

'How long is it since you have eaten something?' he asked, drawing his brows together.

'I don't remember,' Wren admitted. 'Hours ago, I think, on the plane. Not that I had much.' She made a face. 'Everything tasted like plastic.'

'*Allora*, if you think you could walk a little, it will be my pleasure to take you to a small place only a few doors away.'

'Thank you, no,' Wren protested feebly. 'I've already caused you quite enough trouble. Once I have viewed the drawing and performed the necessary checks, I'll leave you to get on with your day.'

'That will not do at all,' Baretti said, his stern tone mitigated by a smile that made her feel weaker than ever. 'Like so many of life's pleasures, art should be enjoyed at one's leisure. It is the Italian way.'

Still dazed, Wren allowed herself to be escorted to the café. Once they were settled in a shady corner, Baretti ordered. 'I hope you don't mind,' he said. 'I've asked for something very light, just a caprese salad, a little pasta and a glass of prosecco. It is a combination guaranteed to make you feel better.'

'Thank you, Signor,' Wren murmured, attempting to hide her discomfort by smoothing back the dark curls that had escaped from their clasp.

'Call me Alessandro,' Baretti said easily. 'Signor is far too formal, especially under the circumstances. It is not every day I have the good fortune to come to the aid of a beautiful Australian woman.' He looked into her eyes. 'Would you tell me your name?'

Wren found it impossible to summon the cold expression she would normally adopt when a man began flirting so outrageously.

'*Mi chiamo Wren*,' she said with a smile.

CHAPTER TWELVE

Her gloved fingers trembled with emotion as she held the sublime sketch in her hands. Roth's photographs had not done it justice – the woman in this picture seemed to live. The curve of her cheeks, the slight tilt forward of her body and the mysterious smile that graced her lips – all were rendered in a way that transcended mere observation. What an extraordinary joy it was to touch this centuries-old work of genius.

Wren brought the sheet of paper up to the light, wrinkling her forehead as she examined its quality and the precise nature of the watermark. She could make out the faintest traces of a grid, an encouraging sign as it meant that the drawing had been intended to be used as a guide for a larger painting – a practice Raphael favoured. Fortunately, the deterioration Roth had mentioned was confined to some pale grey spotting and a little tea-coloured staining along the lower edge. This oxidation, or 'foxing' as it was known in the art trade, was another positive sign, for it indicated the work's considerable age.

Next, after carefully placing the drawing down on a length of white tissue paper, Wren used a magnifying glass and a powerful torch to better assess whether the techniques matched those of Raphael. If the work was truly an original and not a mere copy, the giveaway would be signs of his corrections.

Yes, she thought with a thrill of delight, there were the near imperceptible marks of the steel-point pen the artist used to sketch in the principal forms. What else? She tried not to reveal her growing excitement as she observed the black chalk Raphael famously applied to add depth, as well as the red he used for modelling the body.

As Wren slowly moved the magnifying glass over the work she detected finer details. Added with a pen, they served to emphasise specific elements such as the angle of the woman's right arm and the weave of the basket she was carrying. Finally, a tiny brush had been employed to apply white highlights. She marvelled at the way these delicate strokes made the woman's flowing hair and the drapery of her robe appear to dissolve into the light.

Wren needed no more convincing. Only the master himself could have captured his subject's pensive expression and graceful form, while never once sacrificing anatomical integrity. Only he could have created a composition of such beauty and elegance.

A surge of pleasure made her glow. She'd always felt that great art was like a radiant sun. It was moments like these that filled her heart with hope and nurtured her soul.

'All is in order?' Alessandro said, raising his eyebrows.

Unwilling to reveal how much the drawing had moved her – it seemed too intimate a confession – Wren concentrated on removing her gloves. 'It is an excellent study,' she said, striving for a formal tone. 'I have no doubt that it is genuine.'

'Then we are agreed.' He took a set of closely typed documents from the desk drawer and placed them in front of her. 'Simply add your signature to every page and the work is yours – or at least, the museum's.'

Wren looked down, frowning. The contract was written in Italian. 'I'm not certain I should,' she said hesitantly. 'I don't think I'm up to translating this agreement.'

'Let me assure you, it is a standard contract.' Alessandro's voice had acquired a steely edge. 'As you would expect, we have many,

many clients, but not one of them has ever suggested we might be less than scrupulously honest.'

Wren cursed herself. Clearly, he felt she'd insulted him.

'Of course, if you prefer not to proceed,' he continued in the same stiff tone, 'it will not be a problem. But you must decide straight away. An important Swiss museum has already made a firm offer. I promised the director I would let him know' – he consulted his wristwatch – 'within the hour.'

Wren bit her lip. If she didn't sign, the department would lose the drawing. Bobby would be devastated and the trip – paid for in full by the museum – would have all been for nothing. One glance at Alessandro was enough for her to make up her mind. A distinguished dealer like him was hardly going to lead her astray. 'No, no,' she said quickly. 'I'm sure it will be fine.'

She signed immediately.

Only when they shook on the deal did she feel her stomach tighten. As if her clumsy handling of the contract wasn't bad enough, she'd let herself be wined and dined by Alessandro before she'd even begun her assessment of the drawing. That meant she could be accused of compromising her independence. It was a complete breach of protocol, one that she hoped nobody at the museum would ever discover. As for fainting, she wanted to forget it had ever happened.

'Thank you,' Alessandro said, his voice once again warm and inviting. He moved a little closer to her. 'Though I confess that I struggle whenever I must let something so beautiful leave me.'

During the ensuing silence, Wren decided that imagining Alessandro's words were directed at her was ridiculous. For one thing, what sort of polished man of the world would use such an absurdly florid line?

'Well, goodbye,' she said, conscious of an unexpected pull of reluctance. 'I'm sure you have a great deal to do.'

'I think I mentioned I was due to fly to Milan later,' Alessandro said smoothly as he opened the door. 'But the owner of the collection I was to view tomorrow cancelled due to ill health. As I'll be free now, I could show you a little of our city.'

'No, that won't be necessary.' She could still feel the faint impression of his shoulder where he'd brushed passed her.

'Surely you wouldn't want to offend the hospitality of a Roman,' he protested.

His sombre expression was tempered by a hint of mockery that made Wren pause. Hadn't Jo told her she was too cautious? It couldn't possibly matter if she saw the sights with Alessandro now – after all, their business had been concluded. She'd just have to make sure she kept her unusual attraction to the man firmly under control.

'Well then, for the sake of maintaining good Italo-Australian relations.' She laughed. 'Thank you, that sounds wonderful.'

Alessandro spent hours the next day diligently escorting her through the Vatican's many splendours. He was attentive and amusing, telling anecdotes about illustrious sculptors and painters from centuries past with such verve that they might have been good friends he met up with after work at a favourite bar. Wren's enjoyment was disturbed only by the startling darts of electricity she felt whenever the crowds pressed the two of them together, or when Alessandro touched her arm as he drew her attention to a detail – perhaps the ingenious carving of a Madonna's robe or the brushstrokes that illuminated the tormented eyes of a saint.

Once, he'd taken her hand while he led her to a quiet corner of the Sistine Chapel, smiling as he said, 'Poor Michelangelo. His great work deserves to be contemplated in peace, don't you agree?' But she had not felt peaceful. She'd been so stirred by Alessandro's presence that only by peppering him with a stream of random questions about Roman history and art was she able to maintain her equilibrium.

Finally, after they'd ordered a late lunch in a café with a view of St Peter's, he declared, 'Enough of this talk of monuments. I believe I'm beginning to sound like a tour guide.'

Wren shifted uncomfortably. Her interrogation had bored him.

He poured her a glass of Frascati as their waiter set down plates of grilled seafood. 'Don't you think it's time you told me something about the part of the world you come from?'

Wren sipped her drink while she pondered his question. 'Rome is all pomp and grandeur,' she said. 'Every magnificent building or work of art that we've seen was built by men to serve the glory of God.'

'Emperors and popes, more likely,' Alessandro said wryly.

Wren smiled. 'No doubt you're right. But the place where I grew up belongs to a more ancient culture, to a people who've left only the lightest of footprints behind. Outside the cities and towns, the land is still mostly untamed. It doesn't give up its secrets so easily.'

Her dark eyes became wistful as she spoke of watching cockatoos, black as shadows, gliding high above the sun-dappled waters of the Shoalhaven River, of seeing soft grey rock wallabies leap from behind fallen logs in the moonlight and how, if you were quiet and still, the mysterious rustles and sighs of the bush became a haunting melody.

'Maybe,' she pondered aloud, 'it takes being in a foreign country to truly appreciate what you have left behind.'

'Your country sounds captivating.' Alessandro topped up her glass. 'Just like you.'

Wren looked away. For a moment or two she'd been transported to the wild landscape surrounding Woolahderra. Being complimented so fulsomely by this cultivated man in a chic Roman restaurant was unsettling.

She picked up her napkin and used it to fan herself, wishing she had something cooler to wear than her constricting navy blue suit. Removing her jacket wasn't an option, as after trudging around the Vatican for hours she was sure the fresh blouse she'd put on that morning would reveal embarrassing damp patches. By contrast, Alessandro looked perfectly relaxed and more appealing than ever in his beige linen trousers and white, open-necked shirt. A glimpse of his honey-coloured skin was enough to make her wonder how it would feel to place her hand inside that shirt, but then she silently admonished herself. She really had to stop drinking wine at lunchtime.

'I hope you don't mind me mentioning this,' Alessandro began.

Wren struggled to swallow her mouthful of scampi. She had the unnerving feeling he'd been able to divine what she'd been thinking.

'But you don't appear entirely comfortable.' He frowned slightly. 'I imagined Australian women would wear light, pretty dresses.'

Wren coloured. 'It's not really my thing.'

'So I see. But you will need to change if you are to avoid another attack of heatstroke.' He replaced his frown with a disarming smile. 'As it happens, a designer friend of mine called Luca Morani opened a new boutique on the via Condotti just last month.

'Luca is making quite a name for himself.' Alessandro signalled to a waiter for the bill. 'I propose that I take you to your hotel for a short rest and that I return by, say, five o'clock, when the worst of the heat has passed. Then we can visit Luca and find something charming for you to wear to dinner tonight.' He smiled at her. 'Yes?'

Wren was taken aback. She'd never come across a straight man who exhibited the slightest interest in looking at women's fashions or, for that matter, shopping. Perhaps it was just another Italian custom, like standing at the counter of a bar downing espressos or zipping around the streets on a Vespa. Even so, this was one invitation she would not be accepting.

'That is very kind, but I'd rather not,' she said firmly.

Sightseeing with Alessandro had been a harmless pastime. Hunting for a dress together suggested a far more alarming familiarity.

Alone in her hotel bedroom, she tore off her clothes before managing to coax a trickle of water from the hissing, hand-held shower. As the thin steam of cool liquid slid over her shoulders, the thought of climbing back into that suffocating pantsuit became unbearable.

Still damp, she threw herself onto the bed, wrinkling her nose when a small black insect flew in through the window. The tiny creature's persistent buzz seemed to grow louder and louder in the still room, until she jammed her hands over her ears. What was she doing lolling about in here anyway, when so many new discoveries lay waiting for her in the streets outside?

Wren swatted away the hovering pest, swore when she missed it, then jumped off the bed. Without a ready alternative, she dragged on her crumpled clothes and jammed her feet back into her brogues. Maybe, if she was lucky, she'd find something cheap she could actually breathe in at this Luca Morani's boutique.

But she'd be going there alone.

CHAPTER THIRTEEN

Twirling out of the changing room on her bare toes, Wren was amazed at how delightful trying on wonderful dresses could be. At first, she'd felt horribly awkward each time she presented herself to Luca's discerning black eyes, but the fine fabrics of the frocks had felt so good against her skin, and their vivid colours – aquamarine, hot pink, emerald and more – were so luscious that her self-consciousness had soon vanished.

Happily, there had been a complete absence of The Look. Short and slightly overweight, Luca simply stood to one side, furrowing his thick brows as he assessed each design she appeared in, much as a museum curator might consider whether a particular frame was the right match for a painting. One style was too square, another excessively long, and a third not precisely the right shade. Finally, after nearly an hour, he nodded emphatically. 'You must take the design you are wearing. That tangerine linen could have been made for you.'

Sleeveless, with a short, gored skirt and a long row of tortoiseshell buttons at the front running from its rounded collar to the hem, it was such a dream of a dress that despite both the expense and her usual aversion to donning anything remotely feminine, Wren was seized by an overwhelming desire to possess it. On an impulse, she took out her wallet and began counting out what seemed like a vast number of lire.

'I hope this doesn't bankrupt me,' she murmured under her breath.

Luca assured her that thousands, 'even tens of thousands', meant very little in Italy's overblown currency. Then he shocked her by offering to give her the dress for free.

'I can't possibly accept,' she protested.

'It's a sample.' He shrugged. 'Now that the pattern-makers have finished, I don't need it anymore.' His round face broke into a delighted smile. 'If you really want to repay me, you can tell the fine ladies of Australia that when next in Rome, they must go straight to the boutique of Luca Morani.'

'I'll do my best.' Wren blinked away a tear. She wasn't used to such generosity.

She was lacing up her heavy shoes when she heard the man splutter. 'What in the name of the virgin are those?' He pointed towards her feet with a horrified expression, 'No, no, no!'

Bustling over to a shelf, he picked up a pair of tan, strappy heels. 'Put these on – they look like the perfect size.'

'Absolutely not.' She'd never worn heels in her life.

'Take them,' Luca pleaded. 'I insist. And add this.' He picked up a straw market basket, into which he deposited her shoulder bag, rapidly followed by the offending brogues.

'But I have to buy *something*.'

'This scarf, then. It's very chic.' He tied a silk square of rich terracotta to the basket's leather handles. 'Now, face yourself in the mirror.'

Wren turned around slowly. Then her eyes opened wide. *Well, well,* she thought, staring at her reflection. So this was what that academic in the Fine Arts Department had meant when she'd delivered a lecture on 'the transformative power of clothing'. Wren had always struggled with the concept.

Now she could see it wasn't just that her appearance was markedly different, although this was true enough. The very act of wearing the tangerine dress had changed her in some more intrinsic manner, as if she'd stepped through a magic portal and become someone else. All this time, she'd been imbued with her mother's fears and distrust. But the image she saw before her was of a confident woman who didn't give a damn how any man might look at her. From now on, she resolved, this was the woman she would be.

Wren had waved goodbye to Luca and begun wandering past the stylish shops and cafés of the via Condotti when her eyebrows shot up. Alessandro was hurrying towards her.

'*Ciao*,' he said when he reached her. 'I'm glad that I caught you.' His tone was cool again.

'But how did you know where I was?' The man's sudden appearance had thrown her off balance.

'Luca telephoned to thank me for sending you to his boutique.' Just for a second, the same hard expression she'd seen when she had questioned the contract passed across Alessandro's arresting features. 'Naturally, that made me wonder why you hadn't wanted me to accompany you.'

He was definitely out of sorts, Wren thought, although as his gaze travelled down her expertly cut short dress and on to the long legs she'd previously hidden, his blue eyes brightened.

'But of course, how clever of you. This way is so much better,' he exclaimed, quickly recovering the winning manner she found so appealing. 'What a marvellous surprise! In that dress, and with your colouring, you look like a model who has just stepped out of the pages of Italian *Vogue*.'

Wren's pulse thudded. Alessandro had made no attempt to hide his approval, yet for the first time in her life she wasn't indignant or angry or even embarrassed. Glowing with delight, she merely waved her hand in a gesture that encompassed her surroundings. 'Who knows?' she said airily. 'Perhaps I lived here in a former life.'

Curiously, this wasn't the first time that thought had occurred to her. Ever since arriving in Rome she'd been struck at random moments – perhaps when turning a certain corner or crossing a piazza – by the odd feeling she was revisiting a place she already knew. She'd had flashes of déjà vu before, of course – everyone did. Yet here the experience was different, releasing a jumble of emotions that changed in an instant from delight to desolation.

'Perhaps you are not yet over your jet lag.' Alessandro's quick laugh put a stop to her musing. 'For if you had really been to Italy, you would know that we shouldn't be standing here.'

'Why not?' Wren hid her bewilderment by adjusting the clip into which she'd twisted her hair. She wasn't sure if he was teasing her.

He linked his arm through hers. 'Because, my dear Wren, at the end of each day real Italians like to go out walking – it's called *la passeggiata*. Occasionally people stop for a drink or to greet someone they know, but mainly they simply scrutinise the passing parade – and show off their best clothes.'

Suddenly, she became aware of appreciative glances. One spry older man tipped his panama hat and muttered '*Bellissima*' as he strolled by. Two women wearing smart sundresses actually crossed the road for a closer look at her, nodding their approval before continuing their promenade.

'I am certain that everyone thinks I am out with a young *contessa*', Alessandro said expansively. 'Tomorrow, all Rome with be awash with rumours.'

Wren laughed, mostly at herself. After all this time, how quickly she'd discovered the pleasure to be had from the admiration of others.

She had been so distracted she'd barely noticed they had left the main street behind and begun making their way down a shadowy lane.

'I hope you have worked up an appetite,' Alessandro said. He stopped in front of a solid wooden door, opened it with a large brass key and led her inside a dimly lit lobby. Wren peered at an ancient wrought-iron elevator at the centre of a winding staircase.

'This doesn't seem like the sort of place where we'd find a restaurant,' she said doubtfully.

Alessandro beckoned her forward. 'That is because the most authentic Roman food can only be found in a Roman home,' he said. 'Tonight, I will cook for you.'

Wren's stomach knotted. Alessandro was either an unusually hospitable colleague – or he was setting the scene for seduction.

As soon as she entered his apartment her concerns were forgotten. On its deep-red walls hung such an impressive selection of old prints and drawings, she wished Bobby could see them. Standing beside a brass drinks trolley was a striking black marble sculpture of a rearing horse and there was an elaborate gilded mirror on the opposite wall. But it was the view that drew her forward.

Wren leant against the balcony railing, her eyes sparkling as she gazed out over Rome's red, pink and gold palaces, its classical statues and domes. Lit by a yellow moon, the city looked magical. 'It's breathtaking,' she murmured.

'I agree,' Alessandro said. 'There is nothing like Roma, although many other Italian cities are also very special. As a matter of fact, I am about to make you a cocktail invented in Firenze.'

He busied himself with various bottles before returning with a crystal tumbler. 'It's called a negroni. Tell me if you like it.'

The cold mixture of spirits stung the back of Wren's throat. 'Mmm, delicious, but if I had many of these I might do another of my dying swan impersonations.'

Alessandro looked at her intently with his vivid eyes. 'I wouldn't wish to see you faint, even if it gave me the perfect excuse to hold you in my arms again.'

Wren finished her drink in a gulp. She could no longer pretend to herself that she didn't understand Alessandro's intentions. What she wasn't at all sure of was how she might respond.

Her eyes swept over the glorious Roman skyline once more, although her mind dwelled on the feel of Alessandro's touch, the shape of his mouth and the glimpse she'd had at lunch of his sun-kissed skin. *Oh God*, she thought. *I'm already tipsy.*

Nerves pricked her belly. She was afraid of how much she wanted him, a man she barely knew. She felt too much, her emotions were too unruly. Perhaps she wasn't the bold woman she'd seen in the mirror after all.

'I'm sorry,' she blurted out. 'But I think my heatstroke has returned. I need to go back to my hotel.'

'That is very sad.' A crease appeared on Alessandro's brow.

She inhaled sharply when he reached behind her and undid the clip holding back her dark waves.

'Perhaps that will make you feel a little better,' he murmured as her hair tumbled down around her shoulders. 'Although I think there is something else that might also help.' His fingers grazed her throat. '*Permesso?*'

Alessandro didn't wait for a reply. As he undid her top button, then one more, and then another, longing began to coil through her belly. When his lips lightly brushed each of her cheeks, she knew her last shred of resistance had been vanquished. She didn't want to go anywhere now. What she wanted was for Alessandro to kiss her properly, preferably for a very long time. Instead, Wren felt his hand at her elbow. Too stunned to speak, she realised he was steering her out of his apartment.

Maybe she'd misread the signs. More likely, her silly plea to return to her hotel had convinced him she was someone he shouldn't bother with. He was used to sophisticated women, whereas she'd acted like a child.

It was not until he had hailed a taxi that Wren spoke. 'Thank you for a wonderful tour,' she said, her voice strained. 'I won't take up any more of your time.'

Alessandro seemed bemused. 'But tomorrow is Sunday. I'm not working, and it's your last day in Rome. Meet me downstairs in front of your hotel at ten o'clock. You will not be disappointed.'

A moment later, he vanished into the darkness.

CHAPTER FOURTEEN

'I'm trying to work out where you're taking me.'

Wren braced herself as the taxi Alessandro had hired launched forward into the morning traffic. She was relieved that he'd made no comment on the previous evening, but merely inquired politely as to whether she had slept well during the night. In fact she'd had the sort of dreams about him that she'd be mortified to share with anyone.

'That is my secret,' he said, putting one finger to his lips.

When the car came to a halt near an impressive domed structure Wren exclaimed, 'How did you know I was desperate to see the Pantheon?'

'I didn't.' Alessandro smiled. 'But what I do know is that this is the very best day for your visit.'

'What's so special about the twenty-second of May?'

'Nothing in particular. But this year it happens to fall exactly seven weeks after Easter Sunday, which means that today is Pentecost.'

Wren caught her breath when Alessandro took her hand.

'Come inside,' he said. 'The service will be finishing soon and then something very rare will happen.'

The Pantheon was crowded with excited groups of worshippers chanting mass in myriad languages. There were a flock of nuns wearing habits and wimples like medieval holy women and a scatter of priests in long black cassocks. Alessandro pointed out several diplomats dressed in dark suits and a smattering of sleek politicians, but most of the congregation appeared to be made up of ordinary Italians.

'I'm going to have a closer look at the building,' Wren whispered, slipping away. There was something she needed to do, preferably without the distraction Alessandro was certain to provide. After moving quickly through the throng, she began to examine the Pantheon's intricately decorated, curved walls. There were statues standing in alcoves at regular intervals, topped by rounded pediments and richly painted panels, but where was the one treasure she was seeking?

Her eyes moved from one masterpiece to another until she found it – Raphael's tomb, surmounted by a tender-eyed marble Madonna and Christ child. Feeling a well of emotion, she reached out and touched the shrine's stone surround. Here lay the mortal remains of the same man whose centuries-old work she'd had the honour to hold in her own hands. It didn't seem possible.

'I might have known I'd find you here.' Alessandro appeared at her side. 'Forgive me if I revert to my tour guide persona,' he said with mock seriousness. 'But I feel duty-bound to draw your attention to the diameter of the span, which is exactly forty-three metres.'

She gazed up at the vast coffered dome.

'It remains the largest of its type in the world, even though the construction dates back to the Emperor Hadrian,' Alessandro added. 'He wanted the Pantheon to be a great temple, standing forever in honour of the most important classical deities, but it seems even emperors can be overruled.' He gave her a wry smile. 'The Pantheon was consecrated as a church in 609 AD.'

Wren concentrated on the very centre of the dome, where the famous oculus was located. The circular opening, completely exposed to the elements, revealed an expanse of clear blue sky marked by a solitary wisp of white cloud. It was the building's only source of light.

'How wonderful,' she exclaimed. 'It's even better than I had imagined.'

As the service drew to a close, the ringing chords of the organ joined with the massed choristers' pure voices in a thrilling crescendo.

'Alessandro, that was sublime. I can't thank you enough,' Wren murmured.

She felt a frisson of pleasure when he placed a restraining hand on her arm. 'Wait,' he cautioned. 'The best is yet to come.'

Without warning, a shower of scarlet rose petals began floating from the aperture above, spinning and twirling in the sunlight. As Wren watched, transfixed, more and still more poured down in a scented torrent of such beauty she thought she might weep.

She saw a petal flutter to rest on Alessandro's hair, felt another land like a soft kiss on her cheek. The floral cascade lasted for minutes, until a thick carpet of fragrant rose petals lay in a perfect circle on the marble floor at the very centre of the Pantheon.

'It's an ancient ritual,' Alessandro explained, 'symbolising the Holy Spirit's descent upon the Apostles in the form of tongues of flame. The only day of the year it takes place is Pentecost Sunday.' He smiled. 'We have been lucky.'

'It seemed as if heavenly angels were casting down those glorious petals,' Wren said with a dreamy expression.

'Actually, some of Rome's toughest firemen climb up the dome in harnesses, lugging huge canvas bags filled to the brim.'

Wren's mouth pursed. 'I like my version better.'

'Then perhaps there are no firemen today,' Alessandro said softly. His arresting blue eyes were trained on her upturned face. 'Maybe there really are angels in the sky.'

Wren stared out of the elevator's black wrought-iron grille as it made its painfully slow ascent, her back rigid with tension. Alessandro had suggested they make another attempt to eat dinner on his terrace. 'I still haven't shown off my skill in the kitchen,' he'd said, smiling.

She wasn't stupid. She knew what he was hinting at, and she doubted it included fettuccine carbonara. But her rare sexual encounters had left her feeling let down and empty. Perhaps that had been her doing – she'd never been able to relax and was hopelessly inexperienced. The prospect of failing to please Alessandro made her wretchedly nervous. While in the core of her being she longed for him, her thoughts dwelled on unsettling possibilities.

By the time they reached the terrace she was trembling. 'Are you all right, Wren?' Alessandro asked.

She took a deep breath. 'Yes, I'm fine.'

He touched her cheek. 'And last night – were you really ill?'

'Not really.' Avoiding his gaze, Wren focused instead on the lush beauty of Rome, spread out before her in the fading light. 'I was ... overwhelmed.'

Alessandro looked pained. 'It was my fault. I should have explained myself.'

'What do you mean?' Her heart had begun beating far too quickly again.

'It's quite simple. You have surely realised that I am incredibly attracted to you and, well, I had thought you were not entirely repelled by me. It is a pity I must be so direct, but you will be catching your plane back to Australia tomorrow, which leaves me no choice.'

He took her face in his hands.

'I would very much like to pick up where we left off last night. But is this what you want, Wren? Is it good for you?'

Buying the tangerine dress might have begun her journey away from distrust and doubt. But tonight, with this man, she would complete it.

'*Molto bene,*' she whispered.

Once more they embarked on their dance of desire. She drank a negroni, he let down her hair, then unfastened the same three buttons of her dress. But this time he didn't brush her cheeks with his lips, nor did she make any excuses. As his mouth met hers, she readily melted into his embrace.

'Slowly, slowly,' he murmured after leading her inside. In between passionate kisses, he took his time over releasing each one of her remaining buttons. As her dress fell to the floor he unhooked her plain cotton bra and slid down her white briefs. His fingers traced the fine gold chain and the locket she wore around her neck. She moaned when they fluttered across the sensitive tips of her breasts.

'You have been hiding your beauty, *cara*,' he said, pressing her naked body against him. There was no mistaking his desire, even though he was still fully dressed.

They kissed every step of the way to his opulent four-poster bed.

As she reclined against the indigo sheets, Alessandro studied her high breasts, her rounded hips and her thighs as would a connoisseur, touching and teasing these delicate places with such devastating expertise she could barely breathe.

'The moment I first saw you at my gallery, I had the strongest desire to separate you from your many garments,' he said. 'Now I can see you are just as seductive as Canova's Venus, although, *grazie a Dio*, you are made of flesh and blood and not marble.'

Wren had never felt so aroused. As soon as Alessandro had discarded his own clothes, she avidly ran her hands across his tanned chest and slim torso. The sense of abandonment he provoked in her was new and wonderful. There were no inhibitions. Nothing was forbidden. She savoured his taut muscularity as he kissed and caressed her.

His lovemaking bore no resemblance to the quick, clumsy fumbling of the few boys she had slept with. Alessandro was an artist. He knew exactly where and how to use his skilful tongue and his fingers, just long enough for her to be tantalised while never permitting satisfaction.

'Please, this is torment,' she whispered at last, drawing him towards her. She gasped as he expertly tilted her hips, so she received none of the discomfort she'd previously suffered but only the very deepest pleasure.

Then Alessandro was a part of her, moving with a tempo that made her body sing. He gazed into her eyes, dark as the very centre of a pansy. She clasped his back, her pale body burning. As her longing became molten, Alessandro at last relinquished his self-control and, with a groan, muttered '*Cara!*'

This was the moment Wren felt herself soar, higher and higher, beyond the clouds and the yellow moon and even the sky, until she reached a golden place where scarlet rose petals were consumed by fierce burning flames.

Alessandro stroked her curtain of hair while they lay close to each other amid the tangled sheets. 'You are a divine woman,' he said, 'which makes me sadder than I can say that you must leave in the morning.'

She'd had no illusions. She knew what had happened between them was but a single passionate episode, yet a sharp pain made her chest tighten. 'I wonder if we will ever see each other again,' she said wistfully.

'Who can tell what lies in our future?' Alessandro shrugged his bronzed shoulders. 'But I will never forget you, *mia cara.*' He kissed her tenderly. 'You are far more precious than any masterpiece.'

Alessandro's words were wonderfully poetic. They might even have been sincere, at least as he said them. Yet Wren knew in her heart that another encounter was unlikely. She would never forget Alessandro either – or what she had learnt in Rome. A new understanding of herself, as a woman, had bloomed within her. She had experienced her own power.

CHAPTER FIFTEEN

Sydney

With their lungs straining, the pair gasped for breath.

'Are you sure this new fitness regime is a good idea?' Wren panted as she surveyed the expansive park beside Rushcutters Bay that she and Jo had just jogged around twice. 'I'm still worn out from travelling, and you're trying to turn me into a long-distance runner.'

'Best way to recover,' Jo wheezed, 'is by having a caramel milkshake – with extra malt, of course.'

Wren smiled. 'Now you're talking. I'll go grab a couple at the kiosk.'

Once she returned with the drinks, she flung herself down on the grass next to Jo. As they gulped down ice-cold mouthfuls, she watched a flurry of blue and white sailboats skim past on Sydney Harbour. The view of the bay, with a modern yacht club on one side and a jostle of twentieth-century flats opposite, was as far from the antique splendours of Rome as Wren could imagine.

'So, how was the trip?' Jo asked. 'I've hardly heard a word, and you've been back since Wednesday.'

She tilted her head to one side as she scrutinised Wren. 'Which reminds me, you look different.'

'Really?'

'Mmm. For a start, wasn't that a dress I saw you wearing yesterday? But it's more than that. You're sort of *glowy*, in a way I doubt has anything to do with that new moisturiser you found at the duty-free store.'

Jo raised an eyebrow. 'Now that I think about it,' she said, 'I'll bet something even more thrilling than authenticating a Raphael drawing went on when you were away.'

Wren blushed.

'Ha! I knew I was right.' Jo rolled onto her back. 'Tell me all.'

Wren couldn't help smiling at her memories of Alessandro, the way he looked at her and called her *mia cara*, the touch of his hand, how his warm mouth had pressed against hers …

'Wren?'

'Sorry, I was thousands of miles away.'

'Yeah, back in Italy with Romeo.'

Wren's spirits plummeted. 'You're right. I did meet someone.'

'Let me take a wild guess – he was tall, dark and handsome with an irresistible accent.'

'How did you know?' Wren gave her friend a rueful look.

'Let's cut to the chase. How was the sex?'

'A revelation.' Wren smiled dreamily as she stretched her arms over her head. 'But I'll probably never see him again.'

'I wouldn't worry about that.' Jo gave her a playful look. 'Just think of it as a wonderful interlude. Everyone needs to let themselves go once in a while – even you.'

Wren sighed. 'Now that I'm back here, the entire experience feels more like a movie.

'Seems to me you should go visit that cinema more often.' Jo giggled. 'So, when's the Raphael arriving?'

'Soon, I hope. Apparently, it's caught up in Italian customs.' Wren looked at the cotton-wool clouds scudding high overhead. 'I expect it will be with us some time in the next week or two.'

'That's good. You must have noticed the whole museum is hyped up about the unveiling, from the director right down to the installation crew. Even Tremaine is excited.'

'I suppose he'll be wanting a debrief.' Wren pressed her lips together. 'I've got mixed feelings about that man.'

Jo sat up. 'I know what you mean. There's nothing he likes more than putting you on the spot, which is particularly nerve-racking as you're never sure whether he's going to butter you up or try to make you look a complete dunce.'

'I've experienced both,' Wren said, frowning.

'It's a power trip, that's all.' Jo's mouth formed a moue of distaste. 'Just like the way he hovers over you, especially if you're in a lift or something.'

'How do you cope?'

'I stay out of his way.' Jo hauled herself to her feet, then gave Wren a hand. 'But you're going to have to make nice with him.'

'Me? Why on earth is that?'

Jo gave Wren a look she couldn't read.

'You know how I've been waiting for my US visa,' Jo said. 'Well, it's come through. This time next month, I'll be in the Big Apple.'

'That's fantastic! Except I'm going to miss you big time.' Wren had been miserable at the thought of losing Jo, but she couldn't see what it had to do with her and Tremaine.

The girls strolled out of the park, crossed a tree-lined street and began tackling a hill.

'Actually, I tried to join you,' Wren said suddenly.

There was that odd look from Jo again.

'I didn't say anything before because I knew it was such a remote possibility.' Wren had to raise her voice while a bus lumbered past. 'But after that talk we had about auctions on the night of the InterCon sale, I remembered coming across a notice among Bobby's rubble. It was about interning for Archer's auction house at their New York headquarters.'

Wren recalled the excitement she'd felt when she'd first spotted the flyer. She hadn't been at the museum for long, but somehow the position being advertised had felt *right*.

'Oh?'

Jo sounded curiously off-hand, but now that she'd started, Wren thought she might as well tell her the entire story. 'Anyway,

I did a bit of research. It turns out that the wealthy, widowed mother of one of Archer's most dedicated specialists was a long-serving guide at the Sydney Art Museum. Having lost her husband and, with her son living in New York, it had become a sort of cherished second home for her.

'After she died, the son – an only child – inherited her fortune and retired to the south of France. When he too passed away, his will instructed the executors to set up an endowment in his mother's honour, one that would forever link the museum she had loved with the place where he'd worked so happily.'

'Hmm, what a nice story,' Jo mumbled.

'The way it works is,' Wren ploughed on, 'the auction house provides a six-month internship to a suitable candidate, while the dear departed's bequest pays for travel, accommodation and living expenses. It's only available to young grads who work at the Sydney Art Museum, but if the museum considers there isn't anyone appropriate on staff, there's no obligation to award the grant – even if Archer's has already given the thumbs-up to a candidate.'

They had arrived at Jo's building, a faded Art Deco jewel located next to the dandelion-like El Alamein Fountain in Kings Cross. Jo summoned an aged lift that creaked its way up to the sixth floor. 'Sounds like a sweet deal,' she said, opening the door to her one-room studio.

Wren's face fell. 'Except I sent my application after the deadline, so they're sure to have chucked it out.'

Jo slid down a wall until she reached the floor. 'Um, what would you say if I told you that you'd been accepted?' she said, stretching her leg.

Wren threw up her hands. 'I'd say you were crazy, of course.'

'Well, I'm not!' Jo's expression was triumphant. 'Stephenson's secretary, Cath, told me yesterday afternoon. She'd been looking for you, only Bobby said you'd ducked over to the university to check something in their archives.'

Wren stared at Jo. 'Hang on a minute. Do you mean to tell me that all the time I was running around that damned park, followed by divulging my Roman secrets and then rattling on about the internship, you not only knew about my application but that I'd actually won the thing? Why the hell didn't you say something?'

Jo jumped up and grinned. 'I was bursting to tell, but I wanted to give you the chance to introduce the subject.' She danced over to the milk crate that served as her bedside table, picked up a piece of paper and waved it in the air. 'Here's a copy of the fax Archer's sent. Looks like you were just too good a candidate to pass up.'

'Hey, give that to me!' Seizing the page, Wren took a quick look, then strode over to the window and rested her forehead against the cool glass.

She'd been bitterly disappointed when she'd thought she had missed out on the internship, but now that this incredible chance had opened up, her stomach was churning. Lily seemed vaguer than ever these days – how would her mother cope without Wren checking up on her? She'd be leaving Bobby to his own devices as well, just when the department was at last running smoothly.

On the other hand, the program only lasted for six months – it wasn't as if she was committing to a lifetime. Could she really give up the opportunity for close study of the outstanding works that passed through the auction house? Once they were sold, many would go into private hands and be hidden away forever. At Archer's, she'd also be in the perfect position to immerse herself in the endlessly thrilling way collectors bid for art and obliging auctioneers sold it to them. That thought alone made her eyes shine.

As Wren turned back to Jo, she tried but failed to suppress the small stab of pleasure she felt about something else – surely an international dealer like Alessandro would visit New York from time to time. Maybe there'd be a chance to rekindle their romance …

'I can tell a zillion little cogs are whirring around in that mind of yours,' Jo broke into her thoughts. 'So, what do you think? You are accepting, aren't you?'

Wren smiled. 'Absolutely. Oh my God, imagine the two of us in the Big Apple!'

She pushed back a stray loop of hair. 'Hey, wait a minute. You said something about Tremaine earlier. What's he got to do with the program?'

'The Head of Collections is always in charge of issuing the grant,' Jo said. 'If he doesn't give you the tick of approval, you won't be going anywhere.'

CHAPTER SIXTEEN

Wren made sure she arrived at work early on Monday morning. Bobby never appeared much before ten o'clock, so he wouldn't be around to keep her tied up checking references or sorting out his latest batch of scribbled notes. As she bent down by his desk to pick up the manila folders he'd left strewn on the carpet, she glanced at her new short red skirt, a snappy, barely worn Carla Zampatti creation she'd found at Bondi's Salvation Army outlet. She had paired it with one of her men's white shirts, which she'd tucked in at the waist, and added a pair of long black boots.

She smiled with satisfaction. Whether due to one special dress or the alchemy wrought by Rome itself, this was the new Wren Summers. What did she care if men paid her attention? She could deal with any situation.

Wren picked up the phone and dialled Cath's extension. 'Sorry for the lack of notice,' she said, 'but I need an appointment with John Tremaine, preferably today. How's his schedule looking?'

'Chock-a-block,' the woman replied with a sigh. 'I do know he's keen to discuss the internship, though. Congratulations, by the way.'

There was a pause before Cath said, 'This might work. John's staying back to show a group of museum patrons through the new Australian sculpture exhibition. If you don't mind waiting around, he can see you afterwards.'

'Thanks. That sounds perfect,' Wren said, ringing off.

Yes! She punched the air with her fist. Six months working in a top New York auction house would be incredible. And all she had to do was convince Tremaine she was up to the job.

'*Buona sera,*' he called out in his over-loud voice when Wren entered his office. '*Come sta?*'

He just couldn't help showing off, she thought. She also noted that he'd had some new artworks installed. A fine Ian Fairweather hung behind Tremaine's desk, opposite an early landscape by Arthur Boyd. A small Rodin bronze sat on the coffee table.

'I'm very well, John,' Wren said, making sure she sounded properly respectful. 'It's good of you to see me.'

'Sit down, Wren.' Tremaine gestured towards a modern black leather bench. 'Heard you had a good time in Rome,' he added, smirking as he walked over to shut the door. He seated himself next to her.

Wren began to feel uneasy. Jo had been right. Why hadn't he stayed behind his desk, or at least taken one of the visitor's chairs? The man had no idea of personal space. And what had he meant, exactly, by that crack about 'a good time in Rome'?

'I had a little chat with Alessandro,' Tremaine continued with a sly smile.

'Really?' Wren tried to keep her tone neutral.

'Yes, I needed an update on a few things. He was very … enlightening.'

Wren's stomach lurched. Surely Alessandro would not have said anything about their brief love affair?

She edged away from Tremaine. Even if Alessandro had simply let slip that she had been unwell and he'd been obliged to take care of her, it might be concerning enough to sink her chances for the grant. It would sound as if she wasn't able to handle the stress of an overseas role. This conversation needed to be moved along smartly.

'I believe Archer's has been in touch with you about the internship.' Wren smiled encouragingly.

'Yes, I received a fax from them late on Friday.' Tremaine loosened his tie. 'I must say, I wasn't altogether surprised you applied for the role – I've always had you tagged as an ambitious girl.' He paused. 'The way you reeled in Stephenson at your job interview was masterful.'

Wren stiffened. 'I beg your pardon?'

Tremaine held up his hands. 'No, honestly, I admire you. I don't know who you used your feminine wiles on to winkle out that information about the director's quaint fondness for the little Tom Roberts, but full credit. You pulled it off.'

Wren was aghast.

'It's how the world works, isn't it?' Tremaine shrugged. 'Girls manipulate blokes to get what they want.' He sidled closer. 'But it cuts both ways, you know.'

'I'm not sure I'm following you.' She felt a spike of alarm.

'No? Well, I'll make myself clear. This time, your mate Stephenson is out of the picture.' He gave her a smug smile. 'You have to satisfy me alone.'

'Did you have something specific in mind?' Wren asked blandly, struggling to maintain her composure.

'Oh, for God's sake.' Tremaine put his hand on her bare knee. 'Let's not beat around the bush. What I'm wondering is' – his hand moved up to her thigh – 'how badly do you want it?'

Wren froze.

'Don't start playing the innocent with me,' he said irritably. 'Bloody Baretti's the art world's most notorious womaniser. I'll bet you spent half your time in Rome shagging him.' His voice rose. 'Well? Am I wrong?'

A dart pierced Wren's heart. What she and Alessandro had shared was not a love affair, she saw that now. It hadn't even been a fling. She'd been merely another notch on his belt, a willing little idiot he'd probably laughed about with Tremaine. She should never have allowed herself to be swayed by his looks and his absurd charm. She should have remembered what Lily had told her over and over – men were not to be trusted.

'No one's going to disturb us if that's what you're worried about.' Tremaine leered at Wren. 'I made certain the door was locked.'

Her mind raced. Should she try to laugh off this odious proposal, reason with the man, slap his face?

She took a quick breath. 'Look, maybe you've got the wrong idea about—'

'You?' Tremaine's voice had a new, angry tone. 'Not a chance. The minute you walked in here in that outfit, showing off your tits and your legs, I knew what was on offer.'

Suddenly, he grabbed Wren by the shoulders. 'It's time I got a piece of you, too!'

Lunging forward, he forced her down until his flushed cheeks and wild eyes were inches from her terrified face. Wren struggled to breathe as Tremaine's heavy body crushed her against the unyielding leather bench. His hands were everywhere: unzipping his jeans, pushing up her shirt and bra, groping under her skirt. Panic immobilised her.

Grunting like an animal, Tremaine shoved his hot tongue into her mouth. *This isn't happening*, she told herself. He was hurting her breasts. *This isn't happening.* His thick fingers were fumbling between her legs. *This isn't happening.*

The sound of her underpants tearing snapped Wren out of her trance.

'Get off me!' she yelled.

Fury boiled inside her. If Tremaine thought she was so desperate for the Archer's grant she'd let him rape her without a fight, he had another think coming. She tried to kick him, to slap or punch his face, but he still had her pinned down.

He was forcing her thighs apart, moaning as he tried to thrust himself inside her, when she managed to fling out one arm. She scrabbled wildly for anything she could use to defend herself. Her hand flailed through the air – nothing. There was no way to stop him now.

Then her fingers closed on a cold piece of metal. Mustering whatever remained of her strength, she swung it towards him as hard as she could.

'Christ!' He reared back, groaning.

The Rodin bronze fell from her grasp and toppled onto the floor with a thud.

Wren leapt to her feet. Yanking down her shirt and rucked-up skirt, she stared at Tremaine. Blood was pouring from a gash on the side of his head.

'Don't think I'm finished with you,' he snarled, eyes bulging with pain and rage. 'You've just made a big mistake.'

CHAPTER SEVENTEEN

By the next day, the news was buzzing around the museum. John Tremaine had taken a tumble when he'd hopped up on his sofa in order to adjust one of his favourite landscapes. Those who crossed his path noted both his surly expression and the large wad of gauze attached to his head by surgical tape.

Wren confided in no one other than Jo about his attack.

'I'll warn Cath,' her friend said as they sat on their favourite seat under the magnolia tree during lunch, 'in case Tremaine gets any ideas about her. But you have to tell Personnel,' she insisted.

Wren shook her head vehemently. 'Are you kidding? He'll deny everything.'

'Yes, but—'

'But nothing,' Wren said, her brown eyes darkening. 'I'm a girl, and the most junior member of the museum's curatorial staff. John Tremaine is Head of Collections and a respected man. Who do you think is most likely to be branded a troublemaker and given their marching orders? I might have lost out on New York, but at least I still have my job.'

'So you're just going to keep quiet?'

Wren looked at Jo bleakly. 'What other choice do I have? I'm already suffering the consequences from turning that pig down.'

She reached into her shoulder bag and passed Jo her copy of Tremaine's response to Archer's invitation. She'd found it on her desk first thing that morning. 'I have a horrible feeling this is just the beginning.'

Jo read the pivotal sentence out loud. 'It has been determined that Miss W. Summers is ineligible for a Sydney Art Museum grant.' She looked up. 'What a complete bastard!'

Wren put her head in her hands. Tremaine's message cut every bit as effectively as a bronze figurine that had found its mark.

Forcing her eyes open, she winced at the sunlight streaming through the open window. She had a disjointed memory of the night before, involving eating greasy food and downing a great deal of vodka, followed by a crying jag when she'd wept tears of bitter frustration on Jo's shoulder. After that she couldn't remember anything, but as she'd woken up on Jo's sofa she realised she must have passed out. How embarrassing.

When she swung her legs gingerly over the side of the sofa her foot hit an empty bottle, sending it spinning across the floorboards. No wonder she felt like death. Why the hell had she thought getting smashed would be a good idea?

It was all coming back to her. The way men had wolf-whistled and called out lecherous comments as she walked down the sleazy main street of Kings Cross after work, past the barred windows of pawn shops and lurid neon-lit signs advertising strip clubs called DreamGirls and the Pink Pussy Cat. She'd stopped to buy burgers and chips at a brightly lit takeaway, then once more to pick up the vodka from a bottle shop, before lugging the lot up to Jo's flat.

Wren had always had a horror of 'getting out of it', as Lily would have put it. She'd seen her mother in that state way too many times. But after being knocked back for the grant solely because she'd repelled Tremaine's disgusting behaviour, she had felt so much anger and hurt that oblivion seemed like a reasonable option.

She massaged her temples. What an idiot. If there was one thing she'd known since she was a child, it was that being trashed never solved anything. All she'd achieved was a shattering headache.

She limped over to the minuscule kitchen, poured herself a glass of water, then spotted a note propped up on the electric jug.

Sorry, had to leave for an early meeting – hope you're more or less in one piece. Chuck on anything of mine you want to borrow.
J xxx
    PS There's aspirin on the top shelf.

Wren kept her head down as she trudged through the museum. Usually, there was nothing she liked more than being greeted by the ever-changing array of paintings and sculptures on display – she'd often told herself there could not be a more uplifting way to arrive at a workplace – but today was different. Today she felt so ill, so appalled by the attack and so worried about her future, she walked straight past each piece of art, no matter how breathtaking.

'Gosh, you don't look very well,' Bobby said when she arrived at Prints and Drawings. For once, he'd come in before her.

'It's just a headache.' She crossed the room and slumped into her chair.

'That's no good.'

There was a brief silence while she looked blankly at her messages.

'Um, Wren?'

It was Bobby again, only this time he was looking even more timid than usual. Wren tensed, wondering what was coming.

'Everyone knows I'm not exactly what you'd call a people person,' he said. 'But this department – these beautiful works on paper – well, they're the most important thing in my life.'

'Of course,' Wren said gently. 'I understand.'

'But what I want to say,' he soldiered on, 'is that I really *missed* you when you were in Italy. And then it occurred to me that I might have taken you for granted.' He coughed.

'When you first turned up here, I was so overwhelmed by my own mess that I just hunkered down. But in no time, you had everything perfectly organised, plus you made sure we displayed works on the walls, where they belong.

'So, what I'm trying to say,' he coughed again, 'is thank you. I'd given up hope of ever finding a colleague who not only understood what my prints and drawings meant, but was willing to, well, put up with me.'

Wren felt so touched by these words she thought she might cry. 'That's a lovely thing to say. Honestly, Bobby, it's a privilege to work with you. And you're more than just a colleague. I think of you as a friend.'

Bobby ducked his head behind a book, although not before she caught a glimpse of his half-delighted, half-embarrassed expression. 'Same,' he said shyly.

A quick check of the clock on the museum library's wall told her it was almost lunchtime, although she had no appetite. Wren felt overcome by a wave of nausea as an image of the red-faced Tremaine pawing her came flooding back.

She'd worked for most of the morning on the show that was to open in tandem with the hotly anticipated Raphael's unveiling. Immersing herself in the art she loved had never felt so welcome. The exhibition would survey four hundred years of European works on paper, all derived from the museum's collection, with a special emphasis on drawings that depicted women. As that twist had been her own idea, she'd been thrilled when Bobby had embraced the concept. The two of them had already begun selecting pictures, but there was still a great deal of research to be done before they started writing the explanatory captions.

She rose unsteadily. It was best to keep busy, to try not to dwell on her searing memories. She'd go back to the department and fill Bobby in on her progress.

Though the room was as dim as usual, Bobby's desk light revealed he was searching for something – not an unusual occurrence.

'Anything I can help you with?' she asked as she walked in.

'I can't seem to find the message I took down.' He shrugged. 'Oh well, I suppose it doesn't matter. Cath told me the director wants to see you in one of the old courts. Gallery Three, I think she said.'

The news instantly brought back Wren's headache. Tremaine may have already begun increasing his efforts to undermine her.

'What's this all about?' Bobby's forehead bunched into a frown. 'If it's to do with the exhibition, I should be there with you.'

'Search me,' Wren said, forcing herself to maintain a casual tone. 'It's probably just something to do with my travel expenses.'

'Expenses.' Bobby was already losing interest. 'They're always making a fuss over such unimportant things.'

Wren walked across the creaking parquetry floor of Gallery Three, her head pounding. Whatever Stephenson had on his mind, she doubted it was the extra *cornetto* she'd ordered from her Rome hotel's room-service menu.

As she approached, he turned around from the painting he'd been surveying. 'A remarkable work,' he observed, pointing to a crimson and gold nineteenth-century oil.

'Yes, *Cymon and Iphigenia* by Frederic Leighton,' Wren said. 'There's a theory he was inspired by the *Decameron*.'

'Of course, I should have known that someone like yourself' – he paused – 'someone with so much *promise*, would be well informed.' His usual, pleasant manner had become decidedly distant. 'Which makes it even more painful for me to admit that I am extremely disappointed in you.'

The band of steel at Wren's temples tightened.

'Why don't we walk,' he said tersely, 'while we discuss the matter. There's nothing I like more than a stroll through the collection before the doors open and the public streams inside.'

They passed under an archway that led into another court, this one painted in a burgundy tone. 'I can imagine it is possible to lose perspective on one's first trip abroad,' he began.

Blushing, Wren looked away. Just as she'd feared, the director had found out about her fainting fit, the lunch that had followed and, quite possibly, even more embarrassing details.

'When it comes to finances, however, one has to draw the line.'

Her head whipped around.

'The trustees have a very firm view about any irregularities, particularly when the quantum of money under discussion is significant.' Stephenson removed his glasses, took out a handkerchief from his trouser pocket and began furiously polishing them.

'I have no idea what you mean.' Wren took a step back.

'Now, now,' he admonished her. 'It's always best to own up when you're caught out. Tremaine has told me the whole story.'

Wren's stomach lurched. The man could have said anything.

'What I fail to understand,' Stephenson said as he regarded her reproachfully, 'is why, when your immediate superior had concluded an excellent deal for a prized drawing at a price of three hundred and fifty thousand dollars, you instructed Mr Baretti to alter the paperwork, so it appeared the museum's offer was four hundred thousand.'

'What! But I—'

'Yes, yes,' Stephenson spoke over her as if she were a child. 'By all accounts, Baretti is a charismatic fellow, and you are of course young and inexperienced. Should I be inclined to give you the benefit of the doubt, I would assume you merely wanted to impress the man.' He placed his spectacles back on his nose. 'However, given the large sum involved, youthful folly hardly provides mitigation.'

They had come to a halt in front of a richly coloured monumental painting, *The Visit of the Queen of Sheba to King Solomon*, by Edward John Poynter. Wren wondered if this was Stephenson's way of making a point, and, if so, what exactly he meant by it. Did he think she was some sort of temptress?

'I feel obliged to tell you there has been speculation you may have attempted to benefit personally from this unauthorised transaction,' he said sternly. 'As you can imagine, bringing charges against you has been under serious consideration.'

A shiver of dread ran through Wren. Was this all an invention of Tremaine's? Or perhaps – she felt sick to her stomach – Alessandro had inserted the inflated figure in the Italian contract he'd pressured her into signing.

'Let me assure you, Alastair, I would never dream of doing anything underhand, let alone illegal,' she said emphatically. 'These charges are not just false. They're downright malicious.'

'Malicious, you say.' He raised an eyebrow. 'But why would anyone wish you harm?'

Wren felt a surge of anger. She couldn't prove anything against Alessandro, but at least she could stop Tremaine from ruining her reputation. She would tell Stephenson exactly what he had tried to do to her.

'The sad fact of the matter is,' the director continued, 'I have received information that your personal conduct in relation to Mr Baretti has not been what we would expect from a representative of this institution.'

In a second, Wren's ire turned to dismay. Tremaine had all the ammunition he needed. If she claimed he had attempted to rape her, he'd merely accuse her of trying to seduce him in an effort to chisel the grant out of the museum, just as he had obviously claimed she'd seduced Alessandro so she could secretly pocket another chunk of its money.

They had reached Rupert Bunny's *A Summer Morning*. Wren had always been fond of this pretty pastel paean to the indolent life of upright Edwardian ladies. Now the subject struck her as painfully ironic, considering the vile accusations Stephenson was making.

'In light of your serious misdemeanours,' the man said, 'this is what I propose.'

He waited until a uniformed attendant had passed out of earshot before continuing. 'We have no intention of making your reprehensible actions public – it would only damage the museum's international standing. Therefore, as I understand Archer's has offered you an internship, I strongly suggest that you accept the position.'

Wren's face burned. 'You must know that John Tremaine has vetoed the grant. I don't have the funds to travel anywhere.'

'Well, that is a great pity.' He gave her a withering look. 'Because we no longer have room for you here.'

Wren was so shocked she had to grasp the edge of a plinth bearing a white marble faun so she didn't collapse.

'Alastair, you must believe me.' She raised her voice. 'I am innocent.'

Stephenson merely shook his head. 'So you still don't accept responsibility for what you have done,' he said gravely. 'Nor do you seem to appreciate the consequences of your actions. The reason I asked you to meet me here is because I regard these halls as sacred places. Look around you, Wren. Very soon, that Raphael drawing would have been hanging on one of these very walls – a highlight of the collection.'

His eyes glared indignantly from behind his glasses. 'Now, thanks to you, there's been so much upheaval surrounding its purchase, last night the museum's trustees held an emergency meeting.'

'And?' Wren could scarcely breathe.

Stephenson scowled. 'They vetoed the acquisition.'

Wren stumbled slowly through one gallery after another, her mind reeling. This disaster had happened all because she'd had sex with one man and turned down another. It seemed that women paid a high price, no matter what choices they made.

She tried to imagine how Bobby would react when he learnt about this debacle. Naturally, he'd be distraught – she could hardly blame him for that. But only this morning he'd said they were friends. Surely, Bobby at least would give her the benefit of the doubt.

She came upon him in the corridor outside the Prints and Drawings Department, hurrying towards her.

'Wren?' His face was grey beneath the pendant lights. 'The director just phoned and told me what's happened.'

Bobby looked at her with tears in his stricken eyes. 'You wouldn't wreck our chance to obtain that beautiful Raphael all because you wanted to look important to a dealer you'd started up a, a relationship with – would you?'

Wren shrank back as Bobby's voice dropped to a whisper. 'As for you profiting from the arrangement … Please, Wren,' he urged her in a voice filled with pain, 'tell me it isn't true.'

Wren rushed out of the museum. She needed fresh air, somewhere to sit and be quiet so she could pull herself together. At least the magnolia tree's great canopy of leaves offered a semblance of protection.

She lowered herself onto the wooden bench, shaking. On Saturday, she had imagined she was on her way to a dazzling six months with her best friend at the centre of the New York art world. Now, she was the victim of an attempted rape, her name had been besmirched and she'd lost her job. As for Alessandro, he'd not just taken her for granted, he'd betrayed her.

Outrage contorted Wren's face. One minute Stephenson had accused her of being a silly, irresponsible girl who'd do anything to win an attractive Italian's attention; the next, she was a conniving adventuress determined to line her own pockets. It seemed that stereotypes were not restricted to the depiction of women in nineteenth-century paintings.

She gazed at the row of government buildings opposite. Beyond them were skyscrapers and department stores, hotels, banks and shopping arcades, all filled with the hum of thousands of people going about their daily business.

Wren touched her locket as she turned away. No matter what she'd so foolishly imagined, she didn't belong here – not in this museum, not even in this city. She watched as a predatory seagull pecked at a discarded sandwich wrapper, then rose slowly to her feet. There was only one place she could go.

CHAPTER EIGHTEEN

Woolahderra

A shrieking wind wrenched Wren's flimsy umbrella from her hand as she stepped from the bus. She watched, despairing, as the spoked disk cartwheeled away in the pouring rain before disappearing into the fading grey light. There was nothing for it but to continue.

As Wren trudged down the sodden gravel road to Woolahderra, she thought grimly about that long ago, shocking day when she'd found Lily lying passed out on her bed with a bong on the floor and her latest boyfriend beside her. But was she any better herself? Despite all her years of study and striving, despite the lies she'd told and the fancy accent she'd adopted, she was right back where she'd started.

Wet through and shivering, she thumped on her mother's door.

'Sweet Jesus, come inside,' Lily murmured when she saw her.

Wren was surprised at how faint her voice sounded.

'Did I miss a letter or something?' She looked dazed. 'You didn't tell me you were coming home last time I phoned you.'

That had been weeks ago.

Wren dried herself with a towel while Lily made a pot of herbal tea. 'Sorry, there's not a whole lot to eat,' she said.

Wren looked at her mother, frowning. There was something wrong with her. It wasn't just her voice. Lily was even more lethargic and much thinner than usual. She felt a spear of guilt. Sure, she'd been busy, but she should have made an effort to get down to Woolahderra more often. 'Everything okay?' she asked.

'Just fine.' Her mother gave a strained smile that only made Wren more concerned.

'I might have lost a little weight, that's all,' she added, 'because I'm on a special cleansing juice regime.'

The only food in the shack Wren could see were bunches of celery, carrots and spinach, heaped upon the sole table. Far more unexpected was the sight of the shiny electric juicer sitting next to them, its gleaming modernity at odds with everything else in the shabby dwelling.

Feeling anxious, she poked around on a shelf looking for something she could make into a meal. Lily's latest health kick couldn't be agreeing with her – there were dark shadows under her eyes and lines Wren had never seen before on each side of her mouth.

Wren sighed. She was sick of having to play parent, especially now when she could have done with some advice herself, or at least a bit of comfort. With Lily insisting she wasn't hungry, Wren set about making herself a stew out of vegetables and the rice and nuts she'd discovered. As she spooned up her dinner, Lily chatted over-brightly about inconsequential matters – who had just moved into the commune and who had left, how there was a new baker in town and the way the farmer next door was eyeing off the commune's land, only no one at Woolahderra was sure who owned the title.

After an hour, Wren felt utterly drained. Her mother hadn't once asked about what was happening in her own life, but, considering the events of the past couple of days, maybe that was for the best. 'I'm turning in,' she said.

Her old bed stood behind a faded green curtain. As she lay hunched beneath the blankets, she listened to the rain falling on the corrugated-iron roof with the insistence of drumbeats. She'd expected the sound to be a comforting reminder of the past, but instead the incessant noise was unnerving. While she pulled restlessly at her bedclothes, one anguished thought followed another until she broke out in a sweat of self-recrimination.

Her rash fling with Alessandro had brought unthinkable consequences. As for Tremaine, if only she had stuck to her baggy men's clothes instead of wearing that stupid little red skirt, maybe he would never have attacked her. Perhaps every horrible thing that had happened was her own fault.

A moment later, Wren landed a fierce punch on her pillow. She must be crazy. In what world was a woman asking to be raped because of her fashion choices? It was the egos of bloody men that had ruined her life. The more she dwelled on their treachery, the angrier she became.

When at last she dropped off to sleep, she dreamt she was a child again, hiding behind a clump of murraya because a man in a black limousine was coming for her.

The rain had disappeared overnight, leaving a sky washed so clean it appeared limitless. Although Wren thought a couple of colonial painters came close, the only artist she knew of who truly captured the unique blue depths of the Australian sky was her mother. She'd always wondered how Lily did it.

Smiling to herself, Wren began trudging down the rugged slope that fell away at a sharp angle from the land surrounding the commune. She'd been only a skinny little kid with a tangle of black curls the first time she'd been lured down by the sparkling water below. Back then she had clung to pliant saplings when she wasn't sliding on her bottom, screaming with terrified glee. By now, she'd made the journey so many times she could probably do it blindfolded.

She sat high on her special rock, revelling in the wild beauty of the landscape. The swollen river rushed and swirled, its surface lit by the saffron rays of the winter sun as tiny wavelets lapped against banks edged with lush native grasses.

Her brow creased with worry. Here was all the peace she craved, but if she stayed too long in this bush paradise there was a danger she might succumb to its siren song. At Woolahderra, one day flowed into another, with time marked only by the change of seasons – and the weekly arrival of the dole cheques.

It had been a long time since she'd thought about the reasons why so many lost souls ended up at the commune. Now she found herself contemplating whether any of them had once been just as ambitious as she was. Perhaps some had suffered a devastating experience. Maybe others simply couldn't cope with the dozens of daily slights and hurts that were the result of them marching to a different beat from other people. Whatever the reason her mother had come to Woolahderra, she'd found herself unable to leave its lazy embrace.

Wren tossed back her hair. She'd worked too hard to let herself fall into that trap. And she wouldn't be getting mixed up with another man, either. At least Lily had been dead right about that. They brought nothing but trouble.

What she should be doing was finding a job. The problem was, she couldn't provide a reference from the museum. The last thing she wanted was to drag Bobby into her mess. His own position might be at risk if either Stephenson or Tremaine discovered he was championing her.

Wren untangled a cobweb caught up in her hair. Being thrown out might make her feel wretched, but if Bobby was torn away from his beloved prints and drawings, she doubted he'd survive. Mustering her courage, she'd returned to the museum on the day she was sacked. Although she'd shrunk from revealing either Alessandro's devious behaviour or Tremaine's attack to poor Bobby, she'd known that she must. She couldn't bear it if he, too, thought she was some sort of a money-grubbing floozy.

'Oh Wren, no!' he'd whimpered. 'I'm so ashamed. I should never have doubted you.' Despite his aversion to being touched, he'd actually grasped her hand.

As the mournful cry of a magpie rang out from a treetop Wren brushed away a tear. There was no alternative. She'd just have to find some sort of colourless office job where she'd most likely spend her days typing letters like an automaton.

A nearby rustle interrupted Wren's train of thought. Peering down, she made out the silky ears of a pair of rock wallabies moving up quickly through the scrub. Art set her spirit on fire and gave her life meaning. But she loved this land and its creatures, and she loved Lily. As the sun rose above the far bank, she felt the warmth of its replenishing golden rays. At least there was one small task she could apply herself to right away.

She slithered off the rock and began the climb back to Woolahderra, careful not to slip on the wet undergrowth. The first thing she'd do would be to scrounge some eggs and cook her mother a decent meal. She could already smell the faint aroma of smoke from someone's campfire, though the bracing fragrance of burning gums was tinged with something far sweeter and muskier – home-grown cannabis.

'Breakfast of champions,' Wren muttered.

CHAPTER NINETEEN

'Honey, don't fuss with those eggs. Just leave me alone and I'll be all right,' Lily said above the metallic whirr of her juicer. She was intent on feeding it chunks of raw carrot and celery through a plastic chute.

All the pain and the fury Wren had tried to suppress mixed with her fears for her mother and welled up inside her. 'Can't you see I'm trying to help you?' she erupted. 'If you go on like this for much longer, you'll make yourself really sick.' She turned off the stove with a fierce click, flung the contents of the frying pan into a bin and propped herself against a wall, silently seething.

At last Lily finished with her new toy. After slowly lowering herself onto one of the shack's hard-backed chairs, she said, 'Honey, I'm already sick. This here,' she said as she poured herself a glass of murky green liquid, 'is my medicine.' She winked. 'And the odd toke.'

Wren seized the glass from her mother so abruptly that some of the juice spilled onto the table. 'I suppose your chakras aren't in the right meridian or something,' she snapped. 'These weird mystic fads of yours are driving me mad.'

'I've got cancer, Wren.'

Wren sat down with a thump. A terrible pain gripped her chest and her throat.

Lily leant across and squeezed her arm. 'Hey there,' she said as Wren's shoulders began to heave. 'Everything will be all right.'

'What do you mean, all right?' Wren managed to say in between her choking sobs. 'This is the worst news ever. Oh, Mum!'

Lily gave her a smile. 'I'm kind of tired. Come and sit next to me while I lie on the bed and I'll tell you about it.'

Trembling, Wren settled herself beside her mother's slight form. Lily's light cotton dress failed to disguise either her jutting shoulders or the sharpness of her hipbones.

'You see, I've had these headaches, and pretty often there've been dizzy spells with them.' She gave Wren a small smile. 'Before you say anything – no, not after I've been smoking weed.' Lily took a shallow breath. 'You know I don't like doctors, but I went to a clinic in town.'

Wren looked at her, horrified. Her mother didn't just dislike doctors – Lily loathed every member of the medical profession, sight unseen. She knew then just how excruciating Lily's headaches must have been.

'The quack I saw said I had to go to the district hospital for scans, which was the pits. All those rays, nuking my poor body.' She shuddered. 'After that, well, that's when they told me. It's brain cancer – inoperable, apparently. The doctors wanted to give me a heap of chemotherapy, follow that up with radiotherapy and then more drugs.'

She gave a bitter laugh. 'I haven't got this far to start putting manufactured chemicals into my body. They'll kill me off faster than anything. I've never trusted those rip-off, multinational big pharma companies, you know that. I'm sticking to natural herbs and my juices.'

Wren stared at her mother in disbelief. 'But you can't! You have to do what the doctors say. Mum, it's' – her voice wobbled – 'cancer.'

Lily shrugged. 'The way I see it, there's no point.'

Wren felt racked by a fierce current of guilt. All the time she'd been preoccupied by the challenges of her own life, her mother had been suffering terribly. Wrapping her arms around Lily's fragile body, she cried, 'I don't want to lose you.'

She felt her grow limp. 'Mum?'

Wincing, her mother rubbed at her temples. 'Sometimes I have a bad turn,' she said.

'It's not that I want to die. But I've always lived my life on my own terms.' Using her elbows, she raised herself a little. 'If I'm going to pass, I'll do it in my own way.'

Lily's hollow eyes burned. 'That's all I have to say.'

'But—'

'But nothing. Now, I want to talk about you.' She lay down again and reached for Wren's hand. 'I know you think we're not on the same wavelength, and maybe that's right. Only, I'm not so far gone I can't see that you're not yourself. Something's happened, hasn't it?'

Wren couldn't help it. She found herself pouring out every traumatic detail.

'The worst bit,' she said, snuffling, 'is that I'd been approved for a fantastic internship in New York for six months.'

Lily lifted her head with a jerk. 'New York?'

Wren's eyes rested on one of Lily's glowing canvases. It was all such a waste – her mother's rare talent, her own struggle to escape from the commune and make a success of her life.

She fingered the gold locket tucked inside her shirt. 'There's no way I'm off to America now, not with you being so sick. I couldn't go anyway, seeing as the museum won't give me a grant and I certainly don't have any money.'

Lily made an effort to sit up. 'You do, actually,' she said softly. 'Quite a bit.'

Wren frowned. 'You're not making sense.'

'I guess it's time to come clean about a few things.' Lily dropped back onto her pillow. 'Twice a year, ever since we came to live here, a deposit has been made into a bank account for you – for both of us, really.' She groped in the drawer of her bedside table and brought out a tattered passbook, followed by what looked like an old legal document. 'It's all set out here. I've made arrangements with the bank so you can draw on the funds any time you need to.'

Wren gaped at her mother. 'But who'd give us money – and why?'

Suddenly, she found herself grappling with a single impossible answer. 'Wait a minute, Mum,' she said hesitantly. 'You're not saying it's from my father, are you?'

She'd been telling people he'd been killed in an accident for so long she had almost come to believe it herself. But if she was wrong, if her father really was alive, it meant that for all these years he'd made a conscious decision to stay away from her. The void inside Wren began to hurt, but this time it wasn't an ache. This time it felt as if she'd been stabbed with a knife.

'The money's not exactly from him.' Lily looked away. 'It's paid out of a blind trust operated by a bunch of US lawyers called Clayton and Bane. There's never been much, but over the years it's built up because' – for a second or two her eyes blazed – 'I refused to touch it.'

Wren folded her arms resolutely. 'Then I won't touch it, either.' How dare her father think he could buy off his own child, she thought with a flare of outrage. *As if a pile of money was a substitute for love or tenderness, let alone ever actually bothering to turn up.*

'Not so fast,' Lily said, raising one hand. 'Being ill, like this, it's made me think about a lot of stuff differently. My life got screwed up so badly that I never got the chance to live out my dreams. I couldn't bear it if the same thing happened to you.'

'I'll never forgive my father for ruining your life.' Wren fumed.

'Don't be too hard on him,' Lily said gently. 'It was … complicated. Anyway, I'm talking about what *I* want. This life hidden away down here – it's not for you. I've always known that one day my beautiful girl would need to spread her wings. It's who you are, Wren.'

'I'm not going anywhere.' Wren clenched her jaw. 'I'm staying right here and taking care of you, no matter what.'

'There's a reason I've never spoken about your father and me,' Lily said, her voice catching as she spoke. 'But now things have changed, there's something I have to share with you.' Pausing, she let out a long, sad sigh. 'It's why you must go. Do you understand?'

'Frankly, no.' Wren felt at a loss. 'What could possibly be so important that I'd leave you now?'

'You have a sister.'

Wren doubled over, as breathless as if she'd been punched in the stomach. 'A *sister*?' She gulped for air. 'I have a sister – and you kept her secret?'

Her mother winced. 'I convinced myself it was to protect you from the pain of knowing that somewhere out there was another little girl, one who was a part of you.' Lily uttered every word slowly, as if each one was costing her an unbearable effort. 'Now, I don't know. Maybe I was just protecting myself.'

Her eyes were distant and veiled. 'You see, I adored your father. He was the love of my life – still is, despite everything.'

Wren sat forward. 'Well then, what happened? Mum, tell me!'

'Oh darlin', it was all so long ago and I'm so tired.' Lily took an unsteady breath. 'The times were different then. I was young and idealistic. I thought he was drawn to an evil way of life. Then circumstances beyond our control went to work and …' Lily's voice began to fade. 'I lost him forever.'

Wren stared at her mother. 'What are you talking about?'

'Some things are better left in the past.' Lily's face was a pale oval of pain. 'But the only way this awful situation could be resolved was for an unholy judgement to be passed.'

Her voice dropped to a whisper. 'I was faced with a terrible, terrible choice, one no mother should ever be forced to make. Which child to take, which to leave behind?'

Wren felt numb. How could her father have imposed such a cruel choice?

'You were already a toddler, but your sister was only tiny. I knew she would never remember me.' Lily spoke in a whisper.

'But there's not been a day since, when abandoning my baby girl hasn't tormented me.'

An expression of desperate sadness marked her delicate features. 'I guess that's why I always tried to lose myself by getting high – or in the arms of other men.' Tears seeped from her eyes.

'Mum, I, I don't know what to say.' Wren unconsciously placed her hand just below her ribcage. Perhaps that empty space was not only due to the absence of her father. She must have buried whatever memories she'd had of her little sister, but somehow her body knew she was missing.

'Honey, I have so many regrets I don't know where to start, but there is one thing I am sure about,' Lily said, her voice firmer now and more insistent. 'I want to see your sister again before I die.'

'But I can't just turn my back on you!' Wren wailed.

Desperation made Lily's voice strident. 'Your sister was taken to New York. That's why you have to accept the internship. Please, Wren, I'm begging you. Use that money in the bank for something good.'

Wren tried to focus, though her heart ached to see Lily in such distress. 'Mum,' she said softly. 'I don't even know my sister's name.'

Lily didn't respond.

'Mum?' Wren prompted. 'God, Mum. No!' She watched with terror as her mother's fragile body arced in a series of violent spasms.

'Stay with me, please stay,' she pleaded. 'I'll run and call the ambulance, get help for you.'

Suddenly, Lily's hand gripped Wren's wrist with unexpected strength. Grimacing, she tried to force words from her twisted lips.

'Roma,' she whispered at last. 'Find Roma.'

PART TWO

Chiaroscuro

The tonal contrasts artists use to create the illusion of three-dimensionality. From the Italian chiaro, *meaning 'clear' or 'light', and* oscuro, *meaning 'obscure' or 'dark'.*

CHAPTER TWENTY

New York, June 1988

Wren strode down a canyon of steel and glass skyscrapers. She'd been so worried and depressed about Lily that each time she breathed she'd felt as if a granite boulder was pressing against her chest. Yet now she was here in New York, the pulsing energy of the city acted upon her like a shot of adrenaline.

She'd never avoided hard work. Again and again she'd been tested, but she'd won the Daneford scholarship, had a brilliant university record, landed the job she most wanted and then the Archer's internship – despite John Tremaine's best efforts to thwart her. Now she'd been handed her most difficult task, and she'd tackle it the same way she'd done everything else. Unrelenting application was the key. She would do whatever it took to grant Lily her final wish.

Wren sighed. Good intentions were all very well, but she still didn't know where to start. It had taken her only a few hours in Manhattan to realise the place was all about *more*. The scalloped Chrysler Building was more improbable, Trump Tower glitzier and the thrusting Empire State Building more striking than she'd ever imagined. Everything here was larger, faster, brasher and grander.

Gulping for air, she tried to adjust to the insistent tempo. Stuttering jackhammers and the rumble of subways juddered through her. Exhaust fumes belching from rows of yellow taxis made her head swim. It was overpowering. She had expected

New York to be fast-paced, everyone knew that. But she had not been prepared for this intense mix of competing sensations.

Wren stopped, wrinkling her nose as she sniffed an unfamiliar odour. When she spotted a man beside a small cart topped with a striped umbrella, she realised it was the scent of the hot pretzels he was selling.

'Hey, lady,' a workman in overalls came up behind her. 'Get going, why doncha? You're blocking the sidewalk.'

She set off, swept up by a river of people rushing towards their next destination.

Breathing hard, Wren tilted her head back when she arrived at Archer's famous East 73rd Street premises. Lit by bright morning sunlight, the elaborate Beaux Arts exterior was embellished with clusters of white columns and rows of balconies, but it was the bronze relief of Artemis rising above the arched entrance that drew her attention. With the goddess of the hunt's bow thrust forward and a slender arrow grasped in her hand, no one could miss the connection to the company's name.

Wren wondered what the auction house's founder, the fabled Samuel Archer, would make of the chaotic new world in which his eponymous company now operated. Before she'd left Sydney, she had read a book on eighteenth-century London, learning that Samuel had established his business in the genteel environment of St James's Square in 1768. Despite its centuries-long history and the inconvenience of an occasional war, Archer's had never ceased selling the world's finest objects and artworks to its wealthiest inhabitants. When the first New York branch opened in 1957 it had been a modest operation. Today, Archer's Upper East Side headquarters was the centre of an ever-expanding powerhouse devoted to the twin deities of art and commerce.

Wren's gloomy frame of mind returned and, with it, the weight of that imaginary boulder. How could she possibly track down one girl amid the millions who lived in this teeming city? If only Artemis could pass on her secrets. She still knew only her sister's first name – Lily had slipped into a coma on the night of her terrible stroke at Woolahderra and hadn't spoken a word since. The effort required to utter her final, desperate plea must have cost her dearly.

'*Live*,' Wren whispered, her thoughts flying back to the last time she'd seen her mother, at Sydney's Prince of Wales Hospital.

Although the doctors had assured her that Lily was stable and liable to drift in and out of her comatose state for months, Wren had been reluctant to leave her. Lily had looked frail and terribly alone in her antiseptic room. There was nothing she would have hated more than the myriad tubes that snaked from her shrouded body and the constant monitoring kept up by a battery of blinking screens. 'I'll bring Roma back to you,' Wren had vowed as she'd sat by Lily's bed.

As she continued to gaze at the figure of Artemis, her shoulders drooped. That impetuous pledge had been so easy to make. It would be infinitely more difficult to fulfil.

Wren's mood brightened almost as soon as she passed through Archer's doorway. Something about the mellow interior made the roar of New York's traffic fade and the glare soften. The faint tarry taste on her tongue became fresher – even the air she breathed seemed sweeter and lighter.

The refined antique furniture, polished oak floorboards and deep yellow walls appeared curiously familiar, until she realised they bore an uncanny resemblance to the décor of the stately homes of Britain she'd seen in Jo's magazines. That regal style must go down well with Archer's rich clients, she thought, though she suspected that behind this aura of timeless luxury hummed a very slick, well-oiled machine. Surely no company could have stayed at the top as long as Archer's without exercising ruthless efficiency.

A moment later a slender young woman in her late twenties appeared at the front desk. With straight, shoulder-length auburn hair, she was immaculately clad in a classic beige Armani pants suit and beaten gold earrings.

'Wren Summers?' she said in a clipped English accent.

'Yes, I'm the new intern.' Wren hazarded a smile.

'My name is Lady Amelia Heywood. I will conduct today's orientation, but I will also be in charge of you during your stay with us.' She extended a slim hand.

Relieved she had dashed up to Bloomingdale's that morning, Wren silently thanked Jo for the hours she'd put in bringing her up to date on the latest designers. Archer's didn't seem like the kind of place that would approve of op shop dressing.

Using a strictly limited amount of her trust account's funds, she'd acquired some much-needed clothes, including the tan linen Ralph Lauren jacket and skirt she was wearing. Yet she still felt squeamish about spending the money, as if in some ill-defined way she'd compromised her principles.

'Is it okay if I call you Amelia?' she asked.

'I suppose so,' the young woman said, rather more frostily than Wren thought necessary.

The next hour and a half passed in a blur of introductions and a tour of the building, though it took no more than five minutes for Wren to realise that looking ultra-stylish was not just a quirk of Amelia's. Everyone she met – from Jeanette, the petite brunette receptionist who was dressed in a short blue Galanos dress, to the sleek chief executive, Timothy King – resembled the impossibly well-groomed individuals that upmarket publications like *Town & Country* splashed on their pages. What with the piles of glossy magazines Jo had given her to study, accompanied by what she'd laughingly called 'Miss Draper's personal crash course on the spending habits of the rich and famous', Wren reckoned she could now identify a Bulgari necklace or a pair of genuine Chanel shoes from ten paces.

Eventually they reached the sixth floor, where Amelia showed Wren the cramped room they were to share. It seemed that the building had a hierarchy of spaces, which meant that in contrast to the marble columns and richly detailed cornices of the reception area, the humble sixth floor was strictly utilitarian, with low, oppressive ceilings and harsh fluorescent lights.

'I can't imagine why I always get stuck with the new interns,' Amelia muttered under her breath.

Wren pretended not to hear. She'd just have to hope this chilly aristocrat would warm to her.

'I'm afraid you will be spending most of your time on the more menial tasks that need to be done in an auction house – filing and so on,' Amelia explained when they descended to their final stop, a pre-auction exhibition of outstanding marine paintings on show in one of the grand, ground-floor viewing galleries.

'Perhaps if you demonstrate the right attitude, you will find yourself doing more interesting work,' she added.

Wren paused to admire a stirring seascape painted by J.M.W. Turner. It depicted a tiny boat tossed on turbulent waves and was, she reflected, uncannily similar to the way she currently pictured herself. Amelia's show of disdain had dented her confidence – not that she had any intention of letting her new boss see that.

'At least it is helpful that Impressionism is one of your specialities,' the girl mused. 'Those are the hottest pictures in the art world right now, especially since last October's stock market crash – they're regarded as a far safer bet than equities and a great deal more prestigious. The Japanese are paying astronomical prices, but there are many others equally desperate to invest their money in art.'

Wren nodded. 'We have someone like that at home. He's a West Australian entrepreneur called Alan Bond – I'm sure you've heard of him.'

'Naturally,' Amelia said breezily. 'He spent fifty-odd million on Van Gogh's *Irises* last year, the highest price ever paid for a painting.'

Wren chanced a quick smile before observing, 'Bet you wish that picture had gone to Archer's instead of Sotheby's.'

Amelia gave her a scornful look. 'Quite the contrary,' she said, her accent more clipped than ever. 'Indeed, I hear that our colleagues at Sotheby's are bitterly regretting ever handling the sale. From what my spies tell me, they foolishly loaned your Mr Bond half the money.'

Wren's mouth formed an O of surprise. She'd never imagined that such a distinguished auction house would resort to staking a client. It would allow the work's value to be massively inflated.

'And now, here we are,' Amelia continued, 'nearly a year later and Bond is yet to provide so much as what our American friends call a red cent towards payment.'

A withering glance in Wren's direction seemed to suggest she was personally responsible for the negligence of her countryman.

On her first full day at Archer's, Wren slung another new purchase, this time a white Donna Karan gaberdine jacket, onto the back of her chair. With Amelia nowhere to be seen, she felt a secret thrill. Here was the perfect opportunity to come to grips with the room where she'd work for the next six months without anyone peering over her shoulder.

Yet, as she looked around, something inside her deflated. Pale grey filing cabinets stood in uniform rows and shelves containing properly sorted volumes of books and catalogues were neatly stacked. Amelia's desk, too, presented a picture of order. The place was so tidy it bordered on sterile.

She'd never imagined missing the chaotic conditions that had greeted her at the museum's Prints and Drawings Department but, strangely, she felt an acute pang of nostalgia. If only the recent traumatic events had never happened, once her internship was over she'd have been able to return to dear, eccentric Bobby and the works of art he guarded so fiercely. Even now, some other, eager young graduate was no doubt making herself indispensable to him.

With Amelia still nowhere to be seen, Wren glanced through a few random files. Then she ran her fingers down one of the orderly piles of Archer's catalogues and extracted a volume at random.

Wren whistled. Monet, Degas, Toulouse-Lautrec, Renoir – all the top Impressionists were represented.

Ten minutes later she returned the catalogue to its place and folded her arms. Browsing through pages of glossy pictures was pleasant enough, but she had no idea what she should be working on. Maybe Amelia had left her a note somewhere, but if she had, it wasn't on her own desk – its surface was depressingly bare. Perhaps it was on her boss's?

A cursory glance revealed nothing obvious. She moved a couple of books to one side, looked under a folder and then a pile of mail.

'Exactly what do you think you are doing?' Amelia's voice was icy.

Wren whirled around. 'I'm sorry, I didn't mean to snoop. I was just looking to see if you'd left me instructions or something …'

'I see.' Amelia took the seat behind her desk. 'Well, at least you have initiative, that's something.'

Wren received a brief smile.

'And in this business, being a snoop isn't such a bad thing.' She tapped one finger against her chin. 'What else do you bring to the table, I wonder.'

Wren felt on surer ground here. 'Well, I have a first-class honours degree from—'

'Christ, no,' Amelia cut her off. 'Everyone around here has decent academic credentials. Perhaps I should have made myself clearer.' Her eyes narrowed. 'Who do you know?'

Wren looked baffled. 'Um, I don't follow you.'

Amelia raised her eyebrows. 'You may think all our efforts are expended on creating beautifully produced, learned catalogues. They certainly cost us enough.

'But the catalogues' principal role – apart from enticing potential buyers, of course – is to create the image that we are centres of scholarship and expertise, rather than vulgar commerce. One of the hottest commercial gallery owners in New York right now is Mary Boone, and do you know what she told me? "I had reservations about making art a business, but I got over it." Coming as you do from the rarefied world of a public museum, you may have your own reservations, but you'll have to jettison them quick smart if you're going to get on in the auction world.'

'So, you focus mostly on selling works of art?' Wren pushed back her curls. 'That makes sense.'

'Oh God, it seems I will have to start with the basics.' Amelia gave an exaggerated sigh. 'Eighty per cent of our energy is directed towards winning consignments. Paintings, sculpture, jewellery, porcelain, ancient glass, Eastern rugs, precious manuscripts – you get my drift.'

'Really?' Wren didn't try to hide her surprise. 'Eighty per cent?'

'Auctions are hungry beasts. They need to be fed constantly, and in order to maintain our membership of the Holy Trinity – you do know what that is, don't you?'

'Archer's, Christie's and Sotheby's,' Wren recited.

'Well, to stay at the top only the best will do.' Amelia leant forward, making her slim silver bangles clatter against each other. 'Once you have great artworks to sell, the buyers will follow. It's as simple as that. What isn't simple is getting the art in the first place.'

Wren tilted her head to one side. 'And you go about it – how?'

'Occasionally we receive random inquiries. But the most important way is via our own personal networks.'

She waved one expertly manicured hand. 'Take me, for instance. I'm under absolutely no illusions – Archer's employed me mainly because Daddy is an earl and Mummy's first cousin is a viscount. That doesn't just give me an entrée into Britain's grandest homes. It means that I can easily discover exactly who has which Old Master in their collection and, even more importantly, who could do with a quick injection of funds to stop their heritage-listed roof from collapsing.'

Wren eyed Amelia. It sounded as if she was a refined brand of spy.

'As soon as a case like that comes to my attention,' she went on, 'I alert one of our departmental heads. Once he knows that a certain hard-up aristocrat might be tempted to sell a treasure, we work out a plan of attack.'

Amelia laughed. 'Titles are also marvellously effective with the kind of rich Americans who enjoy boasting to their friends about consorting with Her Ladyship.'

'I'm afraid I don't know a soul – well, not anyone who's wealthy,' Wren said apologetically.

Amelia groaned. 'That *is* unhelpful.' She looked Wren up and down. 'Fortunately, you have other attributes. There's your style; it's discreet, but that's a plus in our trade. A classically beautiful face like yours with those big Bambi eyes is invaluable. And thank God you don't have a ghastly Australian accent.'

Wren bristled. Amelia's description made her feel as if she was a prize heifer who'd just been judged in an agricultural show. 'Come on,' she protested. 'You can't tell me looks are important in this business.'

'That sort of comment just shows how much you have to learn,' Amelia said coolly. 'The very rich gravitate towards those with good looks, charm and impeccable manners. There's no doubt you have the first, but we may need to work on the other two.'

Wren swallowed back the sharp retort she was dying to utter, something along the lines of scholarship and intellect being surely far more relevant. 'Thank you,' she said as sincerely as she could manage. 'I really appreciate your advice.'

'Well done.' Amelia arched one eyebrow. 'Now, that wasn't so hard, was it? I can see you're a quick learner.'

Wren's face burned. Amelia didn't miss a trick.

'There is a strictly limited amount of first-class art to go around,' she said, 'so the competition between the Holy Trinity is cut-throat. Our most important task is to make sure that when the day comes for an owner to sell either an important work or even an entire collection, it will be one of our specialists they will call first.'

Wren looked perplexed. 'How do clients go about choosing between the three of you?'

'Good question.' Amelia nodded approvingly. 'Oh, they'll give all sorts of reasons, talk about a superior catalogue or a more creative advertising campaign and, yes, being able to produce both to a deluxe standard is important. But the reality is, people prefer dealing with someone they like and, most important of all, trust.

'A potential source may need to be cultivated over many visits. Sometimes it takes years to build a relationship. There will be drinks, complimentary appraisals of the works for insurance purposes, special lunches or cosy dinners with the directors – and the board always includes a Lord Something as well as an extraordinarily well-connected American whose family has been on the social register since they came out on the *Mayflower*.'

Wren's forehead wrinkled. 'So, you must establish a rapport, is that what you're saying?'

'It's more than that. Everyone at Archer's, from people like me who focus on acquiring consignments, right through to the auctioneers, must know how to cast a spell.'

Amelia consulted her leather-bound Filofax. 'I have meetings and inspections scheduled for most of the next couple of days. How about I assign you some work – I'm afraid it won't be terribly exciting, though it's still important – and tomorrow night we can continue over a drink.'

Wren made sure to paste on a wide smile. 'That sounds wonderful.'

'No need to over-egg the pudding,' Amelia said tartly.

This time Wren's grin was genuine.

CHAPTER TWENTY-ONE

As she looked around her sparsely furnished single room, Wren had the distinct impression she was back at boarding school. She'd been urged by Jo to join her at the Parkside Evangeline, a 'women's residence' located in a slim Georgian Revival building opposite secluded Gramercy Park, but the number of rules that went with living there made her feel as if she were fourteen again.

It would have been so much easier if Jo hadn't been at a conference in Washington on the day she had arrived. Instead, she'd had to depend on the formidable woman who ruled Parkside's front desk to explain its many regulations.

'I'd better tell you straight up,' Jewel Hoskins had pronounced almost as soon as Wren stumbled inside, worn out by worry, the long fourteen-hour trip from Sydney to Los Angeles and then another flight across the country.

'Evangeline is owned and run by the Salvation Army, and they won't tolerate any nonsense.' Jewel, who had unnatural jet-black hair and was wearing a lime green cardigan, pointed at a typed page taped onto the counter. 'There's no alcohol, no toasters, no microwaves and no candles allowed in the rooms. But, most important of all – no men.'

The woman examined her suspiciously. 'I hope you won't be one of those girls who tries to get around that, because if you are, you'll be marched out of here faster than you can blink.'

'I'll cope,' Wren said with a tight smile. 'I've sworn off men, for one thing.'

'Gee, did you have your heart broken?' Jewel's sudden, friendly demeanour caught her by surprise.

'Let's just say they're more trouble than they're worth,' she said with a frown.

'Well, Amen to that.' Jewel chuckled in a way that made Wren suspect she might well be in possession of a past that, if known, would put her at odds with the Salvos.

'There's plenty of other advantages to living at Parkside.' Jewel held up her fingers and began counting. 'Number one, it's cheap, plus you get breakfast, dinner and maid service thrown in. Two, there's no long-term lease involved and three – well, three is the best of all.'

She opened a drawer. 'You get to use Gramercy Park. It's just lovely, plus it's strictly private; the only private garden in Manhattan. Any time you want to go there, ask me for one of these.'

Wren nodded sleepily as Jewel brought out a silver key hanging from a light-blue cord. 'Sounds great,' she said. 'But I guess they're in demand. How many residents do you have at Parkside?'

'Nearly three hundred ladies, and we're pretty well always full.'

Jewel leant her elbows on the desk. 'We have plenty of college kids, secretaries and salesgirls, some actresses and models, plus a few artists and writers – all sorts, really. Most stay a while and then move on, but around a third are long-term residents. I don't mind telling you' – she raised a heavily pencilled eyebrow – 'there're some characters here.'

'I'm sure there are,' Wren murmured as she dragged her suitcase towards the elevator.

Stretched out on her narrow bed with her hands behind her head, Wren cast her mind back to the bespectacled woman sporting a greying bun she'd seen the night before in Parkside's drab cafeteria.

The woman had been sharing a table with a heavily made-up young blonde who had slavishly copied Madonna's 'Material Girl' look. She'd styled her hair in the same messy way, rimmed her bright blue eyes with sooty black liner and draped an abundance of chains around her neck.

The unlikely couple had laughed and talked together with such relaxed intimacy Wren had wondered if they were mother and daughter. Inevitably, this had led her to thinking about her own mother – and her lost sister. She was still thinking about them, and the more she did, the more she realised it was not only for Lily's sake that she was desperate to find Roma.

Thanks to her healthy bank account, she'd been able to phone long distance to Lily's oncologist, Dr Carmichael, only that morning. Her spirits had been raised when he'd told her that Lily was holding her own, but then he'd spoiled everything by adding that there was no chance she would still be alive in twelve months' time. Wren's chest hurt so much at the thought of losing Lily that she curled herself up into a ball. She would be completely alone in the world – unless she could somehow unearth her sister. Now she knew Roma existed, she ached for that missing part of herself.

A knock on the door broke into her sombre thoughts.

'It's me!' a familiar voice called out.

Wren threw open the door and flung her arms around Jo, who let out a loud whoop of glee.

'Can you believe it's actually happened – the two of us, here in New York City!' Her jubilant tone changed when she saw the strained look on Wren's face. 'I'm sorry, you must be worried sick. Any update?'

'Dr Carmichael thinks Lily will continue as she is for a while, but in less than a year she'll …' Wren's bottom lip trembled. 'I can't even begin to imagine how much Mum's suffered, not seeing her own child for so long. I have to find Roma before it's too late.'

Jo settled herself on the edge of the bed. 'What about you, how do you feel? We didn't have time to talk much before I left.'

Wren sat down on a hard-backed chair, her face pensive. 'At first, the news was just a massive shock. Then I felt wretched because, though I love her to bits, Lily has driven me nuts for most of my life. It's awful that it's taken her getting so sick for me to discover what made her the way she is.'

She sighed. 'Now, it feels as if, even though Mum is still alive, I've already started grieving. I hate being away from her, and there's another thing, too. I'm beginning to think that somewhere deep down I must have known my sister was wrenched away.'

Wren felt an eddy of shame. She still hadn't been able to bring herself to tell Jo that her father had not met his end in a head-on collision but might well be living right here in New York City – unless of course he really was dead.

If, on the other hand, he'd simply opted not to make any effort to contact Wren, his decision amounted to a conscious rejection. Her father's complete lack of interest in her very existence was far more painful than the guilt she felt about keeping a secret.

Wren gritted her teeth. She would not let any man's actions make her feel worthless. Lily had told her so little, but if she found her sister, perhaps it would be different. The girl she'd never known might help her to unravel the past.

'I've been racking my brain over how to start searching for Roma,' she said. 'I've got the name of the lawyers who administer the trust fund, but when I tried to extract more information from my local bank manager, he said these things had strict confidentiality clauses, so there was no point in approaching them.' She paused. 'I don't care what he said – I'm still going to give it a shot. In the meantime, what do you think about putting ads in the classifieds?'

Jo looked unconvinced. 'I guess it's a start, but you can't rely on someone to read a tiny message at the back of a newspaper. This isn't *Desperately Seeking Susan*, you know. We're talking about real life.'

Wren nodded. 'I'll try it anyway, though when you put it like that, the odds don't look good.'

'I've become friendly with a couple of the girls living here.' Jo smiled encouragingly. 'Maybe they'll think of something.'

Wren flung her arms out wide and wriggled her shoulders. She had spent all day bent over, tape measure in hand, checking the dimensions of sixty-four pictures against the master list drawn up for Archer's latest catalogue. Now that she'd finished painstakingly measuring each work down to both the last millimetre and quarter inch, she felt cross-eyed.

'Finished?' Amelia said, strolling through the door.

Wren began massaging her neck with her fingers. 'Thankfully, yes.'

'Good, then let's have that drink I promised while I add to your knowledge about the ways of an auction house. I think we should go to the Pierre. It's an easy walk down to 61st Street and the place is something of an Upper East Side landmark.'

Wren stared at the hotel as they drew nearer. 'Wow, this town definitely goes in for fantasies – and making big statements.'

'Never a truer word,' Amelia said. 'Down here at street level the Pierre looks exactly like your typical seventeenth-century French residence. Just what you would imagine finding on an American city street,' she added wryly, before pointing skyward.

'Way up there, the copper roof is modelled on the Versailles Chapel. Of course,' she said in a sardonic tone, 'being in the Big Apple, there's a forty-one-storey brick tower in between so, yes – this building is a classic case of illusion meets self-aggrandisement. The perfect metaphor for life in 1980s Manhattan, really.'

She turned into the hotel's smart Fifth Avenue entrance. 'The staff here really know how to look after you. We often recommend it to our out-of-town clients.'

They settled themselves on two chairs in the intimate bar while a waiter glided over with a bowl of salted peanuts. Two martinis materialised almost as soon as Amelia ordered them.

'Cheers.' She touched her glass to Wren's. 'Since you're living down at Parkside, I thought you'd appreciate a stiff drink.'

Wren quickly swallowed some of the cold, crisp liquor. 'My very first martini,' she said. 'Is this how your tutorials always begin?'

Amelia gave Wren a penetrating look. 'I like to see how our interns shape up in a situation they might find themselves in with a client.'

She crossed one tapered leg over the other. 'Most people don't realise that acquiring pictures only happens as a result of one of the four d's. Like to guess what comes first?'

Wren drew her brows together. 'I suppose death would be an obvious one, especially if the heirs don't like the artworks – or else just want the money.'

'Well done.' Amelia nodded. 'But what you may not know is that every auction house employs junior staff to go through the newspapers each day and read the obituaries. If they see the name of a prominent collector, a departmental head is notified straightaway.'

Wren's mouth turned down. 'That sounds like grisly work.'

'Depends on how you look at it,' Amelia said breezily. 'We like to think we offer a helpful service to the family. Dealing with a substantial estate is no easy thing, especially when it comes to a man who's had multiple wives and children – let alone mistresses.

'Normally, we would immediately communicate with the estate's lawyers, offering our assistance both for valuation and liquidation of the artworks. Then we send a personal letter of condolence to each heir that we know of. Often one or more of our senior people will attend the funeral, too, though the atmosphere can become somewhat tense when our competitors start eyeballing us across a fresh grave.'

Wren failed to suppress a titter.

'Let me assure you, this is no laughing matter.' Amelia gave her a severe look. 'The next two d's are divorce and debt. They're both extremely lucrative – at least, for an auction house.

'Finally, we have deaccessioning.' She picked up her drink. 'A collector may want to upgrade a piece or alter his collection's focus. Alternatively, his wife might have changed her interior decorating scheme and discovered that the Picasso she loved last year no longer matches her new curtains.'

She sipped her martini, then dabbed at her mouth with a napkin. 'Of course, the owner might merely be after some quick profit taking, much as he'd do if he were a bonds trader.'

Wren frowned. 'I notice you always say "he". Don't women collect art?'

'Not like men do. First, because women rarely control the real money. Second, it's a matter of psychology. As a rule, women want art that makes their homes more inviting, whereas wealthy men establish important collections for the same reasons they might acquire a stable of prime racehorses or a cellar of rare wine. It's the competition with other chaps and the insatiable desire to impress they can't resist.' Amelia drank the last of her martini. 'Must be the testosterone.'

'Tell me about it,' Wren muttered. 'So, what are the pitfalls of the auction business?'

'Far more than I have time to go into now.' Amelia dropped her voice. 'But the absolute worst is selling a fake.'

Wren felt herself relax for the first time since she'd arrived in New York. She wasn't sure if she actually liked the taste of the martini she'd just finished, but it had certainly helped her unwind.

'Surely you would do the same as any museum or major gallery,' she said. 'Check the work's previous ownership, back to the artist's studio if possible; do the forensics, x-rays and so forth; and seek the opinion of experts.'

'I'm assuming you learnt that in class – you make it sound so straightforward.' There was an edge of condescension in Amelia's voice. 'When it comes to maximising a picture's sales potential, it can be a great deal more complicated.'

'Really? How so?'

'There might be some, shall we say, reattribution,' Amelia responded, 'especially when it comes to the Old Masters. There is a world of difference between stating a portrait is painted by Rembrandt, for instance, and claiming that there is *evidence* of the hand of Rembrandt. Usually, this applies to the subject's face, as often pupils were employed to do the clothes and the background.

'Next, we might advise that – in descending order of value – it "comes from the studio" of Rembrandt, then "from the circle", followed by being "in the style" of the painter until, finally we reach "a copy of" a certain picture. Often such a copy might have been executed by another artist who created the work either as an exercise or an homage, but what's important is that the picture is still associated with Rembrandt. His name is pure gold.'

She paused before adding, 'So long as the artist who's painted the copy has used his own signature, there isn't a problem. Otherwise, it would be a forgery and we wouldn't go anywhere near it.'

'So, Archer's has never sold a fake?' Wren noticed another round of martinis had arrived.

'Lesser auction houses have been caught out,' Amelia replied, her pale blue eyes now a steely grey. 'But Archer's? Never. It is unthinkable.'

'Okay, I get that.' As Wren downed her second drink, she had the disconcerting sensation that her mouth was no longer working properly. She really was useless with spirits. 'What about the actual auction?' she asked, ploughing on. 'How is that orcheshtrated?'

She blushed. 'Sorry, I meant,' she enunciated carefully, 'orch-es-trated.'

'From the sound of things, we've probably covered enough for one night,' Amelia said curtly.

Wren felt her cheeks grow warm.

'A word to the wise.' Amelia leant forward. 'One martini is very pleasant. Two is even better. But clearly, not in your case. You have to keep your wits about you in this business, never more so than when you're socialising.' She sat back. 'Try to pull yourself together while I order you a black coffee.'

Wren winced. If she wasn't careful, she'd spoil any prospect of forging a good working relationship with Amelia. There must be something she could say to counteract the impression she had nothing to offer.

'I've realised I do know someone who's on the international art scene,' she said quickly. 'Recently, I went to Italy to authenticate a Raphael drawing.

'So? I saw that on your resumé.'

'Well, dealers work with auction houses, don't they?' Wren asked. She began nibbling the peanuts.

'All the time. They frequently represent their clients, whether buying or selling. Or else they buy for themselves, to sell on later.'

'The dealer I met in Rome handles important works. He's a man called Alessandro Baretti – we got on quite well.' The last thing Wren wanted was to trade on their brief relationship, but Alessandro was the only card she had.

Amelia looked at Wren coldly. 'I'm acquainted with him myself.'

'Do you know him well?' Wren asked, hoping her inquiry sounded sufficiently casual.

'I suppose as well as any fiancée can.'

Wren spluttered and coughed violently.

'Oh dear, a peanut must have gone down the wrong way. You're really not coping very well tonight, are you?' Amelia asked a passing waiter for more napkins.

'Actually, Alessandro will be in town in a couple of weeks,' she said. 'I'd suggest you join us for a drink, but after this evening's performance, I'm not sure that would be such a good idea.'

'I promise I'll be fine.' Wren took a gulp from the cup that had just appeared by her side. 'As it happens, there's something I need to discuss with Signor Baretti.'

CHAPTER TWENTY-TWO

July

Wren lay on a scratchy, blue and red checked picnic rug with Jo and their new friends. Even though she was sprawled in the deep shade cast by one of Central Park's spreading sycamore trees, the summer heat made her throat dry and her limbs feel heavy. The humid weather didn't seem to have affected the roller-skaters rocketing past on the path opposite, or the energetic teenagers who laughed and called out to one another while performing complicated tricks on their skateboards. Locals, Wren thought. Obviously acclimatised.

She let her eyes flutter shut as she imagined herself beside the swirling Shoalhaven River. It was winter there now. The air would be cool and damp, with only the piercing cries of sulphur-crested cockatoos or the snuffle of a solitary bandicoot to disturb the silence.

'Right,' Jo announced. Suddenly, Wren was back in steamy Central Park.

Jo handed out cans of ice-cold Coca-Cola and oversized Reuben sandwiches, saying, 'Brain food, girls. Essential for problem-solving.'

'Thanks,' Wren said.

It seemed she'd rushed her judgement again, for the unlikely pair she'd observed in Parkside's cafeteria on her first night had turned out to be quite different from her initial assumptions. The blonde who modelled herself on Madonna was a real sweetheart named May Floris. Softly spoken and extremely pretty behind all the make-up, she'd explained that when she wasn't waitressing in a diner near the wedge-shaped Flatiron Building, she spent most of her time writing her first novel on a portable typewriter. Her pal, Ava Green, was far younger than Wren had thought. In her early thirties, albeit prematurely grey, she had a razor-sharp wit and wrote reviews for a well-regarded, if obscure, downtown arts journal.

As Jo had already chummed up with the duo, it hadn't taken long for Wren to join the little gang of Parkside residents.

Despite wearing only a skimpy pair of turquoise silk shorts and a vintage-style Hawaiian shirt, Jo looked flushed. 'Have your classified ads led to anything useful yet, Wren?'

Wren shook her head.

'I think posters are the way to go,' Ava said, flicking away bits of sauerkraut from the front of her vintage Women's Lib T-shirt. 'Something with big block letters and a line like "*Do you know Roma?*" Then you could add a couple of sentences saying it's urgent she make contact – put in her age, too, that will help to narrow things down. You can leave Parkside's phone number and address.'

Tugging down her printed, vintage dress, Wren propped herself up on one elbow, feeling gloomy. 'But New York is huge. We'd never be able to put up enough of them.'

'Countless campaigns have taught me you have to be targeted,' Ava said.

'I get what you mean!' Jo swallowed another mouthful of Coke. 'We'll put them up in clubs and cool bars, places someone her age would be most likely to go.'

'I'm beginning to think I shouldn't drag you into this business,' Wren said glumly. 'I don't know if Roma even *wants* to be found.' She was missing Lily and feeling dispirited by her latest conversation with Dr Carmichael. As always, he'd said little other than 'She's stable, for now.'

May patted her hand. 'Hey, don't be sad. I know a journalist on the *Star*. I'll bet I could convince him to write a story about you, and how you've come all this way to New York to find your missing sister. Newspapers love that kind of human-interest piece – at least it would make a change from the endless reporting about who'll be running for president in November.'

'Hell, what will become of us if we're lumbered with four years of George Bush?' Ava broke in. 'The ex-director of the CIA, God help us,' she said caustically. 'Just who we need in the Oval Office.'

'Right now, we've more immediate problems to deal with,' Jo said. 'I think both Ava and May are onto something. Want to give their ideas a go, Wren?'

'Thanks, I do. I've got nothing to lose.' She gave the group a thumbs-up. 'I'll see if Jewel will agree to put some posters up in Parkside. Maybe I'll ask her how she'd go about finding someone in this city, too. She seems pretty cluey.'

'Great.' Jo looked around. 'Speaking of places to hang out – who's going to Nell's tonight?'

'I thought it was impossible to get into unless you were a supermodel or something,' Ava huffed.

'Our mate May might have a contact at the *Star*, but I've got one at New York's hottest club.' Jo grinned. 'We might not have the posters yet, but at least we can check the place out. So who's up for it?'

'Don't tell me you're not already lined up with a cute boy?' Wren asked with a smile. Jo had thrown herself into a whirlwind of dating ever since she hit New York.

'Not tonight, sweetie,' she exclaimed. 'I'm planning on painting this town red with you guys.'

'Count me out,' Ava said, hugging her knees. 'I'll be trying to think of something to write that hasn't already been said about Tom Wolfe's *Bonfire of the Vanities* for the magazine.

'I love his term "social x-rays",' she continued. 'It's the perfect description of all those skeletal ladies like Nancy "Just Say No"

Reagan who lunch at Le Cirque on nothing but the world's most expensive spinach and a couple of strips of steamed carrot.' She took an aggressive bite of her sandwich. 'Man's a genius.'

May nodded enthusiastically. 'Count me in.' She pulled her wallet out of her bag and waved it in the air. 'Just as well I have my fake ID. This city doesn't let you have a drink anywhere until you're over twenty-one,' she grumbled to her friends.

'I have to meet some people for a work drink a bit later,' Wren said. 'But maybe we could catch up after that.'

She took a deep breath. The thought of seeing Alessandro was making her heart thump.

Wren noted the heads that turned towards her when she entered the Plaza Hotel's Palm Court, a glamorous room boasting a small rainforest of greenery interspersed with marble pillars, frosted glass and plenty of gilt trimmings.

Good, she thought as she crossed the mosaic floor. Alessandro would not be seeing an uncertain girl encased in a baggy man's suit this evening, but a woman who was in control of her life. As for Amelia, well, she was ready for her, too.

After a consultation with Jo – followed by a tussle with her conscience – Wren had used yet more of her funds to acquire a chic black Azzedine Alaïa dress that did nothing to disguise her curves.

Once she'd spotted Alessandro and Amelia deep in conversation at a small round table, she squared her shoulders and made her way over.

Looking more striking than ever in a dark suit and deep blue shirt, Alessandro stood up. 'Hello, Wren,' he said with a smile that threatened to undermine her self-possession. 'What a pleasure to see you again.'

Amelia's sharp eyes moved from one to the other. 'This *is* a happy coincidence,' she said. 'Here we are, from three different countries, and we all wind up in New York at the same time. What are the chances?'

She straightened one of the cuffs of her cream silk Chanel blouse. 'We've been drinking Moët & Chandon, Wren, but I'd better order you a Perrier water.'

Wren ignored Amelia's taunt. 'I'd prefer champagne, thank you.'

For the next thirty minutes Wren said little, leaving it to Amelia to monopolise Alessandro. At first she confined herself to showing off her erudition by commenting on a recent exhibition of Italian Old Masters held at the Metropolitan Museum, but before long she began to display a decidedly flirtatious side Wren had never seen before.

'I'm so looking forward to exploring your own art collection again the next time I'm in Rome,' she purred to Alessandro.

Of course she's been to his apartment, Wren thought with chagrin. *No doubt to his bedroom, too.*

Alessandro adroitly sidestepped Amelia's remark, choosing to flatter her instead by expressing his fascination with her views on the High Renaissance.

Wren was so disturbed by his proximity she found it difficult to keep track of their conversation. It was a relief when Amelia excused herself and disappeared to the powder room.

Seizing her chance, Wren said, 'Alessandro, we don't have much time so I'm going to cut to the chase.'

'I'm glad to hear it.' He draped his arm around the back of her chair, trailing his fingers across her bare shoulders as he did so. 'Because I've been fighting the urge to kiss you ever since you walked in. You look incredible.'

'What do you think you're doing?' she said sharply, trying to ignore the way her skin tingled when he'd touched her. 'You must know you've caused me nothing but trouble.'

She took a quick sip of the champagne she'd barely tasted. 'I can't believe you told John Tremaine about us. You made him think he had a free pass to have sex with me, and when I wouldn't do what he wanted I lost an important grant – and my job. Of course' – her eyes flashed – 'he had plenty of ammunition.

'Changing the price of that Raphael so you could add fifty-thousand dollars to your profit and then blaming me for your fraud – there couldn't be a lower act.' She paused. 'Oh, wait a minute, there *is* something worse. It was making love to me when you were engaged to marry someone else.' Wren glared at him.

'I have no idea what you're talking about.' Alessandro gave her an injured look. 'I did thank John Tremaine for sending me such a charming curator. Perhaps I mentioned you were extremely attractive. If that is a crime, I'm guilty as charged.'

He covered her hand with his own. 'But I can hardly be held responsible for whatever conclusions he drew. *Cara*, I swear I said nothing about the magic we shared.'

Wren removed her hand.

'As for the contract, I admit I made sure Tremaine knew that we deserved to be paid more. I'm a dealer, that's what we do.' He shrugged. 'The man turned me down, so I let it go. Anyway, I gather the deal is off.'

Wren shot him a fierce look. 'Alessandro, I'd love to believe you, but how can I? You're obviously a liar. Otherwise you would never have betrayed your fiancée.'

It was so bloody ridiculous. Even though she was furious with the man, she found herself wishing they were alone so he could take her in his arms just as he had in Rome.

'But there is no fiancée,' Alessandro protested.

'Come off it!' Now she felt more like hitting him. 'Amelia told me herself she knew you as well, and I quote, "as any fiancée can".'

She took a surreptitious peek over her shoulder. Amelia was sure to return any minute.

Alessandro held up his hands. 'Yes, it's true, we were engaged.' He looked into Wren's eyes. 'For a brief period, about a year ago. Amelia Heywood is a good-looking woman and very clever. Unfortunately, she is also what the English call a cold fish.' He shrugged. 'Of course, we're still close friends.'

Wren's thoughts whirled. Everything Alessandro said sounded so plausible. She wanted to believe him. No, longed to. But weren't his protestations just a little too glib? They seemed to come close to other people's claims, then slide away towards an entirely different explanation.

Men are not to be trusted, whispered the voice in her head. 'I'm not sure I believe anything you've told me,' she said, aiming for a tone as cool as Amelia's.

'Why not?' Alessandro demanded, his azure eyes flaring. 'Because John Tremaine took revenge on you, or because you made an assumption about me and Amelia that wasn't true?'

Wren remained silent. Maybe she had leapt to another conclusion. Now she wasn't sure of anything, except that the time she had spent with Alessandro in Rome had meant more to her than she cared to admit.

'Wren, I can't stop thinking about you, remembering how good we were,' he said softly, his accent turning the words into music. 'I told myself you have your life on the other side of the world and I have mine in Italy, that there was no possibility of taking things further. But you're in New York now, and I fly here once a month to look at pictures and see clients.' He paused. 'I could arrange for you to visit Rome, too. We could be together, see what—'

'Develops?' Wren broke in.

'Yes, that's it. We could see what develops.' He gave Wren such a sincere look she could feel her resolve wavering.

'You two seem to be getting along famously,' Amelia said pointedly as she took a seat. 'Sorry I was so long – I remembered I hadn't called back a client, so I used one of the hotel's phones. The dreary man took ages.'

She signalled to a waiter for the bill. 'I'm afraid time is moving on. Alessandro and I have a date to catch up with some mutual friends.' She glanced at Wren. 'Were you able to resolve whatever it was you wanted to discuss?'

Wren smiled at her sweetly. 'Do you know, I'm not sure that we did.'

CHAPTER TWENTY-THREE

It was 10.30 pm and the weather was still hot and sultry, though this hadn't deterred the two hundred or more eager patrons queuing outside a doorway that Wren assumed led to Nell's. The club was obviously so famous it didn't need to bother advertising itself with anything as mundane as a sign.

The line of people snaking down tatty West 14th Street pulsed with energy and expectation, despite the presence of overflowing garbage bins, lurid sex shops and cheap liquor stores. Wren spotted uptown socialites wearing the latest Christian Lacroix puffball dresses with fabulous faux jewels, grungy downtown artists in jeans and sweatshirts, cutting-edge designers, and the wannabes – maybe from Brooklyn or the Bronx – who proudly wore their labels. Then there were the smooth junk bonds traders and real estate wheeler-dealers, slapping one another on the backs of their custom-made suits. They looked just as likely to be exchanging the names of their cocaine dealers as sharing gossip about the stock market. Wren recognised other faces from television, the movies and the social pages Amelia had insisted she study.

She was still dressed in her clinging black Alaïa, while May was turned out in a full-on Madonna look, including a dangling earring in the shape of a cross, her usual masses of chains, a short leather skirt, fishnets and Doc Martens boots. Jo had opted for tight gold lamé pants and an off-the-shoulder emerald green satin top worn with teetering Maud Frizon heels. Being in New York had done nothing to temper her style. If anything, it was more flamboyant than ever.

'Okay, girls,' she said, 'Ready to tough it out?'

'You must be mad,' Wren exclaimed. 'Have you seen who they've just turned away? I swear that was Michael Douglas, as in *Wall Street* "Money never sleeps" Michael Douglas. If he can't get in, what hope do we have?'

'Just watch.'

Ignoring the velvet ropes holding the crowd back, Jo sauntered up to an Amazonian woman sporting a black catsuit and diamanté-studded choker who was guarding the entrance with the ferocity of a tiger. Words were exchanged, a list consulted and, to Wren's astonishment, the enforcer nodded.

'We're in!' Jo cried. She took Wren and May by the hand, pulling them through the entrance and down a dark corridor. With the parting of a curtain, the girls were enveloped by a fantasy world of beaded chandeliers, sumptuous oriental rugs, and velvet sofas on which lounged a collection of gorgeously dressed patrons.

'It looks so cool!' May said, twirling around. 'What do you think, Wren?'

'I'm trying to work out how to describe it. Maybe Victorian gentlemen's club meets 1920s speakeasy? Although with all these celebrities on hand, it could only be 1980s Manhattan.' She grabbed Jo by the elbow. 'Isn't that amazing woman with the scuba mask and shaved head Grace Jones?'

Jo squinted in the direction of the bar. 'Oh my God, you're right, and by the look of it she's hanging out with Debbie Harry. Come on, girls, let's find Nell.'

A group of fans were gathered around a striking woman wearing a slinky, claret-coloured satin dress who was draped languidly over a leather banquette. She had flaming red hair cut in a bob with a short, blunt fringe, and had coloured her mouth with a slash of scarlet.

'Darling,' she drawled, waving at Jo. 'It's bloody good to see you.' Her droll tone was accentuated by a voice that combined both Australian and British vowels. 'I see you've brought reinforcements.'

Jo made the introductions.

'Hey, didn't you play Columbia in *The Rocky Horror Picture Show*?' May said, her eyes dancing with excitement. 'I absolutely love that movie. It's on permanent replay at one of the downtown cinemas and I go all the time.'

'Sure, that was me, back when I was a child of twenty-two. As you can see' – Nell made a sweeping, theatrical gesture – 'I've moved on since then. How's tricks, Jo?'

'Never better, now I've moved to the Big Apple,' Jo answered with a grin. 'Maybe we'll catch you later?' She winked as she watched Sting approaching. 'Don't want to keep you from your admirers.'

Jo turned towards her friends, both with stunned looks on their faces.

'How did you get on first-name terms with the famous Nell?' Wren blurted out.

'I've known her since I was a little kid.' Jo smiled. 'When Dad spent a year working at a London hospital, we all went over too. Mum and I were wandering around the Kensington Market one day – Nell was flogging vintage clothes and heard our Aussie accents.'

Jo's face lit up. 'We started talking about London and life back home. Then Freddie Mercury, who was selling stuff from the stall next door, joined in. I thought he was just a sweet guy with crazy teeth until Queen made it big.'

'Unreal,' May murmured.

'Nell was wearing a shocking pink ballgown and I thought she looked like a fairy princess,' Jo added. 'Anyway, I asked her if we could be pen-friends. When we returned to Melbourne, I wrote her the odd postcard – mostly boring stuff about school or the dog. She'd send something hilarious back, but after a while we lost track of each other. Once I hit New York I contacted the club and we reconnected.'

'I thought you said you were Miss Average?' Wren raised her eyebrows. 'Doesn't sound like it to me.'

Jo laughed. 'Cross my heart, that is the only interesting thing that's ever happened to a member of the Draper family. Now, girls, shall we have a drink or go dancing?'

'Drink,' said Wren.

'Dance.' May spoke at the same time.

The three of them burst out laughing. 'Tell you what.' Wren pointed at the bar. 'I'll find you two downstairs. I feel like a quiet five minutes before hitting the dance floor.'

The other girls took off with a wave while Wren hoisted herself onto a bar stool. She was tempted to ask for a cocktail, but as she'd sworn off spirits for the time being, ordered a glass of white wine instead.

It was impossible to know what to make of her exchange with Alessandro, though just thinking about the sensations his fingers ignited when they caressed her bare shoulders made her breath quicken. He was handsome and cultured – perhaps they could have a glorious future. On the other hand, he could well be a cheat and a liar.

'Is this seat taken?' a voice said.

Wren turned her head towards a tall, well-built man. In his late twenties, he looked like a professional athlete, which made sense as May had pointed out a few muscle-bound members of the New York Giants impatiently waiting their turn in the line outside. Nell's club might boast an all-star cast, but if this guy was a quarterback looking to pick up a girl for the night, he was out of luck.

'Doesn't look like it.' She shrugged.

'Well then,' he said with a smile that revealed the perfect, square white teeth that could only belong to an American. 'Can I buy you a drink?'

'Thanks, I'm fine,' Wren replied, turning away as he took the bar stool next to hers.

He touched her arm.

'Hey, what do you want?' She looked back at him, glaring.

'Ouch, sorry.' He grinned. 'It's just that I think I've seen you before.'

'Can't you come up with anything more original than that?' All she wanted was a bit of space so she could sort out her thoughts, not some jock coming onto her.

'No, really,' he continued. 'At Archer's. I saw you in reception, I'm sure of it.'

'You were in Archer's?'

He lifted his glass of bourbon. 'You sound surprised.'

She tilted her head to one side. 'You don't appear like the kind of guy who's interested in art, that's all.'

'No?' He swallowed some of his drink. 'What do you think I'm likely to be interested in, then?'

'Football, maybe?'

He smiled. 'I do like football – a lot.'

It was time to wrap up this little chat. 'Listen,' Wren said, 'I've some friends waiting for me downstairs.'

'You sure you don't want that drink?'

She sighed. 'Quite honestly, it doesn't sound as if we'd have anything in common.'

'Okay, I know how to take a knockback.' He gave her a rueful look. 'I'll see you around.'

'Probably not,' she said coolly.

He raised his glass to her, an amused expression on what she had to admit was a very handsome face. 'You never know in this town.'

Wren slid off her chair, anxious to be back with her friends. The guy might have been good-looking, with his thick fair hair, square jaw and warm hazel eyes, but she couldn't imagine hitting it off with a knuckle-headed gridiron player. She wondered idly what he'd been doing in Archer's, then remembered there had been a recent pre-auction showing of some classic American sporting memorabilia. He must have been after a trophy or two. Well, she wouldn't be making it three.

As Wren headed downstairs, the thump of the music became all-consuming. It was incredibly dark and the dance floor was crowded, but she could see May and Jo shimmying wildly in the light cast by the DJ's booth.

Wren quickly skipped over to them. She wanted to dance, to lose herself in the rhythm. As a bracket of hip hop gave way to the driving sound of James Brown, every beat thudded through her body.

'Don't look now,' May shouted in her ear, 'but see that skinny little guy across the room, the one in the purple satin shirt with the amazing moves?'

'Yeah, he looks just like Prince.'

'It's him!' May giggled.

Wren threw her arms in the air and spun around and around.

CHAPTER TWENTY-FOUR

She heard the telephone as she walked down the corridor. She yanked open the door of her office and dived for the black receiver, but the caller rang off before she could reach it.

'Damn,' she grumbled. Maybe it had been Alessandro. Although she had to admit to a frisson of pleasure when he'd rung the morning after their drink at the Plaza, pleading to see her, she'd refused his entreaties. 'I have nothing more to say to you,' she'd declared, then hung up abruptly.

This had not deterred Alessandro. Since he'd returned to Rome, he'd not only kept on calling several times a week, but also sent her wonderful bouquets of flowers – crimson roses, naturally. Wren was torn. One moment she hated him; she was sure he'd done everything she had accused him of. The next, her memories of the time they had spent together taunted her. Perhaps it was the illusion of safety that the long-distance phone calls provided, because she'd stopped being quite so quick to slam the phone down when she heard his honeyed voice say, '*Ciao, mia cara.* Have you forgiven me yet?'

Alessandro's pursuit had done nothing to improve her relationship with Amelia. She might no longer be engaged to the man, but the dark looks and the way she pressed her lips together when Wren took a call from him revealed just how jealous she was. Wren had told Alessandro not to ring her at work anymore, but the damage had been done.

After slinging her Coach bag beneath her chair, she sat down and looked balefully at her desk. It was covered with piles of newspaper clippings about auction results, every one of them needing filing.

It was so disappointing. All she seemed to do at Archer's was file, check the measurements of artworks and assist with picture hanging. Although Wren had met the renowned head of Impressionist Art, a tiny, rather old Frenchman with a grey moustache named Antoine Ardant, Amelia had warned her away. 'The man has far more important matters to attend to than bother himself with an intern,' she'd said dismissively.

Amelia hadn't once taken her to any country estates or ritzy apartments to scrutinise artworks, either. Sighing, Wren wondered how long Amelia intended to keep on punishing her for capturing Alessandro's attention.

The only silver lining, Wren thought, as she began sifting through the clippings, was that she'd had the chance to watch plenty of auctions. The exhilaration she had experienced back in Sydney felt even more intense now she was in New York, where the artworks were rarer and the prices far higher. She had also made a point of studying the auctioneers. Their smooth patter, dramatic gestures and the effortless way they extracted vast prices from moneyed bidders gave her the impression that each debonair man was, in fact, a devastatingly effective puppet master.

Curiously, though just like at home she might make mistakes summing up someone she met in the course of an ordinary day, she'd become better than ever at determining the outcome of an auction. Once a sale was underway, she had the feeling she'd been provided with a secret script, because she seemed to know what the bidders might say or do before they did themselves.

Wren longed to be the one up on the dais wielding the auctioneer's hammer, but so far playing even a minor role had remained off limits. She'd had to resort to scattering her high heels, sneakers and sandals around her room, pretending the shoes were bidders while she ran her own make-believe sales. She smiled to herself. Anyone who walked in would think she was a lunatic.

When the telephone's ring broke into her thoughts she seized the receiver.

'Wren Summers,' she said, careful not to sound overly eager.

'That's who I'm after.'

The voice had the cadence of Italy, though its raspy timbre didn't contain a trace of Alessandro's liquid tones.

'I assume this is about a delivery?' She felt more bored than ever.

'I think you've got your wires crossed, Miss Summers,' the voice said. 'My name is Tony Mancini. I'm interested in the Degas I saw in your auction catalogue, the one with the ballet girls.'

Clearly, someone had made a mistake. Dealing with a prospective client was way above her lowly position.

'Perhaps you would like me to transfer you to one of our experts, Mr Mancini,' she said patiently. 'I'm sure they would be delighted to help. Or else I could connect you to the Registration Department. An assistant will take your particulars and arrange for you to collect a numbered paddle when you arrive at the auction.'

She heard the man give a harsh cough.

'Sure, sure,' Mancini said dismissively. 'But not until you and I have sorted things out.' He cleared his throat. 'My granddaughter, Mona, she'd do anything for me. Well, Mona was a ballerina, just starting out with one of the state ballet companies. Only dream she ever had, and it looked like it had come true. But six months ago, the poor kid was in a car accident that busted up her leg so badly she's lucky she can walk.'

'I'm very sorry to hear that, Mr Mancini.'

'She's going to have a birthday real soon and I aim to give her that Degas. But I don't like the idea of appearing at the auction myself. Understand?'

'Of course. You can register a third party to bid on your behalf.'

'I want to call the shots,' he growled.

'That won't be a problem,' Wren said. 'You could register a pre-bid, though this would be risky if the price exceeds the limit you have set. Otherwise, you can simply phone in your bids.'

'Yeah, that's what I'd like. But Miss Summers, you have to be on the other end of the line.'

Wren frowned. What was it with this guy? His interest in her was mystifying. 'I'm afraid I don't have enough seniority,' she explained. 'But we have plenty of experienced staff who would be delighted to work with you.'

'No can do. Tell your boss that Tony Mancini wants you.' He paused. 'From the way you talk, you're not a New Yorker. What are you, English?'

'Australian, actually.'

'Well, Miss Australia, most people in this town recognise my name. The way I figure it, you'll be given the go-ahead, no problem.'

'I'll try, Mr Mancini,' Wren said politely.

She heard him cough again. 'You come highly recommended. So, Miss Summers ...'

'Yes?'

'Get me that Degas,' he said with a hint of menace. 'I don't like being let down.'

There was a hum in the room, for this was the last big sale before the summer, the final opportunity for the wives of New York's finest to dress up and display their jewels and their chic little Oscar de la Renta cocktail dresses in this most public of forums. All the most prominent names from both the social and financial pages were there. But not Mr Mancini.

It was Amelia who had told her about his identity. 'The man is as rich as Croesus,' she'd said, eyeing Wren with new interest when she'd revealed their conversation. 'But then, he has been one of New York's leading Mafia dons for decades.'

She'd folded her Armani-clad arms before adding, 'You probably think the Mafia is something dreamt up by Hollywood, but let me assure you, the Mancini family's reach extends from street corner drug peddling to the highest levels of government. They're into extortion, stand-over rackets, illegal gambling – and don't even get me started on kickbacks from the unions.'

Wren felt as if her legs were about to give way. 'No wonder he doesn't like drawing attention to himself,' she said unsteadily. 'But are you sure Archer's will want to do business with a major underworld figure?'

'Really, Wren, you can be so naïve,' Amelia sniffed. 'Although personally I find Mancini and the world he comes from utterly repellent, an auction house cannot afford to be judgemental. We'd hardly have a client left.'

'And what about me? Is it all right if I handle the telephone bidding?' she asked, worried that this rare chance to prove herself would only further provoke Amelia's ire.

'I suppose so,' she responded, her auburn hair lit by the overhead tubes of neon. 'At least it means *I* won't have to deal with that hoodlum.'

Wren had been on tenterhooks ever since. After much consideration, she'd chosen to wear a discreet, navy blue Calvin Klein pantsuit, with a deep pink Dior lipstick her only flamboyant note. She fidgeted nervously with her hair, then put her hands into her trouser pockets before taking them out again. She might look the part, but was she up to the job?

Perhaps focusing on the man commanding the sale room would still her nerves. The auction had been in progress for just fifteen minutes, but he had already knocked down a dozen lots.

Each of the auctioneers had his own set of attributes, but Peter Morgan, known in the trade as 'Morgan the Magician', was Archer's secret weapon. Every time Wren attended one of his sales, she felt the unique thrill induced by observing true genius at work.

Morgan was English. When they had first been introduced, she'd been surprised by his subdued manner, quite the opposite of what Wren expected from a star performer who routinely achieved multimillion-dollar results. He was of medium height and middle-aged, with brown hair and eyes. Rather than memorable, his face was of a type likely to disappear into a crowd. However, somewhat like a gifted actor, once he ascended the podium and picked up his ivory gavel, Morgan transformed into another being entirely.

His voice became stronger and more resonant, his actions resolute. On occasion, his eyes twinkled when he made a witty remark, while at other times, perhaps when a participant seemed uncertain, his expression became bold. But what never changed was the masterly way he played off one bidder against another. Morgan coaxed and cajoled, challenged and encouraged, right up to the moment when, finally, he thundered, 'Sold!'

At a sign, Wren moved swiftly, replacing another employee behind one of the small oak desks. Her pulse quickened. The Degas was coming up next.

'It's about to get underway, sir,' she said quietly after dialling the interstate number Mancini had given her. 'The auctioneer has just identified the painting and announced its lot number. Now he's providing some details.'

She adjusted the earpiece, frowning. There was a great deal of background noise at Mancini's end. From the sound of people talking and knives being scraped on plates, he was in a crowded restaurant.

'The best way for this to work,' she said in an undertone, 'is if we wait until the picture is about to go under the hammer. Then you can decide if you want to top the bid.'

'I got that,' Mancini muttered. Or at least, that's what Wren thought he'd said. His raspy voice made his words hard to catch, and what with the clatter at his end and the alarming degree of static that the line from Chicago had inconveniently developed, deciphering his words was a challenge.

'What's happening?' he croaked.

'There are three serious players,' Wren said.

'We'd better start bidding.'

'No, sir, remember what I told you? It's best to wait,' she cautioned.

Mancini's response was lost amid a burst of laughter and the clinking of glasses.

'Okay, one party has just dropped out,' Wren said. 'The auctioneer is about to knock it down to the highest bidder. When he gets to "going twice" I'm holding up my paddle.'

Within seconds, her arm shot up.

'Yes, Wren, do you have a bid?' Morgan said.

Wren nodded, and another $100,000 was added to the already hefty price.

'It's in our favour,' she whispered into the phone.

But Morgan had turned to the underbidder. 'You wouldn't deny yourself at this stage, would you, sir?' Wren could see Morgan's eyes twinkle. 'One more bid might do it.' Despite the persuasive auctioneer's best efforts, the underbidder shook his head.

It was then that a late arrival with a willowy blonde on his arm took the seat furthest away from her at the end of the fourth row.

'Going once,' Morgan said, lifting his gleaming gavel. 'The bid is with you, Wren.'

He dropped his hand and looked around the room, allowing the tension to build. Slowly he raised the gavel once more. 'Going twice,' he pronounced.

A murmur rippled through the crowd as, suddenly, the late arrival held up his paddle.

Wren's eyes opened wide. It was the wretched quarterback who had tried to pick her up at Nell's.

The price of the Degas continued to ascend. Each time Mancini instructed Wren to raise his bid, the footballer lifted his hand. The cost now stood at $2.6 million.

'It's currently in the other party's favour, Mr Mancini. Will you be placing another bid?' She strained to hear the man's response over the noisy diners and electronic crackles.

'I need a minute,' was the muffled response.

Wren's voice was taut. 'I'm sorry, sir, we can't hold up the auction. You must let me know straightaway.'

'Pull out,' he said. There was a crash, followed by shouts. Then he added, 'Stop.'

Wren was stunned. She had not picked Mancini as the type to lose his nerve. 'Are you quite certain?

'Yes. Those are my instructions.'

At least that was clear. 'Very well. Thank you, Mr Mancini.' Wren put the phone down.

Morgan turned in her direction. 'Wren, do you have another bid?'

She shook her head, trying not to betray her disappointment. Obtaining the winning offer would have been a coup.

'All done, then,' Morgan announced as his gavel came down for the final time. 'Sold to the gentleman on my left.'

Wren's disappointment stung. She dearly wished it could have been Mancini's poor, damaged granddaughter who was the new owner of the exquisite painting. Instead, the picture had fallen into the hands of a lavishly paid, ignorant pro-athlete who was no doubt counting on it to impress his latest girlfriend.

The next morning, still feeling dismayed, Wren pushed a dark curl away from her forehead. She was wearing her hair out rather than in its usual ponytail, but every time she bent over the filing cabinet it fell in her eyes. As Amelia was with Peter Morgan reviewing last night's prices, the office was particularly quiet.

The phone's ring pierced the silence. It was Jeanette calling from reception, with news that a client was waiting to see her in the private meeting room Archer's referred to as 'the library'.

'For me? That's odd,' Wren said, wrinkling her forehead. She only had one client, but as he'd crashed out of the bidding last night, she wasn't sure that Mancini still qualified.

'I've shown him inside and organised coffee,' Jeanette said

hurriedly, 'though by the look of this guy, I'd head down as fast as you can. I think I saw steam coming out of his ears.'

Wren rushed to the lift, her hair flying.

'Miss Summers,' Mancini growled from the depths of a green leather club chair when she entered the room.

With its mahogany shelves full of leatherbound books and ecru walls displaying antique botanical prints, the library had been designed to create an atmosphere of timeless serenity. But Wren's so-called client appeared far from calm. He thrust his coffee cup onto its saucer with a clatter.

'Good morning, sir,' she said respectfully.

Tony Mancini was in his late sixties, with a heavy build, dark hair and eyes the colour of black olives. He was wearing an expensive pin-stripe suit, a little tight around the shoulders, and a thunderous expression.

Wren wondered if he was experiencing a particularly bitter attack of the 'day-after remorse' Amelia had told her about. Apparently, it tended to strike underbidders almost as soon as they had allowed a painting they coveted to slip from their grasp.

'It was such a shame you missed out on the Degas,' she said in what she hoped was a consoling tone.

Mancini glowered at her. 'I'll say I missed out.' His quiet rasp was alarming. 'What in God's name did you think you were doing, going against my instructions?'

There was an uncomfortable moment of silence before he added, 'People who screw me over don't usually come out well, Miss Summers.'

Wren took the chair next to Mancini, unnerved and bewildered.

'But I don't understand,' she said. 'You instructed me to "Pull out". Then I distinctly heard you say "Stop".'

'What sort of fool are you?' Mancini demanded. 'I said, *Pull out all the stops.*'

Wren's heart sank. She had made a horrendous mistake, one of the worst in the auction business. Failing to put a client's bid forward was unforgiveable. If a complaint were lodged, she'd be thrown out immediately.

'I am so, so sorry.' Wren clasped her hands together. 'The line was unbelievably bad and there was a great deal of background noise. I think you must have been in a restaurant?'

'Where I was is none of your business,' Mancini fumed. 'And I'm not interested in excuses. What I want is that picture. So, you go and get it back for me. Otherwise I'll be informing your chief executive that you are guilty of malpractice. Then I will consider how else your life might be ruined.'

Mancini curled his lip. 'I promised my granddaughter that on her birthday she would receive a picture of ballerinas painted by Degas.'

'Yes, but I don't see how I can—'

He jabbed a finger at her. '*I will not break that promise.*'

Wren swallowed. There was nothing she could say.

CHAPTER TWENTY-FIVE

After Mancini stormed out, Wren buried her face in her hands. Her reputation in Sydney's art world had been trashed. Now it looked as if the same thing was going to happen here.

She didn't think she could cope with another disaster. According to Dr Carmichael, her mother would not remain stable for long. Soon Lily would begin slipping away, a little further every day. So far the only responses she'd had to her posters came from weirdos making obscene suggestions and a couple of ageing Italian ladies named Roma who were employed by the clubs as cleaners. As the classified ads had proved just as unsuccessful, and with the doctor's grim words eating away at her, she'd made an appointment at the toney law firm that administered the shadowy trust that had been making deposits into Lily's account all these years.

Wren grimaced as she recalled being met by a pompous junior attorney wearing a flashy silk tie. Almost as soon as he'd taken down her contact details, he'd done everything he could to show her the door. Furious, she had insisted on seeing one of the senior partners but, to her dismay, Henry Clayton III, a craggy, grey-haired man with a demeanour as dour as his countenance, had been equally dismissive. With a shrug of his pin-stripe shoulders, he'd claimed that a combination of client confidentiality and the explicit terms of the trust prevented him from revealing any information. She'd been determined to extract *something* – a detail that might help her find Roma, perhaps a word about her father – but when she'd challenged him, he'd looked at her with disdain.

'Frankly, Miss Summers, I am surprised by your attitude. I would have imagined that a girl like you would be grateful for the benefaction you have received,' he said.

A girl like you. Clayton had made it sound as if she were a particularly repellent variety of parasite.

Wren kneaded her temples, groaning. If this overbearing snob's refusal to offer her the slightest assistance wasn't bad enough, now she had another major problem. Why did the Degas' successful bidder have to be that arrogant footballer? The only option she had was to try to convince him to on-sell the picture to Mancini, which meant that after giving the wretched man the brush-off, she would now have to beg him for an enormous favour. That prospect made her squirm.

She rose reluctantly and trudged up the stairs to the records department.

'Um, Eileen, I wonder if you could look something up for me?'

The archivist was entering a list of names and addresses onto her word processor. Around the same age as Wren, she wore Clark Kent–style black glasses and moonlighted as a saxophonist in an experimental jazz band.

'Sure,' she said, looking up. 'What are you after?'

'It's last night's Degas. I'm curious to know who bought it.'

'Can't say I'm surprised.' Eileen grinned as she took off her spectacles. 'That guy is the original all-American hunk. He might not be my usual type, but I'd be prepared to make an exception in his case.'

Wren raised her eyebrows. 'What, you on a date with a footballer?'

Eileen burst out laughing. 'Oh God, that's hilarious.'

'It is?' Wren looked puzzled.

You honestly don't know who he is?'

'I guess not.' Wren had an uneasy feeling in the pit of her stomach.

'Well, he's not a pro-footballer, that's for sure.' Eileen placed her glasses back on her nose and immediately looked more authoritative.

'Dr Jordan Grant is the private art curator of E.J. Conroy, the reclusive, mega-rich newspaper magnate. He's also a boy wonder Harvard grad who's rapidly become one of the most highly prized bidders on the auction circuit. Just imagine having Conroy's millions to splash around ...' she said dreamily.

Wren struck the side of her head. 'Nooo! I'm such a dope. Please don't tell anyone, but he tried to come on to me in a bar and I was rude as hell to him.'

'Not a good move, sister,' Eileen said, wagging her finger. 'He's probably Archer's top client.'

Wren tried to absorb this information. In a matter of days, she had managed to alienate both an extremely valuable existing client and a prospective one. She was doomed – unless she could somehow sweet-talk this Jordan Grant into cutting a deal.

'Eileen, could you give me Jordan's phone number? I'd better ring and apologise.'

Her colleague looked sceptical.

'What?' Wren said with her hands on her hips. 'I'm not about to ask him out on a date if that's what you think.'

'Can't say I'd blame you,' Eileen said with a wink.

Wren drummed her fingers on the tiny tabletop. She'd been surprised when Jordan had suggested they meet in a hip Soho bar. He looked more like an Ivy League type who would opt for something like the quiet luxury of the Plaza's wood-panelled Oak Room. But then, her assumptions about him being a footballer had proved to be wrong. Maybe, she told herself, he had other surprises in store for her.

Wren glanced at all the cool girls dressed in funky jeans, little singlets and leather jackets, wishing fervently that she was at least wearing her old op shop clothes instead of standing out like some corporate dummy in her sharp-shouldered Donna Karan suit. To make matters worse, Jordan Grant was late. Probably it was one of the stupid power games men liked to play. She drummed her fingers with increasing irritation.

Sipping from her glass of white wine, she tried to remember the persuasive little speech she'd devised for his benefit in the early hours of the morning. It was vital her plea worked, but now every clever line she had come up with sounded trite and unconvincing. Perhaps she'd be better off simply winging it when he turned up. *If* he turned up.

A high-pitched giggle from a couple of girls at the bar made her look in their direction. Then she saw him – that shock of dark blond hair and his height made Jordan impossible to miss. He was wearing chinos and a white Oxford cloth shirt, and the girls were practically drooling, although to Wren's relief he ignored them. The last thing she needed was for Jordan to be distracted by a pair of nubile young women.

'Hello, Wren Summers,' he said, sitting down next to her. 'Hope you haven't been waiting long. I'm afraid I was held up.'

'I was beginning to think you weren't coming.' Wren forced herself to smile.

He had a watchful expression on his classically handsome face. 'I have to admit, I was surprised to hear from you.'

Flustered, Wren didn't bother with small talk but dived straight in. 'Look, about the other night at Nell's ...'

'You mean when you said I didn't seem the type to have any interest in art?' His voice was ironic.

Wren bit her lip. This was not starting well.

'I am really sorry about that,' she began. 'I'd had a big day and I wasn't myself. You see, I only arrived in New York recently and I'm still getting the hang of things. Please accept my apologies.' She tucked a strand of hair behind one ear, feeling anxious.

Jordan hailed a bartender, ordered a Corona for himself and another glass of white wine for Wren, before turning back to her.

'Sure, whatever.' He shrugged. 'Only, I have the feeling you have something else on your mind. I figure a girl who looks like you do must give guys the cold shoulder all the time, but I'll bet you don't make a habit of calling them up to say sorry.' He looked at her as if she were a picture and he was searching for the flaw. 'So, what I'm asking myself is, what is it you want?'

The bluntness of Jordan's question was unnerving. He might not be a star athlete, but he was still too damned sure of himself. On the other hand, at least he hadn't given her The Look or resorted to chatting her up – that was in his favour. Then Wren remembered the blonde he'd had on his arm at the auction. Maybe brunettes weren't his type.

'Oh, and just so you know,' he added, 'I don't make a habit of coming on to girls in bars.' He swallowed some beer. 'After seeing you at Archer's, I thought we'd have plenty to talk about, that's all. You had other ideas. It's no big deal.'

Wren seized her opportunity. 'We do. I mean, you're right. We do have plenty to talk about. More than you know.'

Nervousness was making her trip over her words. Suddenly hot, she shook off her coat.

'It's the Degas, the one you bought at the auction,' Wren said in a rush.

'What about it?'

She grasped her fresh glass of wine, took a large gulp, and confessed her mistake. There was no point trying to charm or to hold something back. A man like Jordan Grant would be likely to see through any ploys in a second.

'As you can gather, I'm in big trouble.' Her face crumpled. 'But to be frank, I feel more upset about Mona's ruined birthday and Mr Mancini's broken promise than I am about whatever might happen to me.'

Jordan gave a low whistle. 'That's brave,' he said. 'If I was on the wrong side of a big-time Mafia hood, I'd be worried as hell.' He had a speculative look. 'What makes you think I can help?'

Wren was struck once more by his direct manner. 'You could ask Mr Conroy if he would on-sell the Degas painting to

Mancini. I can assure you,' she said earnestly, 'he'd be willing to pay a premium.'

Jordan shook his head. 'I can tell you right now, Conroy wouldn't go for it. He had his heart set on buying that painting – it didn't matter what it cost.'

Wren's spirits sank. She was done for.

'Okay,' she said grimly. 'Thanks for hearing me out. I'd better go tell my client the bad news.'

She had risen to her feet and was putting on her jacket when Jordan said, 'Wait. There might be a way through this. Sit down, Wren.' He placed his hand firmly on her arm. 'Take your coat off.'

Wren flinched. Jordan's touch assumed too much. Maybe he would turn out to be just a younger, better-looking version of John Tremaine. What made men think that because a woman depended on their cooperation, they had a right to expect sex on demand?

'Sure,' she said, eying him warily as she resumed her seat. She had not taken off her coat. 'What exactly are you proposing?'

Jordan sat back, his muscular frame dwarfing the spindly bar chair. 'Not what I'm guessing you think I have in mind,' he said wryly. 'You know, you have quite a habit of jumping to conclusions.'

Wren coloured. 'I … I don't know what to say.'

'I think it would be better if you just listened, don't you?' He regarded her steadily with his hazel eyes.

Wren noticed they contained gold and green flecks that might be considered by someone else to be remarkably attractive. 'I'm all ears,' she said.

'No promises, but I think I have a solution.'

When Jordan leant forward she caught the hint of a delicious scent that reminded her of subtly spiced apples.

'Mr Conroy has a significant collection, and recently …'

He spoke for five minutes, laying out his plan clearly and distinctly. When he'd finished, he folded his arms. 'Well?'

'That is a truly excellent idea,' Wren exclaimed. 'If you can persuade Conroy, I'll take care of Mancini.' She pushed back her loose curls. 'I cannot tell you how grateful I am.'

'Well, if it comes off, you can let me know over dinner.' His expression was detached. Wren couldn't tell what he was thinking.

'As long as it's on me,' she said quickly. Under the circumstances, it was the least she could do.

'No, I think fifty-fifty is fair. And I'll pick the restaurant.' Wren glimpsed his perfect white teeth as he smiled for the first time.

She raised her glass and smiled back at him. 'Dr Grant, you have a deal.'

On the following Saturday morning, Wren was swinging one of Jewel Hoskins' precious keys by its blue cord while she gazed at Gramercy Park's well-groomed gardens and lawns.

'Heaven, isn't it?' she said to Jo as she lay back against a dark green wooden bench. 'No overactive teenagers, no roller-skaters and definitely no boom boxes within cooee.'

'Agreed.' Jo smiled lazily from her perch next to her. 'I'm against private parks on principle, but I have to admit, you can't beat Gramercy for peace and quiet.' She prodded Wren's arm. 'Which leads me to say, now is the perfect time to let me know how you wriggled out of the Archer's nightmare. So spill the beans.'

'*Must* you poke me like that?' Wren laughed. 'Come on. Let's have a stroll while I fill you in.'

Ten minutes later, they paused in front of a bronze statue. Peering at the inscription, Wren announced, 'It says this is the famous nineteenth-century Shakespearean actor Edwin Booth.' She straightened up. 'Wasn't his brother the man who assassinated Abraham Lincoln? I'm sure I read it somewhere.'

'Not a top rello to have, then.' Jo chuckled. 'But what I really want to know is, do I have your story straight? Let's see ...' She had a mischievous look on her face. 'In a nutshell, the awful footballer who turned out not to be a footballer but a media tycoon's private art curator and not awful at all, came up with another Degas ballet painting that his boss didn't want anymore, because now he has a better one that he bought at your auction.' She grinned. 'How am I doing so far?'

'Just fine.'

'The art curator persuaded his boss not to put the excess Degas up for auction but to sell it privately to Mancini who was delighted, so now everything is hunky-dory.'

'Thank the Lord.' Wren performed a gleeful skip.

'Hey, I'm not finished yet.' Jo held up one finger. 'We now know the art curator's name is Jordan Grant. Jordan is very tall, with blondish hair and he's really quite nice. How nice, exactly?' She raised her eyebrows.

'He's all right.' Wren didn't mention just how remarkable Jordan's looks were, because then Jo would assume there was something going on, and she had no intention of becoming mixed up with another man.

'Hmm, I'll let that go for the moment.' Jo's voice had the precise degree of suspicion Wren had hoped to avoid.

'And as far as Archer's is concerned, Timothy King – that's the CEO's name, right?'

Wren nodded.

'Right, so you made sure King knew the deal would be happening under the auspices of Archer's and he didn't mind about it being a private sale, because the price was high, and Archer's would still walk away with a nice commission on two million dollars.' Jo flopped down on the nearest bench and stretched her arms above her head. 'Have I missed anything?'

'That's about it.' Wren sat down next to her. 'The outcome feels like some kind of miracle, though Amelia didn't like it one bit – she was revelling in my auction blunder.' Wren smiled contentedly. 'But none of it would have happened without Jordan. The deal was all his doing.'

Jo narrowed her eyes. 'So, when are you seeing him again?'

'Who, Jordan?' Wren said blithely. 'We agreed to have dinner next weekend.'

'Ha! I knew it.' Jo smirked.

'Contrary to what you might think,' Wren said, 'it's merely a meeting of two art-world professionals who have successfully concluded a business transaction.'

'Oh God, listen to yourself.' Jo giggled. 'Even you can't believe that. Anyway, it's time you stopped mooning over your Italian stallion.'

Wren pursed her lips. 'I'm not.'

As soon as the words left her mouth, she realised it was true. Sure, she'd been attracted to Alessandro when they'd met in New York, and for a few weeks that sensation had lingered. But ever since she'd had the time and space to reconsider his claims of innocence, she knew in her heart he was lying. She was certain he'd boasted about their affair to Tremaine, just as she was convinced he'd blamed her for trying to trick the museum into paying too much for the Raphael. Even their lovemaking now struck her as calculated. Alessandro might have provided her with pleasure, but only so he could manipulate her feelings. The reality was they had shared nothing, and so she had come to feel nothing for him.

'Maybe you have gone off Romeo,' Jo said, 'which as far as I'm concerned is good news. Anyway, that bad boy is on the other side of the world and Jordan Grant is right here. Are you certain you're not interested in him?'

'No way,' she said firmly. 'There's absolutely no chemistry.'

Jo rolled her eyes. 'If you say so.'

Wren remained silent while an elderly couple tottered past. Walking arm in arm, they ambled over to examine the petunias in an adjacent garden bed, before slowly making their way to the next bench. The bent, wrinkled gentleman brought out a newspaper, the small white-haired lady took a book from her handbag. Both began reading in companionable silence.

Wren felt a sharp pang. If only Lily could have enjoyed that sort of relationship, built on steadfastness and trust. The kind of relationship that survived countless storms. The kind that lasted.

CHAPTER TWENTY-SIX

On Monday morning at ten o'clock, Wren was pacing up and down the library's thickly carpeted floor. Any moment now, Tony Mancini would be shown in. She pictured him producing a cheque book from his briefcase and signing away two million dollars. Then, at last, this entire nerve-racking matter would be behind her.

She turned around quickly when she smelled a pungent aroma. Mancini had entered the room, puffing on an exceedingly large cigar that he wielded like a weapon.

'It's very good to see you again, sir,' Wren said brightly. Her eyes dropped. To her astonishment, the man was grasping a pair of battered suitcases.

'Going somewhere?' she asked, motioning him to sit down.

Mancini looked at her serenely. 'I've come to pay you.'

He hoisted the bags up and laid them flat on the long black marble coffee table. Next, with the flick of a silver key, he sprang open the locks.

Wren stared. Both bags were stuffed with piles of dollar bills. She had never seen so much money in one place in her life.

'What, you think it's not all there?' Mancini's eyes flashed.

'Not at all, sir,' Wren said, smoothing her hair as she tried to collect herself. 'It's just … quite an impressive sight.' She thought quickly. 'I will have to contact a superior to take charge of it, though.' Surely payment by cash of such a huge sum was at the very least irregular and, more likely, illegal – she couldn't possibly take responsibility for it.

Picking up the telephone that sat on a Georgian side table, she called Amelia's extension. 'Would you mind coming down to the library?' she said. 'I have Mr Mancini with me, and I would like you to authorise his payment.'

Amelia sighed. 'For goodness sake, you should know the procedure. Just take his bloody cheque and give him a receipt.'

'No can do,' Wren said gaily.

'Honestly!' Amelia exclaimed. 'I'll be there in a minute.'

Wren handed Mancini a cup of the steaming coffee Jeanette had just brought in on a red lacquered tray.

'I knew you wouldn't let me down.' He beamed. 'You're the same as my granddaughter – you even look alike.'

He thrust his hand inside his suit jacket. 'Miss Summers, I'd like to give you something to express my appreciation.' Mancini immediately whipped out a bulging Gucci wallet and began counting out a wad of hundred–dollar bills.

Wren gulped. 'Please don't take this the wrong way, sir, but Archer's employees are forbidden from accepting commissions. Honestly, I'm just thrilled that Mona will have such a beautiful Degas to unwrap on her birthday. That's the best reward I could possibly have.'

'It's not a commission. It's a gift,' Mancini grumbled.

Wren smiled politely. 'I'm sorry, but I don't think the company would view it that way.'

'I see.' Mancini shrugged.

He was replacing his wallet when Amelia sailed into the room. Wren saw her eyes flicker towards the open suitcases, although nothing in her demeanour revealed so much as a hint of surprise. Instead she merely told Mr Mancini what a pleasure it was to meet him and that arrangements for payment to Mr Conroy would soon be completed. Then, picking up a suitcase in each hand, Amelia promptly disappeared.

Wren was shocked. She was sure she'd just witnessed at least half a dozen federal income tax laws being broken – for one thing, there hadn't been any documentation provided. There wasn't even any mention of a receipt. On the other hand, she told herself, who was she to question the way Archer's conducted its business?

Mancini rose to his feet and extended his hand. 'Miss Summers,' he began.

'Please, call me Wren.' She was warming to Tony Mancini. He might be a Mafia boss, but he was also a loving grandfather.

'Wren, then.' He tapped the side of his nose. 'I had a good feeling when you were recommended to me. Glad I followed my instincts.'

Wren looked puzzled. 'I've been wondering who that might have been.'

Mancini held out his hands. 'Ah, thought you knew. It was my late cousin's boy. I've always been fond of Alessandro – he's like a son to me, especially since I lost my own son.' The man's black eyes clouded.

'I'm sorry.' Wren felt the unexpected tug of a bond between them. She knew about loss.

'It was kind of Alessandro to put you in touch,' Wren said evenly, though his introduction now made her distinctly uncomfortable. What was Alessandro playing at? Sure, it was helpful of him to send a wealthy potential client her way. But ensuring she was mixed up with a Mafia don was likely to prove a mixed blessing. She bit her lip with sudden alarm. Maybe her Roman lover had connections to the Mob she knew nothing about.

'You know, Wren, not many people would walk away from a stack of money,' Mancini said, rubbing his shadowed jaw, 'which means now I have a problem. You see, I owe you a favour.'

Wren shook her head. 'Not at all, sir.'

'You're probably not too familiar with the way the organisation I run operates,' he croaked, 'so let me fill you in.' Mancini looked at her steadily from beneath his black brows. 'We always settle our debts.'

He stubbed out his cigar and left.

Wren sat stiffly on the edge of her bed as she listened to Dr Carmichael speak on the telephone. She'd been calling the specialist for months now. At the beginning, she'd looked forward to their weekly chat, half-believing he might have something uplifting to impart. As time wore on, though, the task had become onerous, filling her with an increasing sense of dread.

'Everything is much the same,' the doctor said in an even tone.

Wren stifled a groan. He gave so little away during their brief conversations that afterwards she always felt wretched. The man was the opposite of comforting, but she assumed that over the years he'd become careful not to give anxious relatives false hope. His must be a hard job.

'There is a degree of responsiveness,' he continued, 'which means your mother may well recover complete consciousness. But the time she has left is strictly limited.'

'How long?' she asked, gripping the phone with a sweating hand.

'Lily will not see the year out,' Carmichael said.

He cleared his throat. 'I gather from what you told me previously, she has sent you to New York on some sort of personal mission. But I feel I must warn you, if you wish to visit your mother before she dies, the time is fast approaching when you must abandon your quest and return to Australia.'

An awful sense of hopelessness enveloped Wren. *Before she dies.* It was stupid, but the word was so much more confronting than 'leaves us' or 'passes away'.

'I suppose you can't tell me when I should be booking a ticket?' She gulped down some water.

'Not precisely.' The man paused. 'But I wouldn't leave it too long.'

Wren perched on the end of her bed while Jo, May and Ava crowded around her small table, drinking 7-Up and eating cupcakes with violent-pink topping. They had spent yet another Saturday afternoon plastering posters over Manhattan's clubs.

Ava spread out a map of the island. She had inked in a red cross at the location of each nightspot where they'd stuck up signs.

'Gee, we've done an awful lot,' May said, her rosebud mouth smeared with lipstick and icing. 'Want one of these?' As she held up a cupcake, her polished nails gleamed like little red beacons.

Wren shook her head. She'd skipped lunch but had no appetite.

'I'm beyond grateful to you three for what you've done, but I've come to a decision,' she said, her voice breaking. 'The posters aren't working – nothing is. So I want you to stop.'

'Wait a minute.' Jo held up a sticky hand. 'What about May's idea? You know, lining you up with a reporter from the *Star*.'

Wren rolled up the billowing sleeves of her man's striped shirt. 'I did the interview, but I was worried Roma would have no idea about her past. I mean, reading that your mother abandoned you when you were a baby, only now that she's dying she'd really like to catch up?' She shook her head. 'It wouldn't come out right, plus it's not the sort of thing you want to learn while you're eating your granola.'

'I get that,' Jo said. 'So what did you say to the journo?'

'I told him my sister and I had been split up when we were very small and I was trying to track her down. Even to me it sounded lame.' She frowned. 'He probably thought so too, though I guess I didn't help myself when I turned him down for a date. The guy took a picture and said he'd write a few paragraphs, but I'm not getting my hopes up.'

May patted her arm. 'I'm so sorry – I didn't realise he'd hit on you.'

Wren sighed. 'What's worse, I'd already been to a private detective, one of those old ex-cops in a dusty office with his name written on the door in gold letters like you see in the movies. He was a nice guy and straight as a die. But after he'd tried every directory he could lay his hands on, pestered his police force buddies and even some high-up contacts in the FBI, he couldn't turn up a trace of a Roma Summers anywhere in the United States. The poor man felt so sorry about letting me down he wouldn't even take my money.

'Speaking of money,' she continued. 'I also made an appointment to see the law firm that handles the mysterious trust that's made all the deposits into Lily's account.

Wren made a face. 'The senior partner simply glared at me in a superior manner while delivering a five-minute lecture on what he called his "solemn duty" to uphold the trust's confidentiality clauses' – her voice became sententious – '"to the letter, Miss Summers, to the letter."'

She shook her head. 'I'm beginning to feel like a mouse in a maze, running around like crazy but striking only dead ends.'

'So what's next?' Ava asked, chewing the end of her pen.

'Well, Tony Mancini said he owes me a favour,' Wren mused. 'Maybe I could ask him for help.'

'No way!' Ava looked shocked. 'It's one thing for you to sort him out with some pictures – that's part of your work at Archers. But getting mixed up with a Mafia boss when it comes to a personal matter is a really bad idea. The last thing you want is for him to get his hooks into you.

'Anyway,' she went on, 'I doubt he could help. His expertise, if you can call it that, is confined strictly to the criminal world – stuff like drug dealing and illegal gambling – not finding someone's missing kid sister. Believe me, Mancini is not going to take on something that's doomed to fail, and he won't thank you for asking him, either. You'd be worse off than you are now.'

'I have to say, I'm one hundred per cent with Ava on that one,' Jo said, taking a sip of 7-Up. 'Don't even think about it.'

Wren tried to swallow her dismay. Of course her friends were right. Tony Mancini couldn't help her find Roma – no one could.

The tears Wren had held back began to spill down her cheeks.

Jo gave her a hug. 'You never know,' she said, releasing Wren from her arms. 'Something entirely unexpected might happen. Or you could have an amazing piece of luck. Maybe,' she added, with an encouraging look, 'now that everything's turned out so well with the Degas, you're on a winning streak.'

Wren tried to smile, but she had always believed in making plans, working hard and taking strictly calculated risks. Her hand drifted towards her gold locket. She'd never had much faith in luck.

CHAPTER TWENTY-SEVEN

Varenna, October 1967

Stumbling over the cobblestones, the fair-haired girl in the flowing blue dress grasped the hand of the small child. The villagers were used to their appearance, although she could see a pair of sunburnt tourists look at them with surprise. By now, she could read the thoughts of such visitors: *That girl's hair is so light it looks nearly silver in the sunlight, and her eyes are the colour of pale green glass — perhaps she travelled to Varenna from a frozen fiord. But surely the lovely child with the raven curls is Italian. Why, she could be a cherub painted by Raphael.*

The girl smiled to herself when she overheard the woman say to the man, 'The little one must be part of the wealthy family who live in that grand villa we passed. I suppose the girl is her au pair.'

The girl acknowledged that she and her child made a disparate twosome. Had the tourist actually been acquainted with them, she would have noted an even greater divergence, for the child already displayed an intense focus she didn't recognise within herself. Unless she was in the mood for painting, of course. Then hours could pass when she'd be lost in her quest to capture the yellow, apricot and blood plum colours of Varenna's little houses, the sapphire of the lake in whose arms the village sheltered and the deep emerald of the cypress pines.

Despite the beauty of this small utopia, lately she'd felt a churn of restlessness that made her hurry the child along. The sun was high in the sky when she reached the square in front of the medieval church of San Giorgio. She'd always found the austere building of grey stone with its sharp, geometric edges and jutting clock tower to be disquieting, but she'd heard that a fortune-teller often set up in a corner of the square.

'I swear by the woman,' her elderly neighbour had told her. 'If she's about, she'll be in a corner with a market umbrella, a little table and a couple of chairs. You'll know her when you see her,' the old lady had cackled.

The girl quickly spotted a woman who matched this description. Pulling the reluctant child by her hand, she walked towards her. 'If you're very good, I will buy you a gelato afterwards,' she said, patting her daughter's head.

The girl regarded the woman beneath the umbrella with welling doubt, for she was so like the stock image of a fortune-teller she might have been cast by a theatrical agency. Her eyes bore an uncanny resemblance to the hard black marble of San Giorgio's floor, and her skin was dark and leathery. She wore a red scarf tied around her hair and gold hoop earrings. A deep-green blouse patterned with red roses and a gathered skirt in a darker green completed her outfit.

The blue-eyed boy would probably laugh if she told him about her excursion – he'd never been very willing to explore mystical realms. That was all right. In every other way they shared the same ideas about how a good life should be lived – hadn't they both turned their backs on the United States and its corrupt capitalist system? The only reason she was here was, ironically, that their little paradise had brought her an edge of fear she couldn't shake. Perhaps mortals weren't entitled to such perfect happiness. Perhaps the gods would punish them.

'*Buon giorno*,' she said to the fortune-teller as she hovered uncertainly by the umbrella. 'My neighbour told me you can tell the future.'

'*Buon giorno.* Yes, that is right.' The woman's manner was brusque. 'Sit down.'

The fair-haired girl took the free chair, then glanced at the child by her feet. She was her joy and her shadow. The child was squatting on the weathered stones, intent on arranging some sticks she'd found into patterns.

'She's clever, that pretty little one, isn't she?' the woman said, examining the dark-haired child with her flinty eyes.

The girl smiled. 'How can you tell?'

'Each soul has its own way of speaking,' she said, 'if you know how to listen.' The woman's gold earrings gleamed in the sunlight. 'I can tell you a great deal. For a price.'

The girl agreed immediately to the sum she was asked to pay. She didn't like haggling.

'Now, I need something personal of yours, something I can hold,' the fortune-teller instructed.

The girl slipped off the engraved silver ring the boy had given her when the child was born and handed it over. She shifted on her chair, discomforted by an unexpected swell of nausea and something else — that same edge of fear.

The woman held the silver ring in her fist so tightly that her knuckles showed the white of the bones beneath. Some minutes passed before she unclenched her hand, but still she left the ring on her palm. Perhaps she feared severing her connection with an invisible realm.

Then she spoke in a mesmerising, sing-song voice, quite different from her former manner. She told the girl many things, delving into her past and the present until, finally, she pronounced upon the future.

As she related these insights the girl found herself swaying. The bright light bouncing off the cobblestones created flaring halos that distorted her vision and made her feel ill. It was so hard to concentrate, she began wondering if she should ask in the church for a pencil and paper so she could jot down the fortune-teller's prognostications. But it was too late. The woman was already returning her ring.

'And now,' she said, pointing to a tray of trinkets sitting on the table, 'I will choose something for you to buy.' Her gnarled hand hovered over various brooches, necklaces and other bits of jewellery for a moment, then reached for two identical gold lockets hanging from fine chains. 'Take these.'

The girl shook her head, bewildered. 'I couldn't afford them.'

The woman stared at her with her stone eyes.

'Well, perhaps just one.' The girl suspected she was being taken advantage of, especially when the woman picked the two lockets up, put them into separate blue boxes and pressed them into her hand.

'I will only charge you for one, but you must take both.' Her voice was rough and insistent. 'They will bring luck to those who wear them, luck that will be needed.'

The girl hesitated, then did as the fortune-teller had commanded. The woman was so resolute, it had been impossible to refuse her. She said goodbye and bent over the child, whispering, 'We'll go down to the pier now. Shall I buy chocolate gelato? I know it's your favourite.'

As she watched the gleeful toddler totter past bushes thick with purple hydrangeas, she tried to remember the fortune-teller's prophecies. But her mind still wasn't clear; the woman's words had left only vague impressions. Despite the happy child, the sun shining down from a cerulean sky and the knowledge that the beautiful blue-eyed boy waited for her in their lemon-painted house, her thoughts slid towards dark places.

CHAPTER TWENTY-EIGHT

New York, 1988

Wren studied Jordan surreptitiously as he speared a sliver of smoked salmon with his fork and laid it on a triangle of toast. It was a bit like examining an astonishing work of art – Michelangelo's *David*, for instance – for the man was absurdly good-looking. She had detected the tiniest bump in his straight nose, but everything else, from his square jaw to his sculpted mouth and hazel eyes, was perfect. No wonder he had blondes hanging from his arm and girls in bars throwing themselves at him.

That afternoon Jo had insisted she wear 'your awesome Alaïa', adding, 'No man could resist you in that dress.'

Wren had thrown up her hands and told Jo she was incorrigible. 'It's only a thank-you dinner,' she'd admonished her friend. 'Anyway, even if Jordan had designs on me – which I can assure you he does not – after all the dramas with Alessandro, from now on my only relationships with men will be strictly professional.'

Jo had regarded her sceptically. 'Looking the way you do, now you've given up disguising yourself in those awful men's clothes from charity stores? Good luck with that.'

Following this disconcerting conversation, Wren had dragged out the vintage tuxedo from the bottom of her suitcase, the one Princess Diana had admired at the bicentennial fashion show. The summer weather was way too hot for a wing-collared shirt and bow tie, so she had worn just a black silk camisole beneath the jacket.

Sitting opposite Jordan in the Café des Artistes, Wren smiled to herself. She needn't have resorted to the tux after all, because she doubted Jordan was the least bit interested in what she had on. He hadn't once commented on her appearance or tried to flirt.

'You seem amused,' he said. 'Private joke?'

She coloured slightly. 'I was just thinking about these amazing murals,' she said, waving towards the large panels decorating the walls of the restaurant. 'All those voluptuous wood nymphs frolicking naked in pools of water and sylvan glades. They're so desperately kitsch they're actually very good, if you know what I mean.'

'Totally.' Jordan's face lit up as he turned towards the nearest wall. 'This one's called *The Fountain of Youth*.'

Wren gazed at the picture. 'The naughty looks and the joy on the girls' faces remind me of pre-World War Two pin-ups. Can you tell me anything about them?'

A passing waiter cast an appreciative glance at Wren, then disappeared with their empty plates.

'As I would have expected from a fellow art historian,' Jordan said, bowing his head towards her in acknowledgement, 'you are correct about the pictures being pre-war. An American illustrator named Howard Chandler Christy created them in his studio, right upstairs, in the 1930s.'

'That must have been awfully convenient,' Wren said.

'Exactly. But back in the day plenty of famous people lived in this building, including the silent movie star Rudolph Valentino and the avant-garde dancer Isadora Duncan, just for starters.'

'The architecture reminds me of my school,' Wren said as the waiter presented her with a plate of grilled sea bass. 'Even the gargoyles look like the ones at Daneford.'

'Originally, the block contained mainly artists' studios with no kitchens,' Jordan explained, 'so the Café des Artistes supplied meals hoisted up by a dumb waiter.' He gestured towards his roast veal. 'By all accounts the food wasn't nearly as good as it is now, but it still sounds like a neat set-up.'

'What a fabulous way to live,' Wren said, her eyes dancing. 'And the murals,' she prompted. 'Tell me more about those.'

'There are six major panels, but there are also oils on canvas.' Jordan pointed over her left shoulder. 'Chandler Christy called the series *Fantasy Scenes with Naked Beauties* – that about sums them up.'

He had a faraway look in his eyes. 'I used to come here with my parents years ago. The dark wood, the little lampshades on the white tablecloths – even the flowers and bowls of fruit still look the same. It's something of a New York landmark.'

Two normal parents, the sort who even took their child with them to restaurants. Wren was reminded of the blank spaces in her own life. 'I've seen quite a few sights since coming to New York, but nothing quite like this,' she said softly.

'I'm glad I've been able to introduce you to something new.' Jordan lifted his glass to hers. 'Here's to future discoveries.'

'To future discoveries.' She swallowed some wine, grateful for the way it blurred her sudden spear of pain. She doubted she'd ever discover where Roma was now.

'Plenty of people from the arts, politics and media treat the Café des Artistes like a private club,' Jordan said. 'If you look to your left, you'll see the star TV reporter Barbara Walters chatting to the British Ambassador at her favourite table.'

Jordan smiled, which made Wren feel a little better. 'You mentioned coming here with your parents,' she said. 'Do they still live in the city?' She was curious to know more about him.

'Not anymore,' Jordan said. 'They're both college professors – Mom's field is chemistry and Dad's a physicist. When I was younger they worked here in New York at Columbia University, but now they're in Massachusetts, teaching at Harvard.'

Wren raised her eyebrows. 'So, Dr Grant, does that make you the arty black sheep of the family?'

'I guess so.' A look Wren couldn't quite place flitted across Jordan's face. 'Where did you grow up?' he said quickly.

She told Jordan a little about Woolahderra, smoothing out the craziest bits so it sounded as if she'd been raised in a rural idyll rather than a ramshackle commune.

Jordan gave her his full attention, asking engaging questions concerning Australian painters and the Sydney Art Museum's collection, though to her relief, he didn't probe her about anything personal. Maybe it was his reticence that gave her the confidence to tell him about Lily's illness and that she was looking for her sister, even if she was careful to offer only the sketchiest details.

His manners were perfect. He stood when she returned from the ladies' room, made sure she had enough wine and, unlike most men, didn't speak over her. But something about Jordan seemed reserved. It was as if he was on guard, concerned that he might reveal too much of himself. She knew what that felt like.

He was quite different from Alessandro, not just because Jordan was fair and built like an athlete whereas Alessandro was lean and dark. Alessandro set out to charm; he'd made his attraction to her obvious from the start. Jordan had done neither – probably because right now he was looking forward to a late-night rendezvous with his blonde girlfriend.

When they had settled the bill, she walked out of the restaurant feeling happy and content. It was a lovely, mercifully uncomplicated evening. They'd even been visited at their table by George Lang, the restaurant's owner. The dapper, bald-headed man had made a point of asking after Jordan's parents. 'I've missed them,' he'd said with a beaming smile.

Outside, the night air was so steamy Wren slipped off her tuxedo jacket, confident that Jordan was unlikely to notice the flimsiness of her camisole. 'I really enjoyed dinner,' she said. 'Thanks for making the booking at such a special place and, well … you already know you have my undying gratitude for sorting out the Degas debacle.'

'It's okay.' He shrugged. 'You said that you lived at Gramercy Park, didn't you? I'm going that way – we could share a taxi.'

After hailing a yellow cab, he opened the door for her and then levered himself in beside her.

Wren tensed. Now that she and Jordan were thrown together in the cramped confines of the taxi's back seat, her tranquil mood had evaporated. His proximity made her uncomfortable and there were so many potholes and bumps along their route that the taxi kept juddering. Her shoulder hit Jordan's arm, her hip slid against his and her knee grazed his leg. Each time they were thrown together she felt she'd been singed.

Wren stared fixedly out of the window, achingly self-conscious. Perhaps Jordan sensed her embarrassment, or felt the same way, for he barely spoke during the trip downtown.

It was still warm and very dark when, finally, they stepped out of the taxi in front of Parkside. There was no moon and no stars.

'Well, goodnight. That was great,' Wren said, hoping she didn't sound as strained as she felt. 'I guess we'll run into each other some time.'

'Mmm,' he said, noncommittally. He didn't even bother to smile.

This wasn't good. They were colleagues; he'd done her an enormous favour and demanded nothing in return. It wasn't his fault that she'd found the damned taxi ride so unsettling.

She extended her hand. Jordan followed suit. Their fingers and palms folded into each other's. Seconds passed, but neither one broke away.

As she inhaled his apple scent, a tingling effervescence that began in her fingertips swept through her body. She felt strangely altered, no longer herself but more like one of Christy's wood nymphs, bathed in a pool of light.

'You made it clear right from the start you have no interest in me,' Jordan said in a low voice, the gold and green flecks in his eyes shimmering in the darkness. 'But just this once, I have to say something.' His hand pressed hers with the tiniest amount of additional pressure. 'You are the most beautiful woman I have ever seen in my life.'

She didn't think or analyse, only reached for Jordan and kissed his mouth. He wrapped his arms around her and returned the kiss, with a depth of passion she had never experienced, even with Alessandro.

Alessandro. He'd been the cause of more trouble than she could ever have imagined. *Men are not to be trusted*, whispered the voice in her head. But she didn't want to stop holding Jordan and stroking his neck and his hair. She didn't want to be anywhere but on this New York sidewalk, crushed against his broad chest under a dark sky.

Wren tore herself away. She couldn't lose control, not again. She'd done that before and paid a high price.

Without a word, she ran into the Salvation Army women's residence.

CHAPTER TWENTY-NINE

Early the next morning, Wren rolled over in bed and yawned, luxuriating in the knowledge that she wasn't due to go anywhere or do anything for hours.

She was in that delightfully drowsy state when it was still possible to recall the previous night's dream. It came back to her now, vividly. One moment she and Jordan had been standing in front of Parkside, shaking hands. In the next scene, the two of them were in each other's arms, which was truly weird because that was something neither of them would ever do. Even stranger, right now there was a throb in her belly and the strongest sense of yearning.

'Oh God!' she moaned.

Wren sat bolt upright and buried her head in her hands. This wasn't a reverie. The dream was real.

What had possessed her or, for that matter, him? She was sure he must be regretting their fleeting madness as much as she did. And yet … she touched her bruised mouth. Kissing him had felt wonderful, rather like those ridiculously clichéd scenes in old movies when violins played and waves crashed on the sand.

Wren flung herself back onto her pillow and tried to sort out her whirling thoughts. They had both drunk too much wine. The best way to proceed was to ignore the incident. After all, it was only a tipsy late-night kiss.

She blushed. Running away like a teenager was embarrassing, even though she was sure she'd done the right thing. First, because Jordan Grant represented a major client. If something other than friendship existed between the two of them, she might be accused of a conflict of interest, which was the last thing she needed. Second, he'd had that girl on his arm at the auction and the more she thought about it, the more familiar their body language seemed. Third, and most important of all, she had sworn off men.

She jumped out of bed when she heard a rustling sound at her door. Closer inspection revealed that someone had slid an envelope underneath. That was unusual – she barely received any mail and, anyway, it was the weekend. Wren frowned. It couldn't be from Jordan, not after last night.

Her breath caught in her throat. Perhaps it was from Roma. At long last, she must have seen the ad in the newspaper or one of the posters. Maybe one of the trust's lawyers had relented and told Roma where to find her. She could be downstairs at this very moment. Finally, just when she'd least expected it, she was about to meet her sister. Wren tore open the envelope with shaking hands, read the brief note, then slowly sat down.

Why on earth would Tony Mancini be in the lobby waiting to see her?

'I had the idea you might like a drive around New York,' he wheezed as she stepped into his gleaming, chauffeur-driven black Cadillac. 'And then I thought – it's a beautiful day, not too sticky and the sky is clear – why not ask Miss Australia if she'd like to go for a walk?'

Wren was glad she'd decided to wear sneakers when she'd hurriedly thrown on a cream cotton shirt and a matching pair of cut-off op-shop pants. 'But Mr Mancini,' she said with a smile, 'we seem to be driving.'

'That would be because Vito here' – he nodded towards the bulky man seated behind the steering wheel – 'is taking us across the East River. One of the best views you'll ever have of Manhattan is the walk back into the city along the Brooklyn Bridge. It might not be the most obvious place to discuss business, but I'm getting used to doing deals in the open air.' He shrugged. 'The Feds bug everything else these days.'

Mancini's car had butter-soft black leather seats and high-grade suspension that dealt effortlessly with New York's pitted streets. Wren found herself comparing it to her fraught ride the night before, which was a bad idea. She needed to put Jordan out of her mind – especially as she didn't have a clue about what sort of business the head of one of New York's major crime families could possibly want to discuss with a 22-year-old fine arts graduate from Australia.

After Vito brought the Cadillac to a smooth halt, Mancini said merely, 'Time for some exercise.' They began walking across the legendary bridge, but it was not until they reached its centre, where the thick, twisted-steel cables that kept the mighty structure suspended above the East River dipped to their lowest point, that Mancini revealed what was on his mind.

'I'm thinking of putting another opportunity your way,' he said, placing his hands in his pockets.

'That's extremely kind of you.' Wren aimed for an even tone, though she itched with curiosity.

Mancini looked different without his fat cigar and handmade suit. Dressed in an open-necked blue shirt, darker blue trousers and a New York Mets baseball cap, he could have been the retired manager of a hardware store or the kind of man who'd sold sporting goods all his life.

They stopped on the bridge's slatted wooden walkway while he pointed out the Statue of Liberty, a tiny figure off in the distance. 'You know those famous words on her pedestal? "Give me your tired, your poor, your huddled masses …" No American should forget it was hard-working immigrants, people like my parents who worked in construction and factories twelve hours a day, who helped make this city great.'

'So many inspirational journeys,' Wren murmured. She knew she must allow Mancini to proceed in his own way.

He leant on the metal railing, looking thoughtful, then seemed to come to a decision. 'I'm going to tell you a story,' he said. 'It might take some time.'

Wren blinked in the sunlight. 'I'm not in a hurry.'

The breeze had transformed her hair into a dark nimbus of curls. She groped in her bag for an elastic band and tied them up in a high ponytail.

'Then let's start walking again,' Mancini muttered, 'and I'll fill you in.'

Wren guessed from the tightness around his mouth that whatever he planned to speak about troubled him.

'A friend of my family lives in Venice. Not Venice Beach, California,' he snorted, 'but the real Venice, *La Serenissima*. This friend's name is Josephina Fontana. Back in the old country, her father helped my father out with a big problem, so she's well overdue for a favour.'

He gazed out over the dark green water. 'When Josephina was nineteen, she fell in love with the doctor who cared for her during a bout of typhoid fever. He was an Austrian Jew called Simon Hertzberg. She was a Catholic, a *napolitano* like me. Her parents were firmly against their marriage, so the young couple eloped and moved to his hometown, which was Vienna.'

Wren looked at Mancini. 'It sounds very romantic.'

'Simon was a cultivated, intelligent man who had a passion for two things in life: music and Josephina. But then' – he paused – 'Hertzberg discovered art.

'He was mad about the work of Cézanne, Picasso and Matisse, but Josephina was especially fond of an Impressionist painter by the name of Renoir.'

A prickle of excitement put Wren on alert.

'As you are aware, I don't know much about art,' Mancini said. 'But recently, Josephina set all this down in a long letter to me.'

He waited while a flock of shrieking seagulls flapped past, then sat down on a bench and asked Wren to join him.

'Life continued,' he said, pushing his cap further back on his head. 'Josephina became the adoring mother of two little girls. Sophia was dark like her, Maria fair like her father. Simon himself taught them to play the piano, which they took very seriously. When Josephina spotted a Renoir named *Two Young Girls at the Piano* during a trip to Paris, what with one girl being fair and the other dark – well, it captured her heart.'

Wren's eyes shone.

'I see I have your attention.' Mancini gave her a sideways glance.

'I know that picture very well,' she said enthusiastically. 'Renoir painted several slightly different variations, experimenting with the pose and the colour palette. Apart from some sketches he made, there is a beautiful oil in the Metropolitan Museum, another in the Musée d'Orsay, and two in private collections, making four completed canvases in all.'

'Now that is where you are wrong,' Mancini said with a sly grin. His Brooklyn accent had become more pronounced, transforming 'that' into 'dat'.

Wren stared at him. 'Are you telling me,' she said slowly, 'that somewhere in Paris there is another *unknown* version of the painting?' If this were true, it would fascinate the art world.

'No,' Mancini said.

Her face dropped.

'Don't look so sad.' He patted Wren on the back with the affection of an elderly uncle. 'It's in Venice with Josephina.'

'What!' Wren had to stop herself from whooping with glee. 'How did that come about?'

'Simon bought the painting for Josephina from the friend she was visiting – it was a surprise for her birthday. You can imagine how much the picture meant to her.'

They began walking again, though Wren had only a hazy impression of the towers and spires that made the Manhattan skyline so striking. Instead, she pictured Josephina's two pretty daughters playing a Strauss waltz in an elegant Viennese parlour, overseen, as if in a mirror image, by Renoir's painting.

Mancini frowned. 'Sadly, life in Austria was changing. Jews were being thrown out of schools, barred from shops and stopped from practising many professions. But Simon, who wasn't at all religious, brushed off any concerns.'

Wren nodded. The charming vision she'd conjured had grown swiftly darker.

'In her letter,' Mancini continued, 'Josephina explained that the Jewish religion is handed down through the mother's line, so technically her daughters were not of that faith. They were baptised Roman Catholics and, because of this, Simon was convinced the children were safe. As for himself, he simply told his wife that no matter what happened, doctors would always be needed.'

They were nearing the great gothic pylon that marked the bridge's gateway to Manhattan. The city was fast approaching, but Wren remained silent, engrossed in what Mancini was saying.

'By this time,' he rasped, 'Josephina's father had passed away. As her mother came from a very grand Venetian family, the woman decided to move to her late parents' palazzo.'

'When was this?'

'Around 1938, not long before war broke out. Josephina made up her mind that, after all these years, she had to take her daughters to meet their grandmother before she too passed away. But, at the last moment, the Nazi government claimed there was a problem with the children's travel documents, so Josephina prepared herself to go alone.

'Then she had an idea. If she couldn't bring the real girls, she would present her mother with the picture. Josephina brought it with her to Venice, packed in a big suitcase stuffed with tissue paper.'

They had reached the end of the bridge, but not of the story. Mancini motioned for Wren to continue walking with him across the adjoining park.

He heaved a deep sigh, which spiralled into a throaty cough. 'Almost as soon as Josephina left,' he wheezed, 'a band of Nazis burst into the apartment. Can you imagine the terror those little kids felt when thugs wearing jackboots aimed their guns at them?' He shook his head. 'Josephina never saw Simon or her daughters again.'

Despite the sun's rays on her back, Wren shivered.

'She couldn't bear to return to Vienna. It was her neighbours who wrote telling her the Nazis stole whatever works of art in Simon's collection they didn't destroy. So Josephina stayed in Venice, grieving badly, and caring for her mother until the old lady died.'

Mancini looked up. 'There's Vito with the car. I'll finish up in a minute.'

Wren still had no idea what Mancini wanted of her.

'The pair had been living on what remained of the family's fortunes,' he continued, 'but the funds had dwindled to almost nothing. Josephina supported herself by selling off the family's heirlooms – pictures, silver candlesticks, that sort of thing.

'Eventually, she was reduced to living in a couple of rooms. She had to turn the palazzo into a boarding house, but as the place had been slowly sinking into the Grand Canal for years, not much of it could be used. Now that Josephina is too old to cook and clean, she's there all alone, with only her memories to keep her warm.'

'Isn't it possible to sell the palazzo?' Wren's heart went out to the impoverished woman who had endured such tragedy.

'No can do. The terms of a centuries-old deed mean that it now belongs to a distant male cousin. Josephina has tenancy only as long as she lives.'

'But that's terrible,' Wren cried.

'Yes, it is,' Mancini said sadly. 'Josephina is in a bad way, but she's too proud to accept money – believe me, once I received her letter, I tried. The only item of value she could not bring herself to part with is that Renoir. Now she wants it to be put up for sale.'

Wren's mouth was dry. 'Exactly what role do you see me playing?'

Mancini looked at her with his black olive eyes. 'You're going to auction the painting.'

'Me!' Wren gasped. 'Don't get me wrong, sir, it's an amazing opportunity, but I'm not an auctioneer. A picture like that would be used to anchor a major sale, with many other works of art. I've never auctioned one painting, let alone sixty or seventy.'

'You impressed me when you fixed that Degas mess, and that's not an easy thing to do. This time, I want you running the show.' He pulled down his cap. 'Remember when I told you about listening to my instincts? Well, right now they're telling me that, with your smarts, you'll do a great job.'

'I appreciate your confidence in me,' Wren said. It didn't seem the right moment to reiterate her very real doubts that she was up to the job. 'But Archer's would never agree.'

'Oh, they'll play ball, all right.' Mancini hitched up his trousers. 'I find people usually do if you frame a deal in the right way. I'll let them know that if you're not the auctioneer, the painting will be going to one of their rivals. If that doesn't work, I've a few other tricks up my sleeve.'

'This is your way of repaying your debt to me, isn't it?' Wren said slowly.

Mancini winked. 'Got it in one, Miss Australia.'

CHAPTER THIRTY

Amelia shot Wren a look capable of turning fire to ice.

'That is the most absurd, far-fetched idea I have ever heard in my life,' she said, leaning over Wren's desk. '*You*, conduct an auction. There is such a thing as pleasing a client, but in this case the man must have taken leave of his senses.'

Wren shrank back in her chair. She had expected Amelia to be against Mancini's plan, but she hadn't been prepared for such a savage attack.

Amelia eyed Wren with disdain. 'How on earth did you persuade Tony Mancini, of all people, to make that sort of demand?'

'Well, I—'

'No, don't tell me.' She narrowed her eyes. 'I've heard things about you.'

'What sort of things?' Wren felt sick.

'I'll keep them to myself – for the time being,' Amelia said acidly. She folded her arms, inspecting Wren with a hostile expression. 'It seems it wasn't enough for you to steal my fiancé –

'He told me that was over months ago!' Wren said hotly.

Amelia ignored her. 'You're also determined to upstage me at Archer's, which I can assure you, is not going to happen.

'You're not only unequipped to run a sale. Archer's has been in existence for more than two centuries and has never,

I repeat *never*, employed a female auctioneer. Furthermore,' she added imperiously, 'were they to make that leap, it would be to a highly experienced, well-connected specialist like myself, not a conniving little nobody from Australia.'

Clenching her jaw, Wren remained silent. Her mind was already busy formulating a plan that would effectively bypass Her Ladyship.

Amelia paused as she headed for the door. 'As your immediate boss, I won't let you do it. Our chief auctioneer won't let you do it. And Timothy King will not be the first head of Archer's to willingly turn the company into a laughing stock. As a matter of fact,' she hissed, 'I'm going to see Timothy right now.'

Amelia stalked out, closing the door behind her with an exaggerated click.

Wren thumped her desk with her fist. She'd always loathed bullies, whether it was Clara Johnson back in primary school, Daneford's sadistic Miss Hooke or that pig John Tremaine. They brought out her fiercest instincts.

The Renoir's authenticity would have to be verified and it would need to be photographed for the catalogue. Archer's would have to conduct a pre-sale publicity campaign and court potential purchasers. But, if everything went smoothly, the painting could be squeezed into Archer's Important European Art sale in two months' time.

She'd watched countless auctions and learnt a great deal. If her calculations were right, she'd have enough time to pick up the rest. It would be tight, but she'd always found studying came to her easily. Wren allowed herself a moment to dwell on how thrilling it would feel to be up there on the podium conducting the sale – and to provide poor Josephina with a very comfortable old age.

She slumped back in her chair. What was she thinking? Amelia was right; King would never let Wren near the precious painting. He'd rather lose millions in commission to a rival than risk someone who was young, inexperienced and, worst of all, female screwing up in front of the world's wealthiest art patrons.

Tony Mancini had hinted that he'd be prepared to apply pressure, yet that thought made her decidedly uneasy. King might look the other way when it came to cash payments. No doubt he deserved examination by the Internal Revenue Service, though surely not the Mafia's wrath. Anyway, asking Mancini for a favour would only place her back in his debt. Wren unconsciously touched the fine chain around her neck. Just contemplating whatever act the Mafia don might then demand filled her with trepidation.

A knock on the door interrupted her thoughts.

'Come in,' she shouted, hoping it wasn't one of Archer's many secretaries with a pile of obituaries waiting to be scrutinised.

Wren did a double-take. 'Crumbs! Is that really you?'

May had exchanged her funky downtown black leather and torn stockings for a gathered blue skirt, heels and a white blouse with a frilly pie-crust collar.

Wren jumped up. 'What brings you this way – and why the preppy uptown girl get-up?'

May pointed towards the discreet diamond studs twinkling in her ears. 'You've forgotten, haven't you?'

Wren clapped her hands. 'Of course! It's our *Breakfast at Tiffany's* date.'

The timing could not have been better. She desperately needed a lift, and she'd adored the film ever since watching it on TV when she'd stayed for a weekend with a Daneford daygirl. After discovering May was also a fan, they'd made plans to visit the famous jewellery store together.

'That Givenchy dress,' Wren exclaimed.

'The best black dress in the world,' May cooed. 'And all those huge pearls around Audrey Hepburn's swan-like neck.'

'And what about when she steps out of the taxi as the early morning sun rises above an empty Fifth Avenue,' Wren said dreamily. 'I can see it right now. She takes a long look at the jewels in the window, tilts her head sort of nonchalantly and pulls out a cardboard cup of coffee and a pastry from a paper bag. Pure unadulterated heaven.'

'But when I walked in you looked like you'd come down with a case of Holly Golightly's "mean reds".' May looked concerned. 'Is it Lily?'

'Mum's situation is like a dark cloud that never leaves me, especially as it doesn't seem like I'll ever be able to fulfil my promise,' Wren said bleakly. 'Though right now, I've managed to add two more problems. Work – and men.'

'Not to worry.' May grinned. 'Just ask yourself, what would Audrey do?'

'Go to Tiffany's!' they both cried in unison.

Wren gazed at the Tiffany & Co. sign above the store's dramatic double-height entrance at 727 Fifth Avenue. 'I feel like I'm thirteen again,' she said happily, 'only this is so much better because it's real.'

She scrutinised the displays on either side of the doorway. A large, intricately carved doll's house in the form of a golden castle stood in the left-hand window, with magnificent ruby- and diamond-studded earrings, a necklace and a bracelet spilling from its open rooms. In the opposite window were exquisite dolls wearing tiny tiaras and taffeta gowns in a miniature ballroom, its silvery columns encircled by emerald and diamond rings.

'These are extraordinary,' Wren murmured, her mouth forming a delighted smile.

She was wearing crisp black linen pants with her tan Lauren jacket, but thought she really must check out some of New York's more upmarket vintage stores. Wearing a dress by Givenchy, particularly one from Audrey's era, would be guaranteed to raise anyone's spirits.

May grabbed Wren's arm. 'Let's go inside. You can tell me all about your dramas while we take a closer look at the jewels.'

Wren made a face. 'I don't even want to think about work.'

'That's fine with me.' May steered Wren beneath a ceiling dotted with myriad bright lights towards a teak and marble display case in which nestled an eye-watering selection of sapphire bracelets. 'I'd rather hear about your love life, anyway.'

'Also complicated.' Wren grimaced. 'Let's just say I fell for a guy, but afterwards it all went horribly wrong, so I swore off men. Then I met someone else, only I didn't really take to him, and I thought he felt the same way. But we had dinner together and by the end of the night everything had changed.' She paused. 'Just for context, he's an outstanding kisser and incredibly good-looking.'

May screwed up her face. 'Sorry, Wren, you've lost me. I'm not seeing the problem here.'

'Mainly, I'm terrified of being let down.' She bit her lip. 'I saw him once with a girl draped over his arm.'

'But when you're single, you go out with lots of people,' May said. 'Just look at Jo.' They were heading for an assortment of lustrous pearl necklaces. 'It doesn't mean he's in a serious relationship. Maybe you're the person he wants to get serious with.'

'I guess it's possible.'

Wren gazed intently at the display, though she wasn't giving the pearls a thought. She was too busy reconsidering every conclusion she had reached about Jordan.

Face it, she told herself, *you want to see him*. It had been insane of her to reject a man who was as delightful as he was handsome, just because she was unable to get over her stupid, self-defeating anxiety. She couldn't expect Jordan to call after her childish running-away stunt, so she would just have to take the initiative and ring him. It was time she grew up.

'Come on, drag yourself away from those necklaces,' May said. 'Tiffany's is famous for its diamond rings. See, they're laid out in that long glass case over there.'

Wren looked in the same direction as May was pointing. Among the well-dressed lunchtime shoppers, she noticed a tall, blonde couple with their heads down. A sales assistant was slipping one glittering bauble after another onto the fourth finger of the young woman's slender left hand.

'Oh no,' Wren whispered. 'It can't be.'

The man glanced up. Their eyes met. Wren whirled around. The hot lights overhead bore into her as tears pricked her eyes.

Pushing her way through a group of Japanese tourists, she wondered how she could ever have imagined that Jordan was honest and straightforward. For Christ's sake, he was about to get married! *Men aren't to be trusted, men aren't to be trusted*, said the voice in her head.

Suddenly, her mind filled with lurid pictures of Tremaine. He was groping her breasts, bearing down on her, bent on violation. She could smell his sour breath, hear the sound of her underpants tearing.

By the time she reached the doorway she was running. Running from Tremaine, running from every bit of misery and pain. A horn blared and brakes screeched, but she couldn't stop running and then she couldn't stop falling. Her face was scorched by the heat from the grille of a taxi that was almost upon her when she felt a pair of hands whisk her out of its way and drag her back to the sidewalk.

'What were you thinking, charging into the street like that?' May railed. She placed a protective arm around Wren's shoulders. 'You almost got yourself killed.'

Wren was trembling. 'Not long before I came to New York, a horrible man attacked me. When I was in the store just now, it all came flooding back, just as if it was really happening.'

'But why, Wren?' May said more gently. 'What did you see that triggered the flashback?'

Wren took a shuddering breath. 'It doesn't matter. I overreacted.'

CHAPTER THIRTY-ONE

Timothy King rose to greet Wren when she entered his wood-panelled office. He wore a beautifully cut suit and his black hair boasted distinguished silver streaks, but his most striking feature was his dark, hooded eyes. Wren had heard it whispered in the corridors of Archer's that, such was the half-English, half-American man's cunning, should he enter a revolving door after someone, he'd be sure to emerge ahead of them.

She adjusted the skirt of her square-shouldered, red Emporio Armani suit as she took a seat opposite him. Power dressing was essential if she were to have any chance of being taken seriously.

'Well, well,' he said, pouring tea into a bone-china cup and handing it to her. 'You are certainly proving to be a singular intern.' He smiled. 'Milk? Sugar?'

Wren declined.

'I'm very happy here,' she said calmly, though her stomach squirmed as she wondered exactly why she'd been called in to see King and what Amelia had told him.

He steepled his fingers. 'Let me see. You have already brought us a fascinating new client – I refer, of course, to Tony Mancini – and brokered a very nice deal regarding an existing client's surplus painting. Now you have presented Archer's with the tempting prospect of auctioning a significant Renoir, just at a time when collectors are craving Impressionist art.'

He poured a cup of tea for himself. 'What an unusually resourceful young woman you are.'

'Thank you,' Wren murmured, pondering whether King's personal tea ceremony was the way he attempted to lull all his visitors into a state of unsuspecting ease.

'As you would imagine, our forthcoming Important European Art auction would be a perfect fit for the Renoir that Tony Mancini told you about – should it prove genuine, of course,' he said. 'I expect about seventy lots will go up for sale, ideally with *Two Young Girls at the Piano* as the evening's star attraction.'

'I'm sure the owner would be thrilled, Mr King.' Wren sat forward. Maybe this meeting would turn out better than she'd hoped.

'However,' he began.

She knew what was coming.

'Amelia's opinion is that, even with intensive tutoring, you could not run an auction of this magnitude.' King helped himself to more tea. 'This also happens to be my view. It may not appear this way to the onlooker, no matter how many auctions you've seen, but the task is akin to performing a marathon, except you're sprinting all the way.'

Wren stared into her half-empty cup.

'There are a hundred things to keep track of while a sale is in progress,' he said. 'Bids flying around the room; deciding who to play off against whom; watching how the telephone bidders are responding; establishing who might miss out but could be tempted by another lot; determining whether the work has gone as high as it can or, with a little encouragement, the bidding might reach a new level.' King clasped his hands together. 'It's relentless.'

'I understand,' Wren said, sitting up a little straighter. There was something in King's tone that suggested he wasn't finished.

'And yet,' he continued, 'when I discussed the matter with Mr Mancini, he insisted you take part. This put me in a quandary, particularly when he pointed out that if you did not, the Teamsters

Union would very likely suspend all deliveries both to and from Archer's. That,' he said drily, 'would be most inconvenient.'

He looked at her with a quizzical expression. 'You have acquired a powerful supporter.'

Wren tensed. She needed to be ready for whatever King was going to say next.

'This is my solution. Although Peter Morgan will conduct the auction, I would like you to sell the Renoir.'

Wren sucked in a quick breath. The 'little intern from Australia' was actually going to be up on the legendary Archer's podium, taking bids from the world's rich and famous. King's decision had converted a heartfelt dream into gleaming reality.

'I would be honoured,' she said.

'We'll introduce you as a guest auctioneer.' King poured more tea. 'The type of people who attend our high-end sales are easily bored, so from time to time we spice things up a little. The first female to wield a gavel at Archer's, especially one with your – I do hope you don't mind me saying this – arresting appearance, will add just the right *je ne sais quoi.*'

He chuckled to himself. 'On one occasion, we even paid the movie star Sharon Stone to dress up in a ballgown and perambulate the sale room while a porter bearing an Italian Old Master accompanied her – not that I would dream of putting you in that position,' he said quickly.

'I'm relieved.' Wren cringed inwardly.

'I have already run this past Mancini, who I am pleased to say is very comfortable with the idea,' he added.

What a clever man King was, Wren mused. Here was a solution that would satisfy everyone – except Amelia. This new turn of events would surely put an end to any hope of resurrecting their relationship.

'First things first.' King adjusted his striped silk tie as he spoke. 'I want you to accompany our Impressionist expert, Antoine Ardant, when he verifies the painting. It will be a useful experience, especially as you appear to have an aptitude for this business.' He raised his eyebrows. 'I assume you have no objection to flying to Venice?'

'Not at all,' Wren said hurriedly, marvelling at being offered yet another wonderful opportunity. 'But why aren't we bringing the picture to New York?'

'An excellent question.' King nodded. 'Sometimes, if a client is forced by debt to sell a painting to which they have a strong sentimental attachment, they cannot bear to give it up until the last minute. A brief trip to Venice is a minor inconvenience – and cost – when we are dealing with a very rare and valuable work of art.'

Leaning forward, he regarded her seriously with those dark, hooded eyes. 'You *are* up to this, Wren, aren't you?'

Her last Italian sojourn might have led to a disaster, she thought, but she wasn't the same impressionable girl anymore.

Wren lifted her chin. 'I won't let Archer's down, Mr King.'

CHAPTER THIRTY-TWO

Venice

Wren's eyes shone as she stood on the deck of the speeding water taxi, her long cerise chiffon scarf fluttering behind her like a medieval pennant. Monsieur Ardant, a small man with hunched shoulders and a crusty manner, had opted to stay curled up on a seat in the cabin, but she couldn't bear to drag herself away from the same dreamlike vista that had inspired generations of artists from Canaletto to Monet.

Fantastical buildings of pale pink, cream and faded terracotta shimmered in the pearly afternoon light. Ancient palazzos, splendid bell towers and the domed churches of Byzantium beckoned from each side of the Grand Canal. Venice was bewitching and entirely improbable; a thousand-year-old floating world suspended between sea and sky.

The taxi continued ploughing forward, its foamy wake spreading like white lace on the wide silver ribbon of water. Wren smiled as she watched a barge heaped with oranges and plump melons float by, followed by another carrying a carved chest of drawers and, bizarrely, a large brass bed. A moment later she turned her head in the direction of some warbled snatches of Italian opera, happily waving when she realised that the voice drifting towards her belonged to a swarthy man in a blue and white striped jersey, steering a black gondola. Everywhere her eyes rested, she saw one more glorious surprise.

They alighted at the Hotel Alberto, a rose-coloured building lit by the waning sun. Monsieur Ardant had spoken little on the flight, instead burying himself in the books and catalogues he had lugged on board in a canvas bag. Once they had checked in beneath the hotel's golden Murano glass chandelier, he suggested they eat dinner straightaway.

'I hope you do not mind,' he said with a yawn, 'but we have a very full day ahead and I need to rest.' Wren noticed that since landing in Europe, his French accent had become more evident.

She gave a little gasp of delight when they were shown to a candlelit table covered by a pink cloth. The small inner courtyard in which it stood had ochre walls festooned with thick ropes of ivy. Fragrant lemon trees in terracotta pots sat in the corners.

The two exchanged only scraps of conversation while eating their bowls of spaghetti alle vongole. Not until they had almost finished their meal did Ardant give her his full attention.

'If this painting is genuine, then you have led us to a special treasure,' he said, sipping from a glass of sparkling water. 'What I do not understand,' he added with a frown, 'is why you have never come to see me at Archer's.'

Wren's forkful of spaghetti stopped halfway to her mouth. 'Me?'

'I received a charming letter from an Australian colleague with whom I have corresponded for some time,' Ardant continued. 'Unfortunately, although Dr Robert Hawkins is a curator of international standing, his aversion to travel means we have never met in person.'

Wren retained a clear picture of Bobby, bent over his untidy desk as he penned countless letters to art experts from around the world about various arcane matters of scholarship.

'Dr Hawkins not only made a point of mentioning that your studies focused on Impressionist art, but also wrote that he would personally appreciate it if I were to take you under my wing, so to speak,' Ardant said.

Wren smiled inwardly. It was so thoughtful of Bobby, even if, in his typically disorganised fashion, he'd failed to make her aware of either his connection to Ardant or that he'd communicated with the man on her behalf.

Ardant wrinkled his already lined brow. 'I would appreciate an explanation.'

Wren's fork made a sharp little ping when she set it down against the ceramic bowl. 'Let me assure you, Monsieur, there is nothing I would have liked more,' she declared. 'But even if I'd known that Dr Hawkins had written to you – which I did not – Amelia Heywood warned me off. She said you were far too busy to spend time on an intern.'

'I see.' Ardant nodded thoughtfully. 'Lady Amelia has many fine qualities, but she can be overly zealous.' He deftly extracted a glistening clam from its shell.

'Actually, nothing pleases me more than to spend time with our young recruits. I will not be here forever, so I like to pass on what knowledge I have gleaned over the years. In turn,' he said, smiling kindly, 'quite frequently one gains new insights from a person with young, fresh eyes such as yourself.'

'Thank you,' Wren said. 'It would be a privilege to learn from you.'

'*Très bien*. Our partnership will begin tomorrow morning. We are due at the Palazzo Bartolomeo at 10.00 am. I will meet you in the lobby a half-hour earlier.'

Ardant used the arms of his chair to push himself upright. '*La Serenissima* may be incomparable, but it is not the easiest city for someone my age. Where one cannot travel by boat, it is necessary to walk,' he said, 'and, regrettably, my legs are not so agile these days.'

'Never mind, Monsieur.' Wren smiled. 'We shall conquer Venice together.'

Wren had already spent ten minutes after dinner steaming in the orange-blossom-scented bliss of the hotel's extravagantly large marble bath, and was planning to stay for at least that long again, when she heard a knock and a muffled voice calling, 'Signorina Summers?'

She smacked the fragrant water with one hand, annoyance narrowing her lips – but perhaps it was a message from Monsieur Ardant. There might have been a change of plan. With a shout of '*Arrivo!*', she stepped out of the bath, wrapped herself in a thick white towelling robe and shook out her damp curls.

Wren opened the door, then drew in a breath. 'What the hell are you doing here?'

'You wouldn't take my phone calls.' Ignoring her glare, Alessandro gave a dazzling smile. 'When Uncle Tony mentioned you were coming to Venice to look at a picture, I decided to surprise you.'

His vivid blue eyes lingered on the swell of décolletage Wren's bathrobe failed to cover. 'I assumed you would be grateful to me for putting you and Mancini together,' he said. 'Aren't you going to invite me inside?'

He glanced past her at the room, a small Venetian fantasy with a forest-green velvet bedspread fringed in red, matching heavy drapes, pale yellow walls and a gilded Murano glass light hanging from the ceiling.

'I suppose so,' she said tersely. 'I can hardly conduct a conversation out here with practically nothing on.'

As soon as the door closed behind them, Alessandro began nuzzling her neck. 'My God, you are a divine woman,' he murmured.

'We're not in Rome now. Things are different,' Wren said, stepping away. She was surprised she felt nothing but irritation.

Taking no notice, Alessandro immediately slid his hands inside her robe and drew her back to him. 'There's no need to be nervous,' he whispered in her ear while caressing her warm skin. 'Remember, I know how to please you.'

Wren pushed Alessandro away. 'I'm not doing this.'

He held out his arms. '*Cara*, why so shy? You can't have forgotten how good it was.'

'I haven't forgotten anything, Alessandro,' she said, wrapping her gown more tightly around her.

He ran a hand through his hair, looking puzzled. 'You're not making sense. What is it I'm missing?'

Alessandro's charm now seemed too practised; his compliments came too readily. Next week – possibly even the next day – some other girl would be the recipient of his easy flattery. No doubt he called all his lovers *Cara*. It was so much easier than remembering their names.

'I've changed, Alessandro. I had to,' she said.

Since the alarming scene at Tiffany's, she'd had more flashbacks to the horrific attack that was at least partly Alessandro's fault. Each time these hyper-real recollections assailed her she was left shaken, suffocated by dread.

His eyes hardened. 'What you mean is you've found someone else. Let me guess – it's a clean-cut American.' A mocking smile played on his lips. 'Maybe it's E.J. Conroy's new curator – I heard you've been doing business with him.'

Wren shivered. Mancini's patronage was turning out to be a mixed blessing. The man seemed intent on providing Alessandro with whatever information he could about her.

'Oh, my poor little Wren,' Alessandro sneered. 'That college boy would have no idea how to make love to a woman like you.'

Wren ignored the jibe – the last thing she wanted was to alienate him. As she had learnt to her cost, the egos of men could lead to dire consequences. That look in Alessandro's eyes had scared her. Who knew what he might do, especially given his Mafia connections?

'Rome was perfect.' She strived for a tone that might placate him. 'But it's over. I was hoping we could be friends.'

'You're being absurd,' he said angrily. 'Don't you understand how much I desire you? How can I stop wanting you in my arms – and in my bed?

'Try.' Wren smiled, attempting to introduce a lighter note as she opened the door. 'So, are we friends?'

Alessandro's blue gaze was unforgiving. 'Friendship is not what I came for.'

As she watched him walk away, she had the unnerving feeling he wasn't finished with her yet.

CHAPTER THIRTY-THREE

'This is incredibly kind of you, Monsieur Ardant,' Wren chirped from her purple brocade perch.

She was only seated in this sumptuously decorated craft, with its gold-leaf arabesques and brass handles shaped like seahorses, because Ardant had kindly insisted that a ride on a Venetian gondola was an experience Wren must not miss.

'But are you sure you will be okay?' she asked him. 'These boats don't seem very stable and all the steps we've passed have looked awfully slippery.'

They were approaching the Palazzo Bartolomeo, a flamingo-pink, four-storey fantasy rising from a small waterway that branched off the Grand Canal. The barrel-chested gondolier, who'd been expertly negotiating the narrow canal with the help of a long bronze stick and the occasional kick on a bit of passing masonry, called out from the rear. 'Signorina, is fine. I help the signore.'

'*Grazie*,' Wren said, as the man burst into a robust version of 'Nessun Dorma'.

For a split second, she was gripped by the same sense of déjà vu she'd felt on her last visit. There was something about being on the sparkling water and the way the sun lit the vivid walls that was piercingly familiar.

Wren gave her head a shake. Obviously she hadn't adjusted to the fact that two days earlier she'd been sitting in her cramped office reading obituaries, and now she was in this fairyland city, about to set eyes on a painting that had been locked away from the world for nearly a century.

The gondolier tied up his boat at one of the candy-striped mooring posts in front of the palazzo. Next, he expertly assisted Ardant to his feet, guiding him up the mossy stone stairs before returning for Wren.

'*Che bella!*' he muttered to a bemused Ardant with a knowing wink.

Quietly simmering, Wren was thankful that at least he hadn't pinched her.

There was a sign, handwritten in English, at the entrance to the palazzo: *Please ring the bell, then come to the fourth floor.* With no lift, it took some time for the increasingly breathless Ardant to tackle the stairs.

Josephina met them on the final landing. She had thick grey hair worn in a coiled plait, alert dark eyes and high cheekbones. It was easy to see she had once been a beauty.

'*Buon giorno,*' she said. 'Please accept my apologies. I know the stairs are difficult for anyone who is not, like the signorina, in the springtime of their life. But the ground floor is prone to flooding, and the next two are damp and can be cold.'

She sighed. 'Every year, Venice sinks further into the lagoon. Unfortunately, the Palazzo Bartolomeo is worse than most of the other buildings, and I am without the funds to do anything about it.'

Ardant smiled sympathetically. 'It is indeed a great problem, Signora. But we hope, quite soon, we may be able to help you live more comfortably.'

Wren remembered Amelia telling her that everyone at Archer's must be capable of casting a spell. It seemed that even Monsieur Ardant could play Prince Charming when he wanted to.

'Come.' Josephina motioned them forward. 'First, we will have coffee in the sitting room. We will talk, and then you will see my picture.'

The grand room was painted a subtle shade of mandarin. It had a cream and caramel terrazzo floor and long windows opening to an entrancing view of the canal. The furniture, however, consisted of a moth-eaten, tapestry-covered settee, several chairs with chipped gilding, and a coffee table inlaid with peeling mother-of-pearl. The walls were completely bare save for an occasional water stain and a simple wooden crucifix. Wren glanced around quickly, but there was no sign of the Renoir.

The three drank their coffee and nibbled on the buttery S-shaped biscuits known as *bussolai*, which, their hostess explained, were a speciality of the nearby island of Burano. Wren said little as the other two spoke about the city, its culinary specialities and recent spate of floods, although she was conscious of Josephina's keen eyes assessing her.

"'O Venice! Venice! When thy marble walls are level with the waters, there shall be a cry of nations o'er thy sunken halls ...'" Ardant recited, quoting Lord Byron, one of Venice's more infamous residents. 'The world must make certain that this city never surrenders to the sea,' he added, raising one hand with an uncharacteristic flourish.

Josephina struggled slowly to her feet. 'This has been very pleasant,' she said with the smile of a woman with a secret, 'but, Monsieur, you did not come to Venice to recite poetry to an old lady. Please come this way.'

Wren felt a swirl of excitement as they followed Josephina into a pale green room that would have been as stark as the first, if not for one exquisite object.

'It's incredible,' she whispered.

A glorious painting of two girls, lost in a world of their own, hung at the centre of the wall opposite the windows. The hairs on the back of Wren's neck rose as she gazed at the picture.

Monsieur Ardant's light blue eyes gave nothing away, though he murmured to Wren, 'Looks right.'

He'd explained over dinner that 'looks right' or 'looks wrong' was the shorthand connoisseurs used when they first viewed a work of art – in most cases, a few seconds were all that was needed for an expert to tell an authentic painting from a forgery.

'Signora, I can see why you are so fond of this painting,' he said, his words carefully selected so as not to raise false hope. 'I wonder, could you provide me with any related sale documents?'

'I am afraid everything was left behind in Vienna,' Josephina said, wringing her hands.

'I understand.' Ardant's tone was soothing.

'However,' she continued, 'if Signorina Summers will lay the painting face down on the cloth covering the table, you will see that the label from the original dealer is still in place. There is also a date.'

With a fluttering stomach, Wren put on the white cotton gloves she'd brought with her and did as Josephina had asked.

Ardant came closer. 'Ah, a promising sign,' he said. 'The label bears the imprint of Paul Durand-Ruel, the French dealer. He was an ardent supporter of Renoir.'

He pointed to the date. 'This is also interesting. Durand-Ruel kept meticulous records. Luckily, his ledgers are still in existence, so we can cross-reference the painting with any relevant entries.'

Wren stood back respectfully as Ardant spoke. Despite his measured tone, she was certain his original instinct was right.

'It has long been known that Durand-Ruel recorded the purchase of an 1891 Renoir with the shortened title *Two Girls*. As no one has ever discovered a trace of the picture, the consensus is that it passed into a private collection and was subsequently destroyed, possibly during the Nazi Occupation.' He looked up. 'This might well be that painting.'

Wren covered her mouth with her hand so as not to betray her emotion. These were the moments art historians lived for.

'What was the name of the friend that your husband bought the Renoir from, Madame?' Ardant asked mildly.

'André Royère.'

Ardant turned to Wren. 'Also good,' he said in an undertone. 'Royère was an enthusiastic collector of the Impressionists' work.'

With a sign from Ardant, Wren turned over the painting. Although the girls had never been formally identified, their tender intimacy convinced her they must be siblings. It was easy to understand why Josephina felt so attached to the picture, for she, too, felt its spell. Her eyes began to well up with the knowledge that she herself was unlikely to ever experience the unique relationship that existed between sisters. The feeling was wrenching.

'Could you tell us what you see, Wren?' Ardant asked.

'Certainly,' Wren said. Dipping her head, she used the time spent fumbling in her bag for a tape measure to pull herself together.

'An accurate description of a work is essential, particularly when more than one rendering exists,' Ardant explained to Josephina.

'The painting is exactly one hundred and sixteen centimetres by eighty-nine centimetres, which makes it a standard size fifty canvas in the French system, as codified in the eighteenth century.' Wren looked at her superior. 'I believe that means the dimensions vary slightly compared with those of the picture in the Met's collection.'

'Quite so.' Ardant inclined his head. 'Please continue.'

'A fair-haired girl wearing a white dress and a blue sash sits at an upright piano. One hand touches the keys and the other her musical score,' Wren went on. 'A second girl with dark hair and a pink gown leans over her. Her left arm rests on the piano while her right is placed on the back of the pianist's chair.' Wren drew in a sharp breath. 'There is something different about this painting, and it's not just the size.'

Ardant nodded. 'Go on.'

'In the Met's – and every other version – the dark girl's eyes are trained on the music. Here, she looks protectively towards the fair girl, thus endowing the picture with far greater emotional depth.'

'Anything else?'

'The blend of pastel colours is typical of Renoir, but the brushstrokes are much freer than usual during this period. They are more like the technique Renoir used when he made his initial, daring breakthroughs. At the time, critics could see only flaws, but it is this style that brought a special vitality to his work.'

Josephina sat down on a chair. 'Monsieur,' she said, looking bewildered. 'What does all this mean?'

'We are not sure yet,' Ardant responded, rubbing his chin. 'The fact that this depiction presents significant differences from the other versions would suggest it is either a more experimental work – or a forgery.'

Josephina's mouth opened, though no words resulted. Hearing that the painting she loved so much for all these years might be a fake had rendered her incapable of speech. Wren wished Ardant had not been quite so blunt.

He took out an instrument from the small attaché case he'd brought with him. 'If you would not mind, Signora, I will ask my assistant to close the curtains.'

Once the room was in darkness, he switched on a square, hand-held apparatus, moving it slowly across the painting's surface.

'Monsieur is using an ultra-violet light, searching for signs of phosphorescence,' Wren said, hoping her explanation might help to settle the agitated woman. 'This could indicate restoration, damage or overpainting. It is especially important when it comes to authenticating the artist's signature.'

Ardant stood back. 'Thank you. Now, if the curtains could be opened, please.'

He looked at the picture for a long time, then brought out a large magnifying glass. Once more, he examined every inch of the painting, nodding to himself.

Wren's left leg started to cramp. She'd begun to feel every bit as nervous as Josephina looked.

'*Bon*,' Ardant said at last. 'Perhaps we could return to the sitting room for a little talk.'

Josephina resumed her place on the settee, her face drawn. Wren sat anxiously on the edge of one of the chipped chairs.

'First, dear Signora, I apologise for any distress this process may have caused you,' Ardant said with a return to his old-fashioned courtesy. 'It may prove helpful to provide you with a little history.'

He took a moment to compose his thoughts. 'Renoir was asked by his government to create a picture for a new museum in Paris called the Musée du Luxembourg. Aware of both the extreme honour and the intense scrutiny that would follow, he lavished extraordinary care on the painting.

'The artist himself believed the Luxembourg picture of 1892 was overworked, whereas your picture has the appearance of an earlier, far more spontaneous version. If this proves to be the case, then it is an important discovery.'

'Monsieur Ardant,' Josephina said plaintively, 'this talk of dates and versions is all very well, but I beg you, please tell me. Is my picture genuine?'

Tension hovered within the room's mandarin walls as Ardant hesitated.

'I must, of course, check various records when I return to New York,' he said at last. 'But, bearing that in mind, and with the usual qualifications, I believe the answer is' – he paused – 'yes.'

'*Madonna mia!*' Josephina exclaimed. Ardant permitted himself a satisfied smile. Wren would have liked to pirouette around the room but took care not to succumb to this inclination.

As Wren made her way across the Piazza San Marco a flock of silvery pigeons swerved in front of her with such suddenness that she started. Her destination was the Caffè Florian, a gilded meeting place for Venetians and glamorous travellers alike since it opened in 1720 – or so Monsieur Ardant had told her. He'd added that Florian was Italy's oldest coffee house, saying, 'Everyone who is anyone has been there, from Casanova to Andy Warhol. Who knows?' He'd chuckled gently. 'One day they might boast of the visit by Signorina Summers.'

Wren smiled. The longer Monsieur Ardant was in Europe, the courtlier his manner became. He'd been determined to accompany her while sightseeing, but as his endeavours at the Palazzo Bartolomeo had proven taxing, he had reluctantly opted to rest in his room.

She had lingered inside the magnificent Basilica di San Marco, craning her neck as her eyes travelled across the glittering gold mosaics lining its domes, before finding herself equally entranced by the heavily embellished ceilings in the pink marble palace of the doges, rulers of Venice for a millennium.

She'd had to tilt her head back yet again, massaging her stiff neck, while she examined the figures surmounting the lofty granite pillars that guarded the square's waterside entrance. One statue depicted the winged lion of Saint Mark, the other Saint Theodore standing on a slain dragon. She had just set her foot down on the pavement between the two columns when, with a shiver, she recollected Ardant's warning. 'Venetians believe that to walk on that space, where public executions used to take place, is to court the gravest misfortune.'

Wren had immediately jumped back. The commune-dwellers' strange rituals might have put her off superstitions, but considering everything else going on in her life, the last thing she needed was to tempt fate. It was then that she'd remembered, with a sigh of relief, Ardant's recommendation.

A waiter hurried to her side as soon as she arrived at Caffè Florian, insisting he show her through its ornate series of rooms. She'd agreed that the gold-leaf walls and century-old art were '*magnifico*', but said, 'Signor, if you don't mind, I would prefer the terrace outside.'

Wren took a deep breath, relieved to escape the confines of yet more opulent interiors, and studied the menu. A prick of guilt made her frown when she saw the exorbitant amount charged for even the simplest items, until she reminded herself that what she'd really be paying for was one of the world's most enchanting vistas. She promptly ordered an espresso and a plate of Florian's biscotti.

How different this trip to Italy was from the last, she reflected, when she'd been swept away by Alessandro. Shuddering, she recalled his disturbing visit the night before, then told herself she wasn't about to let that snake of a man spoil her only free afternoon in Venice.

If the pigeons would only stay put, her view of the basilica's graceful arches and five exotic domes would be perfect. She bit into a sweet bicsuit as she watched yet another flock swoop past the colonnade opposite before the birds settled on the piazza's stone surface in a cooing grey cloud.

The swelling sound of a lush Verdi opera made Wren lift her head. 'Oh my God,' she whispered, as a line of extremely tall and slender young women dressed in a blaze of scarlet ballgowns began to float across the square.

Wren's eyes opened wide. She might be a newcomer when it came to fashion, but she could recognise works of art when she saw them. Each of the exquisite silk-chiffon and taffeta gowns was the embodiment of a different flower. One was inspired by a rose, another a tulip. Others took their inspiration from an anemone, a poppy, a carnation, and an exotic orchid. The statuesque beauties who wore these creations carried sheaves of matching blooms tied with trailing black satin ribbons that fluttered gently behind them.

Wren forgot her biscotti and her expensive espresso. Immersed in the spectacle, she felt a pang of disappointment when, after a captivating fifteen minutes, the slim-hipped man directing the girls abruptly turned off his tape deck and called a halt.

There was a smattering of applause from onlookers as the mannequins turned to leave in a gorgeous crimson flush, but one girl with spectacular red hair broke away from the rest and approached her.

'Wren? Wren Summers?' It was the mannequin with the tulips.

'Yes?' Perplexed, Wren stood up.

'I knew it!' the girl cried, and suddenly Wren realised exactly who she was.

'MJ!' She threw her arms around her childhood friend. 'So this is what has become of you,' she said admiringly. 'Wow, you look amazing. How long have you been modelling?'

MJ gave a throaty chuckle. 'There I was, waitressing on the Gold Coast about a year after school finished, when I was spotted by an agency scout. I've been flat out ever since, but this Valentino show definitely takes the cake.' She paused. 'We have to exchange phone numbers and addresses. I don't want to lose touch with you again.'

MJ tucked Wren's business card into her bodice. 'How about you?' she said eagerly. 'What have you been up to?'

Wren quickly filled her in. 'I wish I could stay longer,' she said sadly, 'but I have to get back to the hotel. Then I'm off to New York first thing tomorrow.'

'And I'll be flying to Paris the day after.' MJ spun around, making the petal-shaped chiffon panels that fell from her waist drift and swirl. 'Who would have thought that a couple of misfits like us would end up swanning around the world?' She giggled.

'Definitely not Captain Hooke.' Wren smiled as she paid her bill.

CHAPTER THIRTY-FOUR

New York

As Wren ran down the steps to Parkside's bland below-ground cafeteria, she realised that all trace of the low mood she'd suffered ever since returning from Venice had vanished. Even the bizarre view from the dreary room's low-set windows – as usual, confined to a parade of passing pedestrians' legs and the odd dog trotting by – failed to depress her. This morning's news had lifted her spirits as effectively as a glass of cold prosecco.

'Girls,' she said, taking a seat at her friends' table, 'I have something to tell you.'

'If it's a dalliance with a handsome gondolier, I don't want to know.' Jo groaned. 'I'm consumed with envy about your trip to Venice as it is. All that art and the fabulous palazzos, not to mention Valentino ballgowns in the Piazza San Marco – it's too cruel.'

'From the look on Wren's face I'd say she has something more important to tell us,' Ava said.

'You're right.' Wren's eyes shone. 'Lily's out of her coma. She's awake, really and truly awake.'

Beaming, she poured herself coffee from a jug on the table. 'Her medico rang at the crack of dawn. Mum still can't talk, but she's able to drink through a straw and sit up in bed.'

'That's so great. Is there any hope she'll …' May didn't finish.

'Recover?' Wren shook her head, her smile fading. 'But at least now when I fly home she'll know that I'm with her.' Sudden tears blurred her sight. 'Don't mind me. It's just that being reunited with her lost child is the only thing that will bring Lily peace, but now I'll be breaking my promise to bring her back with me.'

'Oh, Wren.' Jo squeezed her hand.

'I'll never stop wondering where Roma is,' Wren said, wiping her eyes, 'what she's like and how she's spending her life. Sometimes I even peer at random girls in the street with dark wavy hair like mine and imagine one of them is her.'

'Even I can see that's ridiculous.' She forced down some coffee. 'The truth is, Roma could be anywhere. She might live on an island by the sea. She might live in the mountains or in a ranch out west or – I don't know – in a grand mansion somewhere like Florida. Of course' – she paused – 'she might live right here in Manhattan, be well aware that I'm looking for her, and simply be appalled at the idea of meeting me.' Wren gazed into her cup as if it might hold an answer, murmuring half to herself, 'It's the not knowing that makes it so hard.'

Lifting her chin, she smiled shakily at her friends. 'But you all did your bit, and so much more.'

'So, what's your plan now?' Ava said. 'I know you always have one in your back pocket.'

Wren sighed. 'Once the Renoir auction is over I'll be cutting the internship short and flying home. Lily's health is just too precarious for me to stay here any longer. Then I'll remain by her side until' – she looked down, unable to meet her friends' sympathetic gazes – 'until I can't anymore.'

She could feel that old void in her side, like a hunger that could never be satisfied. Her sister and father were no more than ghosts – dead or alive, it made no difference. When her mother was gone, she would not have a single person on earth to call her own.

As if she'd been reading her mind, Ava said, 'You do know we'll all be here in New York waiting for you with gin …'

'… and cupcakes …' That was May.

'… and massive girl hugs,' Jo chipped in.

'... because we're family, right?' Ava finished.

The lump in Wren's throat made it impossible for her to speak.

Without a crush of people to animate the space, the huge auction room with its red velvet drapery and bohemian crystal chandeliers looked like an empty stage set in need of players.

'Auctions are strange beasts,' Peter Morgan was saying.

He and Wren had settled themselves on a couple of chairs in a corner with one of the oak desks between them.

'How so?' Wren grasped her pen, poised to write down every word that he uttered.

Morgan laughed. 'They're said to be a mix of a theatre, a trading floor, a slave market – and a bordello.'

He watched Wren scribble some notes. 'Perhaps you shouldn't quote me on that,' he said hurriedly.

Wren felt barbs of excitement in the pit of her stomach. 'I know I have a lot to learn,' she said. 'But honestly? I can't wait to be up on that dais.'

'That's the spirit.' Morgan's brown eyes twinkled. 'Today I'll introduce you to a few basics. After that, each week we can spend an hour or two concentrating on various technical skills. Of course, you'll have to run a couple of auctions, but don't worry. We'll pick a weekend featuring some of the lower-profile sales. The rest is up to you.'

'Have you worked in other cities?' Wren asked eagerly.

'London, of course,' Morgan said. 'That's where I started.'

'What about Paris?'

He shook his head. 'Only French houses are permitted to hold auctions in Paris. Hard to believe, I know, but it's because of a law passed by Henri II in 1556 that's never been repealed. Typical bloody French protectionism, of course.' He tut-tutted.

'It doesn't matter, though, because these days there is far greater wealth and there are much hungrier collectors here in New York than anywhere else in the world. This money-mad decade has been a boom time for Archer's.' Morgan sat back in his chair. 'Which is why we're in the perfect place to auction your beautiful Renoir.'

'*My* Renoir?' Wren raised an eyebrow.

'We all think of it like that,' Morgan said. 'I'm hoping the picture will arrive here at Archer's very soon, and when it does you should give yourself a big pat on the back for being the one who secured such an outstanding consignment.'

Wren grinned. 'Now all I have to do is learn how to sell it.'

'Well, write this down,' Morgan said. 'It is essential you know who your bidders are – most likely there'll be a mix of museums, wealthy individuals, dealers and so on. Sometimes a collector will also nominate a third party to act for them.'

'Like E.J. Conroy's man, Dr Grant?' Wren looked down, pretending to make a note. She didn't want Morgan to see her blush.

'Quite. Once there were many wealthy gentlemen like Mr Conroy who shunned personal publicity, but all that changed when the rich made up their minds – how did that chap in the film put it? Yes, that greed was good.

'The new, moneyed class positively revel in displaying their vast wealth as publicly as possible. And what better place to do that than at an elite, widely publicised auction?' Morgan shook his head. 'You see, it isn't a passion for fine art that drives their desire. It's the chance to obtain status.'

'Status?' Wren wrinkled her nose.

'Look at it this way,' Morgan said, 'when everyone has vast sums of money, how do you stand out?'

He shrugged. 'There are many Rolls-Royces produced every year. Luxury yachts and Lear jets positively roll off the production line. But a rare, newly discovered Renoir with a fascinating back story? That is a truly scarce commodity.'

'Well, I hope *Two Girls* is bought by a collector who has fallen in love with it,' Wren said vehemently. 'Not someone who's just after a winner's trophy.'

Morgan's expression was grave. 'Remember, Wren, your sole

duty is to maximise the picture's price. I'm afraid nothing else matters.' He rested his elbows on the desk. 'There are two key auctioning principles. First, everyone who enters the room will have a top bid in mind that they're determined not to go above. However, once they succumb to the state we call "auction fever", every plan will be abandoned. Their hunger for possession will prove overwhelming.'

He looked at her closely. 'It is your task to induce this sensation.'

Wren nodded. She had often observed the way even the most disciplined collectors lost their heads when in the thick of bidding for an artwork they coveted.

'The second principle,' he continued, 'is related to the first. Individuals behave differently when they are competing in public – none more so than powerful men. I'm not sure if you have read any Gore Vidal?'

'I have.'

'Well, dear Gore put it marvellously well, if a touch cruelly, when he said, "It is not enough to win. Others must fail." In that regard, your appearance confers a unique benefit.' Morgan smiled benignly. 'Let me assure you, no man will wish to appear a failure in your eyes.'

Wren covered up her discomfort by writing furiously. Even though she knew Morgan meant well, she'd always loathed the idea that a woman's looks trumped her other attributes.

'Now, onto the next important matter,' Morgan said. 'Significant lots such as the Renoir are placed at key positions in order to help you create crescendos of excitement. As for actual bids, they must be spaced only seconds apart. You want to give the bidder just enough time to raise his hand, but not long enough to think about it.'

Wren looked up from her notebook. She was beginning to think Morgan would have made an excellent psychologist – or else a witch doctor.

'You must also possess authority, charisma and a certain elegance,' he said. 'The ability to flirt is essential, but with the utmost subtlety. Use no more than a gesture, a certain intonation of your voice or the expression on your face.'

She'd thought she knew so much about auctions. Now she realised how much she had to learn. She didn't dare look at Morgan, for fear he would see the alarm in her eyes and become as apprehensive as she was about her performance.

CHAPTER THIRTY-FIVE

As Wren took the elevator to the ground floor, her shoulders slumped. In order to concentrate on Morgan's tutorial, she'd had to banish every thought of Lily – and her failure to find Roma. Now that granite boulder was back on her chest, crushing her.

She sighed deeply. Despite his deluge of information, Morgan had still to touch on an auctioneer's gestures and all-important patter, how to record bids and manage the gavel, and the way to successfully set one bidder against another. If she were to master all this and more in a matter of weeks, she'd have to abandon all hope of tracking down her sister.

To be honest, she told herself, lack of time was far from her only problem. All she'd ever had to go on was the name of someone who, according to every one of that nice old detective's sources, didn't exist. Maybe, Wren pondered, she didn't have the right name. Perhaps she hadn't heard properly when Lily had made her desperate plea to find Roma – which meant her search was likely to be as successful as catching a rainbow.

Wren came out of the elevator with her head down. It had been pure hubris to assume she'd be able to waltz into a country of over two hundred million people and pluck one girl out of thin air. What had she been thinking?

'See you tomorrow, Jeanette,' Wren said, feeling wretched. She hadn't the energy to stay and chat. If she hurried, at least she could go over her notes before dinner. After that she would probably spend a sleepless night worrying.

As she passed out of the door, she glanced up at Artemis with a look of despair. She'd begun to doubt even the goddess of the hunt herself would be able to find her sister.

'Wren?'

Her head jerked around. Jordan Grant, his blond hair framed by the rays of the late sun, was blocking her path.

Wren's cheeks burned. Her first instinct was to leave as quickly as possible, but she'd already humiliated herself by running away from him twice. She wasn't going to do it again.

'Oh, hello, Jordan,' she said, adopting an expression of supreme indifference. 'Sorry, I'm on my way to an appointment, but Jeanette is still at reception. She'll sort you out with whoever you're meeting.'

She brushed past him.

'Wait.' Jordan grasped her arm.

Wren looked down at his hand pointedly, then gazed into his eyes. *That was a mistake*, she thought, as some wayward part of her brain registered the entrancing green and gold flecks they contained.

'What is it?' By now she'd become fairly practised at mimicking Amelia's most frigid tone, though that didn't mean she couldn't feel the heat of each one of Jordan's fingers pressing on her skin.

'That girl you saw me with in Tiffany's,' he said.

'Who you see and what you do is your business, Jordan. Now, if you would please let go.' Wren looked away. It was becoming increasingly difficult to maintain her cool façade. She wasn't sure if she felt angrier with herself or with him.

Jordan's grasp only became firmer. 'She's my sister.'

Wren caught her breath. 'I beg your pardon?'

'I have three of them,' he said in a rush, 'all older than me, but I'm closest to Harriet. She lives here in New York with her fiancé. They're both medical interns at Sloan Kettering hospital and have crazy twelve-hour rosters that never seem to coincide, so I told Harriet I'd help pick out her engagement ring.'

'That's who you were with at the auction, too,' Wren said slowly. She'd leapt in and made a mistake again.

Jordan nodded. 'I thought Harriet could do with a change from needles and drips.'

'Oh.' Wren wished she could sink through the sidewalk.

Jordan smiled hesitantly. 'Um, if I stop hanging onto your arm, you won't run away again, will you?'

Suddenly, Wren felt a wonderful lightness. She'd never been so pleased to be wrong.

'Definitely not.' She returned his smile. 'You probably think I'm some kind of nut, but in my defence, there's been an awful lot going on in my life lately.'

He released her from his grip. 'Do you want to tell me about it?' His voice was warm and deep.

'Some of it, yes.'

'Over a drink? The Carlyle and the St. Regis aren't far. I'd like to get a few things straight, myself.' He paused. 'That is, if you don't mind being late for your appointment.'

'What appointment?' Wren said breezily. 'I've been locked indoors all day. Let's walk across to the park.'

By the time they'd entered the Conservatory Garden and found a seat in front of a tumbling fountain, she'd brought him up to date about the Renoir, her trip to Venice and the role she would play at the auction. She didn't mention Alessandro.

'Congratulations on discovering that painting.' Jordan whistled. 'It's an important find.'

'I'm not sure I deserve much credit,' Wren said, breathing in his delectable scent. 'All I did was pass on some information.'

Now they were sitting next to each other, she felt intensely conscious of his physical presence. Even a Brooks Brothers suit couldn't disguise his athlete's body. Her gaze wandered to his mouth. She had tried but failed to forget their perfect kiss.

'I'm having a hard time working you out, Wren,' he said abruptly.

For a moment, she couldn't imagine what he was talking about.

'At first, I was certain you didn't take to me at all and, to be frank, I had a few doubts about you. The way you acted at Nell's made me think you were just another spoilt, good-looking girl. Then, when we were sorting out the Degas business, I discovered you were far from being a brat. By the time we'd had dinner I knew you were not only gorgeous but interesting and sweet and, I have to admit, insanely desirable.'

His eyes darkened to a rich caramel colour. 'I knew you saw us strictly as colleagues but, hell, it was a struggle to contain myself.'

Wren went to speak but Jordan held up his hands. 'Sorry, I have to finish this. I want to make sure we both know where we stand.'

'Despite what you thought at Nell's, I'm not a pushy guy when it comes to women,' he said, raking his fingers through his corn-coloured hair.

Wren couldn't help reflecting that any man who looked like Jordan wouldn't need to make much of an effort.

'But when we were thrown together in the back of that cab, all I could think of was how much I wanted to hold you in my arms. By the time we reached your place I had to say something. Jesus, Wren, I was so damned happy when you kissed me and then …' He loosened his tie. 'When you disappeared at something like the speed of light I figured you must have decided I was totally unappealing.'

That was so far from the truth Wren felt like laughing.

'After you turned your back on me in Tiffany's, I knew you'd misunderstood what was going on, but by the time I rang you at work, Jeanette said you'd gone away for a few days. I thought that was maybe an excuse so you could avoid me.'

His expression became sheepish. 'Eventually, I became so desperate, I decided my only option was to ambush you. Which I just did.'

Wren took a deep breath. 'Are you finished yet?' she said.

'Almost.' Jordan looked into her dark eyes. 'By now you must have worked out that I like you – a lot. But if you're not interested, please just tell me.' His smile was endearing. 'I might be miserable for the rest of my life, but I won't bother you again.'

As she slipped her hand into his, Wren felt the same tingling effervescence she'd experienced the first time their fingers touched. 'Jordan,' she murmured, 'there is nothing I would like more than to be bothered by you.'

Then everything sped up. Jordan's mouth was on hers, their lips parted, and they were kissing passionately while she had that luminous wood nymph feeling all over again.

Shadows had reached across the garden's clipped hedges by the time they parted.

'It's not that I want to stop,' Jordan said with an adorable grin, 'but the park's about to close and you might not want to be locked in here with me for the night. Is there someplace else you'd like to go?'

Wren thought how much she'd like to undo Jordan's tie, unbutton his shirt and run her hands over his broad chest. They obviously couldn't go back to Parkside, but his place was near hers …

She sucked in a quick breath. Suddenly, she could see Tremaine's leering face. Her body stiffened.

'Hey, I didn't mean to rush you,' Jordan said, touching her cheek.

'It's not your fault. Not long ago a guy, he …' Her voice dropped to a whisper. 'He tried to rape me.'

'Jesus, no wonder you kept taking off. I'm so sorry that happened to you.' Jordan stood up and pulled her gently to her feet, then kissed the top of her head. 'I promise we'll take things real slow.'

As they walked hand in hand out of the park, Wren touched her locket. Maybe Lily had been wrong. Maybe there were men in this world who could be trusted.

CHAPTER THIRTY-SIX

Varenna, October 1968

When the girl strolled onto the wisteria-draped terrace she felt almost happy. For once, the suffocating fog of sadness that had clouded her every waking moment since the new baby arrived had lifted. Most days, she felt as if an invisible noose had been tied around her neck, and every hour it grew tighter.

She loved her little ones with a passion so all-consuming that it frightened her, but their incessant demands ate away at her energy and her spirit until she had nothing left to give – not to them, not to the boy and certainly not to her painting. Her inadequacy shamed her.

Although the girl jiggled the mewling infant she held in her arms, the baby wouldn't settle. Despairing, she glanced at the older child. At least she seemed content, playing in a patch of sunlight with the purple petals that were drifting down.

But the boy – she wrinkled her forehead. Something was definitely up with him. Glassy-eyed, he sat slumped in a chair with a cup of grappa in his hand. A near-empty bottle and a crumpled telegram lay in front of him on the old wrought-iron table.

'What is it, honey?' she said. 'What's wrong?

'I'll tell you what's wrong,' he answered hoarsely. 'My father's coming.'

'Here?' Her expression darkened. 'That's heavy.' There was no way she could cope with a difficult stranger, not now when she was surrounded by shadows. They needed to talk, but the boy was drinking steadily.

'That grappa's pretty strong,' she said, with another frown. 'How many have you had?'

He threw back the potent drink, muttering, 'As if you're in a position to judge me.'

The girl flinched. She hadn't realised he knew she'd been stealing swigs of liquor during the day. She'd begun smoking a lot more weed, too, but whatever she did, it never kept the darkness at bay.

Just try to hang in there, she told herself, although her chest hurt and her palms were already sweating. 'Hey, you're all upset, I get that,' she said. 'You and your dad have never got on.' She put the restless baby down in a wicker bassinet. 'Lots of unfinished business.'

The boy groaned. 'You don't know the half of it.'

Then her world tilted on its axis.

'I've deceived you,' he said. 'I'm not who I said I was, and neither is my father.'

A moment of silence passed between them before she could bring herself to speak. 'Then who in God's name are you?' she whispered.

'Let's start with Dad.' The boy's face bore a sardonic expression she'd never seen before. 'Think of the American you hate the most,' he said. 'No, wait, I'll make it even easier. He's not a politician, but he's someone with the power to spread lies and corrupt millions of people's minds.'

The girl looked at him, wild-eyed. 'You're talking about that millionaire mogul, the one who's the strongest supporter there is of the war in Vietnam and the ugliest racist around. You're not – no, it's not possible.' She struggled to comprehend the boy's meaning. 'You can't be that monster's *son*?'

'Yep, that's who I am.'

The boy might have slashed her cheek with a blade, so deep and so sudden was her pain. 'I can't believe you lied to me,' she said, raising her voice. 'Lied and lied and lied! You even used to laugh about your last names being the same.' Hurt and resentment made her flower-like face closed and grim. 'Seems like the joke was on me.'

The girl sat down, poured herself a glass of grappa and swallowed it quickly.

When the boy went to take her hand, she snatched it away. 'After all this time, what made you tell me now?' she challenged him. 'Why ruin our perfect life?'

The boy told her he'd learnt recently that his father had suffered a serious heart attack. 'For the first time, I thought about the way I'd run out on him so soon after Mom died,' he said. 'I've been feeling guilt like you wouldn't believe.'

He sighed. 'Sure, the man's got some terrible ideas, but he's still my father. Now he needs me back in New York so that, in a few years, I can take his place at the helm of the company.'

To the girl's horror, he said he was seriously considering the request.

'I'd need a lot of help, especially at first. But if I had a strong team around me, I think I could do it,' he said. 'I'd have a chance to remake the business, pioneer something to be proud of.'

He was gazing at a small craft ferrying people across the shimmering surface of the lake, but the girl could tell he already pictured himself enshrined in a glass and steel skyscraper. She no longer recognised him. Her beautiful boy was a stranger.

'I thought you hated big business.' She took a joint from her pocket and lit it defiantly.

The boy sprang to his feet 'How can you be so naïve?' His words were beginning to slur. 'Don't you see what could be achieved if I ran the organisation? Do you honestly think we're doing anything to change the world while I scribble a few stories and you sit around getting high?'

Long after the whimpering children were fed, bathed and put to bed, their parents' argument raged. Both drank and smoked too much, both said terrible things they shouldn't have.

'You're nothing but a selfish sellout,' she shouted.

'You must be insane if you think I'm going to let you sabotage my future,' he growled.

As the night wore on, their positions hardened. By dawn, the boy was determined to return to the United States and run the empire his father had founded.

'It's what I was born to do,' he said, in a way the girl found unspeakably grandiose.

She flew at her beloved. 'You've broken my heart – and my trust,' she cried. 'If you take this hateful course, don't imagine that the children and I will follow you.'

She was panting with fury. The boy had not just betrayed her. He was abandoning every principle they believed in, every cause they had fought for.

She stared at him with an expression of loathing. Then, blinking, she looked again. The boy's blue eyes had filled with shining tears.

'I'm sorry,' he said. 'This isn't us.'

Reaching forward, he enfolded the girl in the gentlest embrace. 'You and the little ones are more precious to me than life itself.' He took a deep breath. 'When my father arrives, I'll tell him I'm staying here with you, in Varenna.'

CHAPTER THIRTY-SEVEN

New York, November 1988
Saturday

'I seem to recall,' Wren puffed as she jogged beside the East River, 'we haven't been for a run since I came back from Rome.' She stopped abruptly. 'That's it. I can't take another step.'

'Me neither,' Jo said, pulling up. 'Oh God, we're still just as hopelessly out of condition as we were then.' She grinned cheekily. 'Although, looking on the bright side, it hasn't held us back.'

'Well, I am having a hard time keeping up at Archer's,' Wren said, retying her ponytail. 'Naturally, damned Amelia has been piling on the work, so doing my regular job at the same time as I've been trying to learn how to sell a masterpiece has been totally exhausting.'

'In that case, you should be conserving energy.' Jo gave her a mock-serious look. 'Let's go get ice creams at that kiosk and chat.'

Wren laughed. 'Have you noticed that every time we try to get healthy, we end up eating junk food?'

'Junk food?' Jo retorted as she paid for two vanilla cones topped with hot chocolate fudge. 'Nothing that tastes this good could possibly be bad for you.'

She handed one to Wren. 'So, do you think you've got the hang of auctioneering?'

Although Wren's stomach did a sudden somersault, she was sure she'd feel more settled once the Renoir finally arrived.

Josephina had used one excuse after another to delay its despatch, and even after Wren was notified that *Two Girls* had landed at customs, nobody seemed able to tell her precisely when it might be delivered to Archer's. It was impossible not to be worried when they were cutting it so fine.

'You can tell me on Monday,' Wren said, 'once it's all over. Lately, I've been veering between dying to get on with it and sheer bloody terror.'

She threw an arm around Jo's shoulder. 'I've got a lot to thank you for. I really love working at Archer's.'

Jo took an enormous bite of her ice cream. 'It's only the beginning, sweetie,' she mumbled. 'Did Timothy King have anything to say about an actual paid job in the future?'

Wren licked the chocolate drips running down her thumb before answering. 'He said I'm in line to be Monsieur Ardant's assistant, which would have to be about the best position I can think of. Ardant's knowledge of art is incredible. I'd have the chance to study some of the world's greatest paintings in depth, and who knows? Maybe one day I might actually become a real auctioneer.'

A shadow passed across her face. 'King was really good when I explained why I had to fly out of New York next Sunday. Lily hasn't long left. I might not be bringing Roma back with me, but at least I can play Mum some of that sixties music she likes, or just sit with her until, well, you know.'

She threw the remains of her ice cream into a bin.

'Sure I do.' Jo gave her a pat. 'On a happier note, how are things with Handsome?'

Wren smiled as they both sprawled on the ground. 'I'm trying not to let my emotions run away with me. But I have to say, I'm mad about the boy. He's gorgeous and fun and super smart, except—'

'What?'

Wren frowned. 'Even though I'm really attracted to him, the physical side of things is still like something out of a Doris

Day movie.' She sighed. 'It's all my fault. Jordan's been incredibly patient, but I'm scared that soon he will be so over me carrying on like the Ice Maiden, he'll decide I'm too weird and will just walk away.'

Jo's brow creased. 'So you're still getting flashbacks?'

Wren nodded. 'They're so real, Jo. I can see Tremaine's face and smell his breath. I can even feel his fat fingers touching me.' She stared at the river. 'One minute Jordan and I will be kissing, and I can't get enough of him. The next minute I freeze.

'So far, he's hung in there, but that's only because he's had a really hectic time with work. Mostly, Jordan's either out on the west coast seeing dealers or making trips to London and Paris for viewings and auctions. Frankly, I've started wondering if he prefers it that way.' She groaned. 'And then there was that weekend.'

Jo made a face. 'Hell, I'd been forgetting the Great Plaza Fiasco. I mean, what are the chances that your hunk of a boyfriend makes a booking for a divine suite on the one weekend he's in town, hoping desperately you'll be in the mood for romance, and—'

'Argh, don't remind me.' Wren shot her a despairing look. 'It turns out to be exactly the same weekend Peter Morgan has scheduled me to run the practice auctions. I'll never forget that awful phone call when I had to tell Jordan it was off. Worst of all, I'm not even sure he believed me.'

She looked down. 'He knows I'm going home because of Mum, but I'm beginning to worry he won't be waiting for me when I come back to Manhattan.'

Jo caught Wren's hand in her own. 'What I think is you're letting Tremaine win,' she said. 'Even though you fought back – which can't have been easy – he's still screwing you. It's time you reclaimed your power, and you know the best way to do it?'

'No idea,' Wren said gloomily.

'It's for you to be the one who's in control of the situation. If you want your Aunty Jo's advice,' she said, 'once the auction is over, take the initiative and put that poor boy out of his misery – and yourself, for that matter.'

Wren looked at her doubtfully. 'You mean,' she hesitated, 'I should seduce Jordan?'

'Carpe diem,' Jo exclaimed. 'After that big Qantas jet takes off on Sunday, who knows when you two lovebirds will next have the chance?' She grinned. 'In the meantime, you can race me to the bridge. I'm told a speedy run works just as well as a cold shower.'

Wren took off straightaway, shouting over her shoulder, 'I knew there was a good reason why you're my best friend!'

It was the night of the auction, but the Renoir still hadn't been delivered.

Wren paced up and down her office, restless as a runner waiting for her Olympic final. 'That's just great,' she said, clenching her jaw. 'The sale starts in an hour, and the star attraction is missing.'

'Wren, could you please settle down?' Amelia said from behind her desk. 'All that walking around is driving me mad.'

Wren grabbed the phone when it rang.

'It's Antoine,' he said, sounding out of breath. He'd asked her to dispense with Monsieur Ardant, saying it made him feel 'even more ancient than I already am'.

'Is it here?' she asked anxiously.

'The crate has just arrived.'

'Thank God for that.' Wren leant against her desk. The pressure had been draining.

'Make sure you check the picture when it's unpacked,' Antoine said. 'And note any damage it might have sustained on its journey, even if it's only a tiny crack.'

'I'll give it a really thorough look,' she assured him.

Antoine wished her good luck before he rang off.

Amelia glanced up from her desk. 'I hope that little man hasn't asked you to examine the picture. You already look exhausted.'

'He has, actually,' Wren said, feeling rattled. 'I told him I would.'

Amelia frowned. 'Then you obviously cannot imagine the pressure you will be under tonight. Auctioneers need a clear head – that's why they always rest beforehand. I'll bet Peter Morgan told you that.'

'True,' Wren admitted.

'I owe it to Archer's to make sure nothing goes wrong,' Amelia said. 'So it seems I'll have to go to the storage bay and make sure the Renoir's all right.' She gave Wren a disgruntled look.

'Thanks, but verifying the picture is my responsibility.'

Amelia crossed her arms in front of her. 'I can see you're simply not up to it.'

'Well … okay then,' Wren said. Maybe Amelia was right.

She sat back in her chair and closed her eyes, hoping to calm her nerves by reminding herself of her recent good fortune. Timothy King had as good as offered her a job. She had dear friends, a lovely man in her life and tonight she'd be auctioning a painting that was sure to become the talk of the international art world. She had everything she could ever have wanted – except for a mother, a father, or a sister to fill the emptiness inside.

CHAPTER THIRTY-EIGHT

Wren sighed with relief. Thank God she'd recovered from the brief moment of panic that had assailed her almost as soon as she'd stepped onto the dais. A glimpse of Renoir's touching depiction of a sisterly bond she'd never known had torn at her heart, but she'd managed to fight off her turbulent emotions.

Now, standing poised in her dramatic black Jean Paul Gaultier suit beneath the glittering chandeliers of Archer's famous sale room, Wren cast her gaze over the auction's most likely players. On the far right was the young scion of a renowned British banking dynasty, with money to burn and the indulgent habits of a seasoned playboy. On the left sat a once-famous beauty, whose avalanche of wealth had rolled into her Zurich account shortly after the demise of her protector, one of France's leading politicians.

Who else? A white-robed Middle Eastern sheik, accompanied by chunky bodyguards; a Russian oligarch with his latest cover-girl wife; a sprinkling of Hollywood movie stars; a coterie of wealthy Japanese developers; and several of Germany's most successful industrialists.

And of course, she couldn't miss the newly minted American tycoons in their tailor-made Zegna suits and Hermès ties. Each one of them had acquired his fabulous riches during the past gilded years thanks to the frenzied trading of equities, junk bonds or big-city real estate. Dan Blackwell, the operator of one of the largest hedge funds in the country, was the most likely of the group to make a serious bid, though there were others who would take part, if only to make their presence felt. Even if they were not yet in the first league, tonight one or two might be tempted to make the leap.

There was also Jordan Grant. He had all the money in the world to spend, but it was impossible to know how badly his employer wanted the painting. Early on, when she had questioned Jordan about the reason behind the media tycoon's fierce desire for privacy, he'd shrugged, saying he guessed Conroy simply preferred to lose himself in art rather than cultivate a high profile. 'And who can blame him for that?' Jordan had said with a serious look. After he'd added that maintaining his silence on all matters relating to Conroy had been a strict condition of his employment, Wren had let the subject drop.

The crowd murmured eagerly as the two aproned porters who'd been charged with conveying the evening's most important work onto an easel made a final adjustment. Then they dipped their heads towards Wren and departed.

It was time.

Wren took a deep breath. 'Ladies and gentlemen,' she began, forcing herself to ignore a sudden tightness in her shoulders. 'We now come to lot twelve, *Deux Jeunes Filles au Piano* or, in English, *Two Young Girls at the Piano*. The work is by the great Impressionist painter Pierre-Auguste Renoir and dates from 1891.'

Wren glanced down, appalled to see her hands trembling. Her panic must not return now.

'A later version of this remarkable work hangs in the Musée d'Orsay in Paris and another is in the Metropolitan Museum of Art, here in New York. This example is, however, the original and, according to expert opinion, the finest of all known variations.'

As she gestured towards the enchanting pink and blue painting, her ears caught more than one sharply inhaled breath. Thankfully, it seemed that even these jaded collectors could not help but be moved by Renoir's portrayal of youth and innocence.

'The picture's fascinating provenance has been fully detailed in your catalogues,' she said. 'There have been only two previous owners, both private individuals. Tonight, for the first time in more than half a century, a rare opportunity exists to acquire this masterpiece.'

Wren paused, allowing a brief silence to add weight to her words. She was steady now, and resolute. The room was hers to command.

'Shall we open the bidding at nine million dollars?' It was less a question than an inviting demand.

A squat, eager German in the front row immediately waved his paddle.

'I have nine million dollars. Thank you, sir,' she said warmly, though her eyes were already darting towards the British banker.

'Nine million one hundred thousand on my left. Do I hear nine two?

'Nine two on my right, against you, sir. At nine three on my left, four, five, six, seven.'

She turned her head from side to side as the bids flew. 'Madame, is that ten million? Very wise.'

The fading beauty with the Swiss bank account looked pleased, but now the Russian was thrusting up his hand. 'Ten one,' he shouted in a heavy accent.

A few bids more and Madame gracefully retired, leaving room for a tussle between the Russian and one of the new American business titans. The intensity with which they traded offers resembled their own private arms race.

Wren's heart was beating fast. *Use the adrenaline*, she remembered Morgan telling her. *Don't let it master you.*

Another paddle rose. 'Eleven four, thank you, James,' she called out to a staff member manning one of the black telephones.

'Eleven five at the front, six, seven, eight. Do I hear eleven nine?'

Wren's striking face glowed. This was her element. She was an eagle, soaring through space. As the bids flew her arms became wings, her gestures acknowledging a player or encouraging a waverer. Keeping track of the offers required fierce concentration, although, as the Renoir's price continued to rise towards an enormous sum, she did permit herself the briefest moment of self-congratulation.

This evening, Wren Summers would become the mistress of the sale room. She would bend the world's richest, most powerful individuals to her will simply by using her charm, her wit and her skill. How shocked they would be if they knew of the rackety place she had come from, or that beneath her polished appearance she was still the same girl who'd had to fight to belong.

Wren's luminous eyes settled on a Japanese gentleman with his arm in the air. 'Fourteen million five hundred thousand in your favour.' She turned to the sheik. 'Do I hear fourteen six? A painting like this comes up only once in a lifetime.' Her warm voice contained the hint of a challenge.

The sheik nodded.

'Thank you, sir. We have fourteen six. Any advance on fourteen six?'

Sensing a little persuasion was called for, she extended her arm towards the underbidder. 'Think how impressive this Renoir would look in your Osaka boardroom,' she purred. Bowing obediently, the Japanese raised his paddle.

For an instant, Wren allowed her gaze to flicker towards the tall figure standing near the back of the room. So far, Jordan hadn't placed a single bid. But the auction wasn't over yet.

The sheik made another offer. The Japanese bidder declined. Then Dan Blackwell entered the fray. A fierce, eight-bid duel between the two ended with Blackwell the victor.

'In your favour, sir, at fifteen five. Any advance on fifteen million five hundred thousand dollars?' A glance at Blackwell revealed he was already gloating.

Wren felt a tinge of disappointment. It seemed Jordan had decided not to bid on the picture.

She lifted her gavel. 'At fifteen million five hundred thousand dollars, going once.' The hammer came only halfway down before she raised it again.

Every person in the room strained forward.

'At fifteen million five hundred thousand, going twice,' she called out. 'Final chance.' The hammer still hovered.

At last Jordan thrust up his hand.

Wren allowed her arm to float down. 'We have a new bidder.' She smiled. 'Better late than never, sir.' There was a faintly teasing quality in her tone. 'Fifteen six, at the back of the room.'

Blackwell looked shocked. He placed two more bids. Each time, Jordan countered.

Wren felt the onlookers' tension rise to a new level. The contest was nearing its climax.

'Against you, sir,' she said, gazing steadily at Blackwell. 'One more bid might do it.'

The man could not meet her eyes. Shaking his head, he looked down, humiliated.

'Any advance on sixteen million dollars?' Wren turned slowly from left to right, alert for the merest suggestion of a raised hand, a paddle or even a nod, but no one could top Jordan's bid.

'At sixteen million dollars, going once. Fair warning, at sixteen million dollars, going twice.' Wren paused for several long seconds. 'All done,' she called out decisively as her hammer struck the lectern with a crack. 'Sold, at sixteen million dollars, to the gentleman at the back.'

Wren looked boldly at Jordan. As his eyes met hers, they might have been the only two people in the room. 'Congratulations, sir,' she said. 'I believe we have set a new record.'

Spontaneous applause broke out. With a brief smile and a nod of acknowledgement she announced, 'Mr Peter Morgan will now resume the auction.'

Wren fizzed with exhilaration. Everyone had told her she'd be wrung out once her job was over, but she felt on top of the world. Selling the Renoir, especially to someone who treasured art as much as she did, had been the most thrilling achievement of her life. Tonight she might have played the role of a gavel-wielding token female, but she'd sure as hell kicked the door open for other women to take to the stage.

Timothy King drew her aside. 'You're a natural.' He beamed. 'Let's meet in the library after Peter knocks down the final lot. A debut like yours deserves to be celebrated.'

The library was crowded with Archer's staff, plus a few select clients. Wren scanned the room, half-hoping she might find Mr Mancini among them. She would have liked him to see that his belief in her had been vindicated, for Josephina was now a very wealthy woman. Wren resolved to send him a box of the best cigars she could find as a thank-you present.

Once martinis had been handed around, King removed a Montblanc pen from his breast pocket and pinged it against his glass.

'Ladies and gentlemen, history was made tonight,' he declared. 'A toast to Wren Summers, Archer's first lady auctioneer. I am sure you all agree with me that her performance was a veritable tour de force.'

Some raised their glasses, others clapped or murmured their agreement. Wren smiled with grace, tamping down her niggling sense of being patronised yet again.

Peter Morgan's brown eyes twinkled. 'I shall have to watch myself. I fear the pupil will soon outstrip her master.'

Antoine was a little quieter than she would have expected, but Amelia made up for it with a typically backhanded compliment, saying archly, 'I never suspected you had it in you.'

As the heat became intense and the cigarette smoke ever denser, Wren drank her second martini. Everyone seemed to be talking at once, either sharing the jubilation of the auction's successful bidders or marvelling at the prices. Pounding waves of noise rolled towards her.

After a waiter had supplied her with a third cocktail, she spent fifteen minutes circulating, then sought Jordan out. 'I'm dying to leave,' she whispered. 'My head is whirling. I think the pressure has finally got to me. Do you know somewhere more secluded we can go?'

'I think I can arrange that,' Jordan said with a look that gave her butterflies.

They slipped out quietly and hailed a passing taxi.

'Hey, we're at the Café des Artistes,' Wren protested when they drew up in front of One West 67th Street. 'I mean, it's lovely, but it isn't exactly the most private place in town.'

'We're not visiting the café,' Jordan said after he'd paid the driver and helped Wren out. He tilted her chin up with his hand and kissed her on the lips. 'We're going to my apartment in the building above.'

Wren stared at him, puzzled. 'I'm not following. You live downtown, remember?'

Jordan looked sheepish. 'I don't, actually.'

Wren's voice caught. 'But we've been there.'

'That little studio belongs to my ex-roommate. When Paul went to study at Cambridge for six months he gave me a key and asked if I'd look after it.'

'Jordan, you've lost me.' She felt dizzy.

'After that first dinner I couldn't bear to let you go. I had to come up with an excuse so I could leap into the taxi beside you.'

'And that's why you said you lived near me?'

'It's the only lie I've told you, and the only one I ever will,' he said earnestly.

Wren ruffled his hair. 'In that case, I forgive you.'

They kissed on the sidewalk, and then in the elevator. They kissed some more while Jordan fumbled for his key. They were still kissing when they tumbled onto his plush dark blue sofa.

He took off his coat.

Wren told herself that this time would be different. There was no way she'd freeze up tonight, not when she felt so charged with adrenaline and so incredibly attracted to Jordan. She unravelled the knot in his tie and let it drop.

'We need to mark your success with champagne,' he said, breathing quickly, 'and by an amazing stroke of luck, I happen to have some on ice.'

Once he'd filled their glasses he murmured, 'Here's to New York's star auctioneer.'

They touched glasses and drank. Wren slowly undid the top three buttons of Jordan's shirt, savouring each moment of exploration.

'And here's to the handsome man who made tonight's winning bid. I quite fancy him, you know,' she said as her eyes flickered towards the smooth, lightly tanned skin at the base of his throat. Jo had been right. Now she'd taken control, her terror had evaporated.

She slipped off her Gaultier jacket, revealing a black lace bra that subtly enhanced her breasts. This was the night. This was the moment.

'Wren,' Jordan said huskily. 'I hope you want this as much as I do, because you are irresistible.'

'Can't you tell?' she said, teasing him.

Jordan slid down her bra straps. 'I'll take that as a yes.'

Wren's pulse quickened when she felt his lips graze her shoulders and the swell of her breasts. Then his hands drifted down to the hooks on her bra.

She leant her head against the sofa, suddenly light-headed.

'I'm a little faint,' she said breathlessly. 'Do you mind fetching me a glass of water?'

'Don't move an inch,' Jordan answered. 'I'll be right back.'

The imprint of his mouth made her skin burn. She'd never even seen him without his shirt, but very soon now it would be her lips on that chest, her hands caressing him.

CHAPTER THIRTY-NINE

Tuesday

'Ugh!' Wren massaged her temples. Her second ever hangover was even worse than the first. This time, a heavy metal band had taken up residence inside her head.

She moaned weakly. Perhaps she should try opening her eyes.

The thick cream drapes, the double-height ceiling, the Matisse drawing on the wall opposite – nothing was familiar. Wren sat bolt upright, wincing.

She'd gone back to Jordan's apartment. That meant she must be in his bed. Pressing her lips together, she tried to concentrate. What had happened between them? She felt a faint echo of desire as she remembered undoing his tie, drinking champagne, the thrilling way he had kissed her and then – her mind was a blank.

'Ah, so Sleeping Beauty is awake.' Jordan walked in, wearing a white T-shirt and grey boxers. With his broad shoulders and chiselled features, he might have just stepped out of a Calvin Klein billboard.

Wren managed a strangled 'Good morning'.

'How are you feeling?' An amused expression played at the corners of Jordan's mouth as he set down a tray bearing fresh orange juice, hot coffee and a packet of paracetamol.

'I've been better,' she groaned, reaching for a couple of tablets. 'Why I ever drink spirits is beyond me.'

Wren glanced down, then blushed. It appeared she was wearing only her black lace bra and tiny matching pants.

'Um, Jordan.' She cleared her throat. 'This is unbelievably awkward, but did we—'

'Make passionate love?' He pushed back a lock of his thick blond hair as he sat down next to her. 'Sadly, no. After I came back with a glass of water, I found you asleep.'

'Is that a polite way of saying passed out?' Wren sipped some coffee to hide her embarrassment.

'Afraid so, sweetheart.' He began planting light kisses on her neck.

Despite her hangover, Wren felt a ripple of need.

'I took your clothes off and put you to bed,' he added with a grin that made him look around seventeen. 'I'd be lying if I said I wasn't tempted to ravish you, but I did about a hundred push-ups, took a shower and spent a lonely night in the spare room instead.'

As her eyes lingered on his perfect face, Wren realised the tablets were beginning to take effect.

'Would you mind holding that thought? The bit about being tempted to ravish me, I mean,' she said.

She slid out of bed, acutely aware of Jordan's gaze travelling across her near-naked body. 'I'll be right back.'

'Thank God for that,' she heard him mumble.

Ten minutes later Wren had cleaned her teeth, showered and magically thrown off her hangover. As she towelled herself dry in front of the bathroom mirror, a throb in her belly caught her by surprise. Letting her towel drop, she studied her reflection while she imagined Jordan's hands touching her neck, her full breasts and other more hidden places. The pictures she conjured were incredibly arousing.

Wren paused before opening the door of the ensuite. Should she appear with nothing on? Maybe a fresh towel tied tightly around her would be more enticing. Or perhaps she ought to go back to her sexy black underwear. Settling for the towel, she shook her hair out so it flowed in lush waves over her shoulders and stepped forward.

Wren's smile faded. There was no sign of Jordan. She heard noises coming from another room in the apartment. Maybe he was returning with some of last night's champagne?

He strode into the bedroom, white-faced. 'I just took a call from Conroy,' he said. 'The man's desperate.'

Wren felt as if she'd had a bucket of freezing water thrown over her. 'What's happened?' She pulled her towel up a little higher.

Jordan looked grim. 'It's his daughter, Rosemary. I've never met her, but I think she's a couple of years younger than you – and she's been kidnapped.'

'No!' Wren's eyes widened with horror. 'The poor girl. That's unimaginable.'

Jordan frowned. 'The kidnappers have already demanded a ransom.'

She reached for his hands. 'How much money do they want?'

'They don't want money.' He pulled her towards him. 'Wren, they've ordered Conroy to hand over the Renoir.'

'I don't understand. Unless there's some wacko out there who wants to lock the picture away in a secret vault for his own private pleasure.'

'That scenario is a bit of a myth,' Jordan said. 'It's hardly ever the motivation for theft. These days, terrorists and criminal gangs seize high-value pictures so they can be used as collateral, usually for drug deals or illegal arms sales. It's a favourite ploy of the Mafia, especially in Naples and Sicily, but it looks like it might have been adopted by their New York brotherhood.'

Wren lowered herself slowly onto the end of the bed. 'I had no idea.'

Was it possible Mancini had used her? He'd said Josephina had originally come from Naples – so had his family. Perhaps they had both played a part in this crime. Or was this the work of a rival? She felt lost in a maze of possibilities, each one worse than the other.

'Consider the advantages,' Jordan said as he sat down beside her. 'You can take a multimillion-dollar picture out of its frame and hide it easily in a suitcase. It's light, occupies a tiny fraction of the room the equivalent in cash would, plus it won't show up on a security scan. Best of all for these guys, thanks to auctions like yours, the artwork's value has been publicly established – there's no guesswork involved.

'Even if a sixteen-million-dollar painting is discounted by ninety per cent, it's still worth one-point-six million. You'd be able to buy a vast amount of cocaine or heroin at source with that kind of money, then sell the stuff on the street for maybe thirty times what you paid for it.'

Wren ran her hands through her hair. Perhaps Josephina was an innocent dupe. It was horrible to know a painting that had escaped the Nazis and given the poor woman solace for so many years, a painting that had reminded her of the daughters who were lost to her forever, might end up in the hands of vicious thugs.

'What happens now?' she said, struggling to keep her voice steady.

Jordan stood up and began pulling clothes out of his wardrobe. 'The kidnappers have demanded that the Renoir be delivered by midday, but we won't know the address until the last minute. They're also threatening Conroy that if the police are involved, he'll never see Rosemary alive again.'

Wren buried her face in her hands.

'You're welcome to stay as long as you like, but I have to see Mr Conroy,' Jordan said, his voice low and troubled.

'I should leave too.' Wren lifted her head. 'Do you have a spare shirt in that wardrobe? It wouldn't be a good look if I came into Archer's wearing the same clothes as I had on last night.'

'I can do better than that. Sometimes Harriet uses the apartment in between shifts. If you look in the other bedroom, you'll find some of her things in the closet.'

Jordan disappeared into the bathroom and emerged fully dressed. 'I'm so sorry, sweetheart,' he said, touching her bare shoulder. 'Nothing has turned out the way that I wanted.'

Wren's lower lip trembled. It looked like she and Jordan would have few opportunities to be together before she left for Australia on Sunday, but there were far more important things to worry about right now than their love life.

'It's fine,' she said. 'Just go help your boss find his daughter.'

Jordan's mouth brushed hers in a fleeting kiss. 'Okay, I'm off. Remember – until someone else breaks the news to you, act as if you haven't heard a word about it. That will keep things a lot simpler.'

Wren found a pair of Harriet's shoes in the closet. The black moccasins were slightly too large, but as this didn't seem like a day for stilettos, she slid her feet into them anyway. Next, she put on a pink cotton shirt of Harriet's and the skirt from her Gaultier suit, then added a slick of the deep pink Dior lipstick she found rolling around at the bottom of her bag.

The big apartment felt empty without Jordan's presence. *How quickly life can change*, she reflected. One minute she'd been imagining herself wrapped in the arms of the beautiful man she cared so much for. The next, they had both been drawn into someone else's unspeakable trauma.

She picked up her jacket and hurried out.

Wren looked up when she arrived at Archer's, but the sun must have been at the wrong angle as Artemis was in shadow. Roma was still missing. And now Conroy's daughter was being held hostage at an unknown destination. She wondered just how many people were hunting for lost girls in this city. New York seemed different now, darker and more predatory.

'Hey,' Jeanette called out quickly as soon as Wren stepped through the door. 'Timothy King wants you to see him in his office right away.'

'From the sound of your voice,' Wren said, 'it's not about last night's sale. I thought he'd be over the moon today.'

'Quite honestly, I don't know what's happened.' Jeanette wrinkled her forehead. 'But there's some kind of flap on.'

Having first smoothed back her hair, Wren knocked on King's door and entered his room. There were dark circles beneath the man's hooded eyes.

'Ah good, you're here,' he muttered, 'sit down. A terrible thing has occurred.'

King related the details Wren already knew, though there was no need for her to feign distress. The retelling affected her even more deeply than the first time she'd heard the news. 'That is truly horrible,' she said, shaking her head.

'I've been up half the night,' King groaned. 'The Renoir has been repacked in the same crate in which it travelled from Venice. Conroy is sending his own security men to deliver it.'

'What happens to Rosemary Conroy after that?' she asked.

'From what I can gather, once the kidnappers are satisfied the picture is safely in their hands, they'll leave instructions about where to find her.'

Wren shuddered. It was impossible to imagine the girl's terror. 'Is there anything I can do?' she asked.

'It's best if you act as normally as possible.' King took a gulp of tea from his ever-present cup. 'I don't want word getting out under any circumstances. It will only make Rosemary's rescue more challenging than it already is, plus attract the worst sort of publicity to Archer's.

'Just check in with Amelia as usual and see what she wants you to do, but don't mention anything about this matter. The only person in the building other than you and I who knows about the kidnap is Antoine Ardant.'

He wrote something in a notebook and looked up. 'Hopefully, this nightmare will be resolved very soon.'

'I hope so too,' Wren said fervently.

She had her hand on the doorknob when King called out, 'Wren, just a moment.'

'Yes, Mr King?'

'I'm sorry this awful business has overshadowed your triumph.'

CHAPTER FORTY

Wren could hear the telephone ringing as she sloped down the corridor to her office, but this time she wasn't hurrying. She dropped into a chair, unwilling to speak to anyone. With her shock easing, her mind filled with images of a fearful young woman alone in some godforsaken place, probably blindfolded and bound. Bowing her head, she prayed the kidnappers wouldn't hurt Rosemary Conroy.

A note had been left on her desk. It seemed Amelia would be out for most of the day valuing a collection, but she wanted Wren to research two eighteenth-century Watteau etchings for a future catalogue. A pile of reference books had been left next to the message, but Wren couldn't imagine how she'd manage to concentrate.

She was thumbing through the first book in a distracted manner when the phone rang again.

'Wren Summers,' she said, hoping for a routine inquiry. Her headache was returning.

'Thank God you're there.' It was Ava, uncharacteristically flustered. 'I've been calling for ages.'

Wren was puzzled. 'I stayed over at Jordan's. It's no big deal.'

'But May didn't come home last night either,' Ava said.

'I still can't see what you're so worried about.'

'That's because you don't understand.' Ava's voice was ragged. 'May never stays out all night, she just doesn't. The last anyone saw of her was at a party in Soho that she left around 10.30 pm and no one's heard a word since. I'm sure she's in trouble.'

Wren tried to suppress a sense of foreboding. Ava was usually such a cool customer. 'Why are you talking like this?' she said with new urgency.

There was a brief pause. 'Because May is not who you think she is.'

Wren gripped the phone. 'Go on.'

'She swore me to secrecy, but Floris is not her real surname. She wanted a year off from college so she could live incognito and write her novel. Her paternal grandmother was Italian. Floris was the woman's name.'

'And May?'

'When she was little that's what she used to call herself.'

'Ava,' Wren said in a rush. 'What's May's real name?'

'Rosemary,' she said. 'Rosemary Conroy.'

Wren sank back in her chair, struggling to assimilate this appalling revelation. Rosemary was no longer a faceless victim. Now she had a face – May's face, with the same blue eyes and rosebud mouth. May was her good friend. No, more than that. When she'd had the hideous flashback in Tiffany's, May hadn't hesitated to race into Fifth Avenue's alarming traffic. She'd put herself in real danger to rescue her. Hell, she'd probably saved her life.

'Wren, Wren, are you still there?' Ava sounded frantic.

'Listen to me. If you're not sitting down, you should,' Wren said, snapping back to the present. 'You must not say a word to anyone but Jo about what I'm going to tell you. This is what's happened.'

She gave Ava a quick account, then told her to stay where she was. 'I promise, May's father is doing everything humanly possible to find her. If there's any news, I'll let you know as soon as I can.'

The morning inched past. Wren jumped when Jeanette buzzed her, but it was only to say that Alessandro had rung yet again. Although she refused to take his calls, ever since Venice he'd become increasingly fervent. Thankfully, his commitments in Europe had kept him away from New York – she could do without anyone making her life more complicated than it already was. With any luck, by the time she returned from Australia he would have forgotten all about her. She made an attempt to concentrate on her research but found herself reading the same paragraph over and over.

At 11.00 am King rang. 'The Renoir is on its way,' was all he said.

Midday came and went. At 1.00 pm Wren went out, bought some lunch and a bottle of water from a deli, then returned to Archer's. She forced herself to eat half of her tuna salad sandwich before giving up entirely.

At 2.00 pm, the phone rang only once before Wren seized it.

'Come to my office immediately,' King said.

Wren raced to the elevator.

King stood up and beckoned her inside as soon as she arrived. 'The kidnappers have been in touch,' he said. 'Why, I don't know, but they want an Archer's representative and one from Conroy's organisation to go to some sort of warehouse at four o'clock. I'm assuming we'll find further instructions inside, though I guess there's a chance they've left Rosemary there.'

He sucked in his mouth. 'I'm hoping it's the latter, but we can't be certain of anything.'

'Let me do it,' Wren said quickly.

King shook his head. 'It's far too dangerous. You don't have any idea what these criminals might do. I'll go myself.'

'I'm a friend of Rosemary Conroy,' Wren pleaded. 'God knows what state she'll be in. She needs to see a face she recognises.'

'I'm reluctant,' King said, but she could tell he was wavering. 'You do make a good point, though. The girl must be scared witless.'

'So, I'll be Archer's representative?'

King nodded silently.

'Who's Conroy sending?' Wren asked.

'I believe it's Jordan Grant.'

The Archer's van turned into a rundown Brooklyn street lined with boarded-up houses, wretched tenements and empty shops. A light breeze sent bits of paper and empty tin cans spiralling down its cracked sidewalks.

'Better lock your door, Wren,' Jordan warned as they passed hollow-eyed wraiths haunting gloomy street corners. 'We're in Brownsville,' he explained. 'It's one of the toughest neighbourhoods in the city. Lots of poverty, lots of drugs and lots of violence.'

They pulled up in front of a warehouse with broken windows, next to an empty parking lot.

'You should stay in the car,' Jordan said.

Wren pushed her door open. 'No way. May's only met you a few times. If she's inside, I have to come too.'

Ignoring the light rain that had started falling, they passed a cluster of scrawny alley cats foraging in a pile of garbage. The surface of the parking lot glistened with an oily iridescence.

Jordan removed the crossbar slotted through the handles of the warehouse doors, then kicked them open. Fingers of grey light penetrated the dim interior.

'May? Are you in here?' Wren shouted.

There was no answer. She heard a rustle, whirled around, then shrank back as ruby-eyed rats swarmed out of an abandoned packing case.

It seemed that the warehouse's only contents were more packing cases, some rusted tools and rows of disused metal racks. A single light bulb hanging on a cord suspended from the ceiling illuminated a far corner.

Wren looked at Jordan. 'That's strange,' she said in an undertone. 'The Renoir crate has been left over there, and there's something written on the front.'

Their feet crunched on broken glass as they walked forward.

'Christ,' Jordan said. 'What's that all about?'

Daubed on the front of the crate in bright red, two-foot-high letters was the word *FAKE*.

'No idea,' Wren said, perplexed. 'But maybe they've left a message in that shoebox on top.'

She picked up the box and removed the lid. Inside was a bunched-up piece of newspaper and a typed note. 'Listen to this,' she said, her voice taut. '*Don't fuck with us. Deliver the real thing if you want to see your daughter again. We'll let you know the address. No cops or the deal is off. Last chance, Conroy. Check the newspaper. You have until 9.00 pm, Thursday.*'

She looked at Jordan. 'I think I know what's going on. The kidnappers must have a postcard or something of the Met's version of *Two Girls*, and because this one looks different they think Conroy's trying to rip them off.'

'We'll have to take it back to Archer's.' Jordan frowned. 'Antoine will need to provide these creeps with proof, though I can't believe one of the world's foremost experts on Impressionist art will be forced to authenticate a painting for what are most likely ignorant Mafia hoods.'

Hoisting up the crate, he staggered out of the warehouse and set it down in the back of the van.

'Hey!' Wren called, running after him. 'They said to check the newspaper. I think there's something inside.'

Once she'd smoothed out the crumpled page on the van's bonnet, Wren saw that the sheet had been wrapped around a clump of stained cotton wool. She'd begun pulling its fibres apart when her hand touched something cold and damp.

'Oh no, no, no,' she moaned, dropping the package. She lurched back, then threw up violently.

Jordan held her hair until she stopped vomiting. 'Sweetheart, what the hell did you find in there?'

Wren wiped her mouth. 'It's, it's the very top of May's little finger,' she whimpered. 'She always wears that red polish. And there's a broken bit from one of her chains.' The acid taste in her mouth was making her gag.

'Jordan,' she said, trembling. 'We only have a couple of days. What if we can't convince the kidnappers that the Renoir is real?'

'On the contrary, I believe it is essential Archer's maintains complete transparency,' King said. 'I'd like you to remain, Jordan, but it's up to you.'

Wren gnawed the inside of her cheek. If only he would take pity on her and go.

'As Mr Conroy's curator, I believe I'm obliged to stay,' Jordan said. 'However, I feel I should mention I found Miss Summers to be highly professional when she organised the sale of Mr Conroy's Degas. I would be very surprised to discover she was the cause of this problem.'

Wren struggled to breathe. It was bad enough that King and Antoine were about to hear whatever poison Tremaine must have poured into Amelia's ear, but the thought that Jordan, who'd just spoken in her defence, would be bearing witness to a brutal assassination of her character was devastating.

'Information has reached me about the reason Wren was fired – yes, no doubt she didn't tell you that – from the Sydney Art Museum,' Amelia announced to the room.

'I am reliably informed that she compromised an international art dealer of indisputable integrity in an attempt to make money for herself at the museum's expense. She also tried to seduce a senior member of the museum's staff not only so she could extract a financial grant, but also quite possibly with a view to blackmailing the man.'

Wren flinched. Tremaine had struck again. Not satisfied with ending her Sydney career, he was intent on destroying her life.

'Unfortunately, Wren brought her unscrupulous ways with her to New York,' Amelia continued. 'When her Mafia associate, Tony Mancini, came in to pay for the Degas he bought, I personally saw him with his wallet open. I have no doubt she helped herself to a very nice kickback.'

Wren's face went white. The grave misfortune Ardant had warned her about in Venice was unfolding right before her eyes.

Amelia shook her head with a show of sadness. 'Of course, if Archer's had been aware that she'd grown up in an unsavoury hippie commune somewhere in the wilds of Australia, we would have known she'd never fit in here.'

She'd never fit in here. Each word was one more brutal stab.

'When Wren checked the picture before the auction, she was either too ignorant to see it was a fake – unforgiveable in itself – or else she conspired with a third party and knowingly sold a forgery. That would of course allow the real picture to be privately traded, thus earning her a very hefty illegal commission.'

'Amelia, you know that's not true!' Wren cried. 'How can you tell such hateful lies?'

Yet it was all so clear. Amelia had never forgiven her for capturing Alessandro's attention. Once Wren had been anointed Archer's first female auctioneer over her colleague's titled head, the girl's jealousy had escalated into pathological hatred.

Wren silently berated herself for allowing Amelia anywhere near the Renoir. She could just imagine her glee when she discovered the painting was a fake. Amelia would have realised it wouldn't take long for the forgery to be discovered. She would also have been aware that this shocking moment would provide her with the perfect opportunity for revenge. The fact that the picture was now central to the kidnapping of Rosemary Conroy, the daughter of Archer's most important client, only served to heighten Wren's apparent guilt – and Amelia's private triumph.

King took a seat. 'Thank you, Amelia. I only wish you had brought your concerns to me earlier.'

'I'm sorry, Timothy.' She had the temerity to look aggrieved. 'I suppose I found it hard to believe that anyone could behave in such a deceitful way.'

Wren fought the urge to laugh in her face.

'I understand,' King said solicitously. 'It appears we have all been taken in.' He looked in turn at Amelia, Jordan and Antoine. 'I intend following up this matter personally with each of you. But for now, if you wouldn't mind excusing me' – his voice became steely – 'I need to speak to Wren in private.'

Wren couldn't meet Jordan's gaze as he left the room. She was lost. He would despise her forever. She sank into a chair opposite King and waited.

'Well, do you have anything to say?' King's eyes were unrelenting disks of obsidian.

Wren begged him to contact Alessandro Baretti. Despite their exchange in Venice, if the man had even a skerrick of decency he'd vouch for her honesty. Next, she tried to explain that although it was true Mancini had offered her a cash gift, she'd refused to take it. Finally, she once more swore it was Amelia and not her who had assessed the Renoir. 'My only crime,' she said bitterly, 'was to relinquish that responsibility, something I deeply regret.'

Wren scanned King's face, hoping for a sign he had softened, but his stony expression remained unchanged. He had already passed judgement.

'Very well, you have had your turn,' he said coldly. 'Now, put yourself in my position. Why should I believe Wren Summers, an intern I have been acquainted with for only a few months and who, on the surface at least, appears to have a distinctly questionable past – instead of Lady Amelia Heywood, a trusted employee of this firm whose father happens to sit in the House of Lords?'

A black chasm opened before Wren. All she had strived for, every small achievement, meant nothing. She was still that dope-smoking hippie chick's kid, a deadbeat without a proper family, a weirdo who would never belong.

King shrugged. 'I don't know whether any of the accusations levelled against you are true.'

Wren felt a faint glimmer of hope.

'Quite honestly, that is unimportant.' He looked at her with contempt. 'The foundation of the auction business is trust,' he said. 'As head of international operations, my principal concern is preserving the company's unblemished reputation. And the one undisputed fact in this whole lamentable business is that last night, for the first time in Archer's two-century history, you auctioned a *fake*.'

Shame stained Wren's cheeks.

King clenched the hand he had wrapped around his teacup with such force she thought it would break. 'If this is made public,' he snapped, 'Archer's will be ruined – and so will I.'

Having set the cup down, King picked up his Montblanc pen and began tapping his desk. 'You are returning to Australia on Sunday,' he said suddenly.

Wren could sense his shrewd mind at work, assessing every angle.

'In the meantime, do not appear in these premises under any circumstances. Indeed, you would be well advised not to show your face in public.

'As you can imagine, right now E.J. Conroy is fully occupied. He has engaged a crack team of investigators to track down the real Renoir. A separate team, manned by both ex-FBI and ex-CIA agents, are out looking for Rosemary. Unfortunately, I understand they are yet to make progress on either front and, as we both know, time is of the essence.'

King leant forward. 'I hope you realise I'm saying this in your own best interest. Conroy is an extremely rich, powerful man. If he hears even the slightest hint that your actions have either endangered his daughter or – and this has to be a real possibility – led to her death, he will be merciless. The best course for you is to disappear to some remote, out-of-the-way place. Australia must have plenty of them.'

He looked almost sorry for her. 'Even then, I wouldn't count on your safety. A man with unlimited resources like Conroy has a very long reach.'

Wren was numb when she emerged from the subway. She made her way to Parkside like a blank-faced sleepwalker, unable to fathom the reality in which she was trapped. The consequences that followed Tremaine's attempted rape had been cruel and unjust, yet it had been possible for her to recover and make a fresh start. The magnitude of the problems that now engulfed her were of an entirely different order. This time, there would be no second chance.

She looked up quickly when she saw a man's shadow outside her building. Had she been able to run she would have taken to her heels, but she was rooted to the spot like a frightened bush creature caught in the glare of approaching headlights.

When Jordan walked towards her, Wren thought she might faint.

'Hi, sweetheart,' he said softly. 'We have to talk.'

'Stay here,' Wren said, struggling to stay on her feet. 'I'll get a key for the park.'

Once she'd returned, Wren managed to unlock the gates and drag herself to a bench. 'I'm surprised you're prepared to be seen with me,' she said forlornly.

Jordan rocked her like a child and kissed the top of her head. 'Wren, I know you,' he said, stroking her hair. 'There's no way you could have done anything Amelia accused you of.'

Jordan's embrace made her feel blessedly safe, yet it took only a moment or two for her to come to her senses. He could do nothing to save her. Wren's shoulders shook as she sobbed.

'I'm so confused,' she said when there were no more tears left to shed. 'I don't understand what went wrong with the Renoir, or how to clear my name.'

She wiped her eyes with the back of her hand. 'Right now, though, none of that matters. All I care about is May.'

'You know I'll help any way I can.' Jordan's voice was low and urgent.

Wren gazed at the angular trees in the park, their branches almost bare. November was late fall in New York, while at home the fresh spring leaves of willows would be trailing across the surface of the Shoalhaven River. Woolahderra had provided Lily with refuge, but would it do the same for her?

She rested her head on Jordan's shoulder. 'King thinks that, wherever I am, I'll be in danger from Conroy. He'll want me arrested and put on trial.'

'If Amelia's lies reach the man, I'll force him to see sense,' Jordan said quickly.

Wren shivered. 'Please don't do anything.' If Jordan spoke out on her behalf he would only be sucked into this whirlpool of horror. With emotions running so high, he might find himself accused of participating in a cover-up – even of being her accomplice. She already had more than enough on her conscience.

Fear clawed at her throat. 'We'd better go,' she said. 'We're not meant to be in here after dark.'

Wren ate an apple in her room. She couldn't stomach dinner, nor could she cope with facing Ava and Jo's questions. She'd asked Jewel to let the girls know that Mr Conroy was doing everything he could to rescue May, and that Wren needed some time to herself before she saw Lily.

Lying tensely on her single bed, she stared at the ceiling. *So, let's see how you're doing*, sniped the voice in her head. *Your mother is dying. You have no father. You have failed to find your sister. The awful wound May has suffered has come about because you sold a fake picture. The art world career you love is finished. As for the man who means so much to you – if you stick around, you're likely to ruin his life too. Oh, and don't go running to your friends. What would they want with someone like you?*

Like a tape jammed on repeat, these bitter words unspooled through her mind over and over until she buried her head under her pillow. How foolish she'd been to imagine she could escape her destiny. With no hope of finding May, on Sunday she would fly back to Australia and stay with Lily until the end came. Then she, too, would spend the rest of her desolate life hiding in Woolahderra, with only the birds and the bush and the river.

CHAPTER FORTY-TWO ·

Wednesday

Wren woke with a start in the early hours of the morning. She padded over to the sink, gulped down a glass of water, then went to the window and pulled it wide open. A rush of cold night air swirled inside, banishing her torpor. While she gazed at the moonlit trees opposite, a dreamlike procession of women appeared before her. In another age, they might have been summoned by Artemis.

She saw her bruised, talented mother and wise Miss Reiter from the library; MJ and Jewel and the unsinkable Jo; gallant May and the loyal, acerbic Ava.

Other images joined this ghostly parade: her childhood heroes, Sir Edmund Hillary and the *Apollo 13* astronauts; her far-seeing primary school teacher Mr Madden; and dear Bobby Hawkins, with his precious prints and drawings. Jordan's remarkable visage was the final act of conjury. Despite every venomous allegation, not once had he doubted her.

As she considered the gifts each one had bestowed, she felt a spark of self-belief ignite. A moment later, it had become a blazing flame. She would not betray their inspiration, their friendship or their love by allowing pain or fear to vanquish her. What had Hillary said after scaling Mount Everest? *It is not the mountain we conquer, but ourselves.*

Knowing she had broken her promise to find the child her mother longed for seared her heart. But at least her sister's disappearance had not been her fault. By contrast, the realisation that she was the cause of both May's mutilation and her continuing captivity was unbearable. Gripping the hard ledge of the windowsill, she swore an oath that she would not be responsible for May's death.

Wren's breath turned the chill air white. There was one man she could beg for help, a modern-day Hades who ruled over a shadowy underworld. If Tony Mancini was behind May's grotesque kidnapping – which, given he'd pushed Wren towards the Renoir, she couldn't rule out – throwing herself on his mercy might be a perilous course.

But hadn't she known ever since she'd been a fatherless child growing up rough that you couldn't get anywhere without taking a risk?

Wren shut the window with a sharp rap. She'd auctioned the cursed picture, just as he'd wanted. Mancini hadn't done her a favour at all. He *owed* her.

'Where to, boss?' Vito said as Wren sat stiffly on the back seat of the long black Cadillac.

'Brooklyn,' Mancini muttered. 'The shore.'

At the push of a button a screen slid into place, separating Vito from the two of them.

A corkscrew of nerves twisted through Wren as she pondered how many murky secrets must have been shared in the confines of this metal and leather confessional.

They glided across the Manhattan Bridge and were soon skimming along the beltway hugging Brooklyn's coast.

'Okay, Miss Australia,' Mancini growled, his heavy-set shoulders hunched inside his suit jacket. 'I figure this isn't a social call, so what's on your mind?'

She told him everything, including the way Amelia Heywood's pathological envy had made her determined to destroy Wren's life. 'It all started when I became, uh, involved with Alessandro. He never said anything to me about being engaged to Amelia, but I suppose you knew about it.'

Mancini nodded.

'As far as the Renoir is concerned, Amelia has no evidence against me except innuendo and hearsay,' Wren said wanly. 'I doubt it's enough for me to be charged with breaking the law, although I can't be sure.'

She resisted a wave of panic. 'What I do know is that her vitriol can put a stop to any career requiring a reputation for honesty, which means just about every job I can think of – certainly one in the art world.'

'I'm assuming you don't want her taken out,' Mancini said.

'God, no.' Wren shrank back.

'Just my little joke,' he croaked, though it felt as if a cold hand had squeezed her throat.

'Mr Mancini, it's rescuing May that is the absolute priority,' she said. He might not have been equipped to find her missing sister, but this was about a crime – and crime was his speciality. 'Only, that doesn't seem possible without locating the real Renoir.'

Finding it hard to breathe, she lowered her window. 'You know I wouldn't ask if I wasn't desperate. But if May is not found, she'll be dead by tomorrow night. Will you help me?'

The screen dividing them from Vito disappeared.

'Pull up ahead at Coney Island,' Mancini instructed. 'This young lady and I are going to take a stroll along the seafront.'

Wren hugged her camel wool coat around her as she navigated the boardwalk. An icy wind was blowing in from the Atlantic Ocean, whipping up snowy caps on the slate-coloured water. She was accustomed to a coast painted with sparkling blue breakers, pale yellow sand, and green bands of she-oaks and Norfolk pines. Here, the beach was the colour of grey bones, while squat, featureless blocks of apartments ringed the abandoned amusement park.

'Coney Island used to be swell,' Mancini mused. 'See over there?'

Wren looked at a huge undulating structure.

'That's the Cyclone Rollercoaster – or is it the Thunderbolt?'

He sighed. 'It doesn't matter. That big circle with the little cars hanging off it is the old Wonder Wheel and the tower was part of the Parachute Jump. Most of this stuff dates back to the twenties. What use are they to anyone now, sitting there rotting?'

Wren was anxious for Mancini to focus on the kidnapping, but she remembered his tendency to speak circuitously, before seizing upon an issue like a raptor.

'In its heyday, the place was a major hangout for mob families,' he said, shoving his hands in the pockets of his black overcoat. 'There was a man named Mimi Scialo, known as the King of Coney Island. Loan sharks, bookmaking, girls, gambling – you name it, he ran it.

'That's until his body was found encased in cement right up on President Street, inside Otto's Social Club. Mimi was a flashy sort, tough too. He thought he could take over the Colombo family, but its head was Carmine "The Snake" Persico and Carmine was never going to stand for it.'

He bent over, coughing. ''Every wiseguy knows if you don't show respect for a don, you better have an army of hard men to back you up. Mimi forgot that.'

They walked on.

'Interesting story,' Wren said, wondering if he'd just delivered a warning. Her face stung as strands of hair lashed her cheeks.

Mancini edged a little closer. The wind had begun buffeting their words across the sand.

'In case you're wondering,' he said, 'it wasn't me who kidnapped Conroy's daughter. Whatever people might say, that's not my style. God above, if something like that was to happen to Mona ...' He scowled.

Wren had seen a photo of Mancini's granddaughter in the social pages. With her coils of dark hair and soulful dark eyes she looked nothing like May, but Wren could understand why the man felt a connection. Both girls must be around the same age and came from well-known families with vast wealth – reason enough to make them vulnerable.

'Listen,' he wheezed. 'I can find that picture for you. In fact, I already have an idea of where it's likely to be. I can also track down Rosemary Conroy. I've got informers all over this city, the kind who wouldn't speak to some ex-FBI or CIA stooge if their lives depended on it.'

He removed a cigar from his top pocket and tried to light up, but the fierce currents of air made it impossible. 'Getting the girl back is more difficult,' he said. 'Not impossible, I'm not saying that. But tricky, especially if the idea is that no one gets hurt. These things can be unpredictable. You get a few gun-happy guys high on coke or pills, anything can happen.'

Wren swallowed anxiously.

'Sure, I'll admit that even though I gave you a break when you auctioned the painting, you helped me out too.' Mancini shrugged. 'But what you want me to do – locate the real picture, find the girl and then rescue her – are three big asks, with no upside coming my way.'

He looked at Wren appraisingly. 'Which brings us to the question that I figure by now you'd be expecting. What will you do for me?'

'Anything in my power,' Wren declared. 'I'd hope it would be legal, but …'

Mancini chuckled. 'From the way I see it, the thing I have in mind is hardly a favour at all.'

Wren drew her brows together. 'You'll excuse me if I say that sounds too good to be true.'

Mancini gave her a sly smile. 'I want you to get married.'

'Married?' Surely this was another of his so-called jokes. 'Do you have a candidate in mind?' she said, humouring him.

'Come on, Wren. Isn't it obvious?'

She looked at him blankly.

Mancini gave an exasperated sigh. 'Alessandro, of course.'

Wren's shrill laughter mingled with the gulls' cries. 'Alessandro doesn't strike me as the marrying type.'

'This isn't a joke,' Mancini huffed. 'I gather there was a time when you had feelings for him.' He gave her a quick sideways glance. 'It's disappointed me to learn there is someone else in your life.'

Wren coloured. 'Your cousin's son talks too much.'

'He's all the son I have now.' Mancini said quietly.

He gazed out over the cold silver waves. 'Look, let's put the relationship matter aside for a moment. If there's one thing I've learnt since taking an interest in the picture business, it's that the art trade is the perfect way to launder money. You might say that the Degas transaction was a successful trial run.' He chuckled.

'Setting up a clever girl like you in your own little gallery buying and selling high-priced paintings would be an extremely helpful way to deal with our excess cash flow. I'm not talking about small change, either – there's millions of dollars involved.' As he spoke, he jabbed a stubby finger at Wren.

'The beauty of the scheme is,' he went on, 'that it means the IRS need never know the real sum you charge my associates, who will pocket legitimate proceeds when they on-sell their pricey pictures at some later date. Most of this sparkling-clean money will flow back to the family – or rather, your family, as you will be Mrs Alessandro Baretti. You can see why I'd have to insist on that.'

He gave Wren a hard look. 'The laws in this country can make it tricky for a woman to testify against her husband – not that I think you'd be dumb enough to try it.'

Mancini's scheme was so outrageous, Wren was having difficulty believing the man was serious. 'But Alessandro's a dedicated playboy,' she said dismissively. 'I doubt he'll agree.'

'He'll do what I tell him,' Mancini growled. 'I'm through with bankrolling his set-up in Rome. His place is here in New York working with me so that, in time, he can become the next head of the family.'

He took a moment to recover himself. 'You're a good-looking girl,' he said, though it didn't feel like a compliment to Wren.

'But what's more important to me is that you've got fire in your belly, you're smart as hell and you're willing to take a risk. That's what makes you the perfect wife for the next don of the family. And the best thing of all is,' he added with a touch of glee, 'with your know-how, you're in a position to make us more dough than you could possibly imagine.'

Wren's jaw ached with barely suppressed anger. Mancini's proposition was vile. Art was just a commodity to men like him and so, apparently, was she.

'But it's simply not possible.' Desperation made her voice crack. 'I'm leaving New York on Sunday and I don't know when I'll return. It's because of my mother – she's gravely ill with cancer and has no hope of surviving.'

'That's tough on you,' he said, shaking his head. 'It's a big thing, losing your mother.'

Relief flooded through Wren. He'd taken pity on her.

Then he coughed and stuck out his jaw. 'But life must go on,' he said, 'and I don't like loose ends.'

He gave a satisfied nod. 'I'll arrange for you and Alessandro to fly down to Vegas late on Friday and tie the knot. You can spend the night at the Desert Inn's honeymoon suite – I hear it's very romantic – and still be back in New York the next day. That will leave plenty of time for you to catch your flight home.'

Wren felt ill.

He gave her a knowing look. 'By the way, don't get any cute ideas about staying Down Under. If you don't return, your American boyfriend might find himself next in line for a concrete overcoat.'

Wren stared at the decaying carcasses of the old rides. 'What you're asking me to do – it's unthinkable,' she said.

'Really? I don't see it that way.' Mancini's expression was that of a man who held every card. 'Unless you're happy for Rosemary Conroy to be murdered tomorrow.'

Gasping, Wren doubled over as nausea swept through her.

He turned his back, cupped his hands and finally lit his cigar. 'Do you really want her death on your conscience?' A succession of nonchalant smoke rings vanished quickly.

'Oh, and just so you know.' He gave her a quick sideways glance. 'When I called Alessandro last night to tell him my plans for you two, he didn't need any persuading.' Mancini drew back. 'Seemed more to me like he couldn't wait.'

Sick to her stomach, Wren could picture Alessandro, self-satisfied and preening, demanding a husband's sexual privileges whenever he felt like it. The thought made her cold face burn. He didn't love her – she realised with a jolt that she'd seen the look he'd given her in Venice plenty of times before. It was that of a man who would stop at nothing if it meant adding an elusive object to his collection. Alessandro didn't want a wife. He desired a possession.

'I can't see why you wouldn't be all for the marriage too,' Mancini went on in an expansive tone. 'The boy's handsome. He's set to become rich and powerful, and you kids have your art in common. From where I stand, I'd say it's a match made in heaven.'

Wren reeled. *A match made in heaven.* Mancini's words released a jigsaw of emotions that left her temporarily off balance. Stumbling forward, she was able to stay upright only by concentrating hard on placing one foot down after another. It had taken this impossible situation for her to gain one simple insight. She was in love with Jordan Grant. She was meant to be with *him.*

'Please,' she said urgently. 'Don't make me do this.'

Mancini's voice had a threatening edge. 'You're not messing around with your pretty pictures now, Miss Australia.' He flicked ash from his cigar. 'You're playing in the big league. You know the price for my help. So, what's your answer? Will you agree to operate the business I want – and marry Alessandro? Because you can't do one without the other.'

Wren's mind raced. There had to be a way of saving May without binding herself to the Mancini crime family, but the solution wouldn't appear. Instead, she saw only that familiar yawning chasm, blacker and deeper than ever. She was balanced precariously on its edge. One word would send her plunging into its depths.

Wren closed her eyes. 'Yes.'

CHAPTER FORTY-THREE

She wandered blindly through the busy streets of the Upper West Side, her sight veiled by tears. The wound she carried would never heal. She would always feel like this: flayed and raw, sickened by the ugly bargain she'd been forced to strike.

She and Jordan had spent so little time together. They hadn't talked or walked or laughed enough. There hadn't been enough taxi rides or dinners or strolls through the park. They certainly hadn't kissed enough. And now they would never make love.

For a moment, Wren toyed with the idea of booking the same suite at the Plaza that Jordan had reserved for their cancelled weekend. She could order champagne, chocolates and armfuls of orchids, greet him in silk lingerie, her skin scented by roses and violets. At least they would have one unforgettable night together. She yearned to know Jordan in the deepest way possible. She would play out every fantasy she'd ever had about him and, in turn, do anything he wanted. Just one night. Was that too much to ask?

Wren slumped against a doorway in Central Park West. She would never be capable of carrying out this charade. Her only option was to act with quick and clinical brutality.

Reaching into her bag, she pulled out the note she had written as soon as she'd returned to Parkside. It had been a loathsome task, but she knew Jordan too well. If she told him the truth he'd confront Mancini. The gangster had already made clear just how merciless he'd be if Jordan threatened his unscrupulous scheme. This awful letter, filled with cruel half-truths, was her gift to the man she loved. It would make him hate her.

> *Jordan,*
>
> *I know this will be a shock, but I have become engaged to someone I met a while ago.*
>
> *It's always been difficult for me to trust a man, but being away here in New York has given me the chance to come to terms with this fault. I admit that after I met you there was a period when I became confused. However, recent events have helped to clarify my thoughts, and I now realise that you and I cannot share a future.*
>
> *I'm sorry if I hurt you.*
>
> *Please don't call and don't write. We can never see each other again.*
>
> *Wren*

Her quivering fingers made enclosing the note in its envelope difficult. Her legs felt weak as she crossed the street. Her hands shook when she arrived at the block of apartments above the Café des Artistes. She hesitated for one unsteady moment, then cast the letter that would seal her fate into Jordan's mailbox.

Jewel Hoskins barred Wren's way when she stumbled back into Parkside.

'You're not going anywhere, honey,' she insisted, her black hair bunched up around her bright orange collar. 'You look like someone whose cat just got run over, and your friends are worried sick about your disappearing act.'

Wren allowed herself to be led into Jewel's cubbyhole office tucked out of sight behind the reception desk.

'It's not hard to see something bad has happened to you in the last couple of days.' Pulling open the bottom drawer of her desk, Jewel took out a half-empty bottle of Jack Daniel's and a couple of glasses.

'This is strictly medicinal, you understand,' she muttered, 'for emergencies only. I know you're leaving on Sunday to be with your poor mom, but while you're still on my watch, you're my responsibility.'

She pushed a glass towards Wren. 'I've heard more secrets since working here than most people do in a lifetime. You can tell me anything.'

Wren downed the bourbon, gasping as its heat burned her throat. Jewel had always struck her as a woman who'd seen heartbreak close-up.

'There's this man,' she began.

'There's always a man, honey,' Jewel said, patting her hand.

That night Wren threw off her bedclothes, suddenly feverish. A moment later she was huddled beneath blankets, shivering. It was impossible to rest.

Grief was a monster; if she allowed it to overcome her she would be rendered immobile. For May's sake, it was imperative she stay alert and single-minded. She focused on pushing away every thought about Jordan, yet still found no peace. Her mind kept darting back to Coney Island. There was something Mancini had said, something that bothered her like an itch she wanted to scratch. It came back just as she'd begun to despair. He had lost his son. But why was that significant?

Fragments of past conversations began arranging themselves like a trail of breadcrumbs in a fairy tale. Lily had said Roma was taken to New York by her father. She'd also claimed he had chosen to live an evil life – and she wasn't sure if he was still alive. That would explain why he'd never once tried to see Wren or, for that matter, make any contact. He hadn't abandoned her after all – dead men don't come calling.

Then there was Mancini. If anyone in New York knew about evil, it was him. He'd also told her his son had died – that was why he needed Alessandro to take over his crime network. He had even said how much Wren looked like his granddaughter.

Why hadn't it struck her when she'd seen that photo of Mona in the social pages? With the girl's dark curls and haunting dark eyes, the two of them could be taken for … sisters.

'No!' She sat up abruptly, staring into the dark. It wasn't possible, she must be wrong. And yet … Wren doubled over in an agony of realisation. There was one simple reason why Roma had never come forward. It was because her real name was *Mona*. In the throes of her terrible stroke, Lily had been incapable of making her twisted mouth form the right pronunciation.

Wren snapped on her light. Mona Mancini was her sister. *Her sister.* The news was both horrific and wonderful. At least she would have a chance to reunite Mona with Lily. At least something good might come out of this fraught discovery.

A bitter laugh escaped from her lips. She'd thought that 'family' was the most comforting word in the world. Now it had become a painful, stabbing thing. Her family was headed by a pitiless man with a lifetime of blood on his hands.

Wren shivered. If she'd calculated correctly, Alessandro must be her second cousin once removed – not nearly close enough to rule out a marriage. She could not be sure whether devious Tony Mancini already knew they were related, though she did begin to wonder if this was the real reason he'd been so eager to put opportunities her way. He had never dropped the slightest hint, but then, a talent for duplicity was surely a prerequisite for his line of work.

There were a hundred urgent questions for which she needed answers. For now, though, she'd make sure not to betray her knowledge by so much as a look or a word. Two could play at this game. The person she was to meet tomorrow would remain simply Tony Mancini, Mafia don.

Wren's head drooped with exhaustion. When, finally, she fell into a fitful sleep, she was haunted by her old dream about the big car that had arrived at Woolahderra when she was a child. This time, however, the man who'd come to take her away had the black olive eyes of her grandfather.

PART THREE

Pentimento

The uncovering of a drawing or painting hidden by a later work.
From the Italian, meaning 'repentance'.

CHAPTER FORTY-FOUR

New York, Thursday

Wren stared out of the taxi at the bleak neighbourhood where she'd been instructed to meet Mancini. The Meatpacking District might have been only a short distance west from genteel Gramercy Park, but wherever her eyes rested she saw nothing but danger and desolation. She'd heard from Ava that the disastrous AIDS epidemic sweeping through New York's gay community had led authorities to close down the area's most notorious hardcore nightspots such as the Anvil and the Hellfire Club. But it didn't look as if anything had been done to deter the blank-faced men and women she saw openly buying drugs from dealers lounging beneath broken shop awnings. Nor had anyone put a stop to the skimpily dressed girls with vacant eyes touting for business on every other street corner. No doubt the Mafia was paying officials to look the other way, she thought, her lip curling with disgust.

She tried to imagine what transpired inside the anonymous buildings where the meatpackers worked, but could conjure only the stomach-curdling images for which the artist Chaïm Soutine was famous. He had a penchant for painting butchered steers, their blood and guts spilling from slashed cavities. Wren hugged herself, shuddering.

The taxi driver sped off as soon as he'd dropped her outside a rundown club called the Iron Lady. With her jaw set, she pushed open the graffiti-covered door, determined to reveal nothing to Mancini about the appalling realisation she'd had during the night. That confrontation would occur only once May was safe.

The Iron Lady was tawdry and cold. With its grimy little dance floor and a bar topped with smeared aluminium, it had a threatening atmosphere that made her skin crawl. She could see the Mafia boss sitting by himself at a round table. Wearing casual fawn slacks, a checked shirt and a brown leather jacket, he appeared engrossed in that morning's edition of the *Wall Street Journal*. It struck an incongruous note.

A group of men, inseparable in appearance from the hulking Vito, loitered in the background. Wren watched them watching her as she approached. She'd dressed in dark blue jeans with black boots, a sweater and a leather jacket, hoping not to draw attention to herself. All the same, she wasn't sure if the men were assessing her figure or looking for a concealed weapon – maybe both.

'Nice place,' she said to Mancini by way of greeting.

Mancini looked up. 'This joint is many things, but nice ain't one of them.' He folded his newspaper. 'Sit down, Miss Australia. We got a lot to cover.' Turning around, he growled, 'Bring us some coffee, will you?'

A man with a crooked nose ambled behind the bar and began tackling the silver levers of a hissing espresso machine.

Mancini's manner was business-like. 'First of all, the picture is on its way. Should be here in' – he consulted his gold Rolex – 'I'd say half an hour, give or take.'

Wren's eyes narrowed. 'How did you manage that?'

He smiled sardonically. 'You're getting to be goddamn suspicious.'

Two cups of steaming black coffee were put down in front of them.

'I admit, not everything you told me yesterday was news.' He tipped the contents of a packet of sugar into his cup.

'There isn't a lot that happens in Brooklyn I don't know about. Two days ago, I heard a mysterious carton with FAKE written on the side had been lugged through a Brownsville parking lot and thrown into an Archer's van. That got me thinking, so I called Timothy King. He explained what had gone on and asked if I had any ideas.'

Wren almost dropped her cup. 'I don't believe it,' she said. 'You actually discussed this with King?'

'Yeah, well, he and I might have different styles.' Mancini produced a wheezy chuckle. 'But our views about the way the world works have a lot more in common than you might think.'

Wren's mind turned back to the suitcases of dollar bills Amelia had spirited away from the library.

'Yesterday you let me bare my soul when you already knew the whole story,' she said heatedly. He'd *wanted* her to feel desperate. It had made her more susceptible to his shameless proposal.

Mancini was unperturbed. 'After my chat with your boss, it didn't take me long to discover what the scam was.'

'And?' she said. Her fingers moved restlessly, toying with the packets of sugar heaped on a cracked saucer. The Iron Lady's threatening aura intensified the longer she was in the place.

'Turns out Josephina had previously arranged for an accomplished Italian painter – who may or may not be a professional forger – to make a copy of the picture. Her story is she did it so she would always have something to remind her of the children she'd come to think of as her lost daughters. At the last minute, she couldn't bear to be parted from the original, so she sent Archer's the fake.'

Wren looked at him doubtfully. 'Do you believe her?'

'Maybe I'm sentimental on account of our families' old connections,' he said, 'but it sounds likely.' His face darkened. 'I'd probably act the same way if, God forbid, anything happened to Mona. Anyway, all that matters right now is that once it was pointed out to Josephina that she'd never see a dollar from the real Renoir's sale unless she handed it over pronto, she allowed herself to be persuaded. The picture immediately left Venice with the same man who confronted her.'

'If this man is bringing a picture worth sixteen million dollars to New York, you must trust him a hell of a lot.' Wren's pulse accelerated. 'It's Alessandro, isn't it?'

'Quick on the uptake as always. The boy's looking forward to celebrating your engagement.' Mancini rubbed his hands together. 'There hasn't been time to fill him in on the details of this rescue operation, so he won't be taking part today. But don't you worry.' He winked. 'I'm planning a little party so we can toast the happy couple.'

No way, Wren said to herself. She'd come up with some excuse so she didn't have to front up. The thought of playing Alessandro's blushing bride-to-be made her skin crawl.

'I've got all the pieces in place for the snatch.' Mancini leant forward. 'See, I'm tight with John Gotti. He's the don of dons in this town and a man you don't cross. If you were a New Yorker, you'd know Gotti has headed up the Gambino family ever since he ordered a hit on his old boss, "Big Paulie" Castellano, right in front of Sparks Steak House on East 46th Street.'

Mancini placed his empty cup back on its saucer with surprising delicacy. 'I can recommend the ribs.'

Wren felt bubbles of nausea rise in her throat. 'Go on,' she said, swallowing.

'According to Gotti, a group of young hotheads who used to work for his family have formed their own breakaway crew. These are the guys who kidnapped Rosemary Conroy. Gotti's learnt they want to use the picture to finance a massive drug transaction with some Colombians.

'Now, anyone who deals drugs in this town knows they have to give Gotti a slice.' He shrugged. 'That's just the way it is, unless you fancy living a very short life. But these guys, they're planning on cutting him out.

'Dumb pups,' he growled. 'You remember how I told you what Carmine Persico did to the King of Coney Island. Well, John Gotti makes Persico look like a pussycat. He won't let anyone challenge his authority, nor his absolute right to be paid whatever he wants.

'To keep things simple, my guys have been negotiating with the kidnappers. But it's Gotti who's after vengeance.' He rubbed his chin, frowning.

'Something bothering you?' Wren asked. Each sip of the strong coffee sent a jolt of anxiety through her body.

'He doesn't know who's pulling the strings, which isn't like him. A thing like this, it needs someone smart to put it together, someone who knows his way around and has access to information. He thinks it's outside talent, maybe someone from the old country who's got good contacts here.'

A noise at the door acted on Mancini's hoodlums like a starter's pistol. Three men sprang forward, drawing their guns. Another two leapt into position in front of their boss.

'What the hell?' Wren exclaimed. 'Should we be diving under the table or something?'

'It's all good,' Mancini said, as a thickset man heaved the crate from Venice inside the club. 'The boys know we have a job on. They're jumpy, that's all.'

Wren insisted she examine the picture, saying, 'This time, I'm not leaving anything to chance.'

'Be my guest,' Mancini said. 'And while you're at it, I'll explain the set-up.'

CHAPTER FORTY-FIVE

He'd demanded she hide her hair under a woollen cap, growling, 'The less you look like a girl, the better.' But the hat was hot and itchy. She swatted away the droplets of sweat gathering at the back of her neck.

Two cars had already left, both filled with hard-faced men. Each thug had displayed the telltale bulge of a firearm either at one hip or on the side of his jacket. Some had both.

'We're like the Boy Scouts,' Mancini muttered when he saw Wren's raised eyebrows. '"Be prepared" is my favourite motto.'

She sat next to him in the back of the third vehicle. A thin-lipped man with watchful grey eyes occupied the passenger seat. Presumably there'd been some concern about the black Cadillac attracting unwanted attention during the drive through Brooklyn, for Vito was behind the wheel of a beaten-up Ford. By the time he'd parked the car opposite a deserted back-street tenement block, Wren felt like a coiled spring.

'Okay, Miss Australia, let's take this easy,' Mancini said, turning towards her. 'All you have to do is bring the kid out nice and quick, and make sure she doesn't panic. If the shit does happen to hit the fan, no heroics, all right? Just get the hell out.'

His words triggered a new, oddly welcome surge of adrenaline. Danger was infinitely preferable to despair. She was eager for the rescue to begin.

They gathered at the entrance to the tenement on a sidewalk littered with cigarette butts and empty syringes. A stony-faced man with a chunk missing from his left ear was assigning roles to the others – who should be on guard at the building's rear exit, who was covering the front and who would enter.

'That's Angelo, my *capo*, he's like a second-in-command,' Mancini said. 'A lot of guys call him the Angel of Death.' This was added in a conversational tone. He glanced at Wren. 'You sure you're okay?'

'I'm sure.'

She was okay only because the bizarre scene felt surreal. She'd watched plenty of gangster movies, so both the mean street and the mobsters looked absurdly familiar. Wren could imagine Al Pacino or Robert De Niro walking around the corner at any minute holding scripts in their hands.

'Let's go over this again,' Mancini said. 'Our meeting place is on the second floor. Two of my guys are bringing up the crate. They're going first, because that means it lessens the chance of some trigger-happy kid deciding to make like the Fourth of July. Rocky will be next. Then you and me.'

Wren pulled her cap down a little further. 'All right.'

'This should be just a nice, smooth exchange,' he added. 'Any questions?'

She shook her head.

Yet there was one aspect of the operation that puzzled her. Given what Mancini had disclosed earlier, the formidable Mr Gotti must have something truly alarming planned for the men holding May – which meant the operation was infinitely more hazardous than had been suggested. A feather of fear stroked her spine. Suddenly the venture didn't feel like a movie anymore.

'Right,' Mancini muttered. 'We're on.'

Wren stayed close to his side as they mounted the filthy staircase. The odour of rotting food and urine threatened to derail her, but she steadied herself and kept climbing.

The only sounds were the shuffle of footsteps and the grunts of the men at the front as, step by step, they carried the crate up the narrow space.

Mancini nodded at Rocky once they reached the landing.

'Open up,' the bodyguard barked as he thumped on a scuffed wooden door.

Wren sucked in a sharp breath. She heard the metallic clicks of locks being undone and the rattle of chains. Then the apartment door swung open.

Four hard-eyed men confronted them in a dank room that smelled of beer and stale cigarettes. Wren's eyes flitted towards the guns in their hands.

'Take it easy with those pieces, will you? Nobody's looking for trouble,' Mancini wheezed.

The stairs must have taxed him. His face had an unnatural flush.

'We've brought what you asked for,' he said in a stronger voice, intent on asserting his authority. 'Hand over the girl and we're square.'

The group's leader had a heavy gold chain around his thick neck and introduced himself as Marco Pellini. 'Not so fast, old man,' he said, wiping his nose on the sleeve of his coat. 'After last time, we got someone here who's gonna make sure this picture's legit. You'll have to cool it.'

'Watch your manners, sonny,' Mancini snarled.

With her eyes still fixed on the men's weapons, Wren wondered what sort of art connoisseur would lend their expertise to mobsters. Maybe it was a curator, sick of struggling by on the pittance museums paid, but it still felt like a betrayal.

The crate disappeared with Pellini into an inner room while his men glared at them. As the strained silence stretched, the room felt increasingly close. Wren's chest was tight. Waiting for the expert's verdict, waiting for May to appear, waiting to get the hell out of this alarming situation, was excruciating.

Ten long minutes later Pellini swaggered back, sniffing. 'Our guy has given the picture the okay.' He addressed Mancini with such a shocking lack of deference, Wren suspected he'd dealt with his nerves by snorting cocaine.

'Where's the girl, then?' Mancini's eyes were hard, his arms loose by his sides.

Wren's stomach clenched. Pellini was crazy to antagonise a man like him. She could tell he'd welcome any excuse to draw his weapon.

The younger man sneered. 'Quit bugging me. She's coming out now.'

Wren tensed as she heard scuffling footsteps and the murmur of voices.

'May!' she blurted out.

Wren saw her in fragments, like a Cubist painting. A hand bound in a bloody bandage, a stain on the hem of her skirt, a lock of limp hair and then a pair of blue eyes, their pupils reduced to tiny black pinpricks.

Although Pellini snapped open May's handcuffs, she remained where she was, swaying and uncertain. Wren was sure she'd been drugged.

Moving forward slowly, she took May's unbandaged hand. 'It's your buddy, Wren,' she murmured. 'Everything's going to be okay.'

'Wren?' The name seemed to penetrate May's spell.

'It's me, all right.' She smoothed back May's hair. 'You're going home now.' Putting her arm firmly around the girl, she steered her out of the fetid room without a backward glance.

Tackling the stairs proved far more challenging. May was clumsy and uncoordinated, while the slightest noise rendered her rigid with terror. Beads of sweat formed on Wren's top lip as she half dragged and half carried her down.

They were descending far too slowly, and why hadn't any of Mancini's mobsters joined them? She and May had no protection.

'Only a few more steps,' she said in a voice pitched to soothe her own nerves as much as May's. 'You're doing great.'

Then the stairwell exploded with ear-splitting sound. May froze. With gunfire blasting from above, she grabbed hold of the metal balustrade and wouldn't let go.

'Please, we have to keep moving,' Wren begged, but as the staccato onslaught continued, she couldn't prise May's fingers open.

Suddenly, the two burly men who'd brought up the crate thundered down the stairs. They picked May up as if she were a ragdoll.

Another burst of gunfire made Wren look back quickly. A hand grabbed her shoulder. She whipped her head around, eyes blazing. 'What the fuck are you doing?'

Jordan's face was inches away from her own.

'Mancini told Timothy King what he was up to, but said not to let on to Conroy. He thought Conroy might try to take over, which would totally screw up the rescue. But King has his own priorities – he wants that picture back where it belongs. I guess he figured Mancini hadn't said anything about not talking to someone else, so he told me everything and sent me here to get hold of the painting.'

Jordan frowned. 'I've been worried sick about you. Are you all right?'

'Of course I am,' Wren retorted, shaking him off. She felt angry with him, as if he'd been the one who had written that perverse letter instead of the other way around.

'Listen, one of the gorillas carrying May said that Mancini and his enforcer left by the fire escape. They'll be waiting in a car by now and you're expected to join them. You'd better leave straightaway if you don't want to be left behind.' The dim light in the stairwell had turned his eyes bronze.

'You needn't be concerned about me,' Wren said heatedly.

To get through this ordeal, she'd slammed an iron door shut on her feelings for Jordan, yet now his sheer physical presence was threatening to melt her defences. She had to keep her guard up.

'Seeing as it's obvious I'm fine,' she said, 'I guess now you'll be after the Renoir.'

It had grown eerily quiet.

'You're right, but I still think you should get out of here.' Jordan ran one hand through his hair. 'I'm not sure what's prompted your mobster friend to play the Good Samaritan – it could be an excuse to wipe out Gotti's disloyal renegades so the man owes him big time, or maybe he's working some other angle.'

Wren swallowed. The hideous role she'd been forced to agree to *was* the angle, though thank God it seemed that so far Jordan didn't know about it.

'Whatever deal Mancini might have going on the side, he made it clear to King that as long as Josephina gets her money, he's willing to let Conroy have the picture he paid for. So, yes, I'm here for the Renoir.' He glanced up the stairwell. 'The men with May said it should still be up in the apartment.'

'Damn it, Wren,' he said, suddenly fierce. 'I'm not about to let a beautiful work of art that's survived this long be wrecked, or give John Gotti time to decide he'd like to get hold of it himself. That painting belongs with Mr Conroy, and I'm going to do whatever I can to see that's where it ends up.'

Jordan tilted his head, listening. 'Sounds as if the action is over,' he said, turning back to her. 'I'll try and get closer so I can work out what's happened. You have to go.' His voice was urgent. 'It's likely to be dangerous.'

For an instant she was torn. But May was safe; it was Jordan who needed her now.

Wren lifted her chin. 'I was the one who first heard about *Two Girls*. I went to Venice to view it and I sold it to Mr Conroy – or at least I thought I did. So I'm not letting you fly solo.'

'That's a really bad idea,' Jordan muttered, his expression dark, 'but there's no time to argue.' He jerked his head towards the second floor. 'Come on, then, but for God's sake stay behind me.'

Wren's mind buzzed with a single unasked question – why hadn't Jordan said anything about the letter? She let it go. Only her body, its nerves, taut sinews and burning muscles, mattered. She had to be ready for anything.

They climbed steadily, pausing to listen every few steps.

Wren's breath caught when they reached the landing. There were smears of blood on the floor, and more in the corridor. A splintered window leading to an iron fire escape that zig-zagged down the outside of the building revealed how Gotti's gunmen had entered and, together with Mancini and Rocky, had presumably exited. But where was Pellini and his band of hoodlums?

All was silent. Jordan eased the door to the apartment open, releasing a sickly rust-like odour into the hall. 'Don't follow me,' he warned, but she ignored him.

Wren choked. The tawdry room she'd left twenty minutes earlier had been transformed into a slaughterhouse. Pellini and his confreres lay with their arms and legs splayed and blood pooling around them. One man's face had been torn away. Another had lost most of his right hand. There was more blood spattering the walls and the cheap furniture. It could have been the work of a crazed artist, let loose with a spray can filled with garish red paint.

'There's an inner room,' she whispered, as if the dead were merely sleeping and she was afraid they would wake. 'That's where they took the painting.'

Jordan's face was stern. 'Just this once, will you stay put while I go take a look?'

Wren nodded. She didn't think she could move anyway. Anxious to view anything other than the prone, damaged bodies, she cast her eyes around the room. There was a tattered curtain at the window on her left, empty beer bottles strewn around the floor, full ashtrays on a table, a girlie calendar open at July hanging from a hook on the wall …

Jordan's shout interrupted her inventory.

'I have it!' He appeared with the painting clutched between his hands, his face lit by a smile of triumph.

Red footprints trailed behind him. 'We're leaving,' he said.

Wren heard a metallic click. She looked to her right and saw Pellini pointing a gun straight at Jordan.

'Easy does it, pretty boy.' He grimaced as he pulled himself up onto one elbow. 'You don't think I'm gonna let you walk out of here with sixteen million bucks, do you? If you don't fancy being shot, and your pal after you' – he jerked his head towards Wren – 'just put it down and keep going.'

Wren couldn't feel her pulse race, or the stabbing fear in her gut. She was floating on the ceiling, looking down as another Wren Summers began inching her way along the wall behind the gunman.

Jordan held the Renoir in front of him. 'If you shoot,' he said calmly, 'the bullet will go straight through this painting and kill me. But you'll also ruin the picture, so what will you have gained?'

'Don't give me that!' Pellini had a madness about him, the kind brought about by drugs and desperation. 'Put it down or I swear I'll take you out.'

Jordan kept his eyes fixed on Pellini and his hands on the picture. He began walking forward. Pellini lifted his gun.

There was a crash, then a deafening bang.

Wren screamed. She was surrounded by shards of glass from the beer bottle she'd just smashed against Pellini's head.

Jordan tore over to her. 'Christ, are you okay?'

She nodded, dazed. 'I didn't kill him, did I?'

He glanced at the man. 'Doesn't look like it, but I'm not hanging around to find out. Let's go!'

Wren raced down the stairs with Jordan following. Once they were in the street, she pulled off her cap and let her hair tumble free. Bending over, she put her hands on her knees and took great gulps of air, her lungs straining.

Still grasping the picture, Jordan leant towards her. 'I thought I'd come to rescue you and the painting,' he said softly. 'Turns out you were the one who saved me – and the Renoir.'

In a faint voice Wren gasped, 'I know the man waiting in the beaten-up Ford over there. Tell him to take us to Parkside.'

Dusk was falling when they pulled up in front of the Salvation Army women's residence. Clouds hung low in the sky and the nearby trees cast long shadows over the sidewalk.

'I'll just leave this at reception,' Jordan said. Grabbing the painting, he sprinted inside.

After a couple of minutes he returned, opened Wren's door and helped her climb out. The feeling of his arm around her waist, the touch she'd thought she would never again experience, was like a lifeline to a saner, still beautiful world.

Jewel Hoskins approached. 'I'll look after Miss Summers from here,' she said quickly.

Wren longed to be with Jordan, which was part of the reason she'd insisted on coming back here – Parkside Evangeline was the one place where she had no choice but to keep her distance.

'Goodbye,' she said softly over her shoulder, as Jewel began marching her towards the elevators. It was the last word she would ever say to him. She didn't look back. She couldn't bear it.

By the time Wren stepped inside the lift, she was shaking. May had been saved. Jordan would be on his way to meet Conroy with the picture. But instead of jubilation she felt shrouded in a dark cloak of despair. Jordan would have been too distracted to check his mailbox but very soon now, maybe even tonight, he would read her letter and believe their relationship had been an ugly sham. It was exactly the outcome she'd wanted, yet every part of her recoiled at the thought of it.

A tear trickled down her cheek. At least she would always know that, against the odds, she and Jordan had achieved something worthwhile – and they'd done it together.

The elevator door slid open on the fourth floor. Wren stumbled forward, with Jewel grasping her elbow to stop her from falling.

She used her pass key to let Wren inside, saying, 'Sorry, I forgot to mention the maintenance man is coming by. I've been at him for weeks to fix the heating, and your radiator is last on the list. He won't be long, honey.'

Wren didn't have the heart to tell Jewel to send him away. The woman had provided a welcome shoulder to cry on when Wren needed it most, and with three hundred women living in Parkside, her job was difficult enough.

'Thanks,' she mumbled.

Wren headed for the bath and turned on the taps. As soon as the heating guy left, she'd slide into the tub.

Another tear fell as she sat on the edge of the bed, listening to the water gush. She had to give him his due: Mancini had upheld his side of the bargain in full. Now it was her turn. Sure, she could refuse to marry Alessandro, but the consequences of her defiance were unthinkable.

Wren hung her head. If you made a deal with the devil, there was no escape.

'It's open,' she called when she heard a knock, not bothering to look.

Her head jerked up sharply when she inhaled the scent of spicy green apples. 'No!' she said, shrinking back.

Jordan's habit of turning up unexpectedly was playing havoc with both her nerves and her emotions. Of course she badly wanted him to stay, but the purpose of her letter had been to drive him away. In any case, the maintenance man was about to arrive. Once it was known she had a male visitor in her room, she'd be thrown out of Parkside immediately. Jewel would never forgive her.

Jordan placed the Renoir against a wall and knelt down beside her. 'Your friend at reception had a little chat with me when I brought this inside. She told me there was something precious in your room that needed fixing.'

As Jordan put his arms around her, Wren was filled with an intense, bittersweet joy.

'I took the fire escape,' he murmured. 'After everything you've been through, I thought you might like to spend some time with the picture before it disappears to Conroy's.'

He stood up, lifted the work carefully from the floor and propped it against the seat of a chair so it was within her line of vision.

'Sweetheart,' he said. 'Tonight there is just going to be you, me and Renoir.'

Wren's muscles screamed with fatigue. This was all wrong. She was incapable of giving herself to Jordan, not tonight, when she was drained of energy, when each time she closed her eyes she saw a scene of bloody slaughter.

'It's okay,' he said gently. 'All I want is to stay by you.'

She nodded gratefully. This wasn't the first time Jordan had read her mind.

Wren left him gazing at the painting while she took a pair of soft cotton pyjamas from a drawer in her bureau and shuffled into the bathroom. As she went through the motions of bathing, drying herself and then dressing, she felt a growing sense of unreality. She was so very tired, she thought, as she slid gratefully into bed. It had been a huge day, filled with drama and high emotions. The last thing she remembered was the warmth of Jordan's lips softly kissing her mouth.

She woke with a start in the night. It was dark in her room, but she could not mistake the tall figure asleep on the rug next to her narrow bed. Wearing a T-shirt and boxers, Jordan was stretched out on his side, his thick fair hair rumpled like a boy's. The extra quilt she kept at the top of her wardrobe lay bunched up across his torso.

As she watched his broad chest rise and fall, Wren felt the same sense of peace that the river had always provided. He stirred when she traced one of the hard muscles in his upper arm but didn't wake. Now that her eyes had adjusted to the lack of light, she could make out his strong legs, the line of his hips and the shape of his shoulders. She memorised these things, knowing they must be branded on her memory. A great sadness welled within her as she reflected that this would be the only night they would ever spend together.

Wren left her bed silently. She lay down on the rug next to Jordan and folded her slender body into his. Very gently, she placed her arm around him, so that her hand rested on his heart. Like a sea nymph rocked by the rhythm of the waves, she matched her breathing to his, and slept.

CHAPTER FORTY-SIX

Friday

Sunbeams danced through the gaps at the edges of the drapes as the sound of early morning traffic rumbled faintly from the street below. Wren's eyes fluttered open. With a smile, she realised that, just like the night of the auction, Jordan must have put her to bed. Poor man, she thought, it was becoming a habit.

She glanced towards the floor but couldn't see him. When she tried the bathroom, he wasn't there either. Slowly, she returned to her room. She'd been exhausted and deeply shocked when she'd returned from the horrific scene at the tenement. She must have fallen asleep and had a wonderful dream. Then her eyes drifted back to the rug. The quilt was no longer there, but she could swear she saw the faint impression of Jordan's body.

Wren lay down on the plush surface and tried to fit herself to his phantom shape. Folding the rug tightly around her, she sobbed as she imagined that instead of its rough woollen strands she was wrapped in his tender embrace.

After eating some yoghurt and downing a cup of Russian Caravan Tea, Wren pulled on jeans and a sweatshirt and made her way to reception. It was imperative she speak to Jewel.

Dressed in a startling shade of purple, the woman was bent over the front desk, sorting through paperwork. Wren sidled up to her.

'About last night,' she said in an undertone.

Jewel looked up. 'Oh yeah, sorry about the heating guy cancelling at the last minute.' She pursed her lips. 'It's just typical – no one wants to work overtime these days.'

A fog of doubt misted Wren's memory. Had Jordan spent the night beside her? She wasn't sure any longer, and she didn't want to put Jewel in an awkward position by asking her. The only certainty, she pondered with rising disgust, was that by this evening she would be Mrs Alessandro Baretti. She'd always prided herself that, whatever the situation, she had a plan – usually a back-up as well. For the first time in her life, she couldn't see a way forward. Whenever her mind nudged open a doorway of possibility, it slammed shut.

'By the way.' Jewel pointed behind her. 'There's a note in your pigeonhole.'

Wren took the folded piece of paper reluctantly; it would only inform her of the time her flight for Las Vegas was departing. If yesterday was unspeakable, today would prove infinitely worse. 'Who delivered this?' she said.

'No idea.' Jewel shrugged. 'It was on the desk when I came in this morning.

As Wren scanned the brief message, her face drained of colour.

Mr E.J. Conroy invites Miss Wren Summers to join him today at the Penthouse, 'Farlight', Fifth Avenue, at 11.30 am.

Jewel shot her a look of concern. 'Everything okay, honey?'

Alarm made Wren's stomach churn. 'Right now, it doesn't look as if anything's ever going to be okay again,' she murmured.

There was a smell of rain in the air. The morning's sunshine had vanished, replaced by ashen clouds that remade the city in monochrome. As Wren trudged towards Farlight, a landmark Art Deco block of apartments known to house only the very rich, she pictured herself striding up Fifth Avenue for the first time. How eager she'd been to find Roma, and how keen to make her mark.

Since then, hard lessons had taught her that New York was a far tougher town than she'd ever imagined.

Wren reached Farlight feeling drained and on edge. The uniformed concierge guarding the lavish marble lobby checked her name against a list before directing her to a private elevator, its brass doors decorated with fans of geometric sunrays. She stepped inside, studying herself in the tinted mirror set into the rear of the carriage.

After receiving Conroy's summons, she'd gone tearing back to her room, then rummaged through her wardrobe until she settled on the first outfit she'd bought in New York, the tan Ralph Lauren suit. Teaming it with a cashmere Donna Karan bodysuit and her camel overcoat, she'd told herself these smart American clothes would help shield her from Conroy's damning judgement. Now they seemed like the flimsiest of armour.

It had been some time since she'd worn her gold locket. Rather than provide comfort, lately, whenever she touched the smooth surface, it had only reinforced her sense of impending loss. This morning, however, she'd needed to feel close to Lily. Her fingers automatically reached for it – she could do with some of the luck her mother had promised.

The slow ride to the top of the building gave her time to consider the man she was about to meet. She'd still heard almost nothing about him from Jordan. The occasional comment at Archer's had only confirmed the media mogul's reputation for being reclusive – borne out by the fact that she had never spotted him at a single auction – though there had been no suggestion he was an eccentric in the mould of Howard Hughes.

In addition to a string of newspapers in major American cities, he owned a television network and was also reputed to be a significant investor in many other ventures. She thought she remembered his blurred black and white image appearing in the business section of the *New York Times*, and there had been one or two mentions in *The Post*'s social pages, usually noting his appearance at a private dinner party with other leading New

Yorkers such as Jacqueline Kennedy Onassis or the Metropolitan Museum's aristocratic director, Philippe de Montebello. Described as a widower, if he enjoyed liaisons with women, she'd certainly never seen any mention of them.

With his great wealth and power, Conroy might well turn out to be the pitiless figure Timothy King had described. Of course, he was also May's father, though it was hard to know what conclusions to draw about their relationship. Ava had said their friend had wanted to strike out on her own. But when it mattered most, exchanging the name Rosemary Conroy for May Floris had not provided an escape from her father's long shadow.

Wren was met at the door of the penthouse by a man in a dark suit whose white hair belied an otherwise youthful appearance. 'Do call me Sebastian,' he said in a professionally friendly manner. 'I'm Mr Conroy's personal assistant.'

Sebastian took her coat, then ushered her down a hallway with a parquetry floor and a mesmerising collection of museum-quality paintings on its deep green walls. Wren felt the hairs on the back of her neck rise as she passed a Cézanne still-life replete with crimson and gold apples, followed by a dramatic Picasso nude, then a meltingly beautiful waterlily study by Monet and, finally, a Degas pastel of a woman bathing. Surely, she told herself, anyone who loved art this much had to possess at least some admirable qualities.

Sebastian indicated she should follow him across a large room furnished with contemporary Italian furniture mixed with several striking Art Deco pieces. The huge floor-to-ceiling windows allowed her a brief glimpse of Central Park and, in the distance, Manhattan's jagged western skyline. There was more art on the walls: stunning modernist works including a glowing Rothko and a de Kooning. She longed to pause in front of each treasure, but Sebastian was intent on leading her forward, saying 'Mr Conroy is waiting' in a tone of such urgency he might have been referring to the president of the United States.

Wren gasped when she entered the study. It was a handsome room, lined with books and the framed front pages of various

Conroy newspapers, but what struck her immediately was Renoir's *Two Girls*. She had fallen in love with the work when she'd first seen it hanging in Josephina's rundown palazzo. Here, displayed on a beautifully lit antique easel, it looked magnificent.

Conroy rose from behind his mahogany desk and came towards her. He was a fine-looking man of perhaps forty-six or seven, younger than she'd expected. Although dark-haired, he had the same vivid blue eyes as May.

'So,' he said, shaking her hand. 'This is the famous Wren Summers.' He scrutinised her closely. 'Won't you sit down? Sebastian will bring us tea.'

She'd been so entranced by the picture she'd forgotten her nerves, but now she had to concentrate on calming herself. 'You have a very beautiful art collection,' she said, as she settled uneasily on a brown leather sofa.

'Art is my passion.' Conroy took the chair opposite. He offered no further comment, merely continued his examination.

It certainly wasn't The Look. Conroy seemed bent on ascertaining the kind of person she might be, as if studying her with sufficient intensity would provide the answers to difficult questions.

'On Tuesday I was very angry with you,' he said abruptly. 'Very angry indeed. Then, out of the blue, two days later you organised Rosemary's rescue, something that I, with all my considerable resources, was unable to do.' He paused before speaking again. 'Who are you really, Wren?'

Her mouth was dry. She didn't know what he wanted from her.

Conroy ignored her disquiet. 'As you would understand,' he continued, 'I am determined to protect my daughter from harm, now more than ever. Yet I understand her rescue involved members of two of New York's most infamous Mafia families, and ended' – he pressed his lips together as if trying to control his distaste – 'in a bloodbath. It was also you who auctioned the forged painting,' he said tersely. 'Taking these factors into account, I can't help but wonder if you exploited your friendship with Rosemary in order to stage a despicable hoax.'

Wren felt ill. She could see just how dubious her part in the venture must appear to him.

Conroy gave her a severe look. 'I will be very honest,' he said. 'If you and your associates think you have placed me under some kind of debt to the Mafia so they can now use their influence to force either my newspapers or my television stations to ignore their nefarious activities, then you are very much mistaken.'

His eyes flashed angrily. 'I am deeply grateful my daughter has been returned, but I never sought assistance from the Mob – and never will. I won't be blackmailed because of this, and I will not be instructing my reporters to ignore organised crime.'

Sebastian entered with a tray bearing cups of tea and small biscuits.

'Thank you,' Conroy said curtly as the man left the room.

He turned his attention back to Wren. 'I know Rosemary is very fond of you, and my curator, Dr Grant, seems to hold you in high regard, but that is beside the point. Conspiracy to kidnap is a serious offence,' he said, 'with a long prison sentence. So perhaps you would be kind enough to explain why I should not immediately telephone my friend the police commissioner and have you arrested.'

Wren held herself very still, intent on keeping her nerve. If she were to have any chance of avoiding a disaster even worse than the marriage she was already facing, there was one more risk she had to take.

'I came to know Mr Mancini purely because he was a client of Archer's,' she said, choosing her words with care. 'Although recently, I discovered we are related.'

Conroy's expression darkened.

'It's a very long story, and not relevant to what we're discussing.' Wren steeled herself. 'But I believe Tony Mancini is my grandfather.'

'You realise this hardly helps your position,' Conroy retorted. 'Admitting to being a part of a Mob family only implicates you further.'

'I do see that.' She took a breath, hoping it would help slow her thudding heart. 'But I want to be completely open, so you know I have no intention of misleading you. I haven't shared this information with another soul. I'm not even sure if Mancini knows about our relationship.'

'Go on.'

Wren clasped her hands together. He had to believe her. 'When I learnt that May – I'm sorry, Rosemary – had been kidnapped, I was frantic. Then, after I discovered I had unknowingly sold the forgery that led to her horrible injury, I felt personally responsible. I turned to Mr Mancini in sheer desperation, because he was the only person I knew who had both the underworld connections and the sheer ruthlessness necessary to save her.'

Conroy looked sceptical. 'Why would a major Mob figure carry out such an operation for a girl like you, particularly if he had no idea you were his granddaughter?'

'Because I had a brief relationship with someone who, I now know, Mancini wants to groom to become the next don of his family.' Wren coloured. 'Among other unconscionable undertakings I had to give, consent to marry this man was the price I was forced to pay in order to rescue your daughter.'

She brushed a hand across her eyes, concerned Conroy might see the tears that threatened to fall and suspect she was trying to manipulate him.

'As you know, Mr Mancini kept his side of the bargain.' Pausing, she steeled herself to continue. 'But now it is my turn. He's insisting I fly to Las Vegas today and marry his heir apparent. Let me assure you, I am utterly repelled by his unspeakable demands. But I'm terrified of what Mancini will do to me – or worse, to someone I care for very deeply – if I go back on my word.'

Conroy frowned. 'Thank you for your honesty,' he said. 'It seems that, like Rosemary, you too are a victim of this shocking affair.'

Wren allowed herself to relax a little.

'What you promised to do in order to save my daughter's life represents an immense sacrifice,' he said gravely, 'one that I appreciate from the depths of my heart.

'Indeed, now that you have made me aware of the facts, I wish I could help you.' He cupped his chin in one hand. 'Unfortunately, it would be impossible to bring such a matter to court, and I'm certain appealing to Mancini's better nature would meet with as little success as pressure or threats.'

Wren bowed her head. At least Conroy believed in her innocence. But if even he, with all his vast resources, could not see a way to extinguish her Faustian pact, then there really was no hope. Conroy appeared to be a good man, with a quietness about him that projected an unexpected calm. She wished she could stay longer in this tranquil atmosphere, perhaps even view his wonderful paintings, but time was running out.

An expression of revulsion stole across Wren's face. She had a wedding to pack for.

CHAPTER FORTY-SEVEN

A quick knock at the door made them both turn their heads. May wandered inside, still a little unsteady on her feet.

'Wren! Sebastian told me you were here – I'm so glad you called by. How can I ever thank you enough?' She gave Wren a one-armed hug before turning to her father. 'Daddy, you do realise Wren literally saved my life.'

Wren smiled. 'I was only paying you back for snatching me from the jaws of death on Fifth Avenue.'

'But that was nothing!' May protested with a little hop. Despite everything she'd been through, the sheer fact of her survival seemed to be acting on her like an electrical current.

'New York's best plastic surgeon tidied up my finger last night,' she said, holding up her neatly bandaged hand. 'He actually did a house call. And thanks to his magic medication, it hardly hurts now.'

She paled suddenly. 'Oh Wren,' she said in a small voice. 'I've been so frightened. The gang doped me up as soon as they grabbed me, so I barely knew what was going on, but it was still horrible.' A sob caught in her throat. 'Now I just want to put the whole nightmare behind me.'

'And you will.' As Conroy exchanged a loving look with his daughter, Wren couldn't help feeling a twinge of envy. If only she could have had a relationship like that.

'Before I forget,' he added, 'Sebastian had this repaired for you.' He fetched a small blue box from a drawer in his desk and lifted the lid.

'Oh, it's the chain the men broke.' May slipped it on and fastened the catch.

'You and your truckload of necklaces.' Wren laughed. 'They're one of the first things I noticed about you.' Her fingers reached instinctively for the chain around her own neck.

'I think I might be over my Madonna phase,' May said wistfully.

Wren could see she was flagging.

Conroy, who'd seemed lost in his own thoughts throughout the girls' exchange, looked up suddenly.

'Darling, I'm afraid Wren has to leave soon,' he said. 'Would you mind stepping out? I'd like to have a word with her in private.'

'Sure.' May yawned. 'I'm exhausted, anyway. I think I'll go lie down on one of the sofas.' She let herself out the door.

Conroy leant towards Wren. 'Regrettably, I am still without a solution to your problem. But before you leave, perhaps you would like a brief look at some of my paintings. There are a few I would particularly value your opinion on.'

'I'd love to,' Wren said. 'But I—'

She broke off, swivelling round abruptly at the sound of hurried footsteps. Sebastian was bounding towards them without a sign of his previous aplomb.

'I'm sorry, Mr Conroy,' he started in a rush, 'but Joe — you know, the concierge downstairs – well, he's just phoned to tell me that a huge black Cadillac pulled up outside the building a couple of minutes ago. Then a thickset man in a pin-stripe suit marched into the lobby.'

Sebastian wrung his hands. 'He's demanding to see Miss Summers – and he won't take no for an answer.'

'Oh God,' murmured Wren. 'Did he give a name?

'Well, that's just it.' Sebastian took out a handkerchief and wiped his brow. 'It's Tony Mancini. You know, sir, *that* Tony Mancini. The big-time gangster who runs …'

'Yes, yes, I'm quite aware of who the man is,' Conroy said.

He turned to Wren. 'If it's all right with you, I think we should see him.'

She hesitated for a second or two, then nodded.

Minutes later, Sebastian ushered the fuming visitor into the room.

'Sir, would you care for a cup of Earl Grey?' he asked uneasily.

Mancini glared at him. 'I could do with a whiskey.'

'Thank you, that will be all, Sebastian,' Conroy said, 'though you could remove the teacups.'

He addressed Mancini coolly. 'I suggest you take a seat while I fix us both a drink. Wren, how about you?'

She shook her head.

There was a side table in the room, on which rested a silver tray bearing several crystal glasses, a water jug and a decanter filled with amber liquid. Conroy poured out two generous measures. 'Ice?' he asked.

'Not for me,' Mancini growled.

'Well, then.' He handed the man his drink. 'Perhaps you would be good enough to tell me what you are doing here.'

Mancini sat back and drained his tumbler. 'We are both men of the world,' he began.

'Rather different worlds, wouldn't you say?' Conroy raised an eyebrow.

'Yes and no,' the other man said. 'I called on Wren earlier, down at Gramercy Park, because I had some important news. Then I found out she was at your place.' He gave her a half-smile. 'I had to tell the witch at reception it was a family crisis.'

Wren stared at him, speechless.

'Conroy, I figure Wren might have already filled you in on the deal that led to your daughter's rescue,' he croaked.

'She did,' he said, folding his arms across his chest. 'Naturally, I'm very thankful that Rosemary was released. But the conditions you imposed on this young lady …' He nodded towards Wren. 'Even you must recognise they are indefensible.'

Mancini brought out a cigar and lit up, as if to show how little he cared about Conroy's opinion. 'Well,' he puffed vigorously, 'the deal's off.'

'What do you mean, off?' Wren was as relieved as she was shocked. 'How? Why?' Then the answer came instantly to her mind. 'You found out, didn't you?'

'About Alessandro, yes. But how did you know?' he said, his heavy brows bunching together.

Wren was equally perplexed. 'We seem to be at cross-purposes. I'm talking about you and me.' She took a deep breath. 'How long have you been aware that you are my grandfather?'

Mancini sat bolt upright, his eyes drilling into hers. 'What the hell are you talking about?'

The gaze Wren returned was equally penetrating. 'You said your son had passed away, and there were heaps of other details that lined up. You see, I've been searching for my sister ever since I arrived in the United States. Mum told me my father brought her here to New York – he'd decided to immerse himself in criminal activities. I thought she said my sister was called Roma, only now I realise that I made a mistake. She was trying to say Mona – the same name as your granddaughter.'

Pausing, she tried to steady herself. 'Remember how you said I resembled her? When I thought back to the way Mona looked in her newspaper photo, I knew immediately she was the girl I'd spent months looking for.'

'Let me stop you right there.' Mancini settled back in his chair. 'Mona is my daughter Luciana's child – Rocky's her dad. As for my son,' his voice quavered, 'Roberto died of leukaemia at the age of fifteen.'

So complete was the silence that followed, the only sound Wren could hear was the rasp of Mancini's next breath.

She was appalled by the enormity of her mistake. In an instant, the sister she'd been so sure she had found was lost to her again. As for Mancini, the man might be an out and out thug, but that didn't mean it was okay for her to inflict this sort of pain. Why hadn't she resisted her usual rush to judgement? After all her missteps, she ought to have learnt her lesson.

'Please accept my sincere apologies,' she stammered, twisting her fingers with anguish. 'All I can say in my defence is that I was so desperate to find my missing sister, I put two and two together and came up with five.'

The suspicion of a tear hovered at the corner of one of Mancini's black eyes. 'You know, I would have been proud to call you my granddaughter,' he muttered.

Despite everything, Wren felt touched by his declaration. 'Thank you,' she said. 'But it sounds like we should backtrack. You mentioned something about Alessandro?'

Conroy topped up both tumblers, then gestured to Wren. She asked for a glass of water instead.

Once more, Mancini's drink disappeared swiftly. 'A major disappointment,' he said, shaking his head. 'Everything always came to that boy too easily. Sure, he's got good looks and can lay on the charm, but a lot of what's gone wrong is my fault.'

He sighed. 'I made up for losing my son by indulging Alessandro. As you know, it was me who backed his art business. I even bought him his Roman apartment. But the worst thing I ever did was to try to present him with you on a golden platter.'

Mancini rubbed his shadowed chin. 'There's not much room for a conscience in my line of work. But I regret that.'

'So your idea about me and the gallery …' Wren was so on edge she couldn't finish.

Mancini shrugged. 'It doesn't stack up anymore.'

Wren's face registered successive waves of emotion. Elation because she'd escaped from the Mancini clan's clutches, a terrible sadness over failing her mother, horror because of the disastrous note she'd written to Jordan.

Mancini flicked open his gold cigarette lighter and relit his cigar. 'Alessandro knew he only had to perform well, bide his time and eventually he'd become the family's new don.' He glowered. 'But the boy wouldn't wait.'

'I discovered it was Alessandro who masterminded the kidnap when his tame art expert ratted on him. Surprising what people will reveal when there's a gun pointing at their head,' he mused. 'Seeing as Alessandro knew nothing about Gotti's involvement in Rosemary's rescue, he wasn't prepared for what, ah, eventuated.'

His face flushed with anger. 'That little shit thought he could steal Josephina's painting from under my nose,' he said. 'Turns out, he planned to finance a drug deal that would make him so rich he and his band of tearaways would be able to overthrow me.' A balled fist struck the palm of his other hand with a smack. '*Me!* And after everything I did for him.'

His cigar had gone out again, but this time he didn't bother to relight it. 'So that's it.' He sighed. 'You're free, Wren. End of story.'

'Not quite,' Conroy interjected. 'This Alessandro should be charged with kidnapping. He has to be punished.'

'That's family business,' Mancini's tone was ominous. 'I can guarantee he'll be dealt with.'

'Very well,' Conroy nodded. 'The last thing I want is for my daughter to be dragged through a lurid trial. I'll take you at your word.'

Mancini rose to his feet. 'Thank you, I won't forget this.' He paused. 'As Wren is well aware, I'm a man who always pays his debts. Who knows? One day you might need my help.'

'I very much doubt that,' Conroy said. 'Goodbye, Mr Mancini.'

'Goodbye, Mr Conroy.'

The mobster turned towards Wren. 'See you take care of yourself, Miss Australia.'

CHAPTER FORTY-EIGHT

With Mancini gone, the room felt as if a high-voltage light had been turned off. Wren glanced at Conroy, slumped in his chair with that same faraway look in his eyes she'd noticed earlier.

'I'm afraid I've taken up too much of your time,' she said. 'You must have a great many more important things to do than show me your paintings. But perhaps a future visit could be arranged? It might be a while, though, as I'm going away on Sunday.'

Conroy snapped out of his trance. 'Not at all. I want you to see them,' he said hurriedly. 'Please, do follow me.'

Wren was intrigued. She'd been expecting to retrace her steps to the large room with the remarkable modern artworks, then be shown out via the masterpieces in the hall. Instead, Conroy opened a secret door concealed by wood panelling. 'After you,' he said.

She took no more than a couple of paces inside before stopping abruptly. One hand flew to her mouth. She whirled around and faced Conroy, wide-eyed.

He grasped her elbow. 'Sit down, Wren. I'll fetch your water – unless you'd prefer a shot of that whiskey?'

'No spirits,' she managed to gasp. Bewildered, she sat gazing at each wall in turn. They were hung with three large and two smaller canvases of astonishing beauty. The colours were unexpected, but the style was unmistakable.

Conroy returned with Wren's glass and took the chair next to her. Other than a small table, these were the only pieces of furniture in the stark space. It was dominated by the luminous pictures, their palette the umber, terracotta and burnt sienna hues of Italy, blues that evoked a limitless lake, and deep greens that suggested wooded mountainsides and new life.

'Do you know the artist, Wren?' he said quietly.

Steadier now, Wren stood up and examined the pictures more closely. 'The signature says *Sommerville*.' She turned to Conroy, puzzled.

'Were you expecting a different name?' he asked.

Wren nodded. 'I don't understand. Lily Summers is the only person in the world who could have painted those pictures.'

'What makes you so sure?'

A breeze wafted into the room from a partly opened window. 'Because Lily Summers is my mother. I would know her work anywhere.' She looked at him sharply. 'How did you come by them?'

'Please, sit down again,' Conroy urged. 'Maybe I should get you that whiskey after all.'

'I'd rather hear your answer.' Her dark eyes were wary.

'Lily gave them to me. We were living beside Lake Como.'

Wren stared at him.

'I've been waiting half my life for this moment,' Conroy said gently.

'Who are you?' she said in a fierce whisper.

'I think you know.'

He winced when she slapped him hard on the cheek. 'Say it,' she hissed.

'I am your father.'

Her head sank forward. This was the man whose absence had caused her so much pain. This was the monster who had ruined her mother's life. Yet he was also the partner Lily had never stopped loving. She struggled to order these clashing realities.

They both stood at the same time. Although Conroy's cheek was branded with the shape of Wren's hand, he neither admonished her nor attempted to move closer. He waited, drinking her in with the grateful eyes of a parched wanderer who has at last come upon a life-giving stream of cool water.

Wren's mind cleared. She could see Conroy was giving her space to accept their new relationship. But after all these lost years, and with Lily so near death, what use was anger or blame, let alone maintaining her distance? There had been a great ocean of distance between them for too long already.

She touched her father's hand. 'We need to fetch my sister.'

There was so much to say, so much to explain, that for at least ten minutes after her father's startling announcement hardly any coherent words were exchanged. At last May sank into one of the study chairs, shaking her head. 'Dad, why didn't you ever tell me I had a sister? And my mother – you said she was dead.'

Conroy looked grave. 'Even I don't know exactly why Lily left me and took Wren with her. I tried everything in my power to find them, but now I realise Lily had changed her name. Perhaps that explains why no one could find a trace of her.

'You were so young, May, you didn't have any memories of Wren or your mother. Maybe I was wrong, but under the circumstances I thought it was kinder to leave your sister out of it entirely. Instead, I spun a fairy tale about a beautiful soul and wonderful artist – that much at least was true – who died during childbirth. I hope you can forgive me.'

May nodded. 'I think I understand. You were protecting me weren't you, just like you always do. I'm sad, though, and I'm pretty confused.' She brightened. 'But oh, Wren!'

May struggled to her feet. 'We're sisters. That's the best news ever.' The two girls embraced, tears mingling with their smiles.

Sebastian chose this moment to put his head around the door, only to be promptly despatched to fetch champagne. 'And make sure you pour a glass for yourself,' Conroy called after him. Then he and May began peppering Wren with questions.

'Stop,' she pleaded as the indefatigable Sebastian returned bearing an open bottle of Cristal and three flutes on a tray. 'I know we have a huge amount to catch up on, but I'm fast approaching overload. The events of the past couple of days have been overwhelming – for all of us.' She bit her lip. 'May knows I'm flying to Australia on Sunday. She also knows I need to tell you why.'

May blanched. 'I was so caught up with everything, I didn't think,' she murmured.

'I can see that you're both troubled,' Conroy said. 'But before you fill me in, there's something I need to explain.'

He gestured towards the Renoir. 'Now perhaps you can understand the reason I was so determined to have this painting.' His voice was thick with emotion. 'One blonde girl and one brunette. I thought it was only through this work of art I'd at least have the impression you two were back together again.'

Wren felt a lump in her throat. 'The previous owner, Josephina Hertzberg, also had a blonde and a brunette daughter, but they were both killed by the Nazis in Vienna. That's the reason she found it so hard to part with the painting. I think it would mean a great deal to her if she knew it was her Renoir that reunited us.'

'That poor woman, I don't know how she kept going,' Conroy said. 'I'll write to her myself.'

Wren was perplexed. Her father seemed kind and thoughtful, nothing like the man she had imagined.

'Perhaps now would be the perfect time to mark our good fortune.' He raised his glass. 'To my own *Two Girls*, Varenna and Roma.'

'Varenna?' Wren felt the burn of a memory forged long ago. 'I heard that word when I was a little girl, but I never knew who or what it was.'

'Varenna is the village on the shores of Lake Como where you were born,' Conroy explained. 'Your full name is Varenna Sommerville Conroy.' A darkness passed over his face. 'Not knowing Lily had changed Sommerville to Summers meant that

I didn't recognise your name, but you reminded me so much of—'

'Who?' Wren broke in. 'I don't look anything like Lily.'

'No, but you are very like my late mother, Adriana Floris, a great beauty who came from the north of Italy. The resemblance struck me as soon as I set eyes on you. Then I recognised the chain and locket you were wearing. By the time I heard you say you were searching for your missing sister, I'd begun hoping against hope you were Varenna.'

'Showing me Lily's paintings ...' Wren said slowly. 'That was a test.'

Conroy gave her a bittersweet smile. 'When I saw your reaction, I knew at once you were the daughter I'd lost.'

May looked at her father, frowning. 'How does the name Roma come into it?'

'Like Wren, you were named after the place where you were born,' Conroy said. 'When I took you to New York, your great-aunt Caroline moved in and took care of you. She'd never married, and being somewhat conservative—'

'A major understatement,' May said with a sigh.

'Yes, well, Caroline thought Roma sounded, in her words, "unnecessarily foreign". Rosemary was the closest name she could come up with. As for Wren and May, that's what you each called yourselves when you were little children.' He smiled affectionately. 'And as these things tend to do, they stuck.'

Wren swallowed some champagne. She'd need something to help her get through the far more difficult conversation she was about to have with ... She realised she had no idea how to address her father.

'But what should I call you?' she said. 'E.J. sounds as if we're going into business together. There's always Dad or Papa, but Mum likes me to use Lily. Do you have a preference?'

Conroy laughed. 'It's honestly an unimaginable delight to hear you call me anything at all. The E in E.J. stands for Edward, by the way.'

Edward. It was the first time she had heard her father's name. 'I'll try that,' she said, draining her glass.

A shadow had haunted her ever since he'd revealed his identity. No matter what Edward's feelings for Lily might be, explaining that the mother of his children was close to death was a task she dreaded. As for May, her subdued manner spoke more strongly than words. The awful realisation that the mother she'd never known would very soon pass away was revealed by the uncharacteristic droop of her shoulders and the way her head bowed. It was as if the weight of this new knowledge was too great to be borne.

'Let's go next door and make ourselves comfortable,' Conroy said. 'I haven't forgotten there's something you want to tell me.'

Almost as soon as they entered the sitting room, the rain that had threatened earlier began lashing the windows. Sheets of steel-grey water fell relentlessly, obscuring the world outside.

How was she to say the unsayable, Wren wondered despairingly. She could not meet Edward's eyes.

'You're rather quiet,' he said, studying her. 'What is it that's on your mind?'

Wren brought a shaky hand to her forehead.

May stared forlornly at the rain.

'Will one of you please tell me what's going on?' Conroy raised his voice above the gale. 'I'm not without resources, you know. Whatever it is, I'm sure it can be fixed.'

'Not this.' Wren's face crumpled. 'No one can fix this.' For one terrible moment she trembled violently, as if the storm itself had taken hold of her. 'Edward.' She forced herself on. 'Lily is dying.'

Conroy seemed to collapse in upon himself. A heart-wrenching sound escaped from his mouth like the cry of a mortally wounded animal.

'No, no, no,' he moaned. 'Not Lily. For God's sake, not Lily … not now.' Moving unsteadily, he retreated into his study.

May curled herself up in one corner of the sofa, wailing.

Wren went to her. Rocking the distraught girl gently in her arms, she repeated a silent mantra of love. *My sister, my sister, my sister.*

The rain had been reduced to silvery rivulets when Conroy returned. Although drawn and pale, his expression was resolute.

'You're flying to Australia in two days' time?' he asked Wren as he pulled up an armchair.

She nodded. 'But you need to know one thing more. Before I left Lily, I promised her I would bring Roma back with me. It was her only desire.'

'Please, Dad,' May urged him.

'I'll have Sebastian cancel Wren's flight,' he said without hesitation. 'It will be faster and more comfortable for you both if you take the Conroy Gulfstream.'

Wren blinked. Edward's lavish lifestyle was unimaginably far from the impoverished circumstances in which her mother lived. Perhaps they had always been destined to follow different paths. Maybe chance had merely drawn them together at the point where their journeys intersected. There was still so much she didn't know or understand, but now wasn't the time to delve into her parents' troubled lives.

'Thank you,' she said. 'I know this will mean the world to Lily.'

Conroy regarded her intently. 'I would like to come with you.'

Wren closed her eyes. What would her mother want? She had expressed deep regret about her shattered relationship – surely she shouldn't be denied the chance to reconcile with the man she still loved. And Edward – didn't he, too, deserve the opportunity to make peace with the past?

She nodded slowly. 'Then I think you should tell Sebastian the Gulfstream will be carrying three passengers on Sunday.'

CHAPTER FORTY-NINE

Saturday

'Babe, over here! Come and eat breakfast.' Jo was on her feet, pointing to a seat next to Ava when Wren appeared at Parkside's cafeteria the following day.

Wren waved to the girls. If there was one thing she needed now, it was their friendship.

She knew Jordan must have flown to Massachusetts the day before, as he was due to deliver a long-planned guest lecture at Harvard. After that, he was to spend the night with his parents. But he'd told her only a week ago, before her world was turned upside down, that he would make sure he was back in New York by lunchtime so they could have one last stroll in Central Park before she flew to Australia the next morning.

Wren's eyes dulled with pain. As Jordan must surely have opened her letter by now, he would be certain to stay away. The cruellest irony was that she needn't have written to him at all.

'And she hath risen,' Ava intoned when Wren joined them. 'Kiddo, we've missed you.'

'We heard from May last night,' Jo said brightly. 'I know when we were looking for your sister I said she might turn up in an entirely unexpected way. What I never imagined was that Roma, aka May, would be part of our own little Parkside gang. Talk about hiding in plain sight! I mean, what are the odds?' She gave Wren a searching look. 'You must be thrilled.'

'Stunned is more like it,' Wren said. The joy and the grief that followed yesterday's revelations had been overwhelming.

'And you found your dad, too.'

'I am so sorry, Jo.' She had dreaded this moment. 'I made up the car crash tale when I was little because I couldn't bring myself to admit I didn't have a father. As time went on, I guess I couldn't let the story go.' She looked down, too overcome to meet Jo's gaze. 'Once I'd told you, I was afraid to admit I'd lied.'

'You do know you can tell me anything,' Jo said gently. 'But hey, I get it. We didn't know each other very well back then, and everyone does stuff to get by. It didn't hurt anybody.' She paused. 'Your dad's a pretty big deal, though. What's it been like, meeting him?'

'A lot of things.' Wren watched distractedly as a small child toddled past the basement window. 'I suppose I'm still getting used to it.'

'I hear you were quite the hero during the rescue,' Ava said, changing the subject. 'A real Wonder Woman, according to May.'

Wren dismissed Ava's remark with a shake of her head. 'I'm just glad the whole ghastly mess is over, except …' She looked down. 'It's not really over for me. As far as Archer's is concerned, I'm still a pariah. And along the way' – she struggled to suppress a sob – 'I screwed up big time with Jordan.'

The blueberry muffin she bit into stuck to the roof of her mouth when she tried to swallow. 'I'd tell you about it, but I don't even know where to start,' she said, gulping down some tepid coffee.

'That's okay.' Jo smiled encouragingly. 'Jewel told us you ladies had a heart to heart.'

'When she refused to spill the beans,' Ava continued, 'we threatened to rat her out to the Salvation Army about the bottle of Jack Daniel's she keeps stashed in her bottom drawer.'

Wren sat back in her chair. 'You knew about that?'

Jo chortled. 'Once we heard you'd written that letter to Jordan, we decided you were obviously out of your mind, so—'

'What?' Wren looked at Jo with alarm.

'Well, we did think of stealing it.'

Groaning, Wren rested her chin in her hands. 'Maybe you should have. I was trying to shield Jordan from the Mob, but now he'll think I'm a two-timing bitch.'

'Oh, for heaven's sake,' Jo exclaimed. 'He's stuck by you so far. Just meet him wherever it is you were planning before all this happened, and explain the situation.' She raised her eyebrows. 'Don't you think it's time you started trusting that man?'

At exactly 2.00 pm, Wren was walking briskly up and down the sidewalk outside the 72nd Street entrance to Central Park, scowling each time a man gave her The Look or said something pathetic like, 'Want some company, sugar?'

She was sure she was in the right place, but so far there had been no sign of Jordan. Her chat with the girls this morning had cheered her up so much she'd decided that the two of them would end up laughing about that stupid letter. Wren anticipated Jordan's surprise when she shared the extraordinary revelations of the day before. Smiling to herself, she thought she might even tease him about dating the boss's daughter.

Dear God, she wished he would turn up soon. She needed the special connection they shared, wanted to run her hands down his back and feel his arms around her. She had to be sure that nothing between them had changed, that when she returned from Australia he'd be waiting for her. His kiss, the way he touched her and looked into her eyes, would tell her everything.

Wren shivered. Although she'd dressed warmly in boots, jeans, a grey wool turtleneck sweater and her black leather jacket, she was freezing. When a frigid breeze swirled around her ears, she pulled up the collar of her jacket.

So much had happened since she'd arrived in New York she'd barely been conscious of events outside her own intense little world. A flapping campaign poster attached to a lamppost served as a reminder that the week before the Democrats had once more failed to win the presidency. At least the indignation expressed by Ava had been tempered by reports that Benazir Bhutto was about to become Pakistan's first female prime minister. The only other news she'd caught up with had been provided by Jo, who'd told her Prince Charles had definitely returned to his ex-girlfriend and Diana was having a fling with a cavalry officer. 'It's in all the tabloids,' she'd said blithely. As that painful intrusion seemed to be the price paid for having a public profile, Wren thought, it was little wonder her father was so reclusive.

She stamped her chilled feet on the ground. It must have been fifteen minutes, but Jordan still hadn't come. She waited another fifteen minutes, and then another.

Dread began to twist inside her like a poisonous vine. With her head down, she walked the short distance to Jordan's apartment building and hit his buzzer. A female voice answered, presumably Harriet's, but when Wren asked for him the girl said, 'Sorry, he's out of town.'

Wren felt cold, colder even than the day's weather would warrant; the type of cold that freezes the smallest drop of hope. Jo's assurances had been well meant, but Jo hadn't read that letter.

She had told Jordan not to call and not to write. She had said they could never see each other again. He had unclasped his hand from the fragile cord that tethered them, and let her go.

On Sunday morning, Wren farewelled Jewel with a heartfelt hug, before she walked out of Parkside's front door and slid into the back seat of Edward's chauffeur-driven limousine. He was grim-faced and May unusually quiet.

It was raining again, a steady grey drizzle that left greasy pools on sidewalks and sent plastic spoons and used paper cups sailing down gutters. As she rested her head against the back of the buff leather seat, the throb at her temples kept time with the windscreen wipers' relentless beat.

Last night she'd barely slept. First she'd anguished over Jordan, then she'd turned her troubled thoughts to Lily. By presenting the daughter she knew as Roma, Wren would be fulfilling Lily's dearest wish. But her rash decision to include Edward now weighed on her heavily. How might Lily be affected by his sudden appearance after so many long years? Perhaps she wouldn't care. Perhaps she would care too much. There might be joy, but there might just as easily be devastation.

Wren sighed. Anything could happen at Woolahderra.

CHAPTER FIFTY

Woolahderra

Soothed by the darkness and the purr of the engine, Wren had dozed as the big Mercedes hire car glided through the night on its journey south from Sydney Airport. But as soon as she felt the bumpy, gravel road to Woolahderra, she raised her head with a jolt.

During the long flight on the Gulfstream she had begun worrying about the plans she'd made for her mother. Before she had departed for New York, Elijah and Winnie had promised to keep the shack clean and go up to Sydney from time to time to look in on Lily. For her part, before Wren had left for the US she'd made sure the shack was stocked with basic necessities.

Once she'd booked her ticket back to Australia, she'd written to Winnie telling her when she would arrive. Next, she had rung Dr Carmichael and the social worker at Prince of Wales hospital, to make sure that a nurse would both accompany her mother during the ambulance transfer and stay with her until Wren joined her. After that, a district health worker would visit Lily daily. As for everything else, Wren had assumed she'd do it herself.

She bit her lip. Perhaps that wasn't enough. Maybe now her mother was so sick she needed more expert care. Wren couldn't bear for her to suffer.

Frowning, she tapped Edward on the shoulder. 'I'm concerned I haven't put enough medical help in place for Lily,' she said.

Her face registered her surprise when he calmly detailed the arrangements he'd initiated straight after Wren had left his apartment on Friday. It seemed he had seized on the details she'd provided him with concerning Lily's address and the name of her specialist, for he had immediately instructed his private secretary to organise the appointment of an experienced full-time nurse for her, plus any back-up that was necessary. The same efficient woman had arranged to have soft pillows, the finest cotton sheets and delicate linen nightgowns transported to Woolahderra, and for the kitchen to be filled with farm eggs, fresh bread and a cornucopia of fruit and vegetables.

'Thank you, I'm very grateful,' Wren said.

She knew she should be relieved. Instead, she felt a stab of annoyance.

The commune was eerily quiet. Winnie had written back to Wren, letting her know that Woolahderra's inhabitants would be away at a rock music festival when she arrived, but would return the following week. She'd also told her there was a vacant shack she could use 'in case you have to put up a doctor or something'.

The spare shack was a godsend, being just large enough for the three of them. Once Wren and May had opened their bags and washed in the primitive bathroom, they collapsed onto the frayed futon they'd be sharing.

'I went round to our mum's while you were showering,' Wren said, pausing before she continued. The 'our' had sat awkwardly in her mouth. 'But the nurse told me Lily was asleep. I begged her for a glimpse, though all I could make out in the dim light was a lock of blonde hair and what looked like the shape of a child. It was surreal – as if Lily was there, but at the same time, not there at all.' Wren paused. 'It's hard to explain.'

'I feel kind of weird myself, seeing as tomorrow I'll effectively be meeting my mother for the first time.' A furrow of tension appeared between May's pale brows. 'It's exciting but incredibly depressing and strange, all mixed up together.'

'That's a lot to deal with,' Wren murmured. 'I guess I'm struggling too.' Her thoughts turned to her father. The way he had just stepped in and assumed responsibility for Lily – without consulting her – still rankled.

Incongruously, Edward was wearing gleaming black moccasins with jeans and a T-shirt when he strolled into the girls' room. With his thatch of hair still unbrushed, it appeared to Wren that the E.J. Conroy who lived in a ritzy penthouse and had thousands of people at his beck and call had been exchanged for a different edition of himself. He might have been a successful downtown writer or a cool college professor, though something about the confident way he held his head and the set of his shoulders revealed he was used to exerting authority.

'I'm anxious to see your mother as soon as I can,' he said.

Wren explained that she and May were visiting her in the morning. 'But it could be a good idea for you to hold back for a bit,' she added hesitantly. It was difficult to know how Edward might respond if he thought she was dictating what he could and couldn't do. 'Lily probably shouldn't have too many shocks at once.'

'If that's what you think.'

Wren could see the muscles in her father's jaw tighten.

'I'm going for a stroll before I turn in,' he said.

'Hang on, it's dark and we're surrounded by bush.' She frowned. 'You don't want to lose your bearings in this place.'

But Edward remained unperturbed. 'I don't think I'll have too much trouble.'

Rather like a game of dominos, her thoughts began to seek matching patterns. 'It sounds like you've been to Woolahderra before,' she muttered.

Edward took a step towards her. 'I don't know what you mean.'

Wren's eyes narrowed. 'A man in a big car came here a long time ago. He got into a fight with Lily – and he kept saying "Varenna".'

'From what I can gather, this place is a bit unconventional.

Perhaps he was from the welfare department,' her father said with a shrug. 'What made you believe it was me?'

She pointed an accusatory finger at his feet. 'For a start, because nobody around here wears shiny shoes, like you do.'

After a moment of silence, Edward began chuckling. Then May started giggling and soon Wren, too, found herself infected by their near-hysterical laughter.

Only later, when it was still and her sister was sleeping peacefully beside her, did it occur to Wren that families were not formed in an instant. They would all need time to make sense of the tangle of memories that made up their pasts – and forge ways of being together. But tonight had been a beginning, and for now that would be enough.

She slept soundly, dreamlessly.

After a quick breakfast, she dressed in her usual Woolahderra mode of cut-off shorts, a faded shirt and trainers. May wore a simple white dress and sandals. Wren was struck by how much more vulnerable she appeared since she'd given up the Madonna look and the Doc Martens.

'How about you wait outside for a minute,' Wren said to her when they arrived at Lily's shack. 'I'll go and see how Mum is.'

She put her head inside the door, calling, 'Lily?'

A stocky middle-aged woman wearing a white uniform with an upside-down pocket-watch pinned on the front bustled forward. 'Hello there,' she said cheerfully. 'I didn't have time to introduce myself properly last night. I'm Jane, Jane Trundle. Lily has been so looking forward to seeing you.'

Jane glanced over her shoulder. 'You know where to find her – I'll stay here in the front room with these lovely paintings.' She gestured towards two works Wren remembered, glorious studies of turquoise seas beneath a pale duck-egg-blue sky.

'Just one thing, dear,' she cautioned. 'The cancer is very advanced now, so the doctors have asked me to keep her comfortable with morphine. I just felt you should know.'

As Wren entered her mother's domain, she steeled herself for the sour smell of the sick room and for Lily herself to be unrecognisable. Yet the woman she saw reminded her of a heroine from a pre-Raphaelite painting. Although painfully thin, she was still very beautiful. Her ivory skin was smooth and her long fair hair lay over the snowy pillow in silken strands. Only Lily's glazed eyes and the blue shadows beneath them revealed the extent of her illness.

Fresh eucalyptus-scented air wafted in through an open window, sweetened by the white roses that stood in a vase on a small table. Wren sat down beside her.

'Hi, Lily,' she said softly, reaching for her mother's hand. 'It's so, so good to see you.' She could have been holding a small bird with tiny, fragile bones.

The fine skin covering Lily's wasted cheeks stretched tight as she attempted to smile.

'And I did it,' Wren said, ignoring the sudden constriction in her throat. 'I can hardly believe it myself, but due to the most unlikely circumstances' – she took a quick breath – 'I found Roma. I've brought her back with me.'

Lily's eyes opened wide, their sea-green depths revealing all the gratitude and joy she was unable to express.

Wren felt a heady sense of euphoria. At last, her mother might be released from a lifetime of torment. 'Would you like to see her now?'

The blue vein traversing Lily's pale forehead throbbed as she lifted her head.

Wren went to find May, then led her into the bedroom.

Lily gazed at her lost child with an expression of wonder. She stretched out one arm, fine as a river reed, softly touching May's cheek with her fingertips, as she forced her mouth to form the word that she wanted.

'Roma,' she whispered, followed by a low moan. She sank back onto her pillows, drained by the effort.

Tears welled in May's eyes. 'Shall I tell you about myself?'

Lily nodded.

'I grew up in New York,' she began. 'Dad always told me you looked like an angel, and how much he loved you. He has five of your paintings in a special room – I always knew when he was thinking about you because he'd take himself off there sometimes and sit looking at them for hours. I used to stare at them too – they made me feel loved somehow, and connected to you.'

She took a deep breath. 'Dad says I look like you. I hope I do.'

Lily fluttered her eyelashes.

'Yes, the eyes are different. Mine are blue, like his. Now, where was I? Oh yes, I went to the Chapin School in Manhattan until …'

Wren slipped out quietly. Poor May was trying to convey a lifetime of experiences and emotions by sharing tiny scraps of information.

She thanked Jane for the mug of tea she had made and sipped it while she sat on the front step. A cloud of melancholy had settled over her.

'Lily's exhausted,' May said when she reappeared. 'I could see her eyelids start to close as I was speaking. Eventually, she just drifted off.'

'Is she what you expected?' Wren asked.

May considered the question. 'In a way, yes.'

Wren made room for her on the step.

'You see, I came to know Lily through Dad,' May said, gazing at a tangled thicket of purple lantana that had sprung up by the path. 'He used to talk about her and show me lots of photographs – and there were her wonderful pictures, of course.'

She turned towards Wren. 'I am incredibly grateful to have met my mother, but now I realise that because of him, I've always sensed her presence. That's enough for me.'

Wren wondered what sort of person she would be if she'd had her sister's experience. Because of Lily's long silence, she'd felt only absence. Her father had been no more than an empty space, a ghost without either a name or a face.

'What's weird,' May continued, 'is that although Dad's had tons of women after him, you only had to see the expression on his face when he looked at one of Lily's pictures to know she was his one true love. I just can't figure out what went wrong between them.'

Wren sighed. 'I've been asking myself the same thing all my life.'

Edward looked up from the sofa as soon as they returned to their shack. 'How is your mother?' he asked anxiously, while folding the newspaper he'd been reading.

'Lily's beautiful, Dad, just like you told me,' May said. 'But she's so frail.' She brushed her damp eyes with the back of her hand.

'I could tell how much seeing you meant to her.' Wren gave May a hug before turning to Edward. 'How are you doing?'

'Oh, you know,' he said, 'trying to keep myself occupied. I rented a Jeep and I made a few calls from the payphone on the main road. My staff know I will be incommunicado for the next week or so, but I'll ring in to the office every couple of days.'

He flung the paper away. 'Wren, when can I see her?' he pleaded.

His longing made her heart ache. 'Jane said to wait at least an hour – the morphine is making her pretty drowsy. Let's have a sandwich or something, and then we'll go around.'

'I don't want to distress Lily,' he said, sounding on edge. 'But being so close and not seeing her … it's unbearable.'

'I'm sure she'll be fine.' Wren arranged her mouth into a reassuring smile.

CHAPTER FIFTY-ONE

In the short time since she'd left her mother, the shadows beneath Lily's eyes had become the mauve of faint bruises and each breath was a sigh. These reunions had come far too late. Wren felt caught in a spiral of despair so intense that the room swam in and out of focus.

'There's someone else who would like to spend time with you,' she said, clutching the back of a worn blue armchair. 'You haven't seen him for a long time.'

Lily stared at her with burning eyes.

Wren's throat was dry. She would never forgive herself if she was about to bring her mother pain instead of balm.

She found Edward walking up and down the dusty path outside the shack.

'What do you think?' he asked.

Wren felt every bit as strained as her father sounded. 'It might be an idea if I hang about in the doorway for a minute,' she said, hoping she sounded more positive than she felt. 'Other than that – she's all yours.'

Edward hurried into the shack with the light tread of an ardent boy. Not until he reached Lily's room did he slow, approaching her cautiously as if not quite certain he wasn't dreaming.

Lily was spellbound. She had a bloom on her parchment-white cheeks that had not been present a few minutes earlier. Edward sat by her, a dazed expression on his face. 'My darling Lily.' His voice broke when he uttered her name.

Her lips trembled as once more she struggled to speak. 'Edward,' she murmured at last. He put his arms gently around her. She rested her head on his shoulder.

It seemed to Wren the disease that had ravaged her mother had also bestowed a blessing. The past painful decades had vanished. Lily and Edward were sweethearts once more. They had escaped time.

During the days that followed, the sisters rarely left Woolahderra. Wren showed May how to read the currents and eddies of the slow-moving river, where to find tiny orchids in rocky crevasses, and the best time to spot brushtail possums and sugar gliders. One morning she drove May into Nowra to buy freshly baked bread, passing fields dotted with brown and white cows that lifted their great heads as the Jeep sped by. The girls also took turns visiting their mother, although mostly they left Edward and Lily alone. Both sensed that their parents' need was greater than their own.

On the third night Wren asked Edward if she could have a chat to him while May sat with Lily. 'Mum and I used to talk on the front step,' she said. 'If it's all right, we could do that. I'd love to know how you two met and why you went to Italy.'

Edward gave her a smile of such wistfulness that it wrenched Wren's heart. 'I'd like that.'

It was a cool night, with a breeze that rustled the dry leaves on the trees. After they'd settled themselves on the worn wooden plank, Edward told Wren how he'd rescued her mother when she'd been pushed over at a free speech demonstration in the grounds of Berkeley University.

'I have to admit, I welcomed the chance to play Sir Galahad,' he said. 'There wasn't a guy on campus who didn't want to be with Lily Sommerville, but even though she was a passionate believer in all kinds of freedom, she wouldn't go with any of them.' His expression became bashful. 'Until she met me.'

Wren hid her surprise. This chaste paragon of virtue wasn't the Lily she knew. 'And Italy?'

Edward looked into the darkness with an unfocused gaze. 'Believe it or not, I was in trouble with the law,' he said. 'We were both very caught up in the politics of the day, fervent about civil rights and fiercely opposed to the Vietnam War. I burnt my draft card and was arrested, but there was no way I was either going to fight for Uncle Sam or find myself in a jail cell.'

So her father had been a student radical, Wren thought. How much had changed.

'You see, I adored Lily. There was never a chance I would leave her.' His voice had a new, mournful quality.

'Luckily, I had a small legacy from my late mother, Adriana. I'd grown up speaking her language, and Lily and I were both enamoured of art. Italy seemed like the perfect escape.'

Edward's face had acquired a new animation.

'We settled in Varenna because the village was near the big villa where your grandmother spent her childhood. She'd always told me what a special place it was. Once we arrived, I discovered Lily was pregnant – with you.'

He smiled. 'I was thrilled. And for a time, we could not have been happier.'

The loving way Edward spoke about Lily made Wren recall the devoted old couple she had seen in Gramercy Park. Her parents should have been like them. They should have had years and years together. An ache grew inside her, made worse when her thoughts turned to Jordan.

'I wrote an unpromising novel while Lily painted, and of course we had you, our darling baby girl, to take care of. After a while, though, your mother became strangely restless. That was when we went to Rome.'

Edward chuckled quietly. 'It turned out she was pregnant again. I was able to top up my tiny income by writing the odd piece for an Italian newspaper, and as you can imagine, we immersed ourselves in Rome's artistic treasures.'

He gave Wren a fond look. 'We used to take you to the museums and galleries, places like the Pantheon and the Vatican too. Even though you were so young, you seemed to love it, waving your tiny hands around while you pointed at pictures. It made us laugh.'

Wren's thoughts flew back to Italy. No wonder she'd felt so at home. What she'd mistaken for traveller's déjà vu had been the stirring of long-buried memories.

'But Lily grew tired of living in the city, so, after your little sister arrived, we returned to what I thought was our idyllic life in Varenna.' Edward's head sank into his hands. 'It was less than three months before everything we shared lay in ruins.'

On the fourth night both girls joined their father at Lily's shack while Jane kept watch over her patient. A final chorus from a flock of nesting honeyeaters rang out as the dusky night sky closed around the three of them.

'Well, we're obviously not all going to fit on the step,' Wren said, stretching her arms above her head. 'May and I have pulled out some chairs so we can sit under the stars. I'll light the hurricane lamps, and there are blankets inside if we need them.'

Wren had been tense for hours, worried that the question May had insisted she ask Edward would only add to his burdens, yet at the same time desperate to know the answer.

May spoke up as soon as they were settled. 'Dad, there's no easy way of putting this so I'll come straight out with it. We've seen how you and Lily are together – it's beautiful. Which makes it even harder for us to understand why you guys ever parted.'

'I never understood it myself, not really,' Edward said, rubbing his forehead as if trying to expunge the pain of memory. 'Until this morning.'

It struck Wren that he'd been particularly withdrawn all day.

'There's something I need from the other shack,' he said, getting up suddenly.

May gave Wren a puzzled look when, a few minutes later, he reappeared with a carved wooden box.

'I'm sorry to be so mysterious.' He frowned. 'I'll explain. When I was with your mother earlier today, she kept looking towards her wardrobe so intently I was sure she was willing me to open it. I kept bringing out various bits and pieces, but received no reaction. That is,' he said, 'not until I discovered this box hidden away under a pile of scarves and straw hats. Lily nodded when I showed it to her, so I knew it was what she wanted.'

Wren inhaled sharply. 'I've never seen it before, but then, I always knew better than to delve into Lily's personal stuff.' She smiled to herself, remembering. 'I would only have tried to tidy up, and Mum preferred chaos.'

May broke in. 'What happened next?'

Edward's face was grave. 'I put the box down on the bedside table and opened it. At the top was yet one more scarf.' He paused for a moment, as if ordering his thoughts. 'Underneath, I found the silver ring I'd given Lily when you were born, Wren. It was sitting on top of this sheaf of paper.'

The sisters stared as he unfastened the box's lid, reached inside and brought out a stack of pages.

'Girls, it seems that Lily wrote about our life together, I'm not sure where or when. I suppose she hoped that when she was no longer alive' – he cleared his throat – 'at least one of you would know the truth about your parents.'

'Please stop, just for a moment.' Wren held up her hand. 'I'll be back in a second.'

She returned bearing cups and a thermos filled with hot sweet tea, poured them each a cupful, then gulped her own down. Ignoring the flame in her throat, she helped herself to another, and waited.

CHAPTER FIFTY-TWO

'It's best if you read Lily's account yourselves,' Edward said. 'There's quite a bit to take in. For now, I'll just tell you what happened at the end – at least, as I understood it at the time.'

May smiled encouragingly. Wren braced herself for whatever was to come.

'The disaster – for that's what it was – took place not long after I'd finally revealed the true identity of my father to Lily. To say she was appalled is an understatement. James Conroy was the one man in the world she loathed above all others. You see, he wasn't just a big-time capitalist – which Lily didn't approve of anyway – but a hard right-winger, a warmonger really. Dad hoped I'd return to the States and join him working in his media empire.'

Realising he was still holding the pile of handwritten paper, Edward placed it carefully by his feet. 'I felt bad,' he continued, 'because he'd had a recent heart attack and I'd run off with Lily so soon after Mum died.

'I guess I also thought that, despite all our ideals, your mother and I weren't really achieving much, tucked away in our little village.' He shrugged. 'So, for a while there, I was tempted.

'Lily wouldn't hear of it. As she was so upset, I told her we'd stay just as we were. To be honest, though, she hadn't been happy for months, and she wasn't exactly taking care of herself. I couldn't work out what was wrong with her.'

He took a sip from his cup. 'Then my father arrived for a short stay. It was easy to see he wasn't pleased with my decision, but all the same, he appeared to accept it with more good grace than I'd expected. Once he'd been with us for a few days, it seemed we were getting on better than we ever had. I was actually sorry he was flying back to New York so soon.

'Lily was rather quiet but, as I said, she'd been moody for a while. I thought it would pass.'

Edward sighed heavily. 'So there I was, young and ignorant. No doubt I was too self-involved. But you see' — he stared into the night — 'I didn't know then that a terrible depression could follow the birth of a baby. I didn't understand the demons that were plaguing Lily.'

A lone bird began warbling, ending with a single mournful cry.

'Anyway, out of the blue, I was contacted by an editor who said he had an important story for me to write, but it meant setting out for Rome the following day. Lily got all worked up. She didn't want me to go because I'd be away overnight and that meant her being stuck with Dad, who she obviously didn't like. But the assignment sounded too good to pass up and promised a hefty fee. I left first thing the next morning.'

Edward's face was a mask of despair. 'When I returned, Lily had gone — and taken my darling Varenna with her.' He buried his face in his hands. 'All I found was a note saying I'd find little Roma with our next-door neighbour.'

Wren touched his shoulder. 'Reliving this must be terrible. Do you want to leave the rest for another time?'

He shook his head. 'I don't think I could bear it.'

After a deep breath he continued. 'As I said, Lily had been troubled for some time. I imagined she'd had a catastrophic breakdown, that she must have thought I'd lied about staying put with her in Italy and this false belief had tipped her into madness. I fell to pieces myself, but my father was magnificent.

'Dad immediately took charge, activating an intensive search, first in Italy and then abroad. He alone dealt with the local police,

Interpol and the private detective agency he'd engaged. The man was tireless, which was remarkable when you consider his failing health. It was the first time in my life I believed my father truly loved me.'

Edward refilled his cup. 'Despite all his efforts, nothing useful ever turned up. It was as if Lily and Varenna had disappeared from the face of the earth.

'I could barely function for six months. If I hadn't had you,' he said, reaching for May's hand, 'I hate to think what I would have done. Eventually, I went back to New York and buried myself in the business. After everything Dad had done for me, I felt I owed it to him. When he died two years later, I took over.

'I blamed myself for his death, just as I blamed myself for losing Lily and my eldest child. I renewed the search, keeping at it for a long time,' he said forlornly, 'but my attempts were just as fruitless as my father's. There were more dark days and nights than I care to admit, but I managed to go on, living a fairly solitary existence. I threw myself into shaping the company into a news organisation I could be proud of, one that was principled and fair, but only my precious youngest child brought me joy – and the paintings I collected. I suppose I acquired a kind of equilibrium, though I never really recovered.'

A chill wind had sprung up, making the gums creak and sway.

'Then one day,' Edward said, with a poignant smile, 'a girl called Wren Summers walked into my life.'

May went inside and brought out blankets. Wren didn't know what to do. Her delicate mother may have been suffering from post-natal depression, she could well have been drinking to excess or smoking too much dope. But the woman Wren knew would never have willingly deserted the love of her life and her treasured baby.

Lily had spoken of circumstances beyond their control. She'd revealed she had been forced to make a terrible choice. There had to be more to the story.

'Edward,' Wren said softly. 'What happened while you were in Rome?'

'In order to know that,' he said, drawing several pages from the pile next to him, 'we need to hear from your mother.'

As Edward recounted Lily's story, Woolahderra's rickety huts and grey-green eucalypts faded. Wren had the impression that she'd entered a more painterly world, one where a fair-haired girl and a blue-eyed boy lived with their children in a lemon-coloured house by a sapphire lake in Italy.

CHAPTER FIFTY-THREE

Varenna, October 1968

Once the boy left that morning, the old man wasted no time. It was quite simple. He wanted his son back. The girl was the problem. He claimed she'd ensnared his son, turned his head with a swish of her fair hair, and her talk about freedom and love, so he couldn't think straight.

He shouted at her, said she was unstable, irrational, mad. She was an anti-capitalist bitch, a hippie dropout who'd turned her back on the best goddamn country in the world. He said she wasn't fit to raise his grandchildren.

'You are an alcoholic and an addict,' he said to her coldly.

'No!' she protested, even though, to her shame, she had a glass of grappa in her hand.

'I will be believed, not you,' he sneered. 'On the basis of what I have seen, I can easily have you medically certified. You will be sent back to the States and incarcerated in a mental asylum. My tame lawyers and medicos – even the odd judge, if necessary – will make sure you're committed for the rest of your life.'

He continued to taunt her. 'Once the doctors have finished with their shock therapy, you won't have a will of your own. And you won't see your children again – they'll be told it's for their own safety.'

She fell to her feet, sobbing. 'Edward would never allow it,' she said. 'He'll stop you.'

'You don't know Edward like I do.' The old man loomed over her. 'He wants what I want. You think his real identity – and mine – are the only things he's kept from you? Your life together has been a lie.'

'But he loves me and I love him,' she said desperately.

The old man's voice was heavy with scorn. 'He's sick to death of you whining, stopping him from fulfilling his destiny. This trip to Rome? He's not seeing an editor. He asked me to clean up his mess.'

The fair-haired girl knew when she met him that the old man hated her. She'd seen it etched in his eyes. That's why she'd started drinking even more than usual. Barely able to look after her children, she was helpless to do battle against someone so powerful.

He told her she was useless. Bad for Edward, and bad for her little ones. Again and again he repeated his accusations, and his threat – that he'd make certain she spent the rest of her days in an asylum. And always, he added it was what Edward wanted.

She felt the darkness descending, the darkness she dreaded.

'Why do you imagine, ill as I am, that I came to this shitty place?' he demanded.

The girl thought she would faint.

'Because Edward told me you were insane. He begged me to get rid of you.'

Insane. The boy had used the same word when he'd accused her of sabotaging his future. Her fragile heart splintered as realisation struck like a brutal blow to the chest – the old man was telling the truth. Everything he had threatened her with had been said at Edward's behest.

'Please, don't do this,' she cried. 'Don't send me to an asylum.'

The old man paused. 'I am not hard-hearted,' he said, assuming a new, more reasonable tone. 'Perhaps there is another way. If you leave this house before Edward returns I'll persuade him to drop the idea of having you committed. You could simply … disappear.'

He made it so easy. Told her how to change her name, said there would be enough money, that he had people who'd already found a place where she could hide away.

'But I can't leave my daughters,' she said, doubling over as tears streamed down her cheeks.

The old man understood when to appear magnanimous. He'd sealed his harshest deals in just the same way.

'You may choose a child,' he said. 'I can't be fairer than that.'

She knew then that she'd been sentenced to a lifetime of torture. How could a mother choose one child to take, another to abandon forever? This was agony. The cry that erupted from the depths of her being was that of a beast, wild and tormented, caught in a vicious trap.

'Well?' the old man demanded.

What should she say? What should she do? Hanging her head, she whispered, 'Varenna.' It would be so much easier for the tiny infant to forget her than for her sister to do so. But even as the name left her lips she screamed, 'No! I cannot lose my baby. I will die of sorrow.'

The old man ignored her. 'The older girl, you say? Very well.' He shrugged. 'You've probably ruined her by now, anyway. But remember, I won't tolerate trouble. If you ever try to leave your new home or contact Edward and Roma – well, Varenna will be back with her father in no time.'

The fair-haired girl raised her horrified face. She saw only blackness. Her life had ended.

'Don't think I will hesitate,' the old man warned. 'One day, when you least expect it, I'll send a man to make sure you and Varenna are still hidden. If you step out of line in any way, she'll be taken away immediately.'

The girl was broken. Only the boy's pure, sweet love had protected her from the deepest shadows. But that love was now shrivelled and blighted. Grief-stricken, she acted exactly as the old man had forced her to do. She'd known all along there was no alternative, yet each breath that she took brought with it a choke of guilt, crushing her will and her spirit.

Thank God she had one child. This small scrap of life, so intense and so vibrant, would keep her alive. In return, she would protect her from ever knowing the agony inflicted by men. They were not to be trusted, she would instruct her again and again.

Months passed, months of tears. Then years filled with nightmares and dreams. Two missing souls haunted her, two elusive beings she would glimpse in the clouds or the first stars of the evening. They were present in every line and brushstroke of her paintings, in each glowing colour she applied.

That was how she knew that her love for the blue-eyed boy and her lost babe was as infinite as it was for the child she had saved. No matter what befell her, this love would endure, always.

CHAPTER FIFTY-FOUR

Woolahderra

Wren lay awake for a long time that night as she reflected upon her parents' tragic story. Edward had been badly shaken. He was still gripping the pages he'd read from, his hands trembling as he'd said he now believed it was his father who'd set up the meeting in Rome, using his publishing contacts to get his son out of the way. As for the man's seemingly selfless search for Lily — it had been nothing but a meticulously orchestrated sham.

A tear trickled down Wren's cheek. The knowledge that Lily and Edward had lived a blighted life far apart from each other, both believing the falsehoods they had been told by a sick and unscrupulous man, was heartbreaking. Thank God they finally knew the truth — and so did she.

At last she understood why she'd grown up on the commune, and how a terrible burden had scarred Lily's life. It had scarred her life too, making her desperate to prove her worth again and again. Little wonder she'd been brought up by Lily to be suspicious and wary of men. Little wonder it had led her to destroy everything she had shared with Jordan.

His loss was scalding. She had to find a way back to him, but here in this remote place on the other side of the world with Lily so close to death, she was helpless.

Her mind wouldn't still; it held too many searing images of

sorrow. When finally she fell asleep, she dreamt she was locked in a burning house by a fiery red lake in Italy.

On the fifth night, Wren told Edward she'd like a private word with him.

'Back on the step?' He smiled.

'Afraid so.'

With the weather far warmer, cicadas kept up a constant reverberation.

'I need your advice,' Wren said, her voice faltering. 'I am deeply in love – I know you understand what that's like. But everything has gone horribly wrong because of something I did.'

Edward raised an eyebrow. 'I'm very sorry to hear that, but I doubt I can be of much use. As you know, my experience in that domain …' He held out his hands, defeated.

Wren tucked a strand of hair behind her ear. 'You understand loss better than anyone. You also happen to be familiar with the man in question.' She paused. 'It's Jordan Grant.'

'So, you two are in a relationship?' Edward gave her that intent look she'd begun to recognise. 'Well, Jordan is an exceptional young man, but I'm sure you know that already.'

He clasped his hands together. 'I have no idea what's gone on between you, and I don't wish to pry. But I do know that a great love might only come your way once in a lifetime. Don't give up on it too easily.'

On the sixth night, Lily shook her head when Wren and May attempted to leave. They stayed with her until late, talking quietly as she drifted in and out of consciousness, before finally returning to their bed.

Jane woke them just as the first diffident streaks of light appeared in the sky. 'It won't be much longer,' she said. 'Best you go to her now.'

When they arrived a grim-faced Edward was sitting by Lily, holding her hand. May and Wren arranged themselves on the other side of the bed. Silent and motionless, they might have been painted figures from a medieval altarpiece.

Their vigil continued as the pink iridescence of sunrise gradually filled the room.

Wren could see the cool white sheet that lay across Lily's frail body move almost imperceptibly as she took each shallow breath. Then, as the rosy light gave way to a pale blue sky, her mother's eyes flickered open. Two words floated from her mouth, so softly they could have been carried by a breeze from a distant lake. '*Ti amo*,' she whispered.

'I love you, Lily,' Edward murmured, his words a sweet lament. 'I will always love you.'

Lily's eyes closed. Her breaths were no more than a gentle shudder. Then the pause between each breath became greater and greater until the moment arrived when the cool white sheet moved no longer.

May bowed her head.

Edward wept.

Wren felt the air shift. It was as if the downy wings of a bird had fluttered past on the way to a destination far beyond the riverbank.

times since her childhood, but their long hair, beads, embroidered dresses and tie-dyed T-shirts still looked exactly the same.

'It's so retro,' May whispered.

Wren rolled her eyes. 'Please tell me that's not going to be your next style.'

Her face lit up when the now aged Mr Madden, her sixth-class teacher, limped up to her. 'You have soared high, just as I expected,' he said proudly, before turning to pay his respects to Edward and May. When his place was taken by Miss Reiter, Wren's State Library mentor, she clasped the white-haired woman's hand warmly. Sydney to Woolahderra was a long way for an elderly lady to travel.

'I'm glad you were able to move on from that business at the Art Museum,' Miss Reiter said in her Viennese accent. 'Cath told me about the odious Tremaine and what he tried to do to you.' She lowered her voice. 'Did you know that awful man has been shown the door?'

'No.' Wren hands had become clammy at the mention of his name.

'Apparently, he attempted the same thing with a woman he assumed was a secretary from the Department of the Arts.' Miss Reiter's eyes danced. 'The fool had misread his diary. It turned out she was the new departmental secretary – as in, the permanent head!'

Her lined face bore an arch expression. 'I believe one would categorise his downfall under "k", for karma.'

'I always admired your talent for classification,' Wren said wryly.

She had a sour taste in her mouth. Tremaine deserved a graver penalty than mere dismissal. It might temporarily inhibit him from attacking other women, although she doubted a man who felt as entitled as he did would ever desist, unless he was publicly called out and charged with a crime. Given the way the current system was loaded against women, that was unlikely to happen. Wren ground her teeth. She knew that from first-hand experience.

Reporting Tremaine's disgrace to Timothy King wasn't likely to help her, either. She'd always had the feeling King had only half believed the slurs Tremaine and, no doubt Alessandro, had fed Amelia. Her real problem remained the notoriety that came with being the first person in Archer's long history to sell a fake picture. How would she ever live that down?

She was pondering this dispiriting question when her eyes widened with pleasure. Bobby Hawkins, of all people, was sidling up to her.

She had to restrain herself from hugging the dear man, conscious that simply venturing forth into the alarmingly foreign world of the countryside would have presented him with more than enough challenges. When he shyly confessed how much he'd missed her, she had to look away so she didn't cry.

'Wren.' Edward frowned as he consulted his slim gold watch. 'We're already half an hour late. It's time to begin.'

She nodded sadly. She'd known this moment would come, had known for months, yet now Lily's burial was upon her, she felt hollowed out and broken.

The mourners moved into position. The baker called for quiet. Father Shane cleared his throat. The crowd stilled, yet when Wren turned towards the piping sound of a magpie, she glimpsed a blur of movement.

A tall figure was striding down the stony path towards her. Wren's heart skipped a beat when she saw the way his thick blond hair blazed in the sunlight.

'Dearly beloved,' the minister began, but she was already running.

With a wildly beating heart, she stopped when she reached Jordan. 'Is it really you?' she panted, so overcome she could barely make sense of the moment. 'Oh God, that letter—'

'Disregarded. Burnt.' Jordan's eyes signalled the cord of connection that bound them together. 'I *know* you, Wren.'

She felt bathed by a soft rain of elation. On this hard day,

Jordan's unexplained appearance was like a gift from a benevolent goddess. 'Quick, come with me,' she said.

Someone began to strum an Indian sitar. Someone else played a melody on a Balinese flute. There followed a Christian hymn and an Old Testament reading, Hindu prayers and Buddhist chants. Edward spoke tender words of tribute, breaking down only at the very end when he whispered, 'Until we meet once more, darling Lily, farewell.'

Finally, King David's ancient psalm was recited as the simple coffin was lowered into the ground.

The Lord is my shepherd; I shall not want.

With tears spilling from her eyes, Wren cast down a vivid waratah.

He makes me lie down in green pastures.

May added a bough of golden wattle, her hand trembling.

He leads me beside the still waters.

Edward, stricken and pale, took up a spade and scattered the first clods of earth over Lily's casket.

He restores my soul.

The three stood quietly, their arms sheltering each other, as the spade was lifted, and lifted again by one mourner after the other, until the broken ground was filled and became whole again.

Several people set down gladioli and dahlias picked from their gardens. Others brought bunches of hydrangeas. Wren and May placed the bouquet of orange tiger lilies Jo and Ava had sent at the foot of their mother's grave.

A single wreath had also been delivered. A large and elaborate affair, it was made up of magnolia leaves, red roses and carnations. The mystery of who the sender might be was solved when Wren spied the attached card. It read: *With deepest regrets, Anthony Mancini.*

People were complicated, she reflected.

And then it was over. Trestle tables and chairs had been set up that morning with the help of staff from the local bowling club. Now, bottles of wine, cans of beer and jugs of cold water, sandwiches, pies and quiches were laid out, with nuts and berries for the vegans. Next, her old school friends hoisted up a vast bowl of fruit punch, while the baker added trays of pastries and lamingtons.

Wren smiled shakily at Jordan. It seemed the community had made a collective decision to mark Lily's life not with sorrow, but celebration.

When the health food store's owner produced a tape deck loaded with her mother's favourite music, Woolahderra filled with the sounds of the sixties. Husbands and wives, boyfriends and girlfriends began drifting in. Many intended only to collect their partners, but ended up staying. By the time dusk had ebbed into night, a great deal of alcohol had been consumed and the musky aroma of dope perfumed the air. People danced and ate, smoked, drank and reminisced. Nobody looked in a hurry to leave.

'California Dreamin'' was playing when Wren said to Edward, 'I assume you spoke to Jordan on one of those mysterious work calls of yours – and flew him to Australia.' This time, she didn't mind her father's intervention. 'Dad, I'm so grateful.' With a pang, she realised it was the first time she'd addressed Edward that way.

'Guilty as charged.' He attempted to smile, though his eyes pooled with grief. 'If there is one thing I've learnt,' he said slowly, 'it's that love always deserves a second chance.'

As the haunting organ chords from Procol Harum's 'A Whiter Shade of Pale' began to float through the balmy air, Jordan walked over to Wren and took her hand.

'Shall we?' he murmured.

She looked up at the brightest star in the sky and knew that tonight Lily would have wanted her to embrace life.

As soon as she was in Jordan's arms, she realised she'd drunk way too much. Whatever was in that punch had gone straight to her head. It didn't matter. She tilted up her chin, linked her hands around Jordan's neck and kissed his mouth, a kiss that went on and on.

'Get a room,' someone sang out good-naturedly. Wren thought that was a very good idea. Not yet, but soon.

CHAPTER FIFTY-SIX

'Lots of love, you guys,' May called from the open window of the Mercedes hire car as she and Edward departed the following morning.

'See you both next week!' Wren had to shout above the roar of the car's engine and the sound of loose gravel crunching under its wheels.

As the limousine disappeared from sight, she unconsciously touched her side, just below the ribcage. She'd sensed the same aching void for as long as she could remember. But the familiar emptiness was no longer there. Wren smiled wistfully. Her sister and father were a part of her now, just like Lily.

She could feel the sun's heat stinging her bare calves as she walked back to her mother's shack with Jordan. Last night an unspoken promise had been made. Now it hovered in the air between them with a soft hum of tension.

'Want to help me sort out Mum's things?' she asked, her voice overly bright.

The memory of her uninhibited behaviour after the funeral made her self-conscious.

Jordan volunteered to look through any artworks that might be lying around. 'I know I'm meant to be on holiday,' he said, brushing back a lock of fair hair, 'but I'm an art sleuth at heart.'

'Good luck with that.' Wren made a face. 'Lily was always so disorganised, God knows what you'll find. I'll make a start on sorting out her clothes.'

'Mmm,' Jordan said with a distracted look.

They tiptoed around each other all day as they went about their tasks. The shack felt too small to contain the two of them. Unspoken words made the air feel close.

'Now that's a welcome sight,' Wren said when Jordan joined her on the front step at the end of the day with two mugs of freshly brewed coffee.

'Let's compare notes,' Jordan said, putting one arm casually around her shoulders. 'You go first.'

Wren's skin burned. Jordan hadn't touched her since last night.

'I thought it would be hard to part with Lily's clothes,' she mused, 'but now that I've given them to Winnie to hand out around the commune, I'm finding I rather like the thought of all those floaty Indian dresses and scarves setting out on new adventures.'

After swallowing some coffee she continued. 'Other things feel different too. Once, I couldn't wait to pack up and leave Woolahderra. Now, it's good to know I can always visit.'

'I'm not entirely surprised,' Jordan said. 'I've only ever known you in the big city, but I've seen a different side of you here. Is this where you feel you belong?'

Wren's throat thickened. She'd found her father and her sister, but that wasn't the same as knowing where home was. 'No, I haven't found that place yet.'

She gazed at the whispering eucalypts standing beyond the shack and the flashes of bottlebrush. 'But I've always loved the landscape.'

'It's very beautiful,' Jordan said quietly, though his eyes rested only upon her face.

Wren's neck muscles tightened. Tremaine was still haunting her. 'So did you come across anything interesting in the shack?'

She relaxed a little when she saw Jordan's attention had been diverted.

'I did!' His eyes glowed. 'There were boxes of wonderful drawings and watercolours stashed away at the top of a cupboard and under the bed. I'd like to take them back to New York so they can be catalogued properly.' He put down his mug. 'Wait a minute. I have something special you should see.'

He ran into the house, returning with a sketchbook that he passed eagerly to her.

As soon as Wren began leafing through the delicate line drawings of two tiny girls, touching flowers, reaching their little hands up to the sky, sometimes smiling, sometimes with a frown of wonder crinkling a smooth forehead, she felt an ache in her throat. 'They're of me and May when we were together in Italy, aren't they?'

Wren cradled the book as gently as if it were a baby. 'I'm so glad you found this. It means the world to me.'

Jordan tilted her face towards him. 'What do *I* mean to you, Wren?'

Wren knew what he was asking. 'I just need a little more time,' she murmured.

She slept alone in Lily's freshly made-up bed that night while Jordan stayed in the other shack. 'I thought I was ready to let Lily go but I'm not, or at least, not quite,' she'd explained after they'd eaten dinner in an atmosphere inflected by strain.

He'd claimed he understood, but she could tell by the slight hesitation just before he said, 'Sure, whatever feels right,' that it was not what he'd wanted.

Wren had wondered whether by staying in Lily's room she would feel haunted or perhaps comforted by her presence, but when she woke the next morning it was with the knowledge that her mother's spirit no longer rested within the shack's four flimsy walls. Lily had escaped earth's reality for the last time. Her soul was captured only within the transcendent pictures she had left behind.

Wren sat up suddenly. If there was some way she could gather enough of Lily's paintings, she could put them together with a selection of the best of the newly discovered drawings and watercolours and organise a show – then at last her mother would have the exhibition she deserved. The work wouldn't be for sale, of course. It would be held purely to celebrate Lily's talent.

Jumping out of bed, Wren pulled on an ancient pair of denim shorts and a red shirt she found at the back of a drawer, then went to find Jordan.

They saw little of each other that day. Wren took the Jeep and drove into Nowra to buy more provisions, as well as the materials she'd need to safely transport Lily's work. Jordan spent his time in the shack trying to establish a rough order to the material he'd found in the boxes.

It wasn't until late in the afternoon that Wren returned, finding a jubilant Jordan clutching a dog-eared exercise book. 'Look what I discovered,' he said. 'Lily kept a record of people she gave her work to. I don't know if it's complete, and it's a bit of a mess – often there's just a name and nothing else – but if you're going to put that exhibition together it will be invaluable. I think you could create something really special.' As Jordan spoke about these plans, his handsome face became mobile and boyish. 'I could help you, if you like.'

Wren felt her knotted muscles unwind. She had no idea where she and Jordan were headed. She didn't know whether all those work trips he'd taken had been strictly necessary, or why he'd failed to turn up outside Central Park. What she did know was that he was always on her side. He made her feel she could trust him. He made her feel brave.

She would never forget the terror Tremaine had inflicted, but perhaps here, in Woolahderra, she might become free of the dread he'd inspired.

'I'd love your involvement,' she said. 'But right now we both need a break.'

Wren could see a new watchfulness in Jordan's eyes. The pull of attraction between them had transformed into something more tangible. 'It's time I showed you the river.'

⁓

Wren led Jordan down the old track, now so overgrown she had to rely on her body's memory to take her the right way. Her rucksack bumped against her back as she scrambled over fallen branches and tussocks of grass.

'Okay?' she shouted. She could hear the snap of twigs underfoot and the sound of him tramping behind her.

'So far,' he called back. 'Although this is a wild country you have here.'

Wren was panting when she reached the end of the steep incline. 'That just shows what city life does to you.' She laughed and stretched her arms out wide. 'Well, what do you think?'

The majestic rush of water sweeping by was tinted by the sky's first blush of night.

'It's an inspiration,' Jordan said quietly, his hazel eyes reflecting the sparkling surface.

'Follow me.' She was relieved he also felt the river's magic. 'I'll take you somewhere even better. It's actually just a big rock – but a special one. I'd sit on top of it when I was a kid and watch the water flowing past. It was my thinking spot. There's also a flat space on the ground in front that's been worn away. It's surrounded by a glade of trees so you can glimpse the water, but it's still really private.'

They left their rucksacks below, then climbed the rock and sat watching the sunset. Air perfumed by boronia flowers and wild honey cooled their warm skin as they listened to the current rushing through the river reeds. Wren's breath caught when Jordan's fingers grazed hers. It might have been an accident, but it felt more like a question.

Together they saw the sky become brushed with wide swathes of colour, from shell pink to crimson, before fading to violet. 'Thank you for sharing this with me,' Jordan said in a low voice.

Wren's pulse thudded. 'Let's go down to the clearing.'

She was conscious of Jordan's eyes on her as she spread out a blanket beneath the shelter of the overhanging rock, then lit the hurricane lamp. The atmosphere felt the same as it did just before a thunderstorm, still and taut.

He poured mugs of wine. They both kicked off their trainers and stood side by side, sipping their drinks while the shadowed river slipped by.

'Hungry?' Wren asked.

Jordan gave her a tight smile. 'Sure.'

She handed him a yellow peach, then took one for herself. As soon as she bit into the ripe fruit her mouth was drenched with luscious sweetness. She had just swallowed the last, dripping piece when Jordan took her face in his hands.

'Let's see if I can help clean you up,' he said, tilting up her chin.

Excitement rippled inside her as he slowly licked the juice from her lips. As she reciprocated, playfully flicking her tongue over his mouth, they began exchanging delicious light kisses until suddenly Jordan was holding her to him and kissing her passionately, the way a man kisses a woman he has desired for a long time.

His eyes were filled with longing when at last they parted. 'Are you okay with this, Wren?' he asked. 'I know I planned for a swanky hotel with all the trimmings, but you've been wandering around in tiny shorts and tight shirts for the last two days and I'm only human.'

Wren blushed.

Jordan placed his hands on her shoulders and looked into her eyes, soft and dark as a falcon's feather. 'We've had so many false starts when things have gone wrong, or you've kind of shut down, I began thinking maybe you don't want—'

Wren stopped his words by putting her finger to his lips. 'I do.'

Here, beneath a canopy of trees, she had no fear but only a yearning that curled through her like smoke from a fire.

'Thank Christ,' Jordan said. 'Because you cannot imagine how badly I want to make love to you.'

They kissed again as Jordan undid her buttons, his fingers swift and sure. When her red shirt dropped to the ground he stood back and gazed at her, his eyes darkened by desire. Wren's rich mane of curls fell over her shoulders. She hadn't bothered wearing a bra.

'Remember when I told you I thought you were the most beautiful woman I'd ever seen,' Jordan murmured. 'Well, I'd only looked at your face then. Sorry, there's no other way of putting this.' He traced the outline of her flushed nipples with his fingertips. 'You're a fucking work of art, Wren Summers.'

'Now you,' she said as the lamplight played over her face and bare skin. 'I've been wanting to see that perfect footballer's body of yours forever.'

Wincing, he pulled his T-shirt over his tousled blond head. 'Not exactly perfect, is it?'

A drift of white, webbed scars marked the left side of his heavily muscled chest and lean torso. 'Before I discovered art, I'd planned to become a chemist like my mother,' he said in a halting voice. 'But I had a major accident in our home lab when I was around fifteen and, well, you can see the result.'

Wren remembered the shadow that had passed across his face in the Café des Artistes when she'd asked him if he was the arty black sheep of the family. 'Jordan, is this why you thought you needed fancy props like a hotel suite?' she asked.

He quivered when she touched his scar.

'You of all people should know it's the hidden flaw that makes a faultless picture so desirable.' She smiled up at him. The man had no idea how beautiful he was.

Wren trembled as, at last, she ran her hands over the impressive contours of his hard chest. 'That feels so good,' she murmured, clasping him to her and kissing him deeply while stroking his strong shoulders and back. They parted only long enough for

Wren to wriggle out of her shorts and for Jordan to slip out of his jeans. When he drew her onto the blanket and slid down her bikini briefs, then his boxers, her body ached with anticipation.

'Sweetheart, I know I've always said I would take things slow,' Jordan said, his voice husky. 'But I think I should warn you that's going to be a challenge.'

The way Jordan's eyes lingered on her face, her breasts and long legs made Wren feel as if she'd been brushed by a flame.

At first, he touched her so carefully it was like being stroked by wings. Then, very gently, he brought his lips to the base of her throat, the silky inner side of her arms, and her wrists. Only when his mouth met the swollen tips of her breasts did his restraint falter.

Wren's arousal flared. Grasping Jordan's shoulders, she pulled him closer. She needed to feel his body pressed against hers, to feel the weight of him as he lay in her arms.

He moved away abruptly.

'Is everything okay?' she whispered. She couldn't bear to disappoint him.

'I did try to warn you.' Jordan gave Wren a shy grin that made her yearn for him even more. 'It's just that I can't trust myself. And I really, really want you to have a good time.'

She felt scorching darts of desire in her belly as he kissed her lips and her neck while taunting her nipples with his fingers. Then his mouth found new ways to excite her. 'What you're doing, it's divine,' she gasped. Jordan seemed to have an inexhaustible appetite for providing her with pleasure.

He was teasing the softness between her smooth thighs when Wren heard herself moan. A wave of arousal threatened to engulf her, yet still Jordan kept his hand where it was. He stroked her for one more exquisite moment, then another, before yielding to his own desire with a fierce, driving rhythm she matched effortlessly.

Their lovemaking was as intense as it was abandoned. They were creatures of the forest, part of the earth and the river and the trees, joined in elemental intimacy. When Wren's scream rang out and Jordan gripped her, shuddering, both were consumed by the same sweet, savage ecstasy.

She woke in the night. Her eyelashes fluttered as she looked up at the silvered branches swaying high above her in the moonlight. Lying quietly, she luxuriated in her closeness to Jordan, listening as the sigh of the river mingled with the sound of his breath.

Wren smiled to herself. Earlier, once their heartbeats had returned to something approximating normal, they had drunk more wine, eaten fresh bread, plump tomatoes and cheese, then tiny, sweet strawberries. Afterwards, neither of them had wanted to leave their bush paradise.

Their passionate tryst was everything Wren had dreamt of, but so much more than she'd expected. As her mind filled with stirring recollections, she felt the heat of new desire coiling deep inside. Carefully disentangling one arm, she began stroking Jordan's wonderful chest, then moved her hand very slowly towards the fine trail of hair on his flat belly. He moaned when she went further.

'If this is a dream, dear God don't let me wake up,' he muttered.

Wren slid on top of him. Melding her body to his, she moved her hips with an unhurried pulse that made Jordan groan. When he reached for her, she allowed him to caress her breasts only long enough to heighten her own craving, then gently pinned his hands down.

The green and gold flecks in his eyes glittered as she whispered, 'It's my turn now.'

CHAPTER FIFTY-SEVEN

New York, December 1988

Freezing air clawed the back of Wren's throat as she trudged towards East 73rd Street. An icy chill had descended upon New York, sending her flying to Bloomingdale's to buy fleecy-lined boots and gloves, a fur-edged knitted hat and thermal underwear – all items she'd never had any need for in Australia. How strange it now seemed that, only days before, she'd been lying naked, beneath a hot summer sky, making joyous love with Jordan.

The morning after their first perfect night she'd insisted they have a dip in the cool water swirling below them. 'It's a treat you really shouldn't miss,' she'd said, even though Jordan had claimed that the best possible treat in the world was currently wrapped in his arms. After that, they'd formed a routine, revolving around swimming in the river or the nearby surf, working through Lily's sketches and drawings, eating fresh local fruit, salads and fish and, best of all, exploring ever more ways to arouse and delight each other. This ideal life was all that she'd needed.

Not until she'd been driving the Jeep to the coast on their last day did she consider the future. It was impossible to predict what lay ahead for her and Jordan. As he had never said that he loved her, Wren had been careful not to reveal the depth of her feelings for him – she wasn't ready to make herself so vulnerable. Sometimes, as she lay listening to the sounds of the night, this uncertainty led her to sleepless disquiet. But on that final morning, she had something else on her mind.

As the warm breeze rushing in through the windows blew her hair into wild tendrils, she announced, 'I've come to a decision.'

'Really,' Jordan said. 'And that would be?'

'I'm going to convince Archer's to take me back. The only tiny little problem,' she added, wrinkling her forehead, 'is that, just at the moment, I don't have any idea how.'

After she parked the Jeep in a spot opposite rolling sets of emerald breakers and a strip of pale sand, Jordan gave her a quick grin. 'Well, there's one surefire way.'

She felt a sudden eddy of need as she remembered how he had looked at that exact moment. Newly tanned, he was wearing only a pair of board shorts slung low on his hips. She spent the next five minutes kissing him.

'What you mean is,' she said, once she had torn herself away, 'Archer's would take me back in a hot minute if instead of believing I was a decidedly suspect, untamed Australian, Timothy King knew I was really the daughter of his top client.'

Jordan laughed. 'It would be worth revealing all, just to see King's face.'

She lifted her chin. 'I've relied solely on hard work and my own merit all my life. I'm not changing that for anything.'

Wren hugged her camel overcoat more tightly around her. The fact was, since her return to New York she'd been struggling with the notion of a reimagined Wren Summers, eldest child of an unimaginably rich and powerful media magnate. This new version of herself made her feel even more displaced than usual. Hunching her shoulders against the cold, she wondered if she'd ever feel as if she belonged anywhere.

Wren had been stunned when Timothy King had telephoned her three days earlier, requesting a meeting at Archer's. When she entered his wood-panelled office, it was impossible not to remember their last, fraught confrontation, but no matter what the man had to say, she was determined that her composure would not slip by even a fraction.

King greeted her with all the magnificent warmth she'd so often witnessed him direct towards a potential client, adding, 'I must say, Wren, you're looking very well.'

'I've had a short break,' she said in a neutral voice.

'Yes, of course,' he said hurriedly. 'My condolences on the loss of your mother.'

She nodded her acknowledgement, careful to maintain her restraint. King was a plotter – she felt certain he'd never made a move in his life that didn't have a personal motive. Their little get-together was sure to be part of a larger plan.

He walked over to a finely detailed French cabinet. 'I'm having a Scotch and soda,' he said. 'Will you join me?'

'Perhaps a small one, thank you.' This was one occasion when she would not be losing her head.

He handed her the drink, then settled back into his leather chair. 'I'll be brief. You're a whip-smart, talented girl and, most important of all, our best bidders are anxious to see more of you.' King raised his cut-crystal tumbler. 'After that Renoir auction, my phone rang hot for days.'

This was a surprise, but Wren didn't show it.

'You might have missed the Page Six piece in *The Post*, but I'll read it to you.'

He opened the folded newspaper lying on his desk. '*Where did the venerable house of Archer's unearth that luscious young lady, Wren Summers? Not only seductive but smart, Summers achieved a record price at the most talked about auction of the season etc, etc.*'

King put down the paper. 'You get the idea. Ghastly prose, but wonderful publicity.'

'What exactly are you saying, Mr King?' she asked.

'I think we know each other well enough by now for you to call me Timothy, don't you?' he said silkily. 'I'd like you to come back to Archer's. How would you feel about that?'

'I'm interested.' Wren's heart began racing. 'But before I left, I seem to recall some fairly unpleasant allegations were made against me.'

'That was regrettable.'

After Wren declined his offer of another drink, King poured one for himself and returned to his chair.

'I was always somewhat sceptical of the accusations Amelia levelled against you,' he said, 'but nevertheless, discreet inquiries were made. Tony Mancini personally assured me you turned down a cash gift. In fact, he revealed that, in his experience, this was a novel event.' King chuckled quietly.

'I have also learnt that her Australian source, John Tremaine, has left the Sydney Art Museum under a considerable cloud. Unfortunately, he'd completely hoodwinked Amelia.'

He glanced at Wren. 'Quite honestly, it appears the girl had lost her judgement entirely, because it seems she'd become emotionally involved with a fellow who, it turned out, was a leading member of the Mafia.' He shook his head. 'As you can imagine, Amelia was mortified when she found out. I mean, it is one thing to do business with these chaps, quite another to allow oneself to enter into a personal relationship with any of them.'

'Quite,' Wren said, being careful to suppress any note of irony.

'Of course,' King continued, 'once she learnt the truth about Tremaine and this other fellow, she was terribly apologetic about her behaviour towards you. Nevertheless, I strongly suggested to her that, under the circumstances, it would be a good idea if she returned to the UK and did something else for a while. The last I heard she was working behind the scenes for a television program about antiques and stately homes.'

Wren chose not to respond.

King sipped his drink. 'But let us return to the present. In terms of Archer's good name, the matter of the fake picture is irrelevant,' he said. 'Having retrieved the original, largely due to your own intervention, the right painting is now with its owner. Conroy is famous for loathing publicity – he'd never reveal what really occurred. Which means that as far as the art world is concerned, the picture you auctioned was authentic.'

'So are you saying that the entire episode might just as well have never happened?' She put her glass down on a silver coaster, feeling uneasy. There was something King wasn't admitting.

'Yes and no.' He leant forward. 'At the time of the incident, it was necessary to inform the Archer's board about the affair. Although, as I said, I would very much like to offer you a position – and Antoine is particularly keen for you to join his team – the word "fake" is anathema to some of the older directors, no matter what mitigating circumstances might exist. In other words, they simply refuse to have anything to do with you.' He swirled the whiskey in his glass before swallowing. 'It's a matter of trust.'

Wren enjoyed observing King's supple mind at work. The man had a gift for considering every angle, making calculations, and coming up with ingenious solutions. But this time she would emerge from life's revolving door ahead of him.

'Timothy, let me cut to the chase,' she said. 'You find yourself in a bind.' She noted with undisclosed satisfaction his look of surprise.

'Everyone knows that Archer's has announced it is holding a celebrity auction to benefit AIDS research early in the New Year – your publicity people have clearly worked overtime. Naturally, a stellar range of desirable objects is required in order to attract top-drawer bidders. However, I am also aware that potential donors are shying away. All things considered,' she said, drawing out the moment, 'it seems you have a full-scale disaster on your hands.'

There was an unmistakable trace of shock in King's hooded eyes. 'You're well informed.'

In a piece of remarkably good timing, Jeanette had mentioned the matter when they'd met for coffee the day before. 'People carry on all sorts of conversations in front of a receptionist,' she'd said with a wicked look. 'It's the earpiece, you see. They think you can't hear them.'

As soon as Wren had learnt of King's problem, she'd begun to devise a plan that would beat him at his own game. This time around, she'd be the one dictating terms.

'Very sadly, if sufficient outstanding items can't be acquired,' she said to him, 'the auction will have to be cancelled, thus severely undermining Archer's standing – and causing you untold personal embarrassment.'

Timothy adjusted his collar. 'Something to be avoided at all costs.'

'It's the AIDS aspect,' Wren said. 'As you would have realised by now, there's an appalling stigma attached to the disease, although I believe there is a way to neutralise that.' She was frankly surprised that King would have allowed Archer's to support such a controversial, if worthy, cause. The man had risen in her estimation.

'What do you have in mind?' His voice wasn't quite as smooth as usual.

She knew then she had King hooked. 'A key gift from someone who occupies so revered a position, and commands such an extraordinarily high profile, that others will ignore their reservations and clamour to leap on board.'

Wren ignored her pinpricks of panic, just as she chose not to reveal that her chance of actually obtaining a gift from this rare personage was the longest of long shots. But then, she reflected, it was far from the first time she'd taken a risk.

King looked at her with undisguised admiration. 'Such a coup would certainly convince Archer's directors that your ability to source rare and desirable objects for auction was so exceptional that they simply could not afford to lose you – especially not to one of our competitors,' he said.

Wren maintained her best poker face. 'My agreement to save you does not only require a permanent position at Archer's working alongside Antoine Ardant.' She waited a beat. 'But also your written guarantee that within twelve months I will be conducting auctions on a regular basis. Important ones,' she added. 'Oh, and one more thing. A formal withdrawal of all charges previously levelled against me.'

There was a glint in King's eyes. 'Why Wren, you're beginning to remind me of myself.'

He placed his empty glass next to hers. 'Now then,' he said. 'Tell me the name of this incomparable saviour who is to rescue our reputation.'

'Sorry, Timothy.' She smiled enigmatically. 'I'm afraid you'll just have to trust me.'

CHAPTER FIFTY-EIGHT

The beseeching look Jordan gave Wren from across the white damask-covered table of the Four Seasons, New York's most fashionable restaurant, weakened her resolve. 'All right, all right,' she said. 'Seeing as you're paying for lunch, I'll give you a hint. Think stratospheric fame.'

She had bet him a bottle of champagne that he would be unable to guess the name of the person she'd approached to make the key donation for the AIDS auction.

He grinned. 'Too easy. Seeing as every international celebrity from the worlds of publishing, television, finance, fashion and politics – plus the odd movie star – lunches here, all I need to do is scan the room.'

Wren's expression might have graced the Sphinx. 'Be my guest.'

The silly bet helped still the nerves needling her stomach. Although her negotiations with the donor's representative had advanced, so far the result remained inconclusive. Today Wren would either receive confirmation – or a knockback that would destroy her carefully laid plans.

'Although you do realise I'm suffering from a serious disadvantage,' Jordan grumbled. 'I have very distracting memories of that outfit you're wearing.'

She'd decided the occasion called for what she'd come to think of as her lucky tuxedo, adding the tiny black camisole beneath, a red silk rose on the lapel and her Charles Jourdan stilettos for extra panache.

'That's very sweet,' she said primly. 'But I'm not handing out any more clues, if that's what you're angling for.'

'Let's see if I can do something about that.' Jordan smiled as he ordered two extra dry martinis from a passing waiter.

Wren doubted he could truly appreciate how much winning the trust of Archer's board of directors meant to her. When you had parents who were highly respected college professors like his, you were wrapped from birth in invisible layers of approval and protection. She'd always felt exposed and vulnerable.

A quick laugh from behind interrupted her thoughts. She watched as men in sleek suits and women wearing designer labels made a show of table-hopping, though there appeared to be an unwritten rule that nobody stayed for long. Despite the room's constant whirr, it seemed that public recognition was rather more prized than conversation.

Jordan reached across the table for Wren's hand. 'Don't be mad, but I had to pull rank to make this reservation. Saying it was for E.J. Conroy's private art curator instead of plain old Jordan Grant worked wonders.'

'Ah well, desperate times call for desperate measures,' she said airily. 'I forgive you, but only because I have a weakness for extra-tall guys with gorgeous blond hair and hazel eyes.'

'Hey, if you don't quit flirting, I'll be forced to accuse you of interfering with one of the players,' Jordan teased as he released her hand.

'Now, down to business.' He gazed across the room. 'There's a high-powered trio beneath the balcony who are occupying the best seats in the house. I can see the editor of US *Vogue*, Anna Wintour behind the dark classes; Miss Blonde Ambition herself, Tina Brown from *Vanity Fair*; and the Advocate Group's star executive, the dazzling Blaise Hill – she was the first woman to edit a daily newspaper in London and now she's running the group's international division.'

The waiter put down twin martinis.

'Hmm, their table is set for four, which makes me wonder who's joining that little coven,' Jordan said, eyeing Wren hopefully. 'There can't be too many people in this town who'd be brave enough to keep those ladies waiting.'

'I think you should give up right now.' Wren raised her glass. 'Better luck next time, darling.'

'Hey, not so fast. I'm not finished yet.' Jordan tilted his head to the left. 'Joan Collins has been the most famous television star in the world ever since *Dynasty* hit, and right now she's sitting three tables away with her agent.' He paused. 'Is it her?'

'Way too glitzy,' Wren said dismissively.

Jordan flicked his eyes to the right. 'Henry Kissinger? He's at the banquette behind you, lunching with the president of the World Bank.'

'Insufficient style.'

'Ivana Trump is next to the window.'

'Jordan, you're kidding, right?' Wren threw up her hands.

'I can feel that champagne slipping away from me,' he said with mock gloom. 'Maybe I should confine myself to a subject I actually know something about.'

He began to describe the 1950s glass and steel, bronze-skinned Seagram Building that housed the Four Seasons restaurant. 'I'm sure you already know it was designed by the great modernist architect Mies van der Rohe in the International Style,' he said. 'However, you might not be aware that lucky Mies was provided with an unlimited budget. By the time his masterpiece was completed, it was the most expensive building in the world. The owners didn't care, however, as it was universally applauded.'

Wren was thinking how much she liked the way Jordan became so alive whenever he spoke about art, when a sudden hush fell upon the busy room.

'I don't want to turn around and stare,' he said in an undertone, 'but who the hell just walked in? This crowd is too blasé to put down their knives and forks for the Second Coming.'

Wren clasped her hands together anxiously. 'I believe I know who that fourth place is for,' she whispered as a tall, striking blonde in a mint-green Chanel suit began walking towards them.

'Hello there,' the woman said in an upper-class English accent.

Jordan and Wren immediately stood up.

'I'm afraid I have to be awfully quick. Unfortunately, this was the only time my stuffy private secretary could squeeze you into my schedule. You know,' she said to Wren, in a confiding manner, 'he was a little taken aback by your request. But what I like about you Australians is that you're so wonderfully up front.'

She put her hand in front of her mouth, obscuring an errant giggle. 'Gosh, I still remember when you rescued my silly bag at the Sydney Opera House. And I see you're wearing that tuxedo I liked so much.'

Suddenly serious, she added. 'Honestly, though, I was very glad that you wrote asking for my assistance. If I can help to diminish the shame borne by AIDS patients even by a little, I will feel I have achieved something of value. That's terribly important to me.'

She passed Wren an envelope. 'Inside is an official letter of consent. I wanted to hand it to you personally because the cause is so close to my heart.' She cast her pellucid blue eyes in the direction of the publishing mavens. 'Best go now. I'm sure it would be unwise to keep those three waiting any longer.'

It was as if a switch had been turned from off to on. Once the woman was seated, the restaurant regained its former dynamism. Flying waiters resumed normal service while habitual power lunchers returned to discussing deals and exchanging gossip – although more than a few stole curious glances in Wren's direction.

Wren smiled at Jordan triumphantly. 'I believe I've just won myself a bottle of Dom Pérignon.'

'Hell, you're impressive, sweetheart,' he said, with a look in his eyes that made her wish they were back at the river licking peach juice from each other's lips. 'You realise this auction will go down in history.'

Wren's smile slipped. 'This time, let's hope it will be for the right reason.'

CHAPTER FIFTY-NINE

February 1989

Stopping abruptly, Wren glimpsed an exceptionally glamorous image in one of the anteroom's tall mirrored doors. The entrancing creature wore a strapless, hot-pink vintage gown of such elegance that Audrey Hepburn herself might have ordered it from Hubert de Givenchy. Her dark curls were swept up in a manner that drew attention to her cheekbones and the fine line of her jaw, while a pair of magnificent Tiffany & Co. pearl and diamond earrings (possibly borrowed) glittered on her ears.

Wren stared at the reflection with her wide, dramatically made-up eyes. Then she pouted her fuchsia-painted lips and raised one languid arm. As the image in the mirror mimicked her every action, she decided there couldn't be much doubt. That scruffy kid from the crazy bush commune had become this svelte, soignée woman.

Wren winked at herself. She'd come a long way from Woolahderra.

Save for two expressionless security guards in grey uniforms and half a dozen attendants, the private area adjacent to the Plaza's ballroom was empty of people. Archer's had been required to change the location of its celebrity charity auction for AIDS research from its East 73rd Street headquarters to this resplendent Fifth Avenue hotel, so great had been the demand for tickets.

Wren's gaze rested upon the signed letter from the late President Kennedy that Jackie O had sent, then moved to the exquisite little Whistler watercolour donated by a member of the Rockefeller family. Beside these precious objects were many other numbered lots, all laid out on long tables covered with starched cloths.

Wren looked up and nodded as Peter Morgan came into the room. She knew better than to disturb him.

Smiling to herself, she trailed her fingers over a photograph of the left-wing activist Jane Fonda, wearing a bright yellow leotard. The actress had promised six personally conducted aerobics lessons.

'My dear, you look bewitching.' Timothy King, dressed in a black bow tie and a matching dinner suit, appeared beside her.

'Thank you,' Wren said, 'though it's these items that are dazzling. I still can't believe Malcolm Forbes was prepared to part with that gem,' she said, gesturing at an exquisite cigarette case by Fabergé. A deep blue enamel, it was encircled by a gold serpent with scales formed by rose diamonds.

'I've seen one very like it in London, given to Edward VII by his favourite mistress, Mrs Keppel.' King remarked.

'And, speaking of royal connections – how you managed to obtain a personal gift from the most famous woman in the world still baffles me.' He paused. 'Although I suppose by now, I should be used to your mysterious coups.'

Wren did not attempt to enlighten him.

King gave her a sharp look. 'You certainly kept your relationship to Conroy very quiet. I can't imagine why you didn't reveal it to me until last week – it might have saved you a great deal of trouble.' He lifted one eyebrow. 'What with one thing and another, you are quite the dark horse, aren't you?'

Wren was relieved when they were interrupted by a pair of attendants who flung open the anteroom's doors. Her pulse immediately quickened. She still felt that the thrum of anticipation generated by an eager auction crowd was the most thrilling sound in the world.

King immediately strode past her into the ballroom. Out of sight, she began watching as he delivered his urbane welcome.

Somewhere in the audience were her best friends, her father, her sister and the man she adored. As she considered this wonder, Wren became radiant with unfamiliar pleasure. Here she was, about to face a huge test and, for the first time in her life, she felt truly nurtured – no, it was more than that. She felt complete.

A rustle of fabric made her spin around. 'MJ! It's so good to see you, and right on time.' Her childhood pal had flown into New York especially to model the night's most talked about item.

MJ swished across the room in a regal, emerald-green satin ballgown. With its gold-thread embroidery, scooped neckline and low-cut back, the dress set off her long, flaming red hair to perfection. Wren told her she looked stunning.

'You don't look bad yourself.' MJ grinned. 'This will be so cool.'

'When it's our turn, I'll go out first,' Wren explained. 'As soon as you hear me say the lot number, make your grand entrance, do a few fabulous twirls, then stalk up and down the centre aisle, just as if it were a catwalk. I'll be fielding bids while you're doing your bit.'

'No probs.' MJ gave her a thumbs-up.

Positioning herself just inside the doorway, Wren listened intently. Lots eleven, twelve and thirteen flew by. She signalled to MJ when she heard Peter Morgan finalising the sale of lot fourteen.

A crack rang out as his gavel came down. 'Sold, to the gentleman on my left, four hours of private tuition with the illustrious golf champion Greg "The Shark" Norman. Congratulations, sir.' Morgan's brown eyes twinkled. 'I'm sure that slice will disappear in no time.'

The crowd laughed and clapped. Morgan waited until they were quiet, then announced, 'We now come to our auction's highlight, a magnificent Luca Morani creation, personally donated by none other than' – he paused, allowing the audience's anticipation to swell – 'Her Royal Highness, Diana, Princess of Wales.'

Spontaneous cheers erupted.

'And to auction this unique item ...' He paused briefly once again. 'I take great pleasure in introducing Archer's own, incomparable, Miss Varenna Conroy Summers.'

Wren swept into the ballroom. As she ascended the dais, the crowd's wild applause only heightened her exhilarating sense of command. This was her room. She was its mistress.

Silence fell as each member of the audience waited eagerly to hear what the vision standing before them would say. Wren produced her most captivating smile. She could feel their tension, sense their excitement.

In a compelling voice, softened by a hint of seduction, she began. 'Ladies and gentlemen ...'

CHAPTER SIXTY

The dark-eyed girl with the Botticelli face and the handsome fair-haired boy embraced in the Plaza Hotel's loveliest suite. She wore nothing but silk lingerie and the remains of her fuchsia pink lipstick. He was still in his tuxedo and smelled of lightly spiced green apples.

The room was adorned with roses and orchids spilling from cut-glass vases. Champagne stood in an ice bucket on a low table next to two crystal flutes and a box of chocolate truffles.

'I can't believe we're finally here,' the girl murmured as she helped the boy out of his jacket and then undid his bow tie. 'You know,' she continued as she began to remove the studs from his dinner shirt. 'A friend of mine told me ages ago that I should seduce you.'

'Very sound advice,' he said.

The girl kissed him lightly on the mouth as she slipped the shirt from his shoulders and ran her hands across his scarred, beautiful chest. Then she unbuckled his belt.

'The only problem,' he said, sliding his arms around her waist, 'is that you are so tempting I might have to seduce you, instead.'

He pressed open her lips with his tongue, filling her mouth with delicious sensations while his fingers unhooked her blush-pink, strapless bra.

'You're a fast worker.' She raised an eyebrow.

The boy took his time kissing her smooth neck and satiny breasts. 'I can do slow.'

The expression on the girl's face was as impish as it was enticing. 'We'll see,' she said, as she led him towards the bed.

Quite some time later, Wren was stretched out beside Jordan, enveloped by the hazy languor that invariably followed their lovemaking. She thought perhaps it was this sense of deep relaxation that, annoyingly, allowed her mind to wander to a question she'd put off pursuing for months.

Hoping to still her thoughts, Wren drank some champagne, but the matter kept nagging at her until she could no longer ignore it.

'Jordan, I'd like to ask you something,' she said at last. 'Why didn't you turn up outside Central Park on the day before I left for Australia? I waited for ages.'

'Hell, I never apologised, did I?' Jordan picked up his glass of Dom Pérignon. 'My plane had to turn around mid-flight and head back to Boston because of a massive early snowstorm. Half the city's communications went out.' He began stroking her tangled curls. 'I was going crazy, knowing I couldn't contact you.'

Wren masked her relief by changing the subject. 'I can't understand how it can be so incredibly cold here, yet I haven't seen a single flake. Snow must look magical,' she said dreamily.

Jordan made a face. 'Not when you're stuck in Boston.' He set his glass down on the side table. 'Now it's my turn to ask you a question.'

Wren felt a twinge of concern.

'When we were at the commune, you told me you didn't know where you belonged. Do you still feel like that?' His touched her cheek. 'Because you definitely belong up on that auction dais. You were sensational tonight.'

She pouted at him over her glass. 'Only during the auction?'

'I can't believe you need to ask.' Jordan laughed. 'But, seeing as you have – definitely not only then.'

'Thank you, but I think I should stop fishing for compliments,' Wren said with a rueful look. 'I was dodging your question.'

Jordan propped himself up on his elbow and turned towards her. 'Now, why would you do that?'

'Probably because I'm still getting used to a few new ideas.' She took a quick breath. 'You see, growing up, I never felt as though I fitted in anywhere. I convinced myself that scoring a great mark in an exam, winning a scholarship or landing an amazing job would have to be enough – was enough.'

She thought for a minute. 'But that was because I didn't understand what belonging really meant. Now I know better than that.'

Wren rested her right hand on Jordan's chest, just above his heart. 'Belonging,' she said slowly, as she looked up into his uncommonly handsome face, 'is the feeling you have when your hippie mum sings you a gospel song on the front step of your shack, or when you're eating ice cream in the park with your best friend. It's the connection you and a colleague experience when you both see a great work of art in a crumbling palazzo.' Her lips formed a poignant smile. 'Or what it's like to hang out with the sister you never knew you had.'

Jordan gazed into her chocolate eyes. 'Anything else?'

Wren's pulse thudded. She was about to take another big risk. 'Belonging is being in the arms of the man you love, whether you're lying together beneath the stars, or … in a suite at the Plaza.' Her voice faltered. Love was the one, dangerous word that up until now she'd always avoided.

'That's quite a coincidence,' Jordan said quietly, 'because whenever I have my arms around the woman I love, I feel as if I belong too. And I'd like to keep on feeling that way for a long time.'

Wren's apprehension melted as Jordan clasped her to him. 'How long is a long time?' she whispered.

'I'm thinking,' he said, after he kissed her, 'eternity sounds about right.'

As the dark-eyed girl and the fair-haired boy slept peacefully in each other's arms, snow began tumbling over New York City. Glimmering drifts cascaded gently onto the benches in Gramercy Park, the gothic pylons of the Brooklyn Bridge and the roof of the Salvation Army women's residence. Soft flakes also found their way to Archer's auction house, where a flutter of crystals came to rest on the bronze bow and arrow of Artemis.

AUTHOR'S NOTE

I have been thrilled to hear from so many readers saying how much they enjoy the Author's Notes that follow my novels. Quite a few of you have revealed your surprise upon discovering that various events actually took place. This is something that's easy for me to relate to, for during my research I often feel the same way!

Some readers ask about what happened next to the numerous real people or places that feature in my books. Others want to know what inspired various parts of the stories. It is my pleasure to share the following brief details and clarifications regarding *The Artist's Secret*.

The late West Australian entrepreneur (and former signwriter) Alan Bond really did, in 1987, buy what was then the world's most expensive painting, for $53.9 million. Surprisingly, he paid this remarkable price for Van Gogh's *Irises* just one month after the notorious 'Black Friday' stock market crash. Only later was it revealed that Sotheby's had in fact loaned Bond half the money. Many claim that this single act was responsible for the wildly inflated art boom that lasted for the next three years – little wonder prices were running hot when Wren arrived at the mythical Archer's.

As Bond never paid Sotheby's so much as, in Amelia's words, 'a red cent' for *Irises*, his possession of the picture was short-lived. After languishing for many months in a secret location, the work was eventually sold by the auction house in March 1990 to the J. Paul Getty Museum in Los Angeles for an undisclosed sum.

I was intrigued to discover that Sotheby's CEO at the time of the *Irises* sale, Diana D. Brooks, was subsequently sentenced for price-fixing. As for Alan Bond, having been declared bankrupt in 1992, he was convicted of corporate fraud in 1997. Newspapers later reported that he spent much of his four-year prison sentence painting portraits and still lifes.

Sometimes, in an effort to create a coherent narrative, it is necessary to combine a number of real events in a single scene or scenes. For instance, although forty young men from the University of California at Berkeley did illegally burn their draft cards in May 1965, more stringent legislation providing for prison sentences of up to five years was not passed by Congress until August of that year.

The students' act of defiance took place at the Berkeley draft board, whereas in *The Artist's Secret* the scene is set in front of Sproul Hall. This was because that stately building and the area directly adjacent to it was Berkeley's most iconic venue for political demonstrations. It was at Sproul Hall that the Free Speech sit-in, where a bare-foot Joan Baez famously sang 'We Shall Overcome' (and Lily first set eyes on Edward), took place in December 1964. This was also the occasion for almost eight hundred arrests, more than at any other single event in US history. The police were later accused by the students of perpetrating many acts of brutality.

Those readers who are familiar with the Art Gallery of New South Wales may note its resemblance to the Sydney Art Museum. Certainly, the building is similar in appearance as, on the whole, is its collection of artworks. Furthermore, the Modern Masters show that had such an enduring effect upon Wren was exhibited at the Art Gallery, albeit in 1975 rather than in 1980.

Despite these similarities, neither the despicable John Tremaine nor his gullible superior, Alastair Stephenson, was based on any member of the Art Gallery of New South Wales's staff, past or present. Both are wholly invented characters.

Having said that, during the 1980s women in almost every profession endured widespread sexual harassment, including physical attacks, with little or no redress. Although today changing attitudes and new legislation help protect female workers, tragically, numerous instances of blatant discrimination – and far worse behaviour – continue to be reported. While Wren was able to resolve the PTSD arising from her assault, many women live with the devastating effects of such attacks forever.

Tony Mancini's account of various mobsters' lethal transgressions, including the assassination of 'Big Paulie' Castellano at the direction of his underling John Gotti, is accurate. Widely known as 'the dapper don', Gotti's new role as head of the infamous Gambino crime family made him the most high-profile Mafia member in 1980s New York. After escaping convictions three times in courts of law – by ruthlessly intimidating witnesses and jury members – Gotti was eventually sentenced to life imprisonment in 1992 as a result of evidence provided by both FBI wiretaps and, ironically, his own treacherous second-in-command, Sammy 'The Bull' Gravano.

All details regarding Renoir's *Two Young Girls at the Piano* are correct, although there is no record of an early, 1891 version of the painting.

King Henri II's ban on international auctions houses conducting business in France has been overturned.

Although Wren was on track to take charge of her first important auction by the end of 1989, it was not until 1990 that Sotheby's Melanie Clore became the first female auctioneer to conduct a major evening sale of Impressionist and Modern Art.

After being suspended for several centuries, the 'Rain of Rose Petals', as the annual Pentecost celebration in Rome's Pantheon is known, was reintroduced in 1995.

During the 1980s, the whimsical 'no alcohol/no men/no toasters' Parkside Evangeline building where Wren and her friends resided was much as I described it. However, should you be tempted to follow suit, in 2010 the Salvation Army sold the property to developers Arthur and William Lie Zeckendorf for $60 million. The revamped complex was completed two years later, with apartments ranging in price from $10 million to $42 million, way out of reach of the vast majority of the women – thousands over the years, including my youngest niece – who once lived there.

Nell's was widely considered the hottest club in New York during the latter years of the supercharged 1980s. All details regarding the nightspot's décor and stellar clientele, Nell Campbell's starring role in *The Rocky Horror Picture Show* and her stint working in London's Chelsea markets alongside Freddie Mercury are true. (I should add here that, having watched a teenage Nell captivate her audience by dancing exuberantly across the stage at the Sydney school we both attended, her later success was not unexpected.)

The scene where Princess Diana, wearing a mint-green Chanel suit, dines at the Four Seasons was inspired by a real lunch she attended in the same restaurant with Anna Wintour, editor of US *Vogue*, and Tina Brown, then editor of *The New Yorker*, in June 1997. I could not resist adding Blaise Hill, the heroine of my novel *The Royal Correspondent*, to this pair of media mavens.

That high-powered lunch date took place shortly before Christie's famous auction where the sale of many of Princess Diana's most glamorous 1980s gowns raised over $3 million for the Royal Marsden Hospital Cancer Centre and AIDS Crisis Trust. This, too, served as inspiration, for Diana was dedicated to reducing the suffering of those afflicted by AIDS and the stigma attached to them. Indeed, in 1987, at the height of the epidemic and the hysteria surrounding it, she made headlines by shaking hands – ungloved – with patients at the UK's first HIV/AIDS unit.

In a lighter moment, Diana wore a black Catherine Walker tuxedo to a formal charity event in April 1988, just three months after the Australian Wool Board's bicentennial fashion parade.

The Four Seasons restaurant, which first opened in the Seagram Building on 20 July 1959, no longer exists. Steep rent rises and other financial pressures forced the former scene of countless power lunches to close its doors on 16 July 2016.

Some early scenes were inspired by a close friend of mine who was also appointed Assistant Curator of Prints and Drawings at a leading art museum when still in her twenties. After she told me that, to her consternation, during her job interview she was invited to name her favourite work in the collection, I knew this incident belonged in *The Artist's Secret*.

Despite my friend's inexperience, her departmental head – a man who shared Bobby's deep-seated fear of flying – soon asked her to travel overseas to authenticate a work the museum was anxious to acquire. In her case, however, she went to New York not Venice, and the picture was a valuable Dürer etching rather than a drawing by Raphael.

The authentication of artworks still remains a fraught undertaking. When in 2006 the Van Gogh Museum in Amsterdam refused to attribute the National Gallery of Victoria's *Head of a Man* to the famous Dutch painter, the picture's value immediately tumbled from many millions of dollars to a few thousand. By contrast, once a damaged portrait with the attribution 'after Leonardo' was controversially attributed to the great Leonardo da Vinci himself, the price rocketed. After being sold to an art dealer in 2005 by a small New Orleans auction house for a meagre $1500, *Salvador Mundi* passed through several hands before being auctioned in New York for $450 million in 2017. At the time of writing, it remains the world's most expensive painting.

Just as the cost of celebrated artworks has continued spiralling towards ever more stratospheric heights, so has the auction format – and indeed, the concept of art itself – continued to evolve. In 2021, *Everydays: The First 5000 Days*, by the artist known as Beeples, became the first purely digital non-fungible token (NFT) to be sold by a major auction house. Like all NFTs, the work exists only as a digital asset, backed up by blockchain technology. In another first, the venerable 255-year-old firm of Christie's accepted the successful on-line bidder's entire $69 million payment – which included the buyer's premium – in cryptocurrency.

Enthralling as the world of museums and high-stakes auctions may be, at its core *The Artist's Secret* is about elemental needs. To know the identity and the whereabouts of one's parents, sisters and brothers seems little enough to expect from life. Yet, this simple information often remains out of the reach of refugees, members of the stolen generation, adoptees, those affected by war and other calamities, or those who, like Wren, have been impacted by traumatic personal circumstances.

That so many of these individuals have been able to forge a new sense of belonging is a testament to the human spirit. Just like great art, their example nurtures the soul and fills the heart with hope.

A.J.

ACKNOWLEDGEMENTS

I am incredibly fortunate that Anna Valdinger is my publisher. Anna has devoted her extensive skills and unstinting care to all three of my novels. Publishing during the time of a pandemic throws up unimaginable challenges, but somehow Anna's enthusiasm never flags – she is a marvel.

My thanks also go to Alexandra Nahlous for her invaluable structural edit and to Fiona Daniels, an inspirational copy editor who always poses exactly the right editorial questions. I also appreciate Nicola Young's scrupulous proofreading.

As always, working with the HarperCollins team has been a treat. Designer Christine Armstrong has created another gorgeous cover, while Senior Editor Scott Forbes not only brought his expertise to both text and production, but never once complained when various unforeseen events in my life meant he was obliged to produce yet one more publishing schedule. I also appreciated the attention of Fiction Campaign Manager Lucy Inglis, Head of Marketing Jo Monroe and Social and Digital Manager Andrea Johnson, who never fail to give their all.

I am so fortunate to have the benefit of my agent Catherine Drayton's judgement and advice. In addition, it is thanks to Catherine and the great team at InkWell Management that my books are available to lovely readers around the world.

I could never have brought *The Artist's Secret* to life without the enormous help I received from past and present employees and principals of major auction houses. All contributed fascinating behind-the-scenes stories, the odd hilarious anecdote and myriad technical details. My appreciation goes to: Justin Miller, director of Justin Miller Art and former Chairman of Sotheby's Australia; Andrew Shapiro, managing director of Shapiro Auctions and former senior vice president at Phillips New York; Gary Singer, CEO of Smith & Singer (formerly Sotheby's); and Edward Hoddle, managing director at Orpheo UK and a former Sotheby's auction assistant.

Particular thanks are due to Paul Sumner, joint partner of Artvisory, former Sydney manager of Christie's Inc., and former managing director of Sotheby's London (Olympia). Not only did Paul patiently answer a host of questions, but he also provided me with the opportunity to 'walk in the shoes' of my book's risk-taking heroine by inviting me to take charge of some telephone bidding at a significant auction. It was a thrilling, albeit nerve-racking experience and I loved every minute.

Special credit must go to my close friend Jane de Teliga. Jane generously shared much knowledge and many experiences from her time working at the Art Gallery of New South Wales. She also introduced me to the beauty of the Shoalhaven River. Her interest and encouragement have been boundless.

Among the fascinating publications I relied on for material regarding the world of art and art auctions were: *Art Theft and the Case of the Stolen Turners* by Sandy Nairne; *The Art Museum in Modern Times* by Charles Saumarez Smith; *Pictures, Passions and Eye: A Life at Sotheby's* by Michael Strauss; *Pedigree and Panache: A History of the Art Auction in Australia* by Shireen Huda; *Art Forgery: The History of a Modern Obsession* by Thierry Lenain; *The Art of the Con: The Most Notorious Fakes, Frauds and Forgeries in the Art World* by Anthony M. Amore; *The $12 Million Stuffed Shark: the Curious Economics of Contemporary Art* by Don Thompson; and *The Dynamics of Auctions: Social Interaction and the Sale of Fine Art and Antiques* by Christian Heath.

David Dale's *An Australian in America: First Impressions and Second Thoughts on the World's Strangest Nation* supplied many wry insights into 1980s New York. *The American Century* by Harold

Evans provided an excellent overview of the forces shaping the country during the 1960s and 1980s. *The Sixties: Cultural Revolution in Britain, France, Italy, and the United States* by Arthur Marwick was an invaluable source of commentary on the free speech, civil rights and anti-Vietnam protest movements.

My thanks to Nell Campbell of *The Rocky Horror Picture Show* and *Nell's* nightclub fame for agreeing to play a cameo role in this book.

A big shout-out to my ever-loyal early readers and great buddies Lyndel Harrison, Susan Williams and Jane de Teliga, together with my dear daughter-in-law, Anna Reoch. It is a treat to share my book journeys with you.

Writing *The Artist's Secret* has reminded me of how blessed I am to have the support of my entire family, including my mother, Sybil, a former long-term Art Gallery of New South Wales guide who first introduced me to the wonder of art when I was a small child. My own art-loving children, Bennett and Arabella Mason, have shown their (too often) preoccupied mother endless patience. My niece Phoebe Joel kindly provided me with terrific details about the Parkside Evangeline. As always, my husband, Philip, buoyed me up unfailingly throughout the writing process. There is no one with whom I would rather stroll through a gallery or museum.

I am in awe of the many fantastic booksellers who have championed my work, even going so far as posting and hand-delivering volumes when the world began shutting down. You have been amazing!

Finally, I am incredibly grateful for my wonderful readers. Thank you for coming to events and also for sending me your enthusiastic emails and messages – they mean so much. Most important of all, thank you for opening your hearts to the worlds I create and the characters who inhabit them.

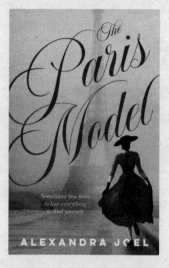

Success would not depend on her beauty.
It would be a test of her wits and her will.

Grace Woods leaves her vast Australian sheep station and travels to tumultuous post-war Paris in order to find her true identity.

Working as a mannequin for Christian Dior, the world's newly acclaimed emperor of fashion, Grace mixes with counts and princesses, authors and artists, diplomats and politicians.

But when she falls for handsome Philippe Boyer, Grace is drawn into a devastating world of international espionage, discovering the shattering truth of her origins – and that her life is in danger.

Inspired by an astonishing true story, *The Paris Model* takes you from the rolling plains of country Australia to the exclusive salons of Paris.

'Gorgeous – the perfect summer escape'
Better Reading

She never dreamt she would become the story …

When Blaise Hill, a feisty young journalist from one of Sydney's toughest neighbourhoods, is dispatched to London at the dawn of the swinging sixties to report on Princess Margaret's controversial marriage to an unconventional photographer, she is drawn into an elite realm of glamour and intrigue.

As the nation faces an explosive upheaval, Blaise must grapple with a series of shocking scandals at the pinnacle of British society. Yet, haunted by a threat from her past and torn between two very different men, who can she trust in a world of hidden motives and shifting alliances? If she makes the wrong choice, she will lose everything.

Inspired by real events, *The Royal Correspondent* is a compelling story of love and betrayal, family secrets and conspiracy that takes you from the gritty life of a daily newspaper to the opulent splendour of Buckingham Palace.

'Combines romance, a splash of espionage and lots of glamour, inspired by real events' *Australian Women's Weekly*